FROM THE CRADLE TO THE CASKET

By Dean Robert

TABLE OF CONTENTS

Acknowledgements

Prologues...Page.......5

Chapter 1: One Love.................................Page........9

Chapter 2: Youngstars..............................Page......16

Chapter 3: Gangsta Love..........................Page......27

Chapter 4: The Streets Are Calling.........Page......50

Chapter 5: No Kids Allowed.....................Page......58

Chapter 6: Dynamite.................................Page......72

Chapter 7: Trapped In The Game............Page......82

Chapter 8: Gangsta Bitches.....................Page......91

Chapter 9: Baby Girl.................................Page.....101

Chapter 10: Mama's Boy..........................Page.....109

Chapter 11: Married To The Game...........Page.....116

Chapter 12: The Game God......................Page....124

Chapter 13: For the Love of Money.........Page....137

Chapter 14: Homies...................................Page....141

Chapter 15: Ain't Nothin But A Gangsta Party...Page....149

Chapter 16: The Syndicate Family...........Page....161

Chapter 17: Who's The Boss.....................Page....170

Chapter 18: Business Is Business............Page....178

Chapter 19: Friends, Foe, and Family......Page....186

Chapter 20: Laugh Now, Cry Later..........Page....204

Chapter 21: Young Ballers   Page....231

Chapter 22: Folsom Lake   Page....239

Chapter 23: There's A Devil in the Ghetto   Page....245

Chapter 24: Sunshine   Page....258

Chapter 25: K-Squad   Page....269

Chapter 26: The Game Is Ugly   Page....278

Chapter 27: Syndicate   Page....285

Chapter 28: Star   Page....294

Chapter 29: Nowhere To Hide   Page....300

Chapter 30: Fuck The Rules   Page....311

Chapter 31: The Game Is Deep   Page....319

Chapter 32: The Heart of a Gangsta   Page....325

Chapter 33: A Teenage Love   Page....329

Chapter 34: Respect The Game   Page....342

Chapter 35: Y.G.'s and O.G.'s   Page....346

Chapter 36: Sugga   Page....355

Chapter 37: The Wedding   Page....377

Chapter 38: Daddy's Lil Girl   Page....389

Chapter 39: From The Bottom To The Top   Page....395

Chapter 40: Gangsta's Paradise   Page....401

Chapter 41: The World Belongs To Us   Page....410

Chapter 42: Two Dimes   Page....420

Chapter 43: Money And The Power   Page....427

Chapter 44: Ain't No Shame In The Game   Page....435

Chapter 45: The Game Don't Stop   Page....445

Chapter 46: Gangstas Make The World Go Round   Page....453

Chapter 47: It's In The Blood   Page....465

Chapter 48: Krystal   Page....472

Chapter 49: Untouchable   Page....477

Chapter 50: Ain't No Free Rides   Page....484

Chapter 51: Spoiled Rotten   Page....489

Chapter 52: Cream   Page....492

Chapter 53: God Bless The Game   Page....500

Chapter 54: Young And Dumb   Page....506

Chapter 55: It's A God Game   Page....513

Chapter 56: The Game Don't Stop   Page....523

About The Author   Page....531

Disclosure   Page....532

Acknowledgments

This book is dedicated to all my mob family, here and gone!

Special thanks to Erin Blackwood. Without you, there would be no book.

A shoutout to my nephew, Gunna 2057 SCRIB BLOCK. Keep ya head up blood!

Lastly, a shoutout to my special friend, Rose. Thank you for all your love and support.

Prologue
November 8th, 1998
Stockton, California

"Daddy, watch out!" Sunshine screamed from inside the car as bullets flew across the parking lot of the liquor store, leaving bullet holes in the walls. And knocking out its windows. Syndicate heading inside the liquor store, reacted to Sunshine's warning and reached inside his waist for his 357 Mag. Just as his assassin's bullets tore into his body, leaving him face down as blood leaked all over the concrete.

Sunshine full of vengeance from seeing hear Father gunned down on the sidewalk, reached under the front passenger seat of Syndicate's Lexus and grabbed his Mac 11. With the extended 30 round clip, she jumped out of the car without hesitation or second thought. Sunshine unloaded her Father's Mac 11, at the two-unsuspecting slow-moving cars.

Sunshine's only experience of shooting a gun being at a New Year's Eve party, held the gun tightly with both hands, and squeezed the trigger. Tears ran down her face as she sprayed bullets wildly, gitting the two cars repeatedly and everything in the vicinity. One of the shooters' car door flew open as a body came tumbling out. Shocked back to reality by Sunshine's onslaught, the two car load of killers returned fire before speeding away.

With the Mac 11, still clutched inside her hands, Sunshine

ran over to where her father was laying face down in a pool of blood. Krystal a pretty-brown skinned girl with big brown eyes, and best friend of Sunshine's ran out of the liquor store screaming out of the top of her lungs. "Is he dead? Is he dead? Is Syndicate dead?"

Sunshine glared at Krystal with murderous eyes. "Bitch, call 911 before you be dead." "It's going to be ok daddy. I'm right here with you." Sunshine held Syndicate's head in her lap and whispered in his ear. "Krystal! Where the fuck is the ambulance?!" Sunshine shouted at Krystal.

Krystal crying unashamedly said, "They're on the way Sunshine. I can hear the sirens now."

Dynamite moaned in pure pleasure as Sugga caressed her soft skin beneath the silk sheets while the phone rang off the hook on the bedside table startling Dynamite. Determined not to let their lovemaking be ruined she ignored it. By the eighth ring the moment had been ruined and Dynamite pushed Sugga off her, as she reached for the phone. Annoyed, Dynamite yelled into the phone, "What?!"

Already feeling anxious behind Syndicate's fate, Krystal trembled with fear after hearing the Notorious Dynamite's voice. "Syn...Syndi...Syndi..." Krystal stuttered unable to gather her bearings.

Dynamite furious at having their lovemaking disturbed rolled her eyes at Sugga. "Krystal, is that you girl? What the fuck is wrong with you?" Dynamite interrupted the stuttering voice on the other end of the phone.

Gathering up the courage to break the bad news, Krystal blurted out. "I said that they shot Syndicate!"

Dynamite stomach dropped to the floor as she heard the words. "Shot? Oh, my god! What happen? How bad is it?"

Krystal exhaled heavily. "It's bad Dynamite. He was walking inside the liquor store, two cars rode up on him and just started shooting."

Dynamite sat on the edge of the bed with her hands trembling around the phone. Standing up naked, she paced the floor and took a deep breath regaining her composer. "Where is Sunshine?" Dynamite asked.

Feeling more relieved now that Dynamite is in charge, Krystal regained some of her focus. "She got into the ambulance with Syndicate."

"What hospital are they going to?" Dynamite asked as she started to get dressed and tossed Sugga's clothes over to her. "Sugga get dressed, we have to go to the hospital! Syndicate's been shot!" Dynamite yelled at Sugga, who was still laying in bed naked with a worried look on her beautiful face.

"Shot? Oh my god! What happened?" Sugga, shot out of bed like a bolt of lightening after hearing the news that Syndicate had been shot.

"No time to talk now Sugga. We have to get the hospital. Krystal, what fuckin' hospital did they go to?!" Dynamite yelled back into the phone.

"Saint Joseph's, they went to Saint Joseph's." Krystal replied. "I'm out the door." Dynamite had just finished putting on her shoes and was about to hang up the phone when she heard Krystal's voice yelling back at her. "Dynamite, Dynamite!"

Dynamite impatiently sighed back into the phone. "What Krystal?! What?!"

Unsure of how Dynamite would take her news, Krystal spoke quietly. "Sunshine killed one of them."

Dynamite shook her head, and her heart grew heavy at the thought of young Sunshine killing someone. Then she responded, "Good for her. That makes one less nigga that I'm going to have to kill."

CHAPTER ONE
One Love

Junior High School

September 16th 1983

D.Dogg, an average in height, solid build, light skinned with a bald head, was hanging out in the school hallway up to no good. Along with him, was his maternal twin brother, Big Time. Big Time, was tall, dark skinned and wore his hair in an Afro. The two brothers, though opposite in character, shared the same experiences of growing up poor in the hood, having a young crack addict for a Mother, and living for the game. The two were inseparable.

D.Dogg, smoking on a Newport, looked down the hallway and nodded. "Who is that white boy walkin' with Michelle?"

Big Time glanced down the hallway and saw the pretty white girl with shoulder length blonde hair and sparkling green eyes. She was flashing her beautiful smile at the tall handsome boy, she was walking with. He couldn't help but notice that the boy was dressed in what looked like a brand new pair of jeans and a button-down shirt. An outfit that was much different than the worn-out bleached pair of black Ben Davis pants and raggedy Oakland Raiders t-shirt, with a big hole in the back that he was wearing. Big Time glanced down at his K-Mart Pro Wings that were long overdue for the trash and spoke jealously.

"I don't know who that white boy is and why do you care anyway?"

"Because that's my girl that fool is walkin' with." D.Dogg replied. Oblivious of his old worn out pair of black 501's, raggedy red Pendleton shirt, and his fifty cent Combat Boots that his mama got from the Salvation Army.

"Your girl? Come on now D.Dogg, you crazy. That white bitch doesn't even know that you exist." Big Time laughed.

Michelle was dressed in a brand-new pair of white Calvin Klein jeans, Calvin Klein shirt, and a new pair of red and white Adidas. Her flashy smile only accentuated by a little gold chain around her neck, and diamond earrings. D.Dogg couldn't keep his eyes off of Michelle's young body, which was full of potential.

"It doesn't matter, she's my girl. So, you need to watch your mouth with all that bitch shit."

Big Time slapped D.Dogg playfully in the back of the head,

almost knocking off his red bandana. "My bad brah. I didn't realize that you were working with feelings. But what makes you think that she's going to fuck with someone like you? That bitch ain't, trying' to fuck with nobody from the hood. Shit look at her D.Dogg, and look at you. She's a have and you're a have not."

D.Dogg gave his twin brother a cold hard stare. Fully aware of his brother's temper, Big Time smiled in vain trying to defuse the situation. "I'm not the one who's trying' to put you down. Shit, I'm broke just like you. I'm just telling you how it is."

"Yeah, well we ain't going to be broke forever." D.Dogg said defensively.

"Yeah, well for now we are, and like I said that lil white bitch ain't fuckin' with you." Big Time cracked up laughing

"Yeah, well she ain't going to be fuckin' with that white boy no more either. Come on blood." D.Dogg waved Big Time forward and started walking towards the young boy who had just dropped Michelle off at her classroom. "Say white boy. What the fuck you doin' walkin' with my girl?"

The young boy looked at D.Dogg and Big Time with a surprised and scared look on his face. "Your girl? What girl? What are you talking about dude?"

D.Dogg impulsive by nature grabbed the boy by his face and slammed his head against the locker repeatedly until he fell to the ground. D.Dogg then kicked him in the face as Big Time kicked him in the stomach. "If I see you talkin' to Michelle again, I'm going to kill you white boy." D.Dogg shouted at the young boy. D.Dogg and Big Time left the injured white boy laying down in the hallway as they walked off towards their next class.

"Damn we fucked that white boy up" Big Time laughed.
"I bet he knows what the fuck I'm talkin' about now." D.Dogg smirked. "I want everybody in this fuckin' school to know that Michelle is my girl and that if I see anybody talkin' to her the same thing will happen to them."

Big Time smiled knowingly at D.Dogg. "You know that we fucked that white boy up for nothing. That bitch still doesn't even know who you are."

D.Dogg smiled back at Big Time. "Trust me Big Time, she knows who the fuck I am."

D.Dogg cornered Michelle after her first period class the next day and confronted her. "Who was that white boy you was walkin' with yesterday?" D.Dogg spoke as if entitled.

Astonished Michelle flashed her anger on D.Dogg. "You stupid fuck! It was you wasn't it? You're the one who beat up Ryan.

"Yeah, me and my brother Big Time. I told that fool to stay the fuck away from you." D.Dogg confessed proudly.

"Why?!" Michelle yelled furiously.

"Because I don't want his punk ass walkin' with you anymore. D.Dogg said smugly.

Confused Michelle changed her tone somewhat. "You don't want him talkin' to me anymore? Why? That doesn't make any sense."

Self-assured D.Dogg begin rubbing his hands together. "Check this out, Michelle. Ryan isn't your boyfriend anymore. I am."

"Boyfriend? You think that Ryan is my boyfriend and that's why you and your brother beat him up." Michelle said feeling kind of flattered that someone would fight for her. "And what do you mean, you're my boyfriend?"

D.Dogg inhaled then exhaled slowly. "Just what I said Michelle. You're my girl now. It's as simple as that." Finding it funny, Michelle started to laugh.

"What's so damn funny?" D.Dogg said irritated.

"You got it all wrong. I'm not even all that attracted to boys. I think that I'm gay. At the least, I know that I'm Bisexual." Michelle spoke seriously full of wisdom beyond her years.

D.Dogg stood open mouth and dumbfounded. "How do you know all of this? You're only what, 14 years old?"

"Well, my mother is a lawyer and my father is psychiatrist, so I have a lot of advantages that most kids don't have."

D.Dogg shook his head in amazement. "This shit is crazy. What part of the game is this, talkin' about you don't like boys?"

"The part of the game where you need to get your facts

straight before you go around beating people up. Ryan and I are just friends. He knows that I like girls. I just used him to keep boys like you away from me." Michelle said honestly.

"I heard the fuck out of that. Are you serious?" D.Dogg asked astonished.

Michelle flashed her beautiful smile. "Just as serious as you are."

"Ain't that a bitch" D.Dogg looked down at his feet as he pondered the whole situation. After a minute he looked at her straight in the eyes. "It don't matter to me. You're still my girl and I will beat a bitch's ass too if I see her trying to talk at you."

"Who are you?" Michelle giggled.

D.Dogg put his chest out. "A gangsta, that's who I am."

"I don't think that my father would approve of my going out with a gangsta." Michelle glanced up and down at the young handsome boy. "So does the gangsta have a name?"

"They call me D.Dogg."

Michelle smiled up at D.Dogg. "I don't want to know what your homeboys call you. What's your real name?

"Derek, my name is Derek."

Michelle laughed as she glimpsed at his soft side. "Well Derek, since you're my new boyfriend, you can hold my books and walk me to my next class."

D.Dogg smiled as he accepted Michelle's books. I still can't believe that you don't like niggas."

"Boys, I don't like boys. And you better get used to it if you're going to be my boyfriend."

"It's all good, Michelle", D.Dogg reassured her. "I guarantee that you're going to like me."

"Boy, you trippin.", Michelle giggled "I just got you to keep the rest of the little thugs away from me."

"Just like you were using that little punk ass white boy huh." D.Dogg teased.

Michelle laughed. "Yep, only you will do a much better job."

CHAPTER TWO

Youngstas

High School

Friday, June 2nd, 1984

D.Dogg, and, Big Time, sat on the school bleachers during lunch contemplating their next move.

"Big Time, how much cash you workin' with?" D.Dogg asked.

Big Time checked his pockets. "I got about forty-five dollars."

D.Dogg replied, "Damn nigga, I only got about twenty bucks. We doin' hobo bad. I'm tired of bein' broke and I'm even more tired of wearing these raggedly ass clothes. It hurts my pride to be walkin' around with Michelle lookin' like this." D.Dogg frowned as he looked down at the worn-out clothes he was wearing.

Michelle ain't trippin' off how you look. I still don't know how you got with her, or why she even fuckin' with your crazy ass. But that's your girl she's down for you like four flat tires. So, don't even trip on that, she ain't goin' nowhere." Big Time reassured his brother.

D.Dogg put his money back in his pocket. "It ain't just that Big Time. We're sixteen years old and we're still sharin' each other's raggedly ass clothes. I'm tired of muthafuckas capping on us about how we look."

Big Time continued counting his money as if it would grow instantly. "You think I ain't tired of that shit nigga? I can't wait to come up on these clowns."

D.Dogg pulled out a plastic bag full of joints. "Nigga, sellin' these goddamn dollar ass joints ain't the way to come up!" Shouted D.Dogg as he fired up one of the joints, despite the fact that he doesn't like smoking weed.

"What's up D.Dogg? Big Time? What you niggas up to?", asked G.; a ruthless, skinny, Mexican kid that everyone took for being black. He walked up, sporting a long ponytail. In public, G. was known as pretty boy. But to those in his circle, G. was known for putting in work for his hood and the best friend of D.Dogg. G. walked up to the bleachers along with Mondo, a brown skinned youngsta with long french braids. Mondo was known for knocking people out. Also, with them was Under. A tall, cut up, jet black youngsta, known to be a brutal enforcer for the street gang that they all belonged to.

"What up G., Mondo, Under. We ain't doin' shit just tryin' to get our hustle on." Big Time answered as he gave the three youngstas daps.

"Nigga, you call sellin' these dollar ass joints hustling?" D.Dogg yelled angrily.

"If it's puttin' money in your pocket, then its hustling." Countered Big Time.

"It's chicken feed blood. Yhat's what it is." D.Dogg disgustedly threw down the joint he was smoking and turned to his best friend G. "You got some butt naked blood? I'm trying' to get my mind right."

G. laughed at his best friend. "You tired of smoking that gold weed huh D.Dogg?"

"Yeah, nigga, you know this shit ain't me." D.Dogg held up the plastic bag full of joints.

"Fuck that gold weed nigga. I got the bomb right here." G. laughed as he reached into his pocket and pulled out a little glass vial with some liquid sherm inside of it. "D.Dogg give me a Newport so I can dip this shit up."

D.Dogg reached into his back pocket and pulled out a pack of cigarettes and gave one to G. "Nigga soak that muthafucka and make it wet." D.Dogg said in anticipation of the high that was coming.

Mondo reached for the sherm soaked Newport. "Give it hear G. and let me fire it up."

"Under snatched the wet Newport out of Mondo's hand. "You ole sherm head ass nigga. You always want to fire something up. I got this G. I already got a lit cigarette anyway." Under said as he fired up the sherm soaked cigarette.

Big Time shook his head in disgust. "That's all you sherm head muthafuckas do is smoke that crazy ass shit."

"We smoke niggas to Big Time," D.Dogg laughed, "Pass that shit Under. I ain't tryin' to hear what this square ass nigga is talkin' about."

"Here you go D.Dogg blood. You niggas goin' to the party tonight?" Asked Under.

"What the fuck you think nigga? Yeah, we going." D.Dogg answered as he inhaled the sherm smoke.

Later that night D.Dogg, Big Time, G, Mondo, and Under stood outside the school gym hanging out waiting to go inside.

"Damn nigga I'm fucked up." D.Dogg laughed

Big Time feelin' good off the gin and juice, put his arm around his brother. "D.Dogg, don't be up in here trippin' blood. Its hoes out tonight and I'm trying' to get my freak on."

Under had his mind on some young pussy just like Big Time. "Yeah D.Dogg. Be cool tonight nigga. I'm not trying' to turn this muthafucka out."

"Damn Under. You startin' to sound like this square ass nigga Big Time."

Under took a drag off his Newport. "I'm just sayin' D.Dogg. You be going insane in the brain off that shit sometime."

Nigga this the Mob. I ain't giving' a fuck what these niggas up in here talkin' about." D.Dogg answered defensively.

"Yeah, niggas this is S.M.G foe life. My nigga can go insane no brain all he wants…and I'm right there with him until the wheels fall off." G. butt in as he gave it up for the Mob.

D.Dogg laughed appreciating G.s loyalty to the hood. "That's what I'm talkin' about G. represent the block. Let these niggas know what time it is."

Don't get it twisted my nigga. It's the Mob on mines to," Under gave it up for the mob. "I'm just saying you be getting out of control when you be on that shit."

"Damn D.Dogg. You know we all down for the block nigga. All the homie's saying' is just kick it tonight." Mondo said as he and Big Time gave it up for the mob.

"Let that shit ride for now D.Dogg. Let's kill off the rest of this gin and mob up in here 'n' holla at some these lil fresh hoes." Big Time joked.

The South Mob Gangsta homies headed inside the gym where they posted up against the wall and checked out the scene. The gymnasium was decorated with long paper chained ribbons in school colors. Basketball championship banners hung from the rafters. High school kids filled the gymnasium dancing to the beat of Michael Jackson's "Billie Jean"

"Big Time ain't that Jazzy over there by the water faucet? I thought that you said she wasn't coming." D.Dogg asked with a smile on his face. As he pointed towards the very pretty Filipino and black girl' She had smooth brown skin, long black hair, and big black eyes. Standing along with five other very pretty girls. All of them belonging to the pretty pimpin' girls. Better known as the P.P.G.

Big Time checked her out from her tight fitting black Jordache jeans that showed off her young curves, to her fully ripe young breast sticking out underneath her High School football jersey. The Jersey she got from making the cheer leading team.

"That's what she told me." Big Time answered with a frown on his face, mad that his girlfriend lied to him.

"Damn nigga who is that new bitch standing' next to her?" Under whistled as he stared at the short, thick, pretty girl with long brown hair and tight eyes, standing next to Jazzy.

"That's her relative from Hawaii." Big Time replied.

"Hawaii? Ain't that a bitch?" Under said surprised as he never met anyone from Hawaii. "Jazzy's relative is a young tender." Under eyes swept from her black jeans that showed off her nice round ass up to the tight shirt that she was wearing that accentuated her juicy, ripe, peach size breast. "What's her name Big Time?" Under asked.

"Denise" Big Time answered, as he strolled towards Jazzy and the other girls. Followed closely by D.Dogg, G., Under, and Mondo.

Jazzy, seeing Big Time approaching flashed her gorgeous smile and walked over to him. "Hey Big, what's up? I been looking for you." Her jet-black eyes looked at him longingly before she reached up and put her arms around his neck.

"I wasn't looking for you, I thought that you said you weren't coming." Big Time said as he started to get an erection from checking out Jazzy's body. A body no fifteen-year-old girl should be allowed to have.

"I wasn't planning on coming, but my cousin, Denise, just joined the P.P.G. She wanted to come and hang out with us so, I changed my mind. I hope you're not mad at me Big?"

Big Time reached out and squeezed Jazzy's nice soft, heart shaped ass. "Naw girl, I ain't mad at you. I'm glad you came."

Jazzy giggled and slapped at Big Time's hand. "Stop playing Big"

Big Time squeezed, Jazzy's ass even harder. "Who's playing? This ass belongs to me and I'll grab it whenever I want to."

"Jazzy, so what's up? Introduce us to your relative." Under asked with a big smile on his face.

"Oh shit! My bad. I'm sorry Under. Denise, this here is Under, and that's G. and that's Mondo. You already know Big's brother D.Dogg." Jazzy pointed out who was who.

Denise smiled and gave everyone a shy wave. "Hi everybody."

"What's going on Denise? You want to dance?" Under asked. A little too quickly for Mondo. "Damn nigga. You didn't even give me a chance to speak to the girl." Mondo cried. Annoyed that he had been to slow to make his move.

Denise laughed. "Sure, Under I'll dance with you."

Under took Denise by the hand and led her out to the dance floor, where the D.J was playing "More Bounce To The Ounce" by the Zapp Band.

D.Dogg laughed as he looked out at the dance floor. Look at my nigga out there getting his freak on with that bitch.

"D.Dogg don't be calling my cousin no bitch." Jazzy said with a lot of attitude. Big Time looked at Jazzy and rolled his eyes. "Don't start with the drama girl. You know that nigga didn't mean anything by that shit."

"So, what. He doesn't have to be disrespecting Denise like that." Jazzy pouted.

"Forgive me sis. Don't be mad at me. Am I still your brah?" D.Dogg laughed as his way of apologizing.

Jazzy gave D.Dogg a big smile and hit him playfully. "Don't be stupid boy. You always going to be my brother no matter what."

Just then, G.'s eye caught some rival gang members, dressed in their blue Crip colors, and walking through the door. "D.Dogg check it out blood." Cautioned G. staring hard at the rival gang members.

"That nigga Silky, you been trying' to catch up with, just rolled up in here with some of his east side homies. D.Dogg's heart started pounding heavily in his chest at the sight of Silky. A tall, muscular, browned skinned, flamboyant, good looking kid with a long perm, and known for putting in work for his east side crip hood. D.Dogg glared over at Silky with a menacing look in his eyes ; highly intensified because of the sherm he had been smoking. "Nigga it's on. I'm about to have that nigga Silky."

"D.Dogg quit trippin' blood. That nigga ain't said nothin'." Big Time said with a worried look on his face not wanting any trouble to get started.

"Yeah D.Dogg just be cool blood. Them niggas don't want no problems." Mondo added as he looked over at the Crips who noticed the mob homies for the first time. Returning the cold stares, they were getting with cold stares of their own.

D.Dogg feeling like a time bomb ready to explode, had been anticipating this meeting with Sliky for days. "Nigga I don't give a fuck if they trippin' or not, because I'm trippin'. I told you Big Time that it's on sight with that nigga Silky."

"What the fuck that nigga do to you blood?" G. was getting more pumped up by the second noticing the change in D.Dogg's demeanor ready to follow his lead.

D.Dogg checked the 9-millimeter revolver tucked in his waist that he had stolen out of a house he had broken into. "That bitch ass nigga keeps tryin' to push up on Michelle. Talkin' to her all crazy. Callin' her bitches and shit, because she won't give his crab ass any game. Plus, he be bad mouthin' a nigga, talkin' about she's a dumb bitch for fuckin' with a broke ass joke like me." "That crab ass nigga said what? I'm with you blood. Let's go smash these fools." G. roared even more. Charged up on hearing how disrespectful Silky had been.

D.Dogg, Big Time, G., and Mondo mobbed over to where Silky and the rest of the Crips were standing. Forgetting for the moment that Under was still out on the dance floor with Denise. Recognizing that D.Dogg and his boys were headed their way. Silky and his crip homeboys stood their ground and mentally prepared for the face off.

"Silky, what's that bitch shit you been talkin' to my girl about blood?" D.Dogg confronted Silky.
Silky cringed at the sound of being called a blood. "Who the fuck you callin' a slob? Ole slob ass nigga." Silky exploded not letting the disrespect by D.Dogg go unchallenged.

Feeling disrespected at being called a slob. D.Dogg reached inside his waist and pulled out his 9-millimeter and started firing at Silky and his crip homeboys. Hitting Silky in the leg as he tried to run away.

Insane, a short little fat crip, pulled out his pistol and yelled. "They dumpin' cuz! That nigga D.Dogg, just shot Silky." Before he started to return fire. Shooting wildly into the crowd of kids.

Madness erupted as school kids dashed for the exists while the two gangs continued shooting at each other. Two Crips grabbed a hold of Silky and carried him out of the gym. While G. and a young crip, by the name of Trigga, were locked in a fierce fist fight in the middle of the dance floor amongst all the chaos. G. knocked Trigga to the ground and kicked him in the face when D.Dogg made it over to where they were fighting.

"That's right G. stomp that crab nigga out and make him bleed!" D.Dogg yelled as he started pistol whopping Trigga.

Big Time, as always more alert than the others grabbed D.Dogg and G. off of Trigga. "Come on blood. Fuck that nigga. Let's bounce before the cops get here."

CHAPTER THREE
Gangsta Love

I told my mother that you were coming over this Friday after school." Michelle stated a matter of factually, while she and D.Dogg stood in line at KFC; along with other students during their lunch period.

"I heard the fuck out of that one. I ain't tryin' to meet your mom lookin' like this." D.Dogg looked down disgustedly at the worn-out clothes that he was wearing.

"So, what's that supposed to mean? Are you trying to imply that my mother is a snob?" Michelle asked defensively.

"All I'm sayin' is that if I had a daughter, I wouldn't want her to be with someone like me." D.Dogg shrugged his shoulders as if that was enough said.

"Well, I'm not your daughter, and I want you to meet my mother. It's been three years, and your always making excuses as to why you can't come over to my house." Michelle countered stubbornly.

"I'm just sayin' Michelle I'm not tryin' to meet your mama lookin' all ghetto and shit." D.Dogg said feeling trapped and trying desperately to wiggle his way out of this unpleasant encounter with Michelle's mother.

Michelle smiled at the irony of D.Dogg's logic. "Boy you are the most ghetto person that I know. So, what are you talking about? And quit tripping on not having something to wear, I'll buy you some clothes. So, stop making excuses." Michelle said determined. Knowing D.Dogg's feelings about her trying to help him out financially.

"Come on now Michelle you know better than that. I'm not going to accept your charity." D.Dogg said as he ordered his food mad that Michelle would even suggest something like that.

"It's not charity Derek it's a gift. That's just your stubborn pride that has you thinking like that." Challenged Michelle. Secretly admiring D.Dogg's defiance.

"Call it whatever you want to call it. I really don't give a fuck. I don't want it. And if I do decide to go, she either accepts me as I am, or she doesn't accept me at all."

Michelle smiled at D.Dogg. "So, is paying for lunch still allowed or is that considered charity now?"

"Girl you really need to watch that big ass mouth of yours.

I don't take kindly to when people make fun of me." D.Dogg glared as they took a seat next to the window.

Michelle looked directly into D.Dogg eyes and gave him a very warm and sincere smile full of compassion. A look that until now D.Dogg had only seen directed at actors on the movie screen or a Soap Opera. "Derek I'm not making fun of you. And I never would. I love you."

"What did you say?" D.Dogg replied wearily, with a trace of a small smile forming across his handsome face.

"You heard me. I said that I love you. I'm in love with you Derek." Michelle spoke softly with a sweet smile that lit up the room.

"You're a little dyke? How in the fuck are you going to be in love with me?" D.Dogg said stunned and confused trying to make some sense out of what he was hearing.

"Derek you might be a gangsta. But you sure are slow when it comes to girls. I been in love with you since the day we first met."

Appalled D.Dogg shook his head and thought for a minute. "Girl that was three years ago. Why you just now tellin' me?" Michelle took a bite of her chicken and giggled. "I had to make sure that you were in love with me too." D.Dogg tried to look hard staring at Michelle with a straight face. Though inside his heart began to beat faster while his stomach was doing flip flops. "And what makes you think that I'm in love with you?" D.Dogg asked trying to maintain his composure and excitement.

Michelle smiled and reached out to D.Dogg with her piece of chicken. "Um this chicken is the bomb. You want a bite?" D.Dogg pushed Michelle's hand away from his face. "Girl fuck this chicken. I asked you a question. How do you know that I'm in love with you?"

Michelle stopped laughing. Her face became serious as she looked at D.Dogg intently. "I heard about what happened the other night at the dance."

"I don't know what the fuck you talkin' about." D.Dogg frowned.

"Derek please don't lie to me. Jazzy told me everything, so stop fronting. It's OK I'm not mad at you." Michelle reassured D.Dogg.

Jazzy has a big fuckin' mouth," D.Dogg snapped before taking a bite of his chicken. Mad that Michelle found out what happened. "I'm goin' to tell Big Time that he needs to check his bitch."

"Don't be mad at Jazzy," Michelle pleaded hoping to calm D.Dogg down enough, so that she could confide in him. "She didn't mean to tell me. She thought that I already knew about it."

Secretly relieved that Michelle knew about the shooting the tenseness left D.Dogg's body as his mood lightened up. "So just because I shot that punk ass nigga Silky, that means that I'm in love with you huh?" D.Dogg questioned, privately hoping that Michelle was impressed that he had defended her.

A great big smile broke out across Michelle's pretty, innocent looking face. "Yes, it does, and it also means that you're my gangsta nigga and I'm your gangsta bitch."

Surprised beyond belief to hear those words come out of Michelle's mouth, D.Dogg started laughing uncontrollably. "I heard the fuck out of that. Whatever it is your smokin', you better leave that shit alone. You got the game fucked up. You're the squarest girl in this whole fuckin' school. You don't have the game or the heart to be a gangsta." D.Dogg shook his head in disbelief as he continued to eat his chicken.

Michelle's brow furrowed and her eyes drew tight as she glared at D.Dogg. "I have enough game and enough heart to know that I'm not going to let another bitch take my place."

"Oh, wow this shit is off the hook." D.Dogg was beside himself as he grabbed his aching side and fell in his seat laughing. "Where is all this shit coming from? What does another bitch have to do with anything? What took place the other night is mob business. You tryin' to say that you want to be a part of the S.M.G.?" D.Dogg said. As he continued to laugh out loud. Michelle frowned and stared at D.Dogg long and hard with intensity she had never felt before. "No! I want to be a part of you. Or is that too hard for someone like you to understand?" Realizing for the first time how serious Michelle was, D.Dogg stopped laughing. And gave her his full attention. "Girl you really need to stop trippin'. You're already a part of me."

Michelle tapped her foot down hard repeatedly on the ground. With her arms folded stubbornly across her sexy young body. "Then why can't I be your gangsta bitch?"

D.Dogg shook his head back and forth and let out a frustrated sigh, throwing his chicken breast down on the table. "Damn girl! Because you're not a gangsta, that's why. But refusing to be denied or dismissed so quickly, Michelle countered. "I can be if you let me."

"That's just what the fuck I'm talkin' about. A gangsta doesn't ask permission to do nothin'. They just do it." D.Dogg cracked a smile, and took a drink from his soda, believing that the conversation was over after making such a viable point on the subject.

Michelle considered the information for a moment and as if on cue or any doubt, she stood her ground. "O.K Fine! Fuck it! From here on out, I'm a gangsta bitch and whoever doesn't like it, fuck um. They can kiss my ass."

In disbelief, D.Dogg again started cracking up. "Michelle, you might not be a gangsta but you are crazier than a muthafucka."

"No, I'm Dynamite! And like it or not I am a gangsta bitch." Michelle announced proudly with a newfound freedom.

Perplexed D.Dogg asked. "What the fuck is your crazy ass talkin' about now?"

Michelle smiled confidently. "That's my new name. Dynamite! And if you want to talk to me, you better get used to it D.Dogg."

Shaking his head in amazement D.Dogg gave up. Looking at Michelle with a new interest and love in his heart, he thought to himself. Fuck it! If she likes it then I love it. "So Dynamite, what time am I supposed to meet your mother on Friday?"

Michelle smiled at the sound of her new name, enjoying the power and respect that she felt when she heard D.Dogg use it. "This Friday after school Why?"

D.Dogg shook his head thoughtfully. "Friday? Aw shit! I can't make it. Me and the homies are going' to the fairgrounds Friday night."

Using her newly found gangsta attitude, Dynamite laid it down. "I don't give a fuck what your homeboys are doing Friday night. You're bringing your black ass home with me."

D.Dogg let out a little laugh and smiled, digging Michelle's new attitude. "Now that's keepin' it gangsta."

Friday came. D.Dogg and Dynamite walked up the front walk of Dynamite's house. D.Dogg's eyes became as big as saucers as he looked up at the enormous two-story stucco mansion. It seemed like there were a million windows with beautiful shutters made out of dark wood that stood out nicely against the beige stucco walls. Underneath each window hung wrought iron baskets, holding brightly colored flowers. This made the home look like something you would only find in the hills of France or Italy. Through the window above the front door, D.Dogg could see a giant chandelier in the foyer, and he couldn't help wondering if it was real, and if so, how much it cost. Nevertheless, it was the bomb.

He finally took his eyes off the chandelier and he began to gaze at the giant wrap-around porch that was accentuated by trendy, white outdoor furniture and luscious green ferns. They were in contrast to the dark, thick wooden pillars holding up the second floor. He barely noticed that the front lawn was a green Granny Smith green, thick, and carefully manicured, when he almost ran into a large fountain in the middle of the stone walkway. He regained his composure, shook his head in disbelief and turned to Dynamite. "Damn this is a big ass house." D.Dogg admitted

Dynamite smiled as she took her keys out of her pocket. D.Dogg looked up and down the street at the other homes and realized that he had never been in a neighborhood this nice. In fact, before now, I wasn't even sure they existed. Dynamite shrugged. "It's really not all that big compared to some of the other homes around here."

In shock, D.Dogg looked at the mansion again. "I heard the fuck out of that. It's like three houses in one." D.Dogg looked at

Dynamite with concern as she opened the front door. "How come you go to a public school and not one of those rich fancy private schools?"

Dynamite stopped and looked at D.Dogg. "For starters, I'm not rich. And secondly, I used to go to a private school up until the 7th grade. The kids and their parents were a bunch of snobs and I couldn't stand it. So, I convinced my parents to let me go to a public school. Since my parents are divorced, it wasn't that hard to play one against the other. Come on, let's go inside."

Leading the way, Dynamite brought D.Dogg into the foyer where he stopped. Wide-eyed, he looked from wall to wall trying to comprehend everything that he was seeing. To his left he saw a plush dining room with a table laid out for twelve. In the corner was a silver tea set and against the other wall, in a glass cabinet, lights shone down on a set of fine China. Next to the dining room he saw an enormous kitchen with every state-of-the-art appliance you could think of all stainless steel. The counter tops were black marble, and a wooden island, the size of D.Dogg's kitchen at home, was in the middle of the room. He noticed another large wooden table in the kitchen and wondered how many tables a person needed to have. The kitchen opened into a large living room furnished with brown leather couches and chairs facing a stone fireplace. Above the wooden mantle was a painting that D.Dogg could only assume was done by a famous artist. D.Dogg turned in the foyer and looked to his right.

Passed the grand piano in the foyer, he noticed a wing in the mansion full of bedrooms   decorated with expensive looking furniture and lush bedding. Awestruck, D.Dogg asked, "How many rooms do you have?" "We have eight-bedrooms and four-bathrooms." Dynamite pronounced modestly. "All these rooms just for you and your mother?" D.Dogg asked, as he scanned all the rooms that he could see, knowing that there were many more that he hadn't seen yet.

"We have guest stay over sometimes. Plus, there's Rosa, the maid who lives with us. Come on, let me show you my room." Dynamite led D.Dogg up the enormous wooden staircase at the opposite side of the foyer. At the top of stairs Dynamite turned left and led D.Dogg down a wing of the mansion that was lined with pictures of Dynamite of her whole life. Proudly, Dynamite directing D.Dogg, "Here's my room."

Smiling at the little girl in the picture with ice cream all over her face, D.Dogg followed Dynamite into her room. Glancing around the room, D.Dogg was pretty sure that her room was at least half the size of his house, if not more. Her bed had more pillows on it than D.Dogg had ever seen. Dynamite threw her back pack on the bed and D.Dogg noticed that it seemed to be moving, then he realized that it was a water bed. There was a desk in one corner of the room with all of Dynamite's homework and textbooks on it.

He also noticed that she had what looked like a computer. On her large dresser opposite of her bed was a big screen television and V.C.R. D.Dogg didn't know anyone who had a television in their bedroom. Dynamite nodded to D.Dogg to take a seat. He looked behind him and noticed a leather loveseat. Tentatively, he sat down, afraid to touch anything in the house.

"Where is your mama at?" D.Dogg asked. Looking around the room, he noticed a new Sony stereo along with a huge collection of tapes.

"She'll be here in an hour or two. Would you like to go swimming?" Dynamite offered.

"Yeah, but I don't have any shorts." D.Dogg responded disappointed.

"Don't worry. I have some boy gym trunks that you can wear." Dynamite went over to her closet and disappeared.

"Where is the maid at? And what are you doing with boy gym shorts?" D.Dogg asked as he looked at the closet, amazed that Dynamite had walked into it like it was another room.

"I like sleeping in them sometimes. They're comfortable. And why are you looking for Rosa, are you hungry or something?" Dynamite yelled from inside the closet.

"No, I was just wondering. I never seen a real live maid before." D.Dogg said feeling just like Dorothy felt when she was lost in the land of OZ. Dynamite stuck her head out of the closet, looked at D.Dogg and laughed. "She looks just like the rest of the people of the world. A head, two arms, two legs, and two feet."

"Funny," feeling more comfortable in the room, D.Dogg teased. "Shit you got it going on up in here. This fuckin' room looks like it just came off the show case of the Price is Right. Gangsta bitch my ass. What you are is a spoiled lil' rich white girl."

Defensively, Dynamite disagreed. "I'm not spoiled, and I'm not rich." D.Dogg shrugged and smiled his deadly smile. "You can call it whatever you want to, but it is what it is. You know what they say, the proof is in the pudding." Dynamite smiled playfully as she walked out of the closet. "Boy be quiet. You don't know what you talking about. Here, put these on." Dynamite tossed D.Dogg a pair of boy's gym trunks. Then they made their way to pool.

"Damn, this is a big ass swimming pool," D.Dogg stated, as they walked through the sliding glass doors and out into the backyard.

The pool was anything, but a normal rectangular shape. It curved around like a jellybean. At one end, it had a waterfall flowing into it from what looked like a hot tub set above the pool. The ground around the pool was all stonework that was beautiful, but supported the, "No running around the pool" rule. A stubbed toe on that stone would really hurt. The yard around the pool held two enormous palm trees and several fruit trees. Botanical gardens could not compare to the beautiful assortment of lilies, roses, and hydrangeas growing throughout the yard.

"It's not that big," Dynamite hollered back at D.Dogg before she jumped into the water. "Girl, this looks like one of those big ass houses on the Lifestyle of the Rich and Famous." D.Dogg laughed as he dove into the pool after Dynamite.

Dynamite smiled, watching D.Dogg swim towards her, glad that she finally got him to come home with her. "You think this is big wait until you see my Father's house."

D.Dogg swam toward Dynamite who stood in the shallow end of the pool showing off her newly developing body in her powder blue bikini. Her blonde hair shinning and flowing free in the sunlight. Her green eyes glowed as beads of water sparkled as they ran down her smooth ivory skin. As D.Dogg came closer to Dynamite, she unmercifully splashed water in his face. "Hey, stop splashing water in my face!" D.Dogg yelled, annoyed with Dynamite who kept splashing water in his face.

"What's wrong? The big, bad, gangsta scared of water?" Dynamite laughed, without letting up on what she was doing.

"You keep playing, I'm going' to show you who's scared of water and dunk your lil ass." D.Dogg threaten.

Dynamite beamed and backed away slowly from D.Dogg, as she splashed him again. "You have to catch me first." Dynamite yelled as she swam to the other side of the pool.

D.Dogg jumped out of the pool, and ignoring the no running

rule, ran around to where Dynamite was and jumped back in picked her up and threw her over his shoulder.

Dynamite kicked and struggled to get loose, laughing and yelling, "Put me down, put me down!" while D.Dogg adjusted her body over his shoulder.

"What's wrong Dynamite? You afraid of water? I thought that you wanted to play." D.Dogg laughed as he held Dynamite tightly who was squirming wildly in his arms.

"Trapped in D.Dogg's grasp and loving every minute of it, Dynamite struggled to get away. "You better not get my hair wet." Dynamite cried, preparing for her fate, but trying desperately without success to. D.Dogg playfully splashed water in Dynamite's face with one hand, while still holding onto her with the other one.

"Look at the big, bad, gangsta, scared to get her hair wet," laughed D.Dogg, while Dynamite fought viciously to get loose. But getting serious, Dynamite yelled, "I'm not playing anymore Derek. Don't get my hair wet!" Dynamite's screams were muffled as D.Dogg dunked her underneath the water. Dynamite gasped as she re-emerged, "I'm going to kill you! Look at my hair." D.Dogg's eyes sparkled mischievously as he grabbed Dynamite and dunked her beneath the water again. "You're going' to kill me huh."

"Stop! Stop! I can't breathe," Dynamite begged between breaths. D.Dogg laughed as he dunked Dynamite again. "OK, I'm sorry, I'm sorry," Dynamite pleaded. "I'm not going to kill you."

D.Dogg let go of Dynamite and teased, "Dynamite, you ain't nothin' but a big ass baby."

"It looks like the two of you are having fun." Surprised, D.Dogg and Dynamite turned around to see a gorgeous woman with a body that made Mariah Carey look like a crack head Whitney Huston. With her perfect tan, sparkling blue eyes, and long sun kissed blonde hair, D.Dogg thought that he was looking at a movie star. "Hi mom how long have you been standing there?" Dynamite asked with a big smile on her face.

"Long enough to see you get your hair wet." Dynamite's mom smiled showing off her perfect pearl white teeth. "And who is this handsome young man."

"Mom this is Derek. Derek this is my mom." Dynamite introduced D.Dogg and her Mother.

D.Dogg looked at the sexy woman in a charcoal gray jacket and skirt, tailored to the curves of her body. She wore a white blouse cut high enough for business and low enough for attention, and black high-heel pumps. With her Diamond-encrusted earrings, little 14k gold chain, fancy watch and gold bracelet. D.Dogg noticed immediately that Dynamite's mother was high maintenance with a capital M. Not wanting to make any bad impressions, D.Dogg hurriedly got out of the pool and dried himself off before walking up to Dynamite's mother and putting his hand out in greeting.

Impressed with D.Dogg's good manners, Dynamite's mother

smiled, as she shook his hand. "Hello Derek. I'm glad to finally get the chance to meet you."

"I'm glad to meet you too Mrs. Anderson," D.Dogg answered, more politely and with more respect than Dynamite had ever heard him use before.

"Please call me Gail. Mrs. Anderson makes me sound like an old lady," Gail laughed to herself.

"You don't look anything like an old lady, Gail. As a matter of fact, I think that you're a very beautiful woman. I can see where Michelle gets her good looks from." D.Dogg said with all earnestly.

Gail smiled a motherly smile toward D.Dogg, "You better watch Derek, Michelle he sounds like a player to me."
Dynamite got out of the pool and wrapped a towel around herself. "He's not a player mom. He's a gangsta, and so am I." Dynamite beamed. Feeling that it was her duty to inform her mother of their true identity.

Gail was amused and fascinated with the young boy standing in front of her who looked like a poster child for the inner-city youth. "A gangster! Is that true Derek? Are you and Michelle gangsters?"

D.Dogg glared at Dynamite. "Your daughter has a big mouth, Gail, and a lot to learn. But yeah, I'm a gangsta. And Michelle is a wanna be gangsta." D.Dogg stated taking a shot at Dynamite for snitching him off to her mother.

The smile left Gail's face as she became serious. "I don't

approve of you being a gangster anymore than I approve of Michelle's claiming to be a gangster. There's so much life has to offer if you just apply yourself."

D.Dogg looked Gail in her eyes and spoke calmly. "I was born and raised to be a gangsta, Gail, it's in my blood."

Not fully understanding nor appreciating D.Dogg's ambition of being a gangsta, Gail persisted. "You're still young Derek, and with a proper education there's no limit on what you could do with your life. You need to expand your vision and look ahead. Being a gangsta is like throwing your life away." Gail smiled to soften her words, not wanting to bruise his young ego. "But who knows Derek, maybe one day you will have a change of heart."

D.Dogg gave Gail a confident smile. "My heart is in it way too deep to change Gail. The only difference is that I'll be rich and live in a house bigger than this one."

Feeling somewhat challenged by the young boy in front of her, Gail felt it her duty to inform D.Dogg of the dangers of being a gangster. "You could also end up dead, or in prison for the rest of your life. Is that what you want Derek?"

Unfazed D.Dogg replied. "No disrespect Gail, but I already told you what I want and what I expect. Getting killed or going to prison is just another part of the game. Some make it and then some don't."

Gail accepting things as they are for the moment shifted

gears to try a different approach. "Your so right about that Derek. But it seems as if you have your mind set on what you want to do. So, I'll tell you what, Michelle why don't you and Derek go inside the house and get dressed. And after that we can decide where we want to go for dinner." Gail gave Dynamite a disapproving look. "Then for dessert, we can discuss this business about you wanting to be a gangster. And rather or not your father should be involved."

D.Dogg and Dynamite walked into the living room and found Gail sitting on the couch, reading a magazine. "Mom, can we go to that fancy new Chinese restaurant that we went to a couple of weeks ago?"

"I'm not really in the mood for Chinese food. Besides the service there wasn't all that great. I was thinking Red Lobster. We can all get us a fat juicy steak, and all the shrimp we can eat. We'll leave it up to Derek. So, what will it be Derek. Chinese or Red Lobster?"

D.Dogg put his head down and started shuffling his feet back and forth. "Why don't we just stay here and order a pizza."

"Pizza? Dynamite whined, with a disgusted look on her face. "I don't want to stay here an order no pizza."

"I'm surprised Derek. I thought that you would enjoy going out to a nice restaurant." Gail frowned. puzzled by D.Dogg's choice for dinner.

D.Dogg heard the concern in her voice, and his stomach

tighten. He looked at his clothes, and looked around the room at the expensive furniture, and had a sinking feeling of inadequacy. "It's not that I don't want to go out and have dinner with the two of you. It's just that, look at me, and look at the two of you. I would feel embarrassed to go out with the two of you lookin' like movie stars, and I look like a hobo."

Gail's heart broke in two as she heard the proud young man put his self down. "You're not a hobo, Derek. It breaks my heart to hear you say things like that about yourself."

D.Dogg nodded towards Gail and Dynamite and protested. "I might not actually be a hobo Gail. But standing' next to you and Michelle all dressed up like that, I sure do feel like one."

Gail known for having a bleeding heart for the underprivileged. Took a mental inventory of D.Dogg's clothing and notice for the first time that they did look a little worn out. "I have an idea. Let's skip dinner for now and take Derek shopping for some new clothes. So, that he won't have to feel embarrassed around anyone, let alone us." Gail offered. Her motherly instinct to protect a child taking over.

Dynamite rolled her eyes. "Forget it, mom. Been there done that. Derek is way too proud to accept anyone's help."

D.Dogg nodded his head in agreement. "Michelle is right, Gail. I don't want anyone's charity.

Understanding D.Dogg's proud nature, Gail, smiled. "Who

said anything about charity. When you make it as a big shot gangsta you can pay me back with interest." Gail said. Taking D.Dogg's ambition to be a gangsta as nothing more than a little boy's bravo.

D.Dogg not aware of the mind game Gail was playing on him. Smiled at her acceptance of his being a gangsta. "That's very nice of you to offer to buy me some clothes, Gail. But I'm afraid that I can't accept."

"You can't accept? Why not?" Gail asked shocked.

"My twin brother is all I got. We been sharin' each other's clothes all our lives. I wouldn't feel right having new clothes and he didn't." D.Dogg said in an attempt to manipulate, Gail, into buying Big Time, some new clothes.

Not missing a beat, Gail, smiled. "I could see how having new clothes might be uncomfortable for you. So, I'll tell you what. Why don't we go out and buy you and your brother a new wardrobe? I think that the both of you are long overdue anyway."

D.Dogg, Dynamite, and Gail walked through the Weber's Town Mall, and the connecting Sherwood Mall on a no-holds barred shopping spree for D.Dogg and Big Time. And being the dedicated shoppers that they were, the mother-daughter duo couldn't resist picking up a few items for themselves.

This was the first time D.Dogg was inside the mall without being up to no good with Big Time, and his homies. With no concerns about money, D.Dogg, got his first taste of the good life.

Completely overwhelmed with joy and excitement, D.Dogg was like a little boy on Christmas morning opening all his gifts. Dynamite was thrilled that he accepted her mother's help and would finally have some new clothes of his own. Gail was just as excited as D.Dogg. Privately, she had always wanted to know how it would feel to shop for a son.

With each one of their hands and arms full of shopping bags full of pants, shirts, underwear, socks, shoes, watches, and two black leather jackets that Gail had insisted on buying for the two brothers. They walked out of the mall into the parking lot, to Gail's, black Mercedes as they put the bags into the trunk of the car. D.Dogg became shocked at the amount of stuff that Gail, had bought. He had been having so much fun during the shopping spree that he hadn't paid attention to the overall amount of clothing he had accumulated. Feeling gratitude in his heart for the first time in his young life, D.Dogg was touched by Gail's generosity.

"Thank you, Gail, for all the clothes and everything. No one has ever done anything like this for me before. You spent over two-thousand dollars on me and my brother, and you don't even really know us." D.Dogg said touched beyond his understanding.

Gail looked at D.Dogg as if he were her son. "The money isn't what's important. It comes and goes like yesterday. What's important is that you and your brother have some decent clothes to wear, so that you can feel good about yourselves. I don't ever again want to hear you say that you feel like a hobo, because of the clothes that you have on your back. And remember clothes don't make the man. Man makes the clothes.

Speechless from the game, Gail had just laced him with, D.Dogg stood there stunned, amazed that this white woman whom he had just met could affect him in such a way. "Thank you, Gail, I won't ever forget this."

Gail smiled and reached into her purse and pulled out a white envelope. "Here take this."

Unsure of what was in the envelope, D.Dogg took it from, Gail's hand and opened it. Inside was ten 100 dollars bills. "Why are you doing' this, Gail?"

Gail's blue eyes sparkled when she smiled. "Even gangstas need a little help occasionally, Derek. There's a thousand dollars in there, five hundred for you and five hundred for your brother. I want the two of you to know what it feels like to look nice and have money in your pocket at the same time. So, that you can get used to it and always have it."

D.Dogg laughed out loud as he opened the back door of the Mercedes "You got a lot of game for a square, rich, white woman, Gail."

Gail smiled that all-knowingly motherly smile of hers as she started the car. "You're right about me being white, Derek. But as far as me being rich, I think not, it's just a matter of opinion. And yes, I do live a square lifestyle. But things weren't always as they are now. I grew up with a very abusive, alcoholic Father, who was good for nothing. All he ever did was beat my mother, and spend all our money chasing women, and buying more alcohol. My mother had to struggle very hard just to make ends meet. For me and my two older brothers who both know what it looks like from inside a jail cell. So yes Derek, I also know what it means to be poor."

Past the point of being surprised by anything Gail said or did, D.Dogg turned his attention to Dynamite. "Ain't that something, Dynamite? The game is in your blood. I never would have thought it. You just might turn out to be a gangsta yet!" D.Dogg laughed. Dynamite turned around in her seat to face D.Dogg. And gave him an, I told you so look. "Might? Boy! I don't know what you're talkin' about. I am a gangsta."

"Whatever you say gangsta. Whatever you say." D.Dogg chuckled.

CHAPTER 4

The Streets Are Calling

1984 Saturday Afternoon The Next Day

D.Dogg rode in the back seat of the Mercedes as, Gail, drove down 8th St., turning left on Phelps. He couldn't help, but to feel a little embarrassed about his neighborhood. Seeing how, Gail, and Dynamite came from such a nice area.

Both sides of Phelps, a narrow little street, was full of gang bangers, dope dealers, and drug addicts. Each in their own little circle, the gang bangers drinking 40 ounces of old English, and smoking on sherm. Dope dealers and hustlers shooting a game of craps. While the drug addicts ran around like roaches caught in the light trying to find a hit of dope.

Up the block at Cutie Pie Park, hood rats, lounged around like Divas. While players barbequed, played Pinocle, and smoked a lot of weed. This was just another day out on the block.

"Check this out, Gail, you can just drop me off right here." D.Dogg said from the back seat of the Mercedes, not wanting Gail to see his house that was only a short block away.

Gail felt insulted that D.Dogg would even suggest that she stop her car amongst all the criminal activity taking place around her; that was forcing her to drive at a slower than cruising pace was terrified. Before she had a chance to respond to D.Dogg's outrageous request. A dirty, bald headed, dark skinned man dressed in only his pajama bottom, no shirt, a pair of old house shoes with a crack pipe dangling out of the corner of his mouth, started banging on, Gail's, window motioning for her to roll it down.

Gail's heart jumped out of her chest upon seeing the angry, shirtless man banging on her window. Securing her door, frantically, Gail, looked around for a way through the jammed pack street. But the car directly in front of her was at a dead stop because, it was involved in a drug transaction. Then cars going in the opposite direction was moving at a snail's pace. There was no way out. Gail, D.Dogg, and Dynamic were trapped.

"What you need lady? What you need? I got it right here. Let me in before the cops come." The shirtless man screamed at, Gail. Trying to get inside the car with the two white girls for a quick sell. Before another faster talking crackhead beat him to the punch.

D.Dogg who had been taking in the scene comfortably in the back seat of the Mercedes behind the tinted windows, opened the back door and jumped out of the car. "Nigga, if you don't get your crack head ass away from this car. I'm going' to have you leakin' blood all over this muthafucka!" D.Dogg yelled at the crack head man that he knew as B.M.

Standing next to the Mercedes. "Oh shit, my bad D.Dogg. I didn't know you were back there."

Standing next to the Mercedes with the back door open. D.Dogg glared at B.M., as other crack heads begin to move in. Swarming around the Mercedes ready to take advantage of the two naive looking white girls. "Yeah, nigga I'm back here. So back the fuck up. And that goes for the rest of you crack head muthafuckas too!" D.Dogg yelled. Prompting B.M. And the rest of the crack heads to back away from the car.

Gail looked disgustedly at the Astro Van that had stopped directly in front of her on the narrow, that had more cars parked on it than a Flea Market, preventing her from moving forward. Hustlers ran back and forth in between the cars trying to out hustle each other. "This is totally insane. I never seen anything quite like it before. These people are out here involved in illegal activity in broad daylight like it's legal. Where in the hell are all the police?"

"If it's in the game, then it's in the game, Gail," D.Dogg hollered back at Gail. As he noticed his best friend G. serving crack to the people in the Astro Van. "Hurry up G.! You holdin' up traffic blood!" D.Dogg shouted at G, who proceeded to handle his business without a second thought to what D.Dogg had said. G. walked over to D.Dogg with a big smile on his face, his eyes glued to Gail's pretty blue eyes the whole time. Who sat shocked, next to, Dynamite, inside the Mercedes, stuck in the middle of the street.

"Nigga what the fuck you talkin' about, I'm holdin' up traffic? You startin' to sound like one of these bitch ass neighborhood watch muthafuckas." G. stopped to admire the Mercedes. "Damn this Mercedes is tight. Who is that bad ass bitch in the car with, Dynamite?"

D.Dogg let out a little laugh. "Blood you trippin'. That ain't some punk rock bitch. That's Dynamite's mama."

G. gave D.Dogg a disbelieving look. "Nigga if that's, Dynamite's mama. Then I'm about to be her step daddy."

D.Dogg, feeling protective of, Gail decided to set the record straight. "Nigga let that shit go. Gail, ain't fuckin' with you."

Hearing a little anger in D.Dogg's voice G. got defensive. "What you mean she ain't fuckin' with me? You speakin' for her now? Are you fuckin' her too?"

Not wanting things to escalate into something more serious. D.Dogg smiled at his best friend. "Yeah whatever you say, blood, "Changing the subject D.Dogg went on. "You seen Big Time out here?"

One of G.'s personal customers drove up in a white Toyota

truck and parked behind, Gail's, black Mercedes. Tired of waiting for the two friends to finish talking. The driver of the truck started blowing his horn to get G.'s attention.

G. frowned at the sound of the horn, and put a finger up indicating for the customer to wait a minute.

"Yeah, I seen that square ass nigga a lil while ago. He said that he was going' home to chill with Jazzy," The driver of the truck impatiently blew his horn again. "Say D.Dogg, I'll catch up with you later. I'm out here on my grind." The two friends gave each other daps and went their separate ways.

Never before being up so close and personal to the game as it is. Gail continued to stare in amazement at all the criminal activity taking place only two feet from her body. "You have some very bold friends, Derek."

D.Dogg looked out the window to the all too familiar scene, and just smiled. "It comes with the territory, Gail, it comes with the territory."

Gail made a left on Superior St. A short narrow street shaded by old trees that stood in front of old houses lining both sides of the streets. "Welcome to the ghetto, Gail." D.Dogg announced as, Gail, pulled in front of a red and white house that was in desperate need of a paint job, where D.Dogg, Big Time, and their mother lived. A 1972 blue Cadillac, sitting on two flat tires with its hood raised up, was sitting in the driveway. There was no fence guarding a well-kept yard despite its surrounding.

Gail's mind quickly flashed back to other rough areas that her legal profession had taken her. As she parked her Mercedes in front of D.Dogg's house. "I agree, Derek. This is a very bad neighborhood. But I been to some very big projects in some very big cities and this isn't the ghetto."

D.Dogg opened the back door of the Mercedes and grabbed his shopping bags before getting out of the car. "The only difference between a poor, messed up neighborhood, and the projects is that we live in some cheap ass houses, and they live in some cheap ass apartment buildings. Wherever you got blacks killing blacks, and dope being served more faithfully than Jesus, it's the ghetto Gail. Please believe it. The game is the same from city to city, and state to state."

Chilling inside the house Big Time, and Jazzy, noticed D.Dogg and Dynamite carrying loads of shopping bags from a black Mercedes. And not wanting to be left out on whatever it was that was going on, the two of them rushed outside to join the others.

"What's this D.Dogg? You and Dynamite hit a big lick or something? What y'all got in all these bags? And where did y'all steal this tight ass Mercedes from. And please don't tell me that the two of you then kidnapped this pretty lady standing' here." Big Time teased.

Dynamite beamed as she smiled at Big Time, whom she was

very fond of and considered him, not only D.Dogg's twin, but her big brother. "No, we haven't hit any licks. And we haven't kidnapped anybody, yet." Dynamite smiled. "This pretty lady here is my mother, Gail. We been out shopping for you and your brother. So here these are for you." Dynamite gave Big Time, the shopping bags she was carrying.

"Thanks." Big Time said. Surprised as well as shocked. Gail smiled at Big Time, and Jazzy, who were going through the shopping bags. "So, I take it that you're Derek's twin brother, John."

Big Time, anticipating how good he would look in his new clothes. Was jolted back to the present upon hearing his real name. He smiled, in uncertainly at the three of them, who were all smiling back at him. "Unfortunately so, but please, call me Big Time. And since Bonnie and Clyde here haven't been out robbing banks. I'm guessing that I have you to thank for all these new clothes."

Gail looked at Big Time curiously, slowly her motherly smile spread across her face, as she appreciated the big difference in personalities between the two brothers. "Thanks really isn't necessary, Big Time, but your welcome all the same. And who is this pretty young girl standing next to you."

Jazzy, smiled shyly at Gail's kind words. "I'm Jazzy, Big's, girlfriend."

Gail had already been wary of letting Dynamite stay overnight at Jazzy's house, but her wariness had dramatically increased since seeing for herself all the illegal activity that was going on in the neighborhood. "Michelle, I know that I told you that you could stay all night at Jazzy's house, but after witnessing what's taking place out here, I'm not so sure that it's safe for you."

Dynamite, blind to the fact that Gail was only concerned with her safety, young heart filled with rage at her mom's suggestion that she wasn't down enough for the streets. "Why mom, because I'm white?" Dynamite fumed.

Gail looked back at the four pair of young eyes staring back at her waiting, for an answer. "I would be lying if I said that wasn't one of my concerns, because it is. But the truth of the matter baby, is that it's not safe for anybody out here. Let alone for a big mouth, spoiled little white girl, like you."

D.Dogg laughed at Gail's assessment of Dynamite. "You're right Gail, it's dangerous for everybody out here. Especially a lil' spoiled white girl. But Dynamite is different. She has me and all my friends to protect her.

OK, Derek I'll let her stay the night. But I'm holding you personally responsible if something happens to my baby." Gail gave in not wanting to embarrass her only child any further.

CHAPTER 5

No Kids Allowed

D.Dogg and Big Time, dressed in their new clothes, strolled through the county fairgrounds later that night with Dynamite and Jazzy by their sides. D.Dogg feeling on top of the world smiled proudly. "Damn nigga we fitted like amuthafucka." D.Dogg said. Sporting a pair of black 501 jeans, San Francisco 49er football Jersey, and a pair of red and black Adidas shoes.

Big Time, also impressed with the way he was looking and feeling, looked down at his silver and black Oakland Raider football Jersey, grey 501 jeans, black and grey Adidas shoes. "Yeah D.Dogg, Gail is cool. She hooked us up with some nice ass fits, plus she blessed us with a thousand dollars. We about to bubble on these fools. With a thousand dollars between us, we can get us three ounces of raw, rock it upoo, and start servin' these fiends. Plus pay Gail, back her G-stack with interest, before the month is out. Ain't no lookin' back from here on out D.Dogg. It's time for us to get paid in full."

D.Dogg admiringly, looked at his brother as he did the math in his head, respecting for the first time that his brother was a bona fide hustler. Just as much as he was a bona fide gangsta. "It's been way past time, if you ask me, blood. I stay down and ready for whatever it takes to make it happen for us. So yeah, nigga you know I got your back to the fullest."

Jazzy, bored with the two brothers talking business, leaned into Big Time's shoulder, hinting for Big Time to put his arm around her. "So, which ride are we going to get on first?" Jazzy asked.

Dynamite taking her cue from, Jazzy, Grabbed D.Dogg, by the hand. "Come on let's go to the bumping cars."

"So, you want to play rough, huh girl? I got something for your lil bad ass." D.Dogg threatened Dynamite after she rammed her bumping car into his.

Dynamite, amused with herself, laughed at D.Dogg as she fled in the other direction. "You have to catch me first."

D.Dogg barreled down in hot pursuit of Dynamite, who was trapped like a deer caught in headlights. "Yeah, I got your lil bad ass now."

Dynamite screamed out loud preparing for the collision that was disrupted, because of Jazzy's life saving heroics. Jazzy slammed her bumper car into the side of D.Dogg's, preventing his goal of a head on collision with Dynamite. Dynamite's safety was only short lived as Big Time came up from behind with a punishing blow that jerked Dynamite in her seat.

Next, the two young couples went over to the roller coaster ride. Riding high up in the sky as they neared the top, Dynamite, smiled at, D.Dogg, grabbing his hand tightly. "I never been on a roller coaster before."

D.Dogg looked at Dynamite as if she were crazy. "What? Girl quit lying."

Dynamite, feeling nervous, scared, happy, and excited all at the same time, held tightly onto D.Dogg for support, and yelled. "I'm not lying! We didn't go to many amusement parks when I was younger and when we did my parents wouldn't let me get on the big rides."

D.Dogg, thinking selfishly about his new clothes, yelled at Dynamite, "Fuck! You better not puke on me," D.Dogg shouted as the roller coaster started downhill. "Shit here we go. I hope you're ready."

Dynamite's screams went unheard, while her breath was sucked out of her lungs, as the roller coaster picked up speed, and zoomed downward moving faster and faster as it zigzagged its way around the maze. D.Dogg hollered just as loud as, Dynamite, while, Big Time, and, Jazzy, yelled from the top of their lungs in the car behind them.

D.Dogg and Big Time waited for Dynamite and Jazzy at the hot dog stand. While the two girl's chit-chatted with members of the P.P.G.

"What's up miss good pussies? What that P.P.G. like?" Said Hot Sauce. A slim goodie, high cheek, red bone.

"Pretty Pimpin' Girls. That's what's up?" Jazzy answered, giving the other girl daps.

"So, what you bitches gettin' into later? Y'all going' to the Roxanne Shantae concert?" Asked Rie Rie, a medium height, pretty, brown skinned girl. With a reputation of fighting like a boy.

"Yeah, we goin' bitch. What you think, we a couple of square-ass bitches or somethin'?" Dynamite laughed.

"So, what's up, Michelle, I see you and Jazzy, be hangin' real tight. Does that mean that your ready to be down with the P.P.G.?" Asked Shorty, A little, short and thick pretty little girl.

"First of all, I don't go by Michelle anymore. From now on, you bitches can call me, Dynamite. Secondly, I'm not tryin' to be some high society ghetto bitch. You bitches act like a bunch of black barbies. Been there done that. I'm a gangsta bitch." Dynamite said. Letting it be known.

"Goddamn bitch what's got into you? Talkin' about you a gangsta bitch." Laughed Angel. A promiscuous, pretty, dark skinned girl.

"D.Dogg got into her, that's what happened. She even startin' to talk like that, nigga." Hot Sauce laughed along with the rest of the P.P.G.

"Whatever bitches. Y'all just jealous that don't none of you have a gangsta ass nigga like I do. Come on Jazzy, let's get back to our niggas. Dynamite said, as the two friends walked off.

"Oh wow! That was wild! I thought I was going to die. I couldn't even feel my stomach when we were on our way down." Dynamite said, as she caught up to D.Dogg and Big Time.

D.Dogg looked at Dynamite as if stunned for a moment by her pure beauty. Then, smiled proudly knowing that this pretty young girl with the sparklingly green eyes was his girl. "You were squeezing my fingers so tightly I thought you were going to break the muthfuckas off." D.Dogg laughed.

"Boy, you were screamin' just as loud as me, so stop tryin' to front." Dynamite teased.

D.Dogg, feeling a little embarrassed that everyone was laughing at him, and also a little angry, wanted to set the record straight. "Girl, I was just bullshittin' with you. I ain't scared of nothin'."

Dynamite, stuck her arm out with some attitude with her hand open as a way of telling D.Dogg, I don't want to hear it. "Talk to the hand D.Dogg. Talk to the hand. Because I don't want to hear it. You're the one who's a big ass baby. You were more afraid than I was."

Jazzy, who was laughing her ass off along with Big Time and Dynamite, at D.Dogg who was trying unsuccessfully to defend his manhood against Dynamite's, brutal assault. Wanting to spare D.Dogg anymore embarrassment interrupted the two of them. "So, what time does the Roxanne Shantae concert supposed to start?"

Big Time who was still laughing at his brother's expense, checked his new gold watch that Gail had bought for him. "I seen a flier earlier that said it starts at 9:00 o'clock. So, we got about forty minutes, maybe more, like an hour before it actually starts."

D.Dogg was standing in the photo booth area along with Dynamite, Big Time, and Jazzy, taking pictures along with a crowd of other people. waiting for the concert to begin. D.Dogg sarted to feel a little edgy. "Say, Big Time, I'm going' to pass on this Roxanne Shantae concert." D.Dogg announced.

"What the fuck you talkin' about, you not going' to the concert? You sick or somethin'." Big Time said feeling a little annoyed.

D.Dogg nodded his head to the grass area where a crowd of people were gathered, waiting for the concert. "It ain't nothin' like that. I'm just not feelin' this big ass crowd. Plus, there's way too many Crips out here for me to get loose and enjoy myself."

Big Time looked over the crowd of people waiting for the concert to begin. "Nigga its homies mobbin' all through this muthafucka. Them crip niggas ain't going' to try nothin'."

D.Dogg grabbed Dynamite by the hand. "I'm not worried about them crip niggas tryin' anything. I don't want to get any blood on my new clothes from dumpin' on them fools. So, check game. I'll meet you at the house after the concert. I'm going' to go and see if I can win Dynamite one of those big stuff animals, I seen her lookin' at. And then I'm out of here."

Big Time knew that it was useless to try and reason with his brother when he got in one of his dark moods. So, he reached over and gave D.Dogg a hug. "Do what you feel."

D.Dogg returned Big Time's hug, before the two brothers went their separate ways. "I always do, blood. I always do."

D.Dogg and Dynamite walked through the county fairgrounds feeling untouchable, as they searched for the booth with the big Bengal Tiger. "Are we really not going to the concert?" Dynamite asked. With a little girl pout.

D.Dogg looked at Dynamite and laughed. "Fuck that concert. You said you just bought her new tape. So, when you get home listen to it. You can have your own little private concert right there in your big fancy bedroom."

Dynamite stepped in front of D.Dogg. Stopping his movement, putting her arms around his neck, guiding his mouth to her eagerly awaiting lips. The two young lovers kissed passionately with no regard to any noisy spectators mingling throughout the fairgrounds. My private concert wouldn't be any fun unless you were there with me."

Holding Dynamite's face close to his own, D.Dogg, whispered into her ear. "I love you."

Dynamite smiled her beautiful smile, and spoke softly into D.Dogg's neck. "I love you too, D.Dogg."

They approached an old, tall white man, with a big fat pot belly, salt and pepper hair dressed in a plain white button up shirt, and a pair of wrangler jeans. He wore black cowboy boots and smiled like the devil as they approached him. The man, yelled out to D.Dogg, and, Dynamite, as they approached his booth.

"Step right up young man, and see if you can win your pretty little gal here a prize. I don't normally do this, but I'll tell you what I'm going to do. I usually give out 3 balls for 5 dollars, but because I'm a sucker for love, and it's obvious for even a blind old coot like me to see that the two of you are in love. Here's what I'm going to do you man. I'm going to give you 5 balls for 7 dollars and all you have to do is make five straight shots. To win your pretty gal here one of these big stuff animals.

"What's your name sweetheart?" The old Carney asked, Dynamite. "Dynamite" Dynamite laughed openly.

The Carney looked over the two youngstas and smiled. "Dynamite, now ain't that cute as a firecracker. I can't say that I ever met anyone with the name, Dynamite, before. And what's your name young man." The Carney asked D.Dogg.

"My name is, D.Dogg." D.Dogg laughed along with, Dynamite. The old Carney chuckled. "D.Dogg, now ain't that cooler than the shade. OK then D.Dogg, are you ready to win Dynamite one of these big stuff animals?"

D.Dogg looked at the big white backboard with the green basketball rim attached to it. "So, what do I have to do to win the Bengal Tiger make 5 straight shots?"

The Carney figuring, he could get at least 50 dollars from the well-dressed, tough looking black kid trying to impress the pretty little white girl. "That's about the way it works, D.Dogg, but like I said I'm a sucker for love, and I'm terrified of Dynamite." D.Dogg and Dynamite bust up laughing at the Carney's joke, as he continued with his hustle. "So, here's what I'm going to do for you. You make 4 baskets in a row, and I'll give cute little Dynamite here the prize of her choice." The old Carney then took a ball and shot it through the basket to show, D.Dogg, how easy it was.

D.Dogg gave the Carney 7 dollars, and the Carney handed him 5 basketballs. D.Dogg's first shot bounced off the rim. "Aw fuck!" Shouted D.Dogg.

The old Carney a veteran at his trade egged, D.Dogg on. "Don't panic, D.Dogg. You still have four shots left. I know you can do it."

D.Dogg missed two more shots leaving him with only two balls to make four shots. "Damn, what you got springs on that back board or something. Let me buy two more balls."

"I can only sell you 3 balls for 5 dollars, or 5 balls for 7 dollars. You don't have to make four straight shots to win a prize. If you make just one basket, you'll still win a prize." The Carney said. Happy to have a young macho mark trying to impress his girlfriend. It made for a good profit. D.Dogg reached into his pocket and pulled out 5 dollars. "Fuck that, I didn't come here to win one of those lil' plastic ass toys. Let me get three more balls."

Dynamite, always fast on her feet, did some quick math in her head. "You might as well get five more balls it will be cheaper. Plus, you'll have more chances to win."

Seeing dollar signs in his eyes, the Carney smiled at Dynamite. "Dynamite's right, D.Dogg. You got a smart gal there. The odds are in your favor if you buy 5 more balls instead of only 3.

D.Dogg handed the Carney two more dollars. "Yeah, imagine that. Let me get 5 more balls then. D.Dogg missed three straight shots, then shouted angrily. "I ain't made a fuckin' shot yet."

The Carney a season veteran at hustling kids with big egos. Grabbed a basketball from underneath the stand and swished it through the hoop. "You see that, D.Dogg, ain't nothing wrong with the ball or the rim. It's your shot. You got to arc the ball."

D.Dogg, feeling frustrated, gave Dynamite one of the balls. "Here, see if your shot is any better than mine."

Dynamite shook her head, smiled, and then handed the ball back to D.Dogg. "No, I want you to win it for me. So here, keep shooting"'

D.Dogg shouted as he missed three out of five shots and slammed seven more dollars down on the booth. "Man, fuck this shit."

The Carney gave D.Dogg 5 more basketballs, and cheered him on. "Come on now D.Dogg I know you can do it." Dynamite gave D.Dogg a kiss for luck, who made his first two shots, and then missed the next three. Angrily, D.Dogg slammed seven more dollars down on the counter. "This shit is getting crazy. We should have went to the fuckin' concert. This old white man is hustlin' me. Let me get 5 more balls."

Dynamite gave D.Dogg a knowing wink. "Poor baby look who's crying' now. I thought that you were a gangsta. You mean to tell me that you can't even win your girl a stuff animal."

D.Dogg took, Dynamite's challenge as a personal insult. "Girl don't ever test my gangstarisim. Which one of these muthafuckin' stuff animals do you want? I'm tired of this square shit."Dynamite pointed to a giant size orange and black Tiger. "I want that big Bengal Tiger right there."

D.Dogg flashed the gun handle of his 9-millimeter stuck in the waist of his pants at the Carney. "Dynamite if I don't win you that Tiger, then I ain't no gangsta, and that's on everything.

The Carney no longer full of fun and games became instantly afraid. Realizing that D.Dogg was on to him after seeing the gun tuck in his waist. Reached underneath the booth and gave D.Dogg a different set of basketballs. "Why don't you try these ones, D.Dogg. They're my lucky ones."

D.Dogg took the basketballs from the Carney and made four straight shots. "Now give my girl her Tiger old man. And next time don't take so muthafuckin' long to give me the balls that's not lop-sided."

Dynamite smiled like she had just won the lottery. "Now that's what I'm talkin' about, daddy, keep it gangsta foe me."

D.Dogg and Dynamite walked past the outdoor concert on their way home with D.Dogg holding Dynamite's Bengal Tiger. Crowds of people were hanging out screaming, and yelling enjoying the concert. Just then, a skinny, dark skinned, young crip, dressed in a brand-new pair of blue Osh over raw jeans, and the strap hanging down below his waist, called out to D.Dogg from amongst his crip homeboys. The crip's light blue sweatshirt had "east side hustler" on the back, in dark blue letters. He was also, wearing enough jewelry to start his own jewelry business. "What's up D.Dogg?"

D.Dogg gave the Bengal Tiger to Dynamite and checked the gun he had tucked in his waist. "What the fuck this nigga want?" D.Dogg said. Recognizing the young crip, as King, one of Big

Time's friends.

King, well aware of D.Dogg's reputation of putting in work for his hood, wanted to set the record straight of the top. Before things got ugly between D.Dogg and his homeboy's, who were staring hard at D.Dogg.

"Don't trip off them niggas D.Dogg, you know I ain't with that set trippin' shit. You know my motto if don't make dollars then it don't make sense."

D.Dogg, still not trusting any of King's crip homeboy's, relaxed a little bit knowing that King is only about his money, and nothing else. "So, what's up, King, you holdin' me up?" Though D.Dogg still his hand on the butt of his gun tucked in his waist.

King looked over at Dynamite holding her stuffed animal, checking her out. "I seen my boy, Big Time, earlier, and he told me that the two of you were ready to come up and start having it your way. I'm glad to see the upgrade in you niggas clothing game. Ya'll lookin' like some real ballers tonight. Like I told, Big Time, I got the plug that you niggas need. Ya'll fuck with me and skies the limit," King smiled a flirtatious smile at, Dynamite. "And you must be, Dynamite? I heard that you had a down lil' white girl on your team, D.Dogg. But I didn't know that she was a dime piece. You got yourself a real winner here."

D.Dogg, feeling disrespected by King's flirting with Dynamite, became angry. "What the fuck that got to do with what you and Big Time was talkin' about."

King, remembering what happened to his friend, Silky, behind talkin' to Dynamite, didn't want to push things. "No disrespect, D.Dogg. I was just givin' you your props."

D.Dogg, already not caring for King as it is, responded defensively. "I don't need your props nigga. I'm outta here. And remember, whatever you and Big Time got goin' on is between you and him. I'm not a dope dealer, nigga. I'm a gangsta, and I set trip."

CHAPTER 6

Dynamite

November 8th, 1998

Standing in a private room at the hospital, Dynamite and G Gunna waited for some news on Syndicate. G Gunna, half black, and half Mexican. Known as a Fly boy. The 28 year-old, stood 5' 7" 160 pounds soaking wet, with short curly hair, was a cold-blooded killer. He was also, the first one to join up with, D.Dogg and Big Time, when they first started the, Syndicate family.

"Does anybody know who shot the boss?" G Gunna asked Dynamite. Dynamite, full of anxiety, paced the room nervously. "It was them punk ass niggas from Richmond, that we had some funk with a while back. Sunshine got off on them with, Syndicate's Mac.11 and killed one of um. He had a Richmond I.D. That's how we know it was them." G Gunna's heart grew heavy from worrying about, Sunshine. "So how is Sunshine holding up?"

Dynamite turned her back to G Gunna and looked out the window. "Not too good. She's takin' it pretty hard. She said that she was messing with the C.D.'s when them niggas rode up on um."

G Gunna lit a cigarette. "If anything, it's my fault I'm in charge of security. I shouldn't have let Syndicate talk me out of keepin' his bodyguards. Sunshine has more heart than a lot of niggas out on the block. If it wasn't for her, we wouldn't know who in the fuck did this."

Dynamite started to cry. "G Gunna, I hope Syndicate doesn't die. They shot him five times. The doctor said that it's fifty-fifty he'll make it through the operation.

G Gunna puffed aggressively on his Newport. "Fuck what the Doctor is talkin' about. My nigga, ain't goin' out like this."

Worthy, a 29-year-old hustler, dark skinned, tall, and, slim, one of, Big Time's, original dope dealers, knocked on the room door with a sense of urgency. "Dynamite! G Gunna! You guys better get out here quick. The police are all over, Sunshine."

Dynamite, forgetting her own pain for the moment, ran past Worthy down the hall. To where Sunshine was sitting down covering her face, rocking back and forth as the police questioned her unmercifully.

Dynamite looked down at the beautiful seventeen-year-old red bone, with the long curly brown hair, and big brown eyes full of tears. Sunshine was her daddy's little angel and Dynamite couldn't stand to see the police braiding her with questions.

"What the fuck are you sons of bitches doing, drilling' my daughter? Can't you see that she isn't in the right state of mind to be asking her questions?"

"We have a job to do lady. There was a big shoot out and a killing. And your daughter is our only witness." Officer Wilson, a big fat, white cop answered. With an air of arrogance and lack of empathy.

"Her Father was also shot 5 times. What about that? You sons of bitches need to be out trying to find the muthafuckas responsible for that. Instead of standing' here breathing all down my daughter's neck," Dynamite shouted at officer Wilson. "And why are you questioning her without her lawyer present? Did any of you read her Miranda Rights to her?"

Poppa Fly, 30-years-old, 190 pounds, solid as a rock, brown skinned, tatted back, with long hair, had the reputation of being the most brutal killer in all of Stockton. His loyalty to Syndicate himself and the syndicate family was legendary. Sat next to, Sunshine, with a protective arm around her. "All these fagots did was ask her who killed that nigga." Poppa Fly told Dynamite.

"I understand that you're upset Poppa Fly, but you better watch your fucking mouth." Officer Wilson said. Poppa Fly stood up in front of Officer Wilson. "Or what. What the fuck you goin' to do."

"Or I will take your black ass down on a parole violation. I'm sure that I can find something that will stick." Officer Wilson said. Trying hard not to show any fear.

Low, 27, 6'1", 235 pounds of muscle, black as tar, with a shining bald head, stepped up from where he was standing next to a T.V. News crew, trying unsuccessfully to cover the story. "You bitch ass nigga. You ain't taking' my homeboy no fuckin' wear."

A short, skinny, Barney Fife, looking cop, with his hand on his weapon, yelled at Low, "We got a cell with your name on it to, Low!"

Whip, 29, 6'2" tall, and bulky, sporting and extra-long perm, standing next to, Low, spoke up. "You touch anybody with the syndicate, and we going' to tear this hospital up."

Blondie, a tall, muscular, white cop. Well-known and respected in the neighborhood tried to ease the tension. "I know that you're not trying to incite a riot are you, Whip?"

Whip, not in the mood to be nice to any cops, regardless of how cool they were. "We just going to finish whatever you bitch ass muthafuckas start."

There a well-built black sergeant by the name of Officer Davis, known to everyone on the block as Officer Tom, wanted to rub some salt into the killer's wounds. "What's wrong, G Gunna? You and your boy's mad that you couldn't protect the boss." "Naw we couldn't protect him, just like that badge can't protect you." G

Gunna said itching to squeeze the trigger on the police officer.

Dynamite shook her hand back and forth across her throat. "Kill it family, that's enough. Ain't none of this shit goin' to help, Syndicate." Dynamite turned towards Officer Wilson. "So, Mr. Policeman, are you going to arrest my daughter or not."

"Where not here to arrest her. We just want to ask her some questions." Officer Wilson said. Starting to feel the pressure in the room.

"Well then, from now on, any questions you want to ask my daughter, you can ask me. I'm also her Lawyer. Poppa Fly, take Sunshine, and get her away from these officers. Any questions you have for me, you can ask me later. Right now, I'm going to go and check on my husband." Dynamite turned and walked away towards the private waiting room.

When Dynamite entered the room, she found Krystal with tears streaming down her face. "Krystal, have you heard anything."

Krystal, quickly wiped a tear off the tip of her nose, "I haven't heard nothin' Dynamite." Krystal said with quivering lips.

Dynamite heard someone coming down the hallway and looked up to see, Nutts, who was a short, medium built, dark skinned man, with dreadlocks. He was dressed in a black tailored suit, a black gangsta Fedora, and a pair of alligator shoes fitted perfectly on his feet. He has a giant gold, Nutts Mandolin hung around his neck, a diamond-encrusted pinky ring rested on his finger to go along with his diamond-encrusted Rolex watch.

"Dynamite what the fuck happened?" Nutts asked impatiently.

Dynamite rushed over and gave, Nutts, a hug. "Nutts, when did you get here? I'm sure glad to see you."

"I was in the Town when I heard what happened through the wire. So, I smashed down here as soon as I heard. So, how is he?" Nutts asked, pushing Dynamite back from him so that he could look her in the eyes. "We don't know yet. Lynette is still in there operating on him." Dynamite said as tears came to her eyes.

"Nutts, unfazed by life and death situations was all business. "Do you know who shot him?"

"Looks like it was them Richmond niggas, we had some funk with a while back." Dynamite said, folding her arms to keep herself together.

"Where the fuck was his bodyguards at?" Nutts, shouted angrily, as he gave his walking cane, custom made from Elephant Tusk trimmed in gold, to one of his bodyguards. And his mink coat, and Fedora to another.

Dynamite closed her eyes and shook her head. "Syndicate wouldn't let G Gunna do his job. He said that he didn't want anyone following him around all day."

Nutts paced back and forth across the floor. "That nigga still thinks that's he's a fuckin' gang banger. He's in charge one the biggest operations in the Central Valley. Everybody and their mama is gunning for him. Once he gets back on his feet, I'm goin' to have a long talk with him. And explain to him that he can't be taking unnecessary risk."

Dynamite walked to the window and looked out as tears started to run down her face. "He has to pull through Nutts, I don't know what I would do without him."

Nutts, not used to seeing Dynamite so vulnerable, was disturbed "Come on now, Dynamite, keep it gangsta. Now's not the time for you to be falling' apart. You have to be strong for Syndicate and the rest of the family. Besides if, Syndicate was goin' to die, he would have died out there on the streets. Not in the comfort of this hospital with all his family and friends around." Nutts gave Dynamite a comforting smile.

Dynamite turned from the window and gave Nutts a small smile. "I'm sure glad you're hear, Nutts."

Nutts sat down in a chair with his back against the wall. "How's my God daughter doing'?"

Dynamite wrapped her arms around her shoulders. Trying hard to keep it together. "She went into shock. The Doctor gave her a shot. Hopefully, she'll be alright. I told Poppa Fly to get her out of here. The police were all over her trying to get information on that nigga that got smoked."

Leaning back in the chair, Nutts gave Dynamite his full

attention. "Did she make a statement?"

Dynamite looked up at Nutts, offended that he would even ask such a question. "She didn't tell them shit."

Unfazed by Dynamite's rudeness, Nutts Smiled a fatherly smile. "That's my girl. Syndicate's schooled her right."

"The game schooled her right. Sunshine is her daddy's lil girl. She's going to always keep it gangsta."

"I've known Syndicate for 15 years now, and the only time I seen him show any kind of emotion was when he found out, Sunshine was his daughter." Nutts reminisced.

"Yeah, he had a hard time dealing' with that. Especially with the way she was living, and those terrible things she was doing' out on the streets." Dynamite sighed, as she remembered Sunshine's troubled past. Nutts stood up and walked to the window, looking out at the cars below. "Shit that nigga was only, what 14-years-old, when that bitch Kat got pregnant. He was still young in the game. He had to learn the hard way that bitches are not to be trusted."

"The thing that really bothered him the most was that he used to see Sunshine out on the block turning' tricks for weed, and basically just being a little hoe. He told me that he used to always wonder where in the fuck her father was. And it turns out he was standing right next to her the whole time." Dynamite remembered sadly.

"Everybody in Stockton knows who Sunshine's father is

now. It's been four years since Syndicate found out that Sunshine was his daughter. And them same niggas that were takin' advantage of her, be shakin' in they boots every time Sunshine walks by." Nutts turned and faced Dynamite. "Syndicate cried me a river when he told me his little girl wanted to be a gangsta. He was like, I love her way too much to tell her no. Besides it's in her blood."

Hearing footsteps, Dynamite and Nutts, turned to the door. As the Doctor entered the room along with the syndicate family. "Lynette! How is Syndicate?" Dynamite asked, as she rushed over to the Doctor.

"The good news is that he made it through the operation." Dr. Lynette said in a calm professional voice.

Dynamite covered her mouth with her hand afraid to ask the question. "And what's the bad news?"

Tenderly, but still professionally, Dr Lynette, held Dynamite's hand. He lost an awful lot of blood, Dynamite. And I'm afraid that he slipped into a coma."

Dynamite fought back the tears, as the rest of the family stood shock still. "A coma, oh my god, Lynette. How long will he be in a coma?"

"You never can tell about these things. It could be days, weeks, months, or sadly even years. We just have no way of knowing. All we can do is be thankful that he's still alive and pray that he wakes up soon. Dr. Lynette said. Fighting back tears of her own.

As if a switch had been flipped on, the tears stopped running down Dynamite's face, and her resolve returned. The only thing on her mind was revenge. "When can I see him?"

"Give me twenty minutes to prepare him Dynamite, and then I will come back for you. Anybody else wanting to visit will have to wait until another day. Syndicate needs his rest and we still have to monitor him closely to make sure there aren't anymore complications." Dr Lynette said as she walked out of the room.

About a half hour later, Dynamite sat next to Syndicate in the hospital room, holding his hand. "I'm right here daddy, the whole family is here. I love you so much. I know that you can hear me. I can feel your warrior spirit living in my soul. So, get your rest daddy and let your mind be at ease."

"Because even though I want to break down and cry. Like the lil spoiled, rich girl, that you used to call me. I promise you, daddy, that I'm going' to keep it gangsta foe you. Them niggas who did this won't live out the week. Like you told me a long time ago daddy, some time you have to say fuck your feeling's and that business is business. Only this here is personal, just like you made it personal when them niggas killed Big Time."

CHAPTER 7

Trapped In The Game

May 17th, 1985

Kicking back on his black leather, butter soft sofa, Big Time, relaxed in his duplex watching the Celtics play the Lakers on his new Zenith television. While he counted his dope money, that was sitting on the coffee table in front of him, he heard a loud pounding at the front door. Pissed off about all the noise, Big Time, got up to see who was disturbing his peace of mind. Looking through the peep hole, he became even angrier to see that it was his twin brother, D.Dogg.

"Why the fuck you bangin' on the door like a goddamn fool, nigga?" Big Time, yelled while holding the door open for D.Dogg. "What you lost your key again?"

D.Dogg strutted into the duplex like he didn't have a care in the world. Walked over to the wet bar and fixed himself a drink.

"Naw, nigga, I didn't lose my key. I forgot it," See its right here," D.Dogg held up his key that was sitting on the bar. "What you doin' over there with all that money out? Waiting for a nigga like me to come along and rob you?" D.Dogg laughed.

"Yeah, nigga, funny. Naw I'm just getting this money together for Juan. I been waitin' on his fat ass to call me back, he's late."

"That fat ass Mexican still chargin' $550 dollars an ounce. D.Dogg questioned Fat Juan's prices. A 350-pound drug dealer, whose family ran a drug cartel from Mexico.

"Yeah" Big Time, said as he turned off the television and turned on the house stereo.

D.Dogg downed his shot of Tangeray. "I thought that your Crip potna, King, was supposed to supply you with a boss plug. We payin' damn near five G's for nine ounces, that ain't no love."

Big Time placed rubber bands around thousand-dollar stacks of money. "Business is business, and what you talkin' about, we? I don't see you doing' no hustlin'.

D.Dogg poured himself another drink. "What the fuck you talkin' about I be getting my hustle on."

Big Time let out a sarcastic laugh. "Nigga, it takes you a whole week just to get off one ounce. That ain't shit. Plus, you fuck off half the money gambling and what not."

D.Dogg sat down next to Big Time, on the sofa. "Blood, you

already know I ain't no muthafuckin' dope dealer, I'm a gangsta."

"Nigga, real gangstas get money. You ain't nothin' but a wanna be, gangsta." Big Time, said. Pouring salt on D.Dogg's wounds.

D.Dogg, offended by Big Time's honesty, stood back up. "Nigga, gangsta's kill muthafuckas too, and if you wasn't my brother I would smoke your ass from comin' at me sideways like that."

Nigga, fuck you and what you talkin' about." Big Time, answered; starting to get angry himself. As the phone started to ring breaking the tension between the two brothers. Big Time picked it up on the first ring. "Fat Juan, what's up? Why it take you so long to get back at me?"

Fat Juan laid back in bed at his hotel suite at the Ramada Inn. "Chill, amigo. The money ain't going nowhere. All work and no pleasure is bad for business, "Fat Juan, smiled at the pretty black girl that was giving him a blow job. "So, what's what amigo, you ready for me?"

"Nigga, I stay on my grind 24-7, I'm always ready." Big Time said. Still eyeing, D.Dogg closely.

"I got this lil black bitch sucking my dick right now. I should be done busting' my nut in about twenty minutes. So, meet me at the spot in the Vista, in about forty minutes." Fat Juan grabbed the girl by the back of her head, pushing up and down on it.

"You ain't nothin' but a fat ass trick, Juan. You took too long with your lil black bitch. I have to pick up my girl, from getting her hair done. So, I'm sendin' my brother D.Dogg." Big Time said taking charge.

"Aw fuck naw, amigo. We can do this another time. I'm not trying to deal with, D.Dogg that fool be tripping." Fat Juan said, pushing the girl off him, as he sat up in bed.

"Don't worry about it, Fat Juan. D.Dogg is cool, as long, as he isn't loaded." Big Time said, as he looked over at, D.Dogg, who was fixing himself another drink.

"You better make sure that he isn't loaded then." Fat Juan said no longer in a jovial mood.

"Chill out, blood. It's cool. I wouldn't send him if he was loaded." Big Time said. As he stuffed money inside a rainbow bread bag.

"If he's late, you just going to be ass out, because I'm not waiting' around." Fat Juan complained.

"He'll be there." Big Time answered. Hanging up the phone. D.Dogg looked at Big Time, with accusing eyes. "What the fuck you and that fat Mexican tallkin' about?"

"He said that you be trippin'," he doesn't want you handling the transaction. Big Time handed D.Dogg the bag full of money.

"Nigga, who in the fuck said that I was going' to handle the transaction. What we need to do is lay his punk ass down and take his shit." D.Dogg tossed the bag of money on the coffee table.

Big Time poured himself a drink. "Come on now, D.Dogg. That ain't staying' true to the game."

D.Dogg, walked over to Big Time, and poked him in the chest. "Nigga, what the fuck you talkin' about, that ain't stayin' true to the game? That soft heart of yours is going' to cost you one day. These punk muthafuckas, out here robbin' us, chargin' these high ass prices. And we supposed to just accept that as business as usual. Nigga, I don't know what part of the game you livin' by, but you got me fucked up."

"Blood, all we got is our balls, and our word. We keep stackin' like we doin now, and one day we going to be on top of all these fools." Big Time put his arm around his brother, trying to re-assure him.

D.Dogg shook his head disapprovingly. "You got some big dreams Big Time. But we a long way from the top."

Big Time walked over to the coffee table and picked up stacks of money. "We a long ways from the bottom too," Big Time, spread his arms out wide. "Look at us blood. We got our own spot, we both driving' somethin' cool. Bitches be jockin' non-stop and we got over twenty thousand between us. This time last year all we had was that thousand dollars that, Gail blessed us with. The grind takes time, blood. It's like anything else in life. The more you put into it, the more you going to get out of it. So, stop treatin' it like a game of dice, and start treatin' it like the business it is."

"Nigga, this your business." D.Dogg downed his drink and pulled out a little vial of sherm out of his pocket. Before dipping his Newport into the liquid.

"Blood, what the fuck you doin' I told Fat Juan that you wouldn't be loaded." Big Time was beside himself.

"Nigga, fuck you, and fuck fat ass Juan, this is my business." D.Dogg lit up the sherm soaked Newport. Grabbed the rainbow bread bag from off the coffee table and walked out the front door.

Later that night, Big Time, laid back on his king size bed, with his hands locked behind his head staring at the ceiling, deep in thought.

"What's wrong, Big. Why you so quiet?" Jazzy asked. Laying next to, Big Time, in one of his oversized sweatshirts listening to Jodeci's 'Forever My Lady'

"It's D.Dogg." Big Time confessed.
Laying with her head on, Big Time's hairy chest, Jazzy looked up at him. "D.Dogg, what's wrong with D.Dogg. What happened to him?"

"Nothin' happened to him. Not yet anyway." Big Time's voice trailed off.

"Then what's wrong." Jazzy asked again starting to get worried.

"He's out of control. He has his mind set on being this big bad gangsta. I thought that once things started to get a little better for us, he would calm his ass down. But shit, it seems as if the more money we get the crazier that nigga gets." Big Time said. Still staring at the ceiling

"Maybe you can ask Dynamite, to talk some sense into him." Jazzy, suggested. Full of concern for Big Time's well-being.

Big Time, laughed. "That's like askin' Bonnie, to tell, Clyde, to stop robbin' banks. It's not going' too happened."

"Yeah, I guess you're right, Dynamite thinks she's a gangsta too. She told me the other day that she wanted to do a drive-by." Jazzy said, as she rubbed on Big Time's chest.

"Yeah D.Dogg, has turned that girl out," Big Time, shook his head. Then again, maybe it's just me. For the first time in my life, I'm finally starting to feel alive. Like I'm somebody."

Unbuttoning Big Time's pants, Jazzy using her small delicate hands reached down and caressed his balls. "You always been somebody to me, Big."

"Yeah, I know Jazzy, but it's different now. I have power, nigga's respect me, some of them even look up to me. And I'm not even on top yet." Big Time, said, as his dick started to get hard.

"So, what does D.Dogg have to do with all this?" Jazzy asked, while continuing to massage Big Time's balls and stroking his dick.

"Me and D.Dogg, aren't only brothers. We're also business potna's. Whatever he does, affects me, and whatever I do, affects him. D.Dogg is a killa, I'm not. We have different ideas on how to get rich. His way is going' to get us killed one day." Big Time reached underneath the sweatshirt Jazzy was wearing and slid a finger through her pink panties and started playing with her clit.

"Then why don't you quit bein' his business potna." Jazzy moaned.

"Because he's my brother. We came into this world together and if it comes down to it, we'll leave it together." Pushing, her panties to the side, Big Time slid a second finger inside of Jazzy's sweet, hot, wet pussy.

"Damn, Big, you making me so hot. I'm about to cum all over your fingers. I don't want to talk any more, your making' me scared." Jazzy said. As she pulled, Big Time's pants down to his ankles and took him in her mouth.

"Oh, hell yeah, baby, that's what I'm talkin' about. I don't want to talk anymore more either." Big Time, moaned.

Flipping, Jazzy, over to a 69 position and pulling her panties off her sexy young body. Big Time licked, and sucked on Jazzy's little pussy, like it was Chicken Noddle soup.

Grinding her pussy on Big Time's face, Jazzy came hard. "I want you inside of me." Jazzy, moaned. As she continued to grind her wet pussy all over Big Time's mouth and tongue. Switching positions, Jazzy lay on her back with her sexy legs wide open. Big Time, pulling his pants from around his ankles and with his dick harder than a tree log, he entered Jazzy's tight, sweet, pussy.

Jazzy, with her legs and pretty little, painted feet, dangling over, Big Time's shoulders, screamed out in ecstasy, as Big Time went deep inside of her. "Oh Big, yeah, yeah, I'm cumming again, Oh god fuck, yeah!" Jazzy, cried. As she came for a third time.

"Aw fuck, shit, goddamn, girl, you got some good ass pussy," Big Time grunted.

With sweat dripping off his dark, handsome, face. Big Time, held, Jazzy's legs high in the air and far apart, as he continued to pound on her young pussy. "Oh, yeah baby, fuck, you got the best pussy in Stockton." Big Time panted. As he exploded inside of Jazzy.

"Stockton? Boy you trippin' I got the best pussy in the world." Jazzy pouted. As she held on to Big Time tightly.

CHAPTER 8

Gangsta Bitches

1985

It was an ordinary day at Cutie Pie Park. Young Tenders, lounged throughout the park smoking weed, and getting caught up on the latest gossip. Mob homies played basketball, Northern Mexicans played handball and Junkies shot up in the pissed covered bathroom, where paraphernalia, and condoms, littered the floor. While, D.Dogg, Dynamite, G., Mondo, and Under hung out in the little cul-de-sac parking lot with the rest of the hustlers, slanging rocks.

"D.Dogg, double me up for $50.00 dollars." Stroker, a jet-black crack head, with big bubbling eyes, and a mouth full of yellow teeth, whined.

"I ain't got no double ups, Stroker. All I got is dove, for, dove." D.Dogg explained.

"Come on, D.Dogg, show your O.G., homie some love."

Stroker begged.

"Man fuck! Y

ou crack heads always want somethin' for nothin'. I'll give you four doves, Stroker, that's the best I can do." D.Dogg wanting the sell gave in a little bit.

"Come on, D.Dogg, blood. Let me get the five doves?" Stroker persisted.

"Nigga, you better hurry up and take these four before I change my mind." D.Dogg threatened. Stroker did some quick math in his head before answering. Seeing how he was still coming out on top, he agreed. "OK, then youngsta, shoot me the four doves."

D.Dogg, nodded towards Dynamite. "Dynamite, give this, nigga, four of them twenty-dollar rocks."

Dynamite reached down her baggy sweatpants, and pulled out a plastic bag full of rocks, tied in a knot from in between her legs. Untying the knot, she gave Stroker four little crack rocks. Wasting no time, Stroker put the four crack rocks in his mouth for safe keeping, before reaching out with the money to pay, D.Dogg.

"Nigga, don't give me the money, I didn't give you any dope." D.Dogg responded aggressively.

"My bad, youngsta, here you go, Dynamite." Stroker said. Handing Dynamite the $50.00 dollars, before quickly walking away.

Dynamite put the plastic baggy back up between her legs, and gave D.Dogg the money. "You want something from the store daddy. I'm hungry, I'm going to go and get me a burrito."

"Yeah, have one of those old crack head muthafuckas buy me a 40 ounce." D.Dogg reached into his pocket and gave, Dynamite, the keys to his smoked black, 1964, box Chevy Impala, hydraulics lifted all the way around.

"What kind of 40 ounce do you want?" Dynamite said. Regretting the question as soon as she asked it.

"I thought you were pass all that, white girl, square shit? Old English. What other kind of 40, do you see me drink?" D.Dogg frowned, giving, Dynamite, a hard time.

"Bring us back one too, Dynamite." G., spoke for, Mondo, and Under.

"Y'all niggas better come out y'all pockets. Because I'm not buying you niggas shit." Dynamite replied harshly, not one to be taken advantage of.

"Come on, Dynamite, we got you on the next one." Mondo laughed.

Dynamite, fully laced by D.Dogg of all the game out on the streets, put her foot down. "Don't be trying to play me, Mondo. You niggas can't pimp me. Y'all out her hustling just like us. Besides I don't drink beer."

"Ya nigga drinks beer." Under put his two cents in.

"Well then tell him to buy you niggas a 40, because I'm not buying you niggas shit." Dynamite warned.

D.Dogg laughed at his three best friends trying to get over on, Dynamite. Reached into his pocket and gave, Dynamite, a $10.00 dollar bill. "Here you go, Dynamite, buy them niggas all a 40, and quit trippin' on small shit.

Dynamite looked up at the big billboard sign on the corner of 8th and Airport Way that read "Welcome to Stockton" South Side Merchants Serving you. And thought it funny with all the drug dealers in the area. Dynamite pulled D.Dogg's, 64, Box Chevy into Ralph's Liquor store. A small, mom and pops, establishment with bullet holes in the walls, and steel bars blocking the windows. Groups of young men were hanging out next to the liquor store, at Sticky Fingers Bar-B-Que, shooting dice.

Kat, a 17-year-old, pretty, nicely shaped, light skinned girl, with long brown hair. Known as a gold digger, wore gold rings on each one of her fingers, and ten small gold chains around her neck. Dressed in a blue and white, Fila sweatsuit, and blue and white Fila shoes. Kat was hanging out in front of the liquor store with her cousin Jeanette, the Young Vette. A 17-year-old, pretty, dark skinned, dope dealer, known as a hustler. Fitted in a tight pair of acid washed jeans, and tank top tucked at the waist showing off her well-developed curves. She was also with Shaka, a 16-year-old beast, dark skinned, and full figured with a big ass, big breast, big afro, a a beast. She was known as a beast for her a reputation of knocking girls out. Shaka was dressed in a pair of camouflaged army pants, combat boots, and white tee-shirt.

"No, this punk rock bitch not mobbin' up in here like she from the hood." Kat smirked. As Dynamite pulled the bouncing car to a stop in front of the three girls.

"Where the fuck you think you going', you punk rock, white bitch." Shaka said. Stepping up to D.Dogg's car.

Dynamite mentally prepared herself for the worst as she exited the car. "Who the fuck you callin' a bitch. Bitch!" Dynamite stood toe to toe with Shaka.

"Bitch you better get the fuck out my face. Before I slap the white of yo ass." Shaka threatened.

"Yeah, bitch this is the mob, and we don't want your fake ass out here." Kat stood next to Shaka.

Dynamite, a student of the game, realized that her time was now, to prove herself as a real gangsta bitch. Turned her attention to, Kat. "The only thing fake about me, is that I didn't keep it gangsta and whoop yo, scantless, ass when you fucked my, man."

Kat stepped up to, Dynamite. "Bitch, you ain't nothin' but a punk ass, fake, white hoe. Out here acting like you down. You ain't no gangsta bitch."

Dynamite's face turned beet red with rage. Her green eyes blazed with fire at being disrespected at not being accepted as a gangsta bitch. Dynamite with no thought of the danger she was in, balled her fist up tightly. She hit Kat with all her might, with lightening speed, a left right combination. Kat, stumbled backwards as Dynamite charged towards her, only to be knocked down by, Shaka's hard right hand.

"Oh shit! Come on, them bitches squaben." yelled Deja, A 20-year-old, dark skinned, muscular young man, with a bald head. Known to be the best fighter, and one of the hardest gangsta's in the hood. Jumped up from the dice game, with a wad full of money in his hands. And ran over to where the girls were fighting, along with the rest of the dice shooters.

"Who is that? Dynamite? The lil' homie's, D.Dogg's girl. That lil' white bitch got hands." Hollered Mad Murf, a 22-year-old, light skinned hustler, with a long perm, known for having bitches. Just as Dynamite made it to her feet and started trading punches with Kat and Shaka. Dmove, a 16-ear-old, self-proclaimed pretty boy, with black wavy hair, and high ambitions of being a pimp yelled to no one in particular, "Somebody needs to break that shit up. Dynamite, is already leakin' like crazy."

"Watch out!" Young Tre, a 13-year-old hustler, with a long wild afro, yelled. Too late to do Dynamite any good. As Young Vette, came up from behind her, and hit her with a big wooden stick across her back, knocking her to the ground.'

"Alright that's enough! You bitches break that shit up! Y'all going' to kill that girl!" Deja shouted, as the three girls kicked, and beat Dynamite half to death. "I said break that shit up!" Deja shouted again, as he forcefully pulled the three girls off, Dynamite, helping her to her feet. Dynamite, stood in her bra, exposing her sweet tender white breast from her shirt being torn off her back. Face swollen, nose and mouth full of blood. Dynamite, leaned against, D.Dogg's 64 box Chevy Impala, full of pain. "You alright, Dynamite? Where is the lil homie, D.Dogg, at?" Deja gave Dynamite his red bandana to wipe the blood off her face.

He's at the park," Dynamite said. Spitting blood out of her mouth.

"Give me the keys, and I'll drive you around the corner to the park." Deja offered.

"I'm not going' no fucking where until I get what I came here to get. And I can drive myself back, thank you." Dynamite, reached in her pocket, and gave the neighborhood wino, Batfink, money for a 40 ounce.

"I don't hear you talkin' shit now, you punk rock bitch." Kat taunted.

"Yeah. bitch this is the mob, and you ain't in it. So, go back to the suburbs." Shaka joined in.

G Gunna, 13-years-old, and D.Dogg's lil' homie, spoke up. "It's looks to me like you bitches just jumped her in. So, from here on out, Dynamite is a South Mob Gangsta.

"I'll follow you in my car." Deja told Dynamite as Batfink, gave her the 40 ounce.

Dynamite pulled up at Cutie Pie Park in D.Dogg's 64 box Chevy with Deja and Mad Murf, following close behind. "Dynamite what the fuck happened to you?" D.Dogg snapped, seeing, Dynamite, half naked, bloodied and bruised.

Moving slowly and holding onto her ribs, Dynamite, gave, D.Dogg, his 40 Ounce. "Here's your 40."

"Girl fuck that 40 ounce," D.Dogg took the 40 Ounce from Dynamite and smashed it on the ground. "What the fuck happened to you?" D.Dogg yelled. Pulling his shirt off and placing it over Dynamite's naked shoulders.

"She got into with, Kat, Young Vette, and Shaka." Deja volunteered. As he walked up to D.Dogg, and, Dynamite.

"Come on, I'm taking you to the hospital, I'm going' to kill them bitches. Where my keys at?" D.Dogg yelled, out of control.

Dynamite wincing in pain gave, D.Dogg, his car keys. "No, you're not."

"No, I'm not what? What the fuck you talkin' about?" D.Dogg said. Ready to explode.

"I'm going to handle it myself." Dynamite said barley able to stand up.

"Handle it yourself? Yeah, I heard the fuck out of that one. Get your ass in the car!" D.Dogg shouted. While opening the passenger side door of his 64 box Chevy.

Holding on to her side in obvious pain, Dynamite stubbornly

held her ground. "I'm not goin' nowhere until you promise me, that you'll let me handle it."

Deja, impressed with Dynamite's not give a fuck attitude, came to her defense. "You got yourself a lil' ride or die bitch, D.Dogg. Give her a lil' credit. She was holdin' her own with all three of them bitches."

"You call barely able to walk, leakin' blood all over the place, and her face swollen like she just went 15 rounds with Marvin Hagler, holdin' her own? Because I don't," D.Dogg yelled. "Now get in the goddamn car, before you fuck around and bleed to death.

"I already told you, I ain't going' nowhere, until you promise me." Dynamite stated flatly, refusing to budge.

Deja, let out a small laugh. "Nigga, Dynamite got the heart of a gunslinger. Let her handle her business on her own with them bitches."

"Check this shit out Deja, you might be a little older than me. But you not callin' shots out here. So, stay the fuck up out my business. "D.Dogg threatened.

"Lil' nigga, who the fuck you tryin' to put in check. You can't even check ya bitch. You way out of your league fuckin' with me, boy." No longer laughing, Deja showed a little muscle.

"D.Dogg more concerned with Dynamite than he was with Deja turned his attentions to her. "Fuck it then Dynamite, you want to handle it, then handle it. Now get your ass in the car."

Deja, secretly believing that D.Dogg wasn't gangsta enough for Dynamite, plotted on a way to steal her away from him. "It's about time you start acting like you got some nuts, nigga. And let your girl earn her stripes like the real gangsta bitch she is."

"Nigga I know you not tryin' to question my, nuts? Don't forget, I play with guns just like you do."

Deja, realizing that now wasn't the time, to try and impress, Dynamite, played it off. "Lil nigga, quit trippin."

"Just remember big homie," D.Dogg said mockingly. "I ain't to lil to make change out of a five-dollar ass nigga." D.Dogg not trusting Deja, or his motives answered in kind.

"Yeah, lil' nigga, I'll make sure to warn all the five-dollar ass niggas. Deja laughed, underestimating D.Dogg's bravo.

D.Dogg closed the door behind Dynamite and walked back around to the driver side. Before yelling back over at Deja, "Yeah blood, you make sure you do that!"

CHAPER 9

Baby Girl

Dynamite laid back in her pajamas on her Victoria, Queen size water bed, watching music videos, when D.Dogg walked into the room. "You bring me my ice cream." Dynamite asked excitedly.

"Yeah, I brought your ice cream. What you think I got in these Baskin Robbins bags, Hamburgers?" D.Dogg joked.

Dynamite's green eyes lit up the room when she smiled at, D.Dogg. "Oh, you got jokes, huh, funny man."

D.Dogg pulled the ice cream out of the bags. "I brought you those big chocolate chip cookies that you like too."

Dynamite reached for the cookies and ice cream. "Ow wow, that's a special treat, thanks."

D.Dogg gave Dynamite a spoon. "So how long you plan on stayin' locked up in your mama's house? It's been 3 months since them bitches jumped you."

"Um this ice cream taste good. You want some." Dynamite put the spoon up to, D.Dogg's mouth.

D.Dogg pulled his head back. "No, I don't want any ice cream."

Dynamite smiled her innocent smile at, D.Dogg. "You want a cookie."

D.Dogg slapped, Dynamite's hand away from his face. "Quit playin' with me, Dynamite. If you changed your mind, just tell me, and I'll handle it."

No longer laughing, Dynamite turned serious. "I told you that I would handle it. If you think I'm going' to let them bitches get away with jumping me, then really got me fucked up."

"Then what's the problem? You not still hurting' are you?" D.Dogg reached for Dynamite's ice cream.

"Yeah, I'm cool. I just been doing' a lot of thinking lately." Dynamite said softly, while she spoon fed D.Dogg.

D.Dogg reached for one of Dynamite's, cookies. "Thinkin'? What you been thinkin' about?"

"I been thinking' about, us." Dynamite spoke softly.
"Us? What about us?" D.Dogg questioned.

Dynamite looked into, D.Dogg's eyes.

"I just been thinking about how much I love you and want to spend the rest of my life with you."

"What you trippin' on girl? That ain't nothin' new. We

already decided to get married after you graduate. Let me get another cookie." D.Dogg said. More focused on the cookies, than what was on, Dynamite's mind.

"Here greedy," Dynamite gave D.Dogg another cookie. "I don't want to wait."

"What the fuck you talkin' about, you don't want to wait? You want to get married now?" D.Dogg, looked up at Dynamite shocked.

Dynamite shook her head adamantly. "That's not what I'm talkin' about." Confused, D.Dogg frowned at Dynamite. "Then what the fuck you talkin' about?"

"I don't want to wait until were married to have sex." Dynamite said with a straight face.

Surprised with what Dynamite had to say, D.Dogg jumped up off the bed. "You don't want to wait until were married to have sex? Where is all this comin' from?"

Dynamite reached up and grabbed, D.Dogg's hand guiding him back to the bed. "I don't want to lose you."

"Lose me! Them bitches, must of did more damage than we thought." D.Dogg chuckled.

Dynamite sat next to D.Dogg with a hurt look on her young, pretty, face. "Quit laughing, it's not funny."

Recognizing the seriousness in Dynamite's voice, D.Dogg, became serious too. "Dynamite can't no bitch take me away from you. You're my best friend. Waiting until you get married to have sex has always been a dream of yours. And I promised you that I will make all your dreams come true, even if it kills me."

Dynamite held her head up high. "That's the problem, that isn't my dream anymore. You are my dream come true. The last thing I'm worried about is losing' you to another bitch." Dynamite said. Then she looked into D.Dogg even deeper.

"No, that's not it at all. I'm worried about losing' you to the game. Before I met you, I was living in a fairytale, being daddy's little girl. You introduced me to a whole new world and gave me a whole new identity. You taught me how to do things that I wasn't supposed to learn. You showed me things that I didn't know existed. I fell in love with the game, and I fell in love with your struggle." Dynamite admitted to D.Dogg.

D.Dogg just looked on as Dynamite poured out her heart to him for the first time, listening as she continued.

"I know that at any given moment we can lose our lives out there on the streets. And I embrace that just as you taught me it's just another part of the game. So, what I'm afraid of is that I might not ever know what it feels like to make love to the man I love. You're my daddy now. You taught me the game To have heart and to be down for whatever. And now I need for you to teach me how to be a woman. Daddy, I love you so much, there's absolutely nothing that I wouldn't do for you."

Dynamite stopped talking and just starred at D.Dogg, waiting for what he was going to say.

D.Dogg, hard as a brick after hearing Dynamite's testimony, full of passion and lust, ripped her pajamas off her and pushed her back onto the waterbed. Seeing Dynamite fully naked for the first time, D.Dogg buried his face deep inside of her golden triangle. Licking on her sweet, pink, virgin, pussy like he was a starving young lion.

Dynamite, caught off guard, though well pleased by D.Dogg's enthusiasm, moaned loudly, as her trembling thighs locked around D.Dogg's bald head. "Oh, my god, daddy, that feels so goddamn good. I'm cumming already."

D.Dogg reached up and caressed Dynamite's soft, white, breast with his hands, playing with her little pink nipples. While he continued to lick and suck on her throbbing clit.

Dynamite, in pure bliss, threw her head back hard against the waterbed, as her eyes rolled in the back of her head.
"Oh daddy, what are you doing' down there. I can't take it. I want you inside of me."

Smiling proudly, D.Dogg stood up and got undressed. "Your wish is my command." D.Dogg stood in front of the bed asshole naked with his nuts hanging and his big, black, dick sticking straight out. "Damn, daddy, you think your hard enough." Dynamite smiled innocently, as D.Dogg crawled on top of her, kissing her passionately on the mouth at the same time fingering her virgin tight pussy getting it ready for him to penetrate.

Dynamite, cumming twice already and full of lust and curiosity, reached down and grabbed, D.Dogg's hard, dick. "Come on daddy, make me a woman."

D.Dogg, full of lust himself, used all his will power to maintain some form of control not wanting to hurt Dynamite, as he entered her slowly, for the first time. "Am I hurting' you, Dynamite."

Dynamite, hating the pain, but loving the pleasure, cried out as she wrapped her legs around D.Dogg's waist "Oh daddy yes, but please don't stop."

D.Dogg kissed Dynamite on her small lips as he penetrated deeper inside of her. "Mmm, Dynamite, this pussy is like dope, and I'm hooked.

Dynamite, on an emotional roller coaster, held on to D.Dogg for all she was worth. "Oh daddy, oh daddy, goddamn, I love you so much."

D.Dogg, feeling the time is now to bust, Dynamite's, cherry, and make her a woman. Quit holding back and with full force went as deep as possible inside Dynamite's tight, sweet, pussy. "I'm makin' you a woman now, Dynamite. Whose gangsta bitch, are you? Whose gangsta bitch are you?" D.Dogg ranted.

Dynamite screamed out loud and dug her nails deep into D.Dogg's back. "I'm your gangsta bitch, daddy, I'm your gangsta bitch! Oh god yes, you're so fuckin' big inside of me."

D.Dogg held Dynamite by her ankles and spread her legs far apart her pretty, little, white feet dangling high in the air and dug in the pussy with the rhythm and motion of the waterbed. "Yeah, you a real gangsta bitch now. I should have got this pussy a long time ago."

Out of breath and out of control, Dynamite screamed out of the top of her lungs. "Oh God, daddy, I can't take it, you're too big, your to fucking big."

Turned on beyond control by Dynamite's screaming confession, D.Dogg turned Dynamite over to a Doggy Style position. Holding on to her small waist and with a bloody dick, he entered her from behind. "You like this big black dick inside of you, Dynamite. Don't you." D.Dogg, rocked back and forth on the waterbed, as he fucked Dynamite, like she was a porn star.

"Aw goddamn, yes, fuck me, daddy! I'm cumming, fuck me! It hurts so fuckin' good!" Dynamite yelled, with her sexy, creamy white ass, high up in the air, and her face buried in the pillows. D.Dogg placed his hands on Dynamite's slender white shoulders, and rammed his dick repeatedly inside of her soft, sweet, pink, pussy, as far as he could. "Aw goddamn Dynamite! Aw fuck, goddamn! This lil' pussy is tight. Aw god yeah!" D.Dogg hollered, before shooting his load inside of Dynamite.

Dynamite laid back comfortably on the waterbed, next to

D.Dogg. "Damn that was intense."

"Intense? What the fuck does intense mean. Was it good or not?" D.Dogg laughed.

"It was great daddy, I'm glad we did it." Dynamite wrapped her arms around D.Dogg, and snuggled up under him.

"Yeah, I'm glad we did it too. I don't know how we made it this far. Now we can work on havin' us some kids." D.Dogg said. Half-jokingly.

"Kids, I don't want a bunch of bad ass kids." Dynamite laughed.

"Girl you trippin', we can have our own crime family. A bunch of lil' D.Dogg's and Dynamite's." D.Dogg laughed along with, Dynamite.

"You crazy, daddy." Dynamite cooled.
"I'm just crazy for you, Dynamite." D.Dogg said, with all seriousness.

"I'm crazy for you too, daddy." Dynamite said as she closed her eyes and went to sleep.

CHAPTER 10
Mama's Boy's

September 1985

"Big Time, what's up, blood." D.Dogg spoke into the pay phone.

"Just checkin' paper as always. What's up with you?" Big Time answered.

D.Dogg pulled his dick out and took a piss on the sidewalk. "Keepin' it gangsta as always. Where the fuck you at Big Time."

Checkin' my traps, tryin' to stack a meal ticket. Where the fuck you at.?" Big Time asked. As Vera, a pretty Mexican girl, with long black hair, gave him a wad of money. Then put her hands down his pants, urging him to hurry up, and get off the phone.

"I'm out on the West Side, on my way to that lil' bitch Poison's house. She's been blowin' up my pager all day, tryin' to be a part of the team. I'm about to beat that pussy up." D.Dogg said shaking his dick free of any lingering piss. Before putting it back in his pants.

Lil' Poison is a dime piece." Big Time, grabbed his dick thinking about, Poison.

"Check game, blood. I didn't page you to talk about, Poison." D.Dogg cut Big Time, off.

"What up then nigga, holla at me, I'll holla back." Big Time was all ears.

D.Dogg looked suspiciously at the pay phone. "We need to talk face to face. I don't want to talk on this phone."

"Everything alright?" Big Time, questioned.

D.Dogg checked his pager. "Yeah everything is cool. I just need to talk to you about some paper, that we need to go get."

"Nigga, what the fuck you talkin' about now?" Big Time, frowned.

"Blood! Just meet me at the apartment at 2:00 in the morning'." D.Dogg said impatiently.

"Nigga, at two in the morning' I'll be knee deep in some pussy," Big Time looked down at Vera who was busy giving him a blow job. "Holla at me when the sun rises." Big Time said as he hung the phone up.

Later on, Big Time walked into his mother's house unannounced later that night. A picture of Martin Luther King Jr. stared back at him from hanging on the wall. He glanced into the big, gold, rimmed, painted mirror, hanging on the wall next to the picture of Martin Luther King Jr., and checked himself out. Admiring his reflection in the mirror, he noticed O.Z. A big, muscular, light skinned man, with a short afro, sitting on a worn out, red couch. Watching a very old, black and white television set.

Winky, 32 years of age, very pretty, flawless dark brown skin, big black eyes, and straight black hair, worn down her back in two long french braids. Seeing, Big Time, got up from the back table, where she was smoking crack. And walked barefooted across the old brown carpet. Proudly flaunting her sexy body, in her black spandex tights and tight-fitting black tank top. "Well hello stranger." Winky smiled at, Big Time, before giving him a big hug.

"Let me get another hit, Winky." Yelled Glen. A crack head sitting at the back table.

"Yeah, let me get one too Winky." Yelled Rock. Another crack head sitting at the table.

Winky reached into her bra and pulled out a little plastic bag full of rocks. Taking one of the small rocks, and breaking it in half, she gave one to Glen and one to Rock. "I see you finally made it over here, to see me."

Big Time glanced over at the old blue and white curtains, that's he's been seeing all his life. "Don't start with me mama, you know why I don't like comin' over here."

Winky patted Big Time on the side of his face. "I know you

don't like seeing your mama getting' high.

"That and I don't like being around all these crack head muthafuckas, you got hangin' around over here." Big Time, kissed Winky on the cheek.

"You niggas heard, Big. Now make like a ball and bounce." Holding the door open, Winky, shouted for everyone to leave. Glen, and, Rock, left the house without argument, already knowing how Winky, was behind her two sons.

O.Z. Sat on the couch without budging. "Winky, you need to stop babying that nigga, and quit letting him think that he's running somethin' around here."

Winky put her hands on her hips. "Nigga, you sure in the fuck ain't running shit around here. Now get you big ass up out of here, so I can talk to my son."

O.Z. Stood up as if to leave. "I ain't goin' nowhere without no dope."

I got your dope right her, nigga." Winky, held up the 2 by 4 that she kept behind the front door. Big Time grabbed the 2 by 4 from, Winky. "You heard my, mama, nigga, get you crack head ass up out of here.

"Big Time, you real lucky that Winky is your mama, boy." O.Z. walked up to Winky and reached in her bra and pulled out the little plastic bag full of rocks. Taking out four $20.00 dollar rocks, he kissed her on the mouth, put the plastic bag back down her bra, and walked out of the house.

Big Time, slammed the door behind O.Z. "Mama, why you fuck with that big, sorry ass nigga?"

Winky sat down on the couch, and waved for, Big Time, to sit down next to her. O.Z. is alright. Plus he keeps the rest of the niggas in check around here."

Big Time sat down next to, Winky. "So, what you sayin', mama, you got that nigga, for protection.

Winky let out a small sigh. "Big, I might be your, mama, but I'm only 32 years old. I still like having' sex, as much as you do."

"Mama, I know that you're still young, and all that, but damn. How do you think I feel seeing' you waste yourself on these nothin' ass niggas?" Big Time cried.

"So, what the fuck am I supposed to do, Big? Wait on Prince Charming to come rescue me? In case you haven't noticed, Big, Prince Charming, don't fuck with no ghetto bitches. Especially the ones that smoke crack, and been to the pen." Winky starting to get irritated by Big Time's fussing.

"Come on mama, you don't need, Prince Charming, to rescue you. You got me for that," Big Time smiled at his mother. "All I'm sayin' is that you can do a lot better than that nigga, O.Z. Like you said mama, your only 32 years old and you still got it going' on. I know a lot of real niggas that be payin' you compliments even now. You clean yourself up and them same niggas will be fighting' each other to get with you."

Winky smiled her motherly smile at Big Time and patted his hand. "You really are a sweetheart, Big. No wonder you got all these lil' bitches chasing after you."

Big Time frowned at Winky. "We ain't talkin' about me, mama, we talkin' about you cleaning yourself up. I know that you had it hard comin' up. Getting pregnant at 15 and havin' to raise two twin babies on your own, taking penitentiary chances just to be able to give us what little we had. And I love you for that, mama. You could have easily given us up for adoption. Or worse yet, you could have had an abortion. I'm grateful to you, that you chose life for us, when a lot of other young women in your position would have chosen death." Big Time told his mom honestly.

Winky looked in her son's eyes and knew his was being sincere. Most of all, speaking the truth about her needing to get clean.

Big Time continued, "The struggle that you been through, and are going' through, is in my blood. It's what motivates me to be somebody. The game is deep, mama, you taught me and D.Dogg, that. Your boys aren't babies anymore, mama, we holdin' our own out there in the streets. And it's time for you to grow up and join us. Put all this crack head bullshit lifestyle behind you. It's time to move forward, mama, and not look back." Big Time put his head down disappointed.

Winky place her right hand under, Big Time's, chin and raised his head back up. "I see you out there making your money, Big, and havin' it your way. I'm proud of you for being on top of your game. It shows me that you paid attention when I told you to live big, and to always get your money. Just like I told your brother to keep it gangsta at all time. That way the two of you will always take care of each other. And your right, Big, I never grew up." Winky admitted.

"This is the only lifestyle I know and I'm sorry if you don't approve, but like you said my boy's ain't babies no more. I know it's a hard lesson for you to accept, but havin' a crack head for a mama, is just another part of the game. So, stay true to it, Big. You don't always have to like it, but you better always respect it." Winky finished with sincerity and Big Time his mom mind was made up.

Big Time, stood up, and reached inside his pocket. Pulling out a wad of cash he counted off a thousand dollars, and gave it to, Winky. "Here, mama, this is for you."

Winky, took the money from, Big Time. "What's this for?" "It's for the game that you just laced me with. I don't like it, but I will always respect it. I love you, mama."

Big Time, gave Winky, a hug and walked out the house.

CHAPTER 11

Married To The Game

"So, what's on your mind, nigga? What's up with this paper you was talkin' about we need to go 'n get.?" Big Time shook D. Dogg, to awake, who was laying in bed sound asleep.

D.Dogg, half sleep, and irritated at being woken up stirred in bed. "Damn nigga, what time is it? Why the fuck you wake me up."

Big Time, snatched the covers off, D.Dogg. "Nigga, its damn near 10:00 in the morning, get your punk ass up. You told me last night that you had some important shit, you wanted to holla at me about."

D.Dogg, grabbed the covers back from, Big Time, and fell back onto the bed. "Damn blood! You didn't have to wake a nigga up, though. That shit could have waited until later."

Big Time, snatched the covers off D.Dogg again. "What's wrong nigga, that lil' bitch, Poison, was too much for you?"

D.Dogg, laughed out loud thinking about, Poison. "Aw man, Poison, is a freak.

I'm going to start callin' that bitch Mad Head. That bitch sucked my dick so muthafuckin' good last night."

"What you didn't fuck her'?" Big Time asked. Wanting to know the details.

D.Dogg reached for the pack of Newport's sitting on the nightstand. "Come on now ole square-ass, nigga. What the fuck you think. I told you I was goin' to beat the pussy up."

Big Time smiled mischievously. "So, was the pussy cool?"

D.Dogg, put on a pair of short pants and lit up a Newport. "Aw blood, the pussy was great! I had that lil' bitch sounding like a Coyote, when I was hittin' it from the back," Both brothers started laughing. "Nigga, if you want to fuck her, I'll hook it up for you. I told you that she was tryin' to be a part of the team."

Big Time, closed the bedroom door, and put his finger to his lips for, D.Dogg to be quite. "Nigga, keep that shit down, Jazzy is in my room sleep."

D.Dogg got up to go to the bathroom. "My bad, I didn't know that sis was here."

Yeah, she's here but hook that shit up. I want to get sucked up, by Mad Head." Big Time grabbed his dick thinking about Poison sucking his dick.

"So, what the fuck you do last night?" D.Dogg yelled from the bathroom.

"Went to the gamblin' shack for a minute. Then stopped by mama's house. After that I hooked up with Jazzy." Big Time walked out of the bedroom into the kitchen.

D.Dogg walked into the kitchen where Big Time was having breakfast. "So how did you do at the gamblin' shack?"

Big Time poured milk into his bowl of cereal. "I won close to a G stack."

D.Dogg poured himself a bowl of cereal. "You won a thousand dollars, nigga? Break me off a couple of hundred."

Big Time ate a spoonful of Captain Crunch. "What's wrong, you fucked off all your get high money."

D.Dogg sat down next to Big Time at the round table. "Naw nigga, I didn't fuck my money off. Every time I come up at the gamblin' shack, I break you off."

Big Time looked at D.Dogg, and laughed. "I gave it all away."

D.Dogg looked at Big Time like he was crazy. "You gave it all away, you fuckin' nice ass nigga."

"I gave it to mama, so shut the fuck up." Big Time said defensively.

"Mama! What, that's supposed to make it better? All she going' to do is fuck it off smokin' crack," D.Dogg continued eating his cereal as if he didn't have a care in the world. "So, what's up with mama?"

Big Time poured himself another bowl of cereal. "Nothin', still fuckin' with that sorry ass nigga, O.Z."

D.Dogg gave, Big Time, a disapproving look. "Nigga, what the fuck you got against O.Z. That's the O.G. That nigga is a salvage, he be knockin' fools out."

Big Time, not interested in D.Dogg's assessment of O.Z. spoke his mind. "That nigga is in the way. Mama needs to clean herself up, and as long as O.Z. is around she ain't going' to do it."

D.Dogg looked at Big Time as if he were an alien. "Nigga, mama is a gangsta bitch. She's going' to do whatever she wants to do. No matter what nigga, she's with."

Big Time held his hand up cutting D.Dogg off. "Just let it go, it is what it is. So, what's up with this paper you was talkin' about?"

D.Dogg quickly became more alert, as he looked up from eating his Captain Crunch. "You know that fool Nutts, from up out of Oakland?"

Confused that D.Dogg would mention Nutts' name. Big Time asked wearily. "Who that ballin' ass nigga?"

D.Dogg smiled a sinister smile at Big Time. "Yeah, that ballin' ass, nigga."

Big Time looked at D.Dogg, suspiciously. "What are you

tryin' to say D.Dogg, that you're plugged in with that, nigga?"

D.Dogg crunching on his Captain Crunch, spoke nonchalantly. "Naw nigga, I don't know that fool. We goin' to kidnap his ass and hold him for ransom."

Big Time, laughed out loud, besides himself that D.Dogg would even consider something so foolish. "You really are out of your fuckin' mind, aren't you? Nutts is a Boss. A Tycoon."

"That's why we're going' to kidnap his ass and hold him for a million-dollar ransom." D.Dogg spoke with all the confidence of a well-trained athlete.

Bewildered, Big Time just laughed. "You really are tryin' to get us killed, aren't you?"

D.Dogg, no longer smiling, gave Big Time a cold hard stare, "I'm tryin to get rich, quick, nigga. I'm tired of getting stepped on. It's time for these niggas, to share the wealth."

Big Time, stared back at D.Dogg. "This shit is unbelievable; you really are serious ain't you?'

"No nuts, no glory, Big Time, you got to pay the cost to be the boss. I'm tired of lookin' up to these ballin' ass niggas, it's our time to ball, blood."

Big Time sat there stunned. "Blood, you really are crazy, ain't you? What other crazy ass nigga you got riding' with you on this."

D.Dogg shrugged his shoulders. "Just me and you Big Time,

blood in, blood out."

Big Time let out a long breath. "This is a suicide mission."

D.Dogg stood up from the table. "Life is a suicide mission nigga, you live, and then you die. I thought you wanted to be this big time Kingpin. After we do this ain't no lookin' back, we'll be on top. Be able to do whatever we want to do."

Big Time sat at the breakfast table deep in thought. "Even if I say no, you're still goin' to do it ain't you?"

D.Dogg walked over and leaned against the sink. "I'm all in blood. I'm married to the game for better or worse, from the cradle to the casket. If you ain't down with me, I'll get Dynamite."

Big Time felt disrespected that D.Dogg would include Dynamite before he even knew about it. "You told, Dynamite, about this?"

D.Dogg picked up on the anger in Big Time's voice. "The only way that she'll find out about it. Is if you ain't down to do it."

"What you tryin' to say, D.Dogg? That, Dynamite has more heart than me?" Big Time asked. Not appreciating the fact that D.Dogg was questioning his heart.

D.Dogg looked at Big Time with a poker face. "I don't know Big Time, you tell me."

Big Time got up in D.Dogg's face. "I ain't no killa D.Dogg, but don't push me. I put my life on the line every muthafuckin' day out there on them streets, tryin' to get this paper. I'm just as down as you nigga, I'm just not crazy like you."

D.Dogg pushed Big Time back off him. "Nigga, I'm a gangsta! You can call me crazy all you want I really don't give a fuck. But you still haven't answered my question, nigga. Are you with me or not?"

Big Time cleared his place at the breakfast table. "What the fuck, nigga. You think that I'm going to let Dynamite put herself out there like that. So yeah, blood I'm down with you. Now tell me how in the fuck we supposed to do this without getting ourselves killed."

D.Dogg rubbed his hands together eager to share his plan with someone. "We goin' to ride down to Oakland. Watch that nigga patterns, find a soft spot in his routine, and snatch him up."

"That's it! That's your master plan. You know that fool is going' to have bodyguards riding' with him 24-7. It won't make sense to get into a shootout with them niggas, especially since it's just going' to be me and you." Big Time tried in vain to talk some sense into his brother.

D.Dogg, unfazed by Big Time's attempt to shatter his dream, continued on. "I might be crazy Big Time, but I'm not stupid. Naw, blood what we goin' to do is wait this fool out. I don't give a fuck how game tight this nigga is. He's goin' to slip. And when he does, we're going' to be there."

"And how long are we supposed to follow this fool?" Big

Time asked knowing there was no turning back now.

Like the cat that swallowed the Canary, D.Dogg smiled. "For however long it takes Big Time, for however long it takes."

CHAPTER 12

The Game God

Standing at a pay phone, at 1:00 o'clock in the morning, at a spirit of 76 gas station, not far from where Nutts was having dinner at a Sizzler Restaurant, D.Dogg scanned the area while he waited for Big Time to call him back. Directly in front of him stood a shopping center, with a Marshall's clothing store, a Radio Shack, a K-Mart, and a Thrifty. Surrounded by a bunch of suburban homes, he glanced to his left at the one-way intersection where a Burger King sat at one Corner, and a Pizza Hut at the other.

"Blood, we been down here for 10 days, and Nutts ain't made a move without his bodyguards yet. Big Time stood at a Denny's restaurant talking in the pay phone, after receiving the page from D.Dogg.

D.Dogg eyed Nutts' bodyguards closely. "We got to be patient Big Time, like you always say it will be greater later!"

Big Time frowned into the pay phone. "Nigga, we down here losing money. Renting two different cars a day, constantly changing motel rooms, and all the other miscellaneous shit. We down here spending money on. Nigga, we got to get back on the grind. We keep this shit up and we not even going' to have enough money to re-up." Big Time said angrily.

Freezing cold, D.Dogg zipped up his leather coat. "After this, skies the limit. We ain't goin' to have to worry about havin' enough money to re-up. We goin' to be able to do whatever we want, whenever we want."

Big Time, with a growling stomach, looked inside of Denny's window, thinking about a Grand Slam. "D.Dogg, between the two of us, we been on this nigga 24-7, and he hasn't slipped yet. The only way we goin' to snag that nigga, is in a shootout."

D.Dogg laughed at Big Time's restlessness. "It sounds like you getting kind of edgy, Big Time. There ain't going to be no need for a shootout. I think I found that soft spot that we been waitin' for."

Big Time's heart started pounding in his chest at the prospect of kidnapping, Nutts. "You bullshitin'."

D.Dogg, weary of being watched, puffed on his cigarette while looking out for any strange movements or slow-moving cars. "Yeah, I'm serious. I wanted to wait a couple of more days. But since you talkin' about, we going' broke, we might as well go for broke."

"What the fuck you talkin' about we might as well go for broke? You found a soft spot or not?" Big Time yelled into the phone.

"Just be out here at 4:00 in the morning. And be ready." D.Dogg said, as he hung up the phone.

Later that morning, Big Time walked up to where D.Dogg was parked, not far from Nutts' house, and knocked on the driver's side window. Caught off guard, D.Dogg's heart skipped a beat, before regaining his composer. "Where the fuck you been? Its 15 minutes to 5. Why you so fuckin' late?" Big Time, motioned for, D.Dogg to scoot over. "I been out here since 3:00 in the morning watching your back. Let me in, it's cold out here."

D.Dogg slid over and let Big Time in the car. "You see anything?"

Big Time closed the door behind him and locked it. "The only thing I seen was you getting' high. I'm shocked that Nutts' bodyguards didn't notice all the little flames inside the car."

Guiltily, D.Dogg looked at Big Time. "I didn't think about that. I was just getting into gangsta mode."

Big Time looked down the street at Nutts' house. "Yeah, that's what I'm worried about. So, what's the plan?"

D.Dogg's eyes followed Big Time's. Every mornin' since I been watchin' this nigga, he's been comin' out of the house between 5:00 and 5:30. Then, he walks down the street to the vending machine and buys a newspaper. Son of a bitch be all by himself like he's untouchable."

Big Time rubbed his chin thinking. "So, you want to snatch him then?"

D.Dogg inhaled and then exhaled trying to stay calm. "It's about the only opportunity we goin' to get."

Big Time nodded his head in agreement. "OK, so what's the plan?"

D.Dogg blew on his hands trying to keep warm. "We ride up on him, I jump out, and make him get in the fuckin' car. Then, you smash out."

"OK, say it works, then what?" Big Time tapped his fingers on the steering wheel.

D.Dogg checked his 357 Magnum that he had sitting on the front seat. "Then we take him to the spot that we already checked out. Wait for his people to get the ransom together. After that we do it movin'."

Big Time started busting up laughing. "Just like that huh, D.Dogg. That's your master plan? Blood, you goin' to get us killed."

D.Dogg placed the gun in his lap. "Nigga, if you scared go to church. Because he's goin' to be comin' out of that house any minute now."

"I ain't scared." Big Time answered truthfully. "I just don't like your plan."

"It's too late to change it now, Big Time. He's comin' out of the house now." D.Dogg's adrenaline was at full blast from seeing Nutts walk out of the house.

Big Time pumped up as well from seeing Nutts. They watched as Nutts made his way down the street. "I wouldn't believe it if I wasn't seeing' it for myself. Nutts, really is slippin."

D.Dogg, in full gangsta mode, put on his black ski mask, and slapped Big Time on the arm. "Put your ski mask on, drive slow, and keep your distance. As soon as he puts the money in the machine rolled up on him."

Putting his ski mask on, Big Time started the car, and followed Nutts down the street at a safe distance. "Yeah, I got him, D.Dogg, I got him."

"NOW NIGGA! PUNCH IT! PUNCH IT!" D.Dogg yelled at, Big Time.

Big Time pressed on the gas pedal of the Buick Skylark. Speeding up the street to where Nutts was caught like a deer in the headlights. "Get in the fuckin' car nigga and hurry the fuck up!" D.Dogg shouted while pointing the 357, at Nutts' forehead.

"What the fuck! Are you serious lil nigga? Do you know who I am?" Nutts spoke without showing any fear.

D.Dogg pressed the gun hard into, Nutts' temple. "Does it look like I give a fuck, Nutts? Now get your ass in the goddamn car before I turn this kidnapping into a murder scene."

Nutts, relaxed somewhat knowing that he still had some time, to play his way out of this. "A kidnapping? That's what this is all about? Just calm the fuck down youngsta, I'm gettin' in the car."

D.Dogg jumped in the back seat with Nutts and made him lay face down on the floor. "Smash out, blood, we got him."

"Yeah, we got him, baby, we got him." Big Time announced proudly. Excited to be doing some gangsta shit.

"Where you youngstas takin' me?" Nutts shouted from the floor of the back seat.

D.Dogg pressed his 357 into the back of Nutts head. Nigga, I strongly advise you to shut the fuck up and keep your eyes close. If you raise your head up even one inch, I'm sendin' your ass straight to hell.

Big Time pulled up at an old, abandoned armory and turned the car off. Putting their ski mask back on, D.Dogg and Big Time got out of the car. "Alright nigga, we here. Get the fuck out." D.Dogg said, as the two brothers escorted, Nutts to a little beige room, without windows, a paint-stained concrete floor, with papers thrown all around. A big green file cabinet without drawers, was laying on the floor next to an old wooden desk. A medal chair sat in the middle of room, with a big rope sitting in the seat that D.Dogg, and Big Time, had bought especially for this occasion.

Hog tie that nigga. D.Dogg said to Big Time. If you got any problems with it, Nutts. I'll blow your fuckin' brains out and still make your people pay ransom for your dead body. That's always an option of mine's anyway." D.Dogg pointed his 357 at Nutts' head while Big Time hog tied him.

Big Time, not wanting to be a part of a murder scene, spoke up. "Be cool blood that's the sherm talkin'. Don't start trippin' on some crazy shit."

"I'm glad to see that one of you youngstas is level-headed. I can promise you that my people not going to pay for a dead body. Who are you lil' niggas workin' for anyway? Whatever he's payin' you, I'll triple it all you have to do is give me a name." Nutts, caught up on the wrong side of some gangsta shit, tried to wiggle his way out.

"What? We give you his name, and you convince him to give you our names, and you kill all of us. We might be young, but we're not stupid." Big Time, as always, respecting the game and respected, Nutts, the gangsta.

D.Dogg, checked to make sure that Nutts' rope was secure. "Blood, quit talkin' to that nigga. All he's doing' is tryin' to save his own life."

"Actually, young blood, I'm tryin' to save the lives of you two niggas. It's obvious that you niggas didn't plan this shit out thoroughly. Whoever put you up to this is tryin' real hard to get you killed." Nutts spoke from a hog tied position.

"We don't work for nobody, this come up was my idea."

D.Dogg full of bravo spoke to fast.

Recognizing D.Dogg's mistake, Nutts gained confidence. "You got a lot of heart youngsta, but you're in way over your head. You should have never told me that you were the mastermind of all this. Now I know who to come lookin' for."

Not in the mood for games, D.Dogg pressed his 357 to the back of Nutts' head. "You keep talkin', you won't have to worry about comin' and lookin' for me."

Big Time, seeing how things were about to get out of control, looked for a way out. "Blood chill the fuck out for a minute," Turning to, Nutts, Big Time, continued. "Nutts, what was you talkin' about when you said you were tryin' to save our lives."

Nutts, winced in pain, as he tried to wiggle free from being hog tied. "How much ransom money, you lil', niggas asking' for?"

"A meal ticked." Big Time answered causally.

"Nutts let out a small laugh. "A million dollars, you lil' niggas are a lot dumber than I thought. First off, there's no way in hell that my people are going to let you leave the Town without being followed. But let's just say the game god blesses you to pull this shit off. How long do you think it's going' to take my people with or without me, to hunt you lil' niggas down? I got connections throughout all of Cali, and across the country. As soon as you lil' niggas pop, y'all head up, my people will be there to chop it off."

D.Dogg, clicked his 357 that was aimed at, Nutts' head. "I

might as well scatter your brains all over this room right now, then. Because what you sayin' is that were both dead men walkin'.

"Yeah, none of us is goin' to win with the way things are right now." Nutts prayed to the game god for D.Dogg not to squeeze the trigger.

"Why are you tellin' us this shit, Nutts? Why not just have your people pay the ransom and come deal with us later?" Big Time questioned Nutts, still trying to figure him out.

Turning his head to face D.Dogg, who still had the gun pressed against the back of his head. Nutts spoke with the knowledge of a real O.G. "Because I'm loyal to the game. I was just like you niggas when I was a youngsta. Starving with a giant size appetite for money, power, and respect. And down, and dirty, to do whatever it took to get it. The game god blesses them that are true to it and puts to shame those that are fake in it. I wouldn't be the man that I claim to be if I had you niggas killed without first trying to bless you. Like the game god wants me too."

"Ain't no free rides in the game, young bloods. How many niggas you know got away with taking a million dollars? None! And the two of you won't get away with it either, unless you're down to earn it. If you niggas got the hustle, to go along with your heart, it won't take you to long to get it. With the deal I'm about to bless you with."

Big Time, recognizing game when it was in his face, seen

nothing but dollars signs. "Bless us? Bless us how? What the fuck you sayin' Nutts?"

Nutts, breathed a little easier, at having their attention. "You youngstas put down some real gangsta shit. Only a chosen few have the heart let alone the balls to do what you two lil niggas did. And rather see you die for it, the game god wants to see you get paid for it."

"We hear you talkin' Nutts, but you still ain't said nothin'." Big Time hurried Nutts along wanting to hear what his deal was.

Nutts, now in full control of the situation, laid it all on the line. "It's like this, young bloods. I have warehouses full of kilos'. I'm going' to bless you lil' niggas for havin' the heart that you have. I only hope that you have the brains to accept my offer. I'll give both of you 10 kilos' each. You can sell them anywhere from 10 G's to 20 G's. It all depends on the customer, and how you conduct your business. My shit is pure Peruvian Flake, you can step on it 2 or 3 times, and it will still be better than the shit that's out on the streets now. Even if you sell them for 10 G's apiece, which would make you a damn fool, you would still come out with $200 thousand apiece. That by itself is a nice come up for anybody out on the block. But if you're serious about getting that meal ticket and down to hustle for it, I'll make it happen for you. I could sell you a kilo for 7 G's, and it wouldn't hurt my profits."

"What the fuck you talkin' about? You just said that you was going' to give us 10 kilos' apiece." D.Dogg cut in, forgetting for the moment that he was the one holding the gun.

Nutts smiled at D.Dogg, glad to see that he was paying attention. "You're right youngsta, I am going' to give you 10 kilos' apiece. But what are you going' to do with them? Get your money or waste this golden opportunity to be some young bosses in the game. You show me that you're about your paper, and I'll sell you a kilo for 10 G's, apiece. Pure Peruvian Flake, you can't beat that nowhere in the States. The catch is that I will only sell you 20 kilos' at a time, anything less will be a waste of my time.

"If you show me that you're serious about havin' money, and start out buying' 20 kilos' at a time, I'll come down on the prices until it reaches 7 G's. The more product you buy, the more the prices will drop. You two lil niggas not the only one's that's goin' to make money, if the game god blesses us to come out of this alive."

Big Time looked at Nutts suspiciously. "What we're supposed to just trust you at your word? How do we know that you're not just running game on us to get from up under this gun?"

Nutts, turned his head to look at Big Time. "You don't know, and I don't want you to trust me. This game is way too deep to be trusting people, especially a gangsta like me. All you youngstas can do now is trust yourselves, stay true to the game as you know it and, pray that the game god shines on us."

"I'm married to the game Nutts, and I praise the game god

faithfully. And I'm also a gambler. I can feel the realness in you by the way your handlin' yourself up under the gun. I wouldn't be a real nigga if I squeezed this trigga now," D.Dogg put his 357 back on its safety. "Help me untie him, Big Time."

Shaking the ropes free and getting to his feet, Nutts looked at the two brothers, who were now unmasked. "Like I said, be true to the game and the game will be true to you. You lil' niggas made the right choice, I'm as real as the day." Nutts walked up to D.Dogg. "And listen here, lil' nigga, I'm not afraid of no goddamn gun. If it's my time to go then I'm just shit out of luck. You niggas handle your business and everything will happen just like I said it would."

Big Time reached out and shook Nutts' hand. "You keep your word with us Nutts, and I promise you, we'll earn that meal ticket.

Nutts turned his attention to D.Dogg. "And what about you, lil' nigga? You in it for the quick come up, or are you in it for the whole ride?"

D.Dogg, looked Nutts in his eyes. "I already told you that I'm married to the game. From the cradle to the casket. The only thing that I'm promisin', is that if you don't keep your word, and give us them 20 kilos', I'm goin' to kill you.

Nutts let out a hearty laugh and slapped D.Dogg on his back. "I don't have any doubt that you would try, lil' nigga. Now let's go and get somethin' to eat. I haven't had my breakfast yet and I'm starving."

CHAPTER 13

For The Love Of Money

September 1985

Driving North on the I-5 freeway, D.Dogg relaxed as he pulled off on the Charter Way exit. "Damn it feels good to be back in Stockton."

Big Time leaned back in the passenger seat of the rental, thinking about the million dollars he was about to make. "Ain't no lookin' back for us, D.Dogg. Once Nutts' folks drop that off its on and crackin'. We got two weeks to put a family together and find out which homies are down to get organized."

"That nigga, Nutts, is a real nigga. I'm glad I didn't kill him." D.Dogg reflected.

Big Time let out a small whistle. "I'm glad that you didn't kill him either. Did you see all those soldiers? That fool got killas on the payroll for real."

D.Dogg pulled the rental behind his 64, Box Chevy, parked in front of his and Big Time's, duplex. "Yeah, I seen um. I don't give a fuck about them niggas. I'm a killa my muthafuckin' self. What impressed me is that he took us to his home to meet his wife and kids. That's more than just love for the game, that's some gangsta shit."

D.Dogg walked through the door and smiled at Dynamite, who was playing cards at the round table with Jazzy. "Dynamite what you doin' here?" D.Dogg smiled.

"Jazzy told me that you and Big Time were comin' home today and I wanted to see you." Dynamite eased her way up from the table and with a look of innocence, walked seductively over to D.Dogg, kissing him passionately. "Why didn't you call me?" Dynamite pouted.

D.Dogg and Dynamite followed Big Time and Jazzy into Big Time's room. "Because I didn't want you distracting me while I was out handlin' my business." D.Dogg answered defensively.

Dynamite stood in the middle of the room with her hands on her hips. "You could have called me, Big Time called Jazzy every day."

D.Dogg let out a little grunt. "I'm not Big Time. And why you so worried about me, did you handle your business with them bitches?"

"Fuck them bitches. I got all the time in the world to get at them hoes. Besides, I was too worried about you to think about anything else." Dynamite, grabbed a hold of D.Dogg's face and looked into his eyes.

D.Dogg pulled Dynamite's hands away from his face and kissed her hungrily on the mouth. "And that's why I didn't call you. I didn't need you worryin' about me."

"Can the two of you please shut the fuck up or take that shit to another room. I want to hear about this big business deal that took the two of you a week and a half to handle. I bet that you were out fuckin' some hoes!" Jazzy shouted. Standing toe to toe with Big Time.

"Girl go on with all that drama. You know damn well I wasn't out fuckin' no hoes." Big Time, laid back on his bed and closed his eyes, daydreaming.

Jazzy, feelings hurt, sat next to Big Time on the bed. "I don't know shit, Big. All I know is that I couldn't never call you back. And every time I asked to talk to, D.Dogg he was always busy."

Big Time opened his eyes, mad that Jazzy was disturbing his million-dollar dreams. "If you don't believe me, then why are you still here talkin' to me."

Jazzy laid down next to Big Time. "Because I want you to tell me what you were doing down in Oakland, that took so, goddamn long."

"We went to Oakland, to pick up some dope. The nigga we

were supposed to meet, was hard to catch up with. So, it took us a lil' longer than we expected." Big Time spoke, with money on his mind.

"Come on now sis, you know it wasn't like that. There wasn't no hoes involved. Like Big Time said, it was strictly business, and that's the truth." D.Dogg laughed at Big Time, getting checked by his woman.

"Fuck it Jazzy, just drop it. I haven't seen my nigga in almost two weeks. I'm not trying to spend the rest of the night listening to you bitch. Just because they had to handle some business." Dynamite, tired of hearing Jazzy complain, walked out of the room.

D.Dogg, following Dynamite out of the room, yelled over his shoulder "Yeah sis, because believe it or not, business went great."

Big Time jumped up off the bed and grabbed the keys to his new caddy. "Yeah, let's go hang out for a while. I need to holla at the homies anyway.

CHAPTER 14
Homies

D.Dogg and Big Time pulled their cars into Ralph's liquor store with Dynamite and Jazzy by their sides, and parked backed in side by side, where the neighborhood hoodlums were enjoying the summer breeze. G. walked up to the two brothers just as they exited their cars, along with Dynamite and Jazzy.

D.Dogg, Big Time, where you niggas been? Shit we thought y'all went somewhere and got caught up in some bullshit." G. passed, D.Dogg the 40 Ounce he was drinking.

"Naw, blood we just been handlin' some business." D.Dogg, took a long swig of G.'s 40 Ounce.

"Righteous, righteous! What kind of business?" G. wanted to know.

Big Time put his arm around G.'s shoulder. "The kind of business we not goin' to talk about right now. The only reason I came out here tonight is to tell all the homies that me and D.Dogg is callin' a meeting tomorrow at Cutie Pie Park. You niggas hear that?" Big Time yelled at the top of his lungs catching the attention of everyone in the small parking lot. "Me and D.Dogg is callin' a mob meeting tomorrow at 1:00 O'clock. All you niggas would want to be there."

Dmove, walked up to where the three homies were standing. "Blood, what you niggas so excited about?"

Big Time gave Dmove daps acknowledging his presence. "Don't even trip, Dmove, all you need to know is that it's going' to be beneficial for all the homies that's down with what we have to say."

Dmove flashed his million-dollar smile. "You know I'm down with the benefits. So, foe'sho, I'll be there."

Hearing Big Time announce a mob meeting, Under came walking up, along with Chip, a young dope dealer. "Blood fuck y'all meeting. You niggas ain't callin' no shots out here."

D.Dogg, caught off guard by Under's disrespectful remarks, came back with some of his own. "Nigga fuck you, ain't nobody tryin' to call shots. Ever since you been hangin with this punk ass nigga, Chip, you been acting' funny style."

"What's wrong D.Dogg, you mad that me and Chip out here pushing weight? And you and Big Time still stuck on 9 of um?"

"D.Dogg, boy you know you ain't tryin' to see Under about nothin'." Chip said with all the confidence of knowing that his father, is well respected in the hood.

D.Dogg, looked at the 15-year-old, stocky, medium height, red skinned youngsta, with disgust. "You ole punk ass nigga, who the fuck you callin' boy. Don't let that big mouth of yours override your punk ass."

"Be cool D.Dogg," Big Time warned. "Chip, if it wasn't for your pops Steele Bill, you wouldn't have it like you have it out here. And Under, me and D.Dogg, never said that we was callin' shots. We just callin a meeting, if you not interested, then by all means don't come."

Mondo, already secretly jealous of the two brothers for having it better than him, decided to back Under and Chip. Why in the fuck y'all just don't say what the fuck y'all want to say right now. Just because y'all dressed a lil' better, and got a couple of cars, y'all still ain't shit."

G. threw up the mob gang sign. "Why you niggas trippin on the homies? If they want to call a meeting, so fuckin' what. Count me in blood, you know I'm there."

"Yeah, right on G. That's one love, blood." D.Dogg threw his hand high in the air and gave it up for the S.M.G.

Dynamite and Jazzy sat on the hood of D.Dogg's 64, Box Chevy, watching their surroundings when, Teayana, and Sweet Ass, two 17-year-old gangsta bitches, dressed identical, in red tee-shirts, tight fitting blue jeans, showing off their sexy young curves, and red

Rebox shoes, walked up to them.

Dynamite smiled upon seeing the two girls. "Teayana, Sweet Ass, what's up?"

"Nothin' much. We just out here chillin', checkin' out the scene." Teayana smiled at the two girls and fired up a fat ass joint.

"Bitch, fuck the scene. I'm lookin' for Cleptoe's fine ass." Sweet Ass took a drink from her tall can of Old English.

"Sweet Ass, you need to stop runnin' behind that nigga like he's the only nigga with a dick." Teayana said. Passing the joint to Dynamite.

Dynamite took the joint from Teayana. "Yeah girl, you know that's D.Dogg's Uncle. I see him all the time with all kinds of bitches. You don't have to take that shit." Dynamite passed the joint to Jazzy.

"Me and Big was at the Mall this weekend. And who do we see walkin' in with two bitches by his side? Cleptoe, that's who." Jazzy said as she took a couple of big puffs off the joint.

Teayana fired up another joint. "I been tryin' to tell this bitch that Cleptoe ain't nothin' but a pimp."

Sweet Ass took the joint out of Teayana's hand and fired it up. "Yeah, well if he's a pimp, then I'm his bottom hoe, because I ain't going' nowhere."

Teayana took a drink from her tall can of Old English. "So, what's up with that punk rock bitch Kat, and them other two coward ass bitches that jumped you?"

"Yeah bitch, you know we got your back." Sweet Ass joined in.

Dynamite jumped down off the car. "Yeah, I know you guys got my back, and that's one love. But I'm not going' to come lookin' for you when I handle my business."

Jazzy jumped off the car and started dancing. "Damn who is that slumpin' like that."

The mob homie, pretty boy L, pulled into the parking lot in his original money green, 68' Chevy Caprice. He was hitting switches, bouncing high off the ground. One Way's 'Cutie Pie' could be heard a half mile away. The 15-year-old, tall, muscular, dark skinned, dope dealer, with braided hair, pulled in next to where, D.Dogg, and Big Time stood along with G. and Dmove.

"Damn L., You got that 68, lookin right. You poundin' boy, what size woffers you got up in the trunk?" Big Time asked while giving L. daps.

L. laughed, and passed D.Dogg a bottle of gin. "I got some custom-made shit back there Big Time. If I told you all my secrets, I'll have to kill you."

D.Dogg poured himself a cup of gin "Look at my sis out there getting' her boggy on." The five homies watched Jazzy put on a one woman show in the middle of the parking lot. "Go sis, go sis." D.Dogg egged, Jazzy on.

"Girl you need to sit your hot ass down somewhere. Every time you hear music, you got to start shakin' your ass." Big Time, with a drink in his hand hollered at, Jazzy.

L. turned his music up louder. "Quit being' a square Big Time, go ahead Jazzy and turn this muthafucka out."

"Come dance with me, D.Dogg." Jazzy shouted over the loud music.

D.Dogg started bouncing his shoulders back and forth. "Come on sis, let's turn this muthafucka out. Show these square-ass niggas how we do it."

Dynamite leaned back against L's car with her arms crossed. "Boy you need to sit your drunk ass down somewhere. Out there acting' like a goddamn fool."

Jazzy walked up to Dynamite, shaking her whole body. "Quit being a dud Dynamite and come out here and get down with us."

Dynamite laughed at Jazzy and pushed her back. "That's what I'm not going' to do."

Big Time watched Jazzy's provocative dancing and scowled. "That's right Dynamite don't be a clown like these two idiots."

Jazzy backed her ass up into Big Time, rubbing up against him." Aw, Big, you just mad, because D.Dogg can dance better than you."

"The only thing that nigga can do better than me is act a

goddamn fool. Look at him! Out there lookin' like a fuckin' jerk. And you, all you want to do is shake your ass in front of these niggas out here." Big Time pouted.

Jazzy grinded her sexy ass up against Big Time's dick teasing him. "You're the only nigga that I'm shakin' my ass for."

D.Dogg walked up to, Dynamite who was sitting on L's car, and stood between her legs. "I'm done sis. I had enough of that." Dynamite wrapped her arms around D.Dogg's neck.

"So, what's up with this mob meeting tomorrow, Big Time." L. took a sip of his gin and juice.

Big Time, squatted down in front of D.Dogg's car, where L. was sitting in the driver's seat. "It's about paper, L. and about the mob getting organized."

L. laughed and fired up his joint that he had been holding. "Good luck, blood. These niggas out here on some other shit. They ain't tryin' to come together on no real shit."

"What about you L. You wit it?" Big Time took a sip from his cup.

L. let out a cloud of smoke. "Nigga, you know I'm down with the mob 100%."

D.Dogg and Dynamite walked over to his car where Big Time and L. were discussing the meeting. "Big Time, I'm about to bounce. L. watch out nigga, so I can get up out of here."

Big Time stood up and let L. get out of the car. "Bounce?

Blood, I thought you wanted to hang out and kick it."

D.Dogg got behind the steering wheel of his 64. "Blood, this gin is kickin' in. I just want to go and kick back with Dynamite."

Big Time slammed D.Dogg's car door. "Take that drunk ass nigga home, Dynamite."

"Alright then D.Dogg, I'll holla at you tomorrow." L. said laughing.

"Alright then L. catch you tomorrow. Big Time, I'll see you later." D.Dogg started his car and pulled out of the parking lot.

CHAPTER 15

Ain't Nothin But A Gangsta Party

Pulling his 64 up in front of his duplex with Dynamite by his side, D.Dogg recognized his sassy, Filipina' neighbor, Lara. 5'5", long straight black hair, pretty black eyes, sexy lil body. Wearing a short cut, colorful summer dress, blowing in the wind, showing off her sexy, model looking legs.

D.Dogg, half drunk, and with a big teenage crush on, Lara. Sat in his car starring at his neighbor while she watered the grass. Dynamite reached over and slapped D.Dogg in the back of his head. "See somethin' you like?"

D.Dogg, rubbed on his dick with a big cool-laide smile on his face. "Yeah, and she sittin' right her next to me."

"Good answer," Dynamite smiled as they both exited the car. "Hey Lara, what's going' on?" Dynamite asked, ignoring D.Dogg's lustful stares.

"Nothing much. Just out here watering the grass. Watching these bad ass kids play, in the streets. What's up with you, girl." Lara spoke with a heavy accent.

"Oh nothing, we were out kicking it, then D.Dogg got drunk and wanted to come home." Dynamite laughed. Thinking to herself why Lara, as fine as she is, wasn't married.

"What's up with that, D.Dogg? I thought you were a young gangster. If you can't handle your liquor, how you going to handle your woman. Where I come from you lose respect for shit like that." Lara teased.

D.Dogg, walked over and slapped Lara playfully on her sexy, ass. "I might not be able to handle my liquor, but I bet I can handle your lil' Chinese speakin' ass."

"Boy, you couldn't handle me if I paid you and for your information, I'm not Chinese, I'm Filipina." Lara, sprayed D.Dogg with the water hose. "There, that should sober his ass up."

Dynamite, used to the flirting between D.Dogg and Lara, laughed openly. "Yeah, that's it Lara, cool his horny ass off."

"You know our bedroom door is always open for you, Lara." D.Dogg shouted behind him as he ran into his duplex.

Dynamite walked into the house, behind D.Dogg, and sat on the leather sofa. "So, what's up with this big mob meeting tomorrow? It has something to do with what you and Big Time was doing in Oakland, doesn't it?'

D.Dogg sat next to Dynamite on the sofa and leaned his head back. "Girl, what the fuck you talkin' about."

Dynamite turned to face D.Dogg. "Come on D.Dogg, you can't play me, the way Big Time played Jazzy. I know damn well it didn't take almost two weeks for you niggas just to buy some dope."

A big smile crossed D.Dogg's face. "We jacked this boss nigga."

"You jacked a boss nigga?" Dynamite smirked.

"Yeah, we kidnapped this ballin' ass nigga and he made a boss deal with us, to let him go." D.Dogg shrugged his shoulders as if no big deal.

Dynamite jumped up off the sofa and yelled. "Kidnapped! Who in the fuck did you niggas kidnap?"

D.Dogg grabbed Dynamite, by the arm. "Sit your ass back down and calm the fuck down. We kidnapped this nigga named Nutts. He's out of control, Dynamite. A real fuckin' Tycoon. For a minute there, I thought that I was going to have to kill him. I'm glad that I didn't, it would have gotten all of us killed one day."

Listening to D.Dogg, Dynamite calmed down. "So, what kind of deal did he make with you."

D.Dogg leaned back and put his arm around Dynamite, pulling her close to him. "He put us in the game, Dynamite, me and Big Time, are goin' to be some real mob bosses."

D.Dogg smiled as Dynamite stared at him with bewildered

eyes.

The little cul-de-sac parking lot was full of cars. Mob homies were posted in the middle of the small park, some standing and others sitting on the little concrete picnic tables, waiting to hear what D.Dogg and Big Time had to say.

Deja waited impatiently for the meeting to start. "You niggas got us all out here, so what the fuck is up?"

Big Time, standing tall, stood in the middle of the mob homies gathered around. "Organization, Deja! That's, what's up. It's time that we represent the mob's name for what's it worth. Me and D.Dogg got blessed with a golden opportunity to be some real ballers. And like the Marine's, we lookin' for a few good men to start a real family."

"Real ballers, nigga I'm already ballin." Under laughed mockingly.

Ignoring Under's disrespect, Big Time continued. "Me and D.Dogg is starting our own crime family. We're takin' this shit to another level. Where the real will be separated from the fake. We callin' ourselves "The Syndicate", for organized crime.

"Blood you niggas is trippin. This South Mob Gangsta, foe life. How y'all going' to change the name." G Gunna shouted out.

"Blood, back in the day, we was called 8th street mob. So, it's not like S.M.G. is an original name." D.Dogg pointed out to G Gunna.

"Yeah, but it still got the mob in it." G Gunna argued.

"What you niggas doin' is disrespectful. Y'all tryin' to break up the mob, that's what y'all doin'. And we ain't havin' that shit. So y'all can take that syndicate shit back to where y'all got it from." Deja looked around to see who was with him.

D.Dogg, feeling that the time was now to show a little muscle if the syndicate had any chance at making it, got pumped up. "Check this shit out, Deja. I respect how you feelin', but you got it all wrong. We ain't tryin' to break up the mob, we tryin' to bring it back together. And who ever ain't with that is going to have to just deal with it, because we ain't going no muthafuckin' where."

Big Time, not tryin' to see his million-dollar dreams fail due to old customs spoke up. "Like, D.Dogg said, we ain't going' no muthafuckin' where. I ain't no killa like my brother, but don't push me. And getting in the way of the syndicate family is pushing' me. Like I said earlier, we lookin' for some solid homies that's down to get rich."

"Big Time is recruiting dope dealers, I'm recruiting killas. That's down to kill whoever and whenever our only business is to protect the family's interest." D.Dogg said feeling like the God Father.

G Gunna's eyes lit up at the idea of getting paid to kill people. "How much you payin' for killas, D.Dogg."

D.Dogg laughed at G Gunna's enthusiasm to kill people.

"First rule G Gunna, syndicate business ain't everybody's business. I'll put it like this, me and Big Time about to have so much money, that we can sink a battleship and there ain't a goddamn thing that anybody can do about it."

Big Time, feeling like a young boss, cleared the air. "The only reason that we called this meeting. Is to find out which homies is down to get paid in a major way. Those of you that are interested in the details of what we have in mind, there will be another meeting tonight at our spot. Like D.Dogg said, syndicate business ain't everybody's business."

G., quiet up to this point, felt betrayed by D.Dogg not including him earlier. "So, D.Dogg, where you niggas get all this dope y'all supposed to have?"

"The only way to find that out G. is to hook up with us." D.Dogg said, past the point of working with feelings.

"Blood, you sellin' your soul, D.Dogg. This is the mob, nigga. Fuck the syndicate." G. yelled with a vengeance.

D.Dogg, fully aware that it was now or never to establish the syndicate as something real, and not a joke, gave his best friend G. a cold hard stare. "That's the last time anybody is goin' to disrespect the syndicate without havin' to defend themselves. I wouldn't give a fuck who it is."

Big Time stepped between D.Dogg and G. "Me and D.Dogg love the mob just as much as you niggas do. Shit, D.Dogg put in more work for the hood than most of you, niggas. We might not be bangin the mob no more, but we still representing the south side. Trust me, we ain't tryin' to start no war with the homies. All we doin' is tryin' to take the mob to another level."

"You ain't from the mob no more, Big Time, so don't let me hear it come out of your fuckin' mouth. Unless you want to get knocked the fuck out. As a matter of fact, you niggas better raised up out of here while you still can. You marks ain't wanted out south no more." Mondo warned.

"Like the homies said, Mondo. The syndicate family ain't leavin' the south side. So why don't you take your punk ass and whoever is down with you and get the fuck out of the park before I start shittin' on you niggas." G Gunna pulled out his 40 Cal. with a 16 round extended clip.

"It's like that G Gunna. You down with these niggas." Mondo, looked confused, as everybody started heading for their cars in the small parking lot.

"You that slow nigga that you got to ask the question. You already heard the young homie. The real recognize the real welcome to the syndicate, G Gunna." D.Dogg, smiled as they walked to the parking lot with Big Time and Dynamite.

"You know I got you niggas back, D.Dogg. You and Big Time raised me like I was your lil' brother. We family blood." G Gunna laughed. Amused by all the loud commotion going on around him.

G., walking close by, along with Under and Mondo. Others over heard the conversation between D.Dogg and G Gunnda and exploded. "These sucka's' ain't your muckafuckin' family, nigga. I'm your blood relative and you going against the grain for these niggas. Nigga, I'm lettin' you know now, if you do this, ain't goin' to be no love lost between us."

G Gunna gave G. a cold hard stare. "I'll be sure to remember that the next time I hear you disrespect the syndicate family."

"Nigga fuck the syndicate family and fuck you to lil' nigga. D.Dogg, you ain't shit for tryin' to break up the mob. After all the work we put in, we spilled blood for the hood, nigga. The mob been here for over 30 years, its tradition. And its goin' to be here when we dead and gone." G. promised, angry and hurt that D.Dogg didn't want to be a part of the mob anymore.

D.Dogg, flashed back to all the times he and G. put in work for the hood. "Out of all the homies G., I thought you would be down with me."

"You thought wrong nigga. It's from the cradle to the casket on mine. I ain't never goin' to turn my back on the mob and go against the grain like you doing right now. I wouldn't give a fuck what the reason is." G. spit on the ground as a sign of disrespect.

D.Dogg's temper flaring, but not wanting to lose his best friend, tried to get his point across to G. "Blood the syndicate family, is the mob. We just makin' it tighter."

"Don't get shit twisted D.Dogg, if it ain't South Mob Gangsta, then it ain't the mob. And the syndicate damn sure ain't the mob." G. argued looking for a fight.

"I got mad love for you, G., we been homies since preschool. You one of the downest, niggas out here. You got a lot of heart and I respect the fact that your stayin' true to what you believe. But things change blood and that goes for the rest of you niggas too. The syndicate is real just like the mob is real. Only we goin' to function like a real fuckin family!" D.Dogg yelled across the parking lot.

"What you talkin' about, D.Dogg. The mob is family." Said Tro. A 15-year-old, short and stocky, ruthless, mob gang member.

"Ain't no real love in the mob, Tro. Only a chosen few is eatin' while the rest of us is still starvin'. Everybody in the syndicate is going to eat." D.Dogg, spoke his mind.

D.Dogg is right, Tro. You out here risking your life for the hood, along with a lot of other down ass homies and don't have shit to show for it. Any of you niggas that want to make some real bread, be at our spot, at 8:00 O'clock tonight. That's all I have to say for now." Big Time announced before walking to his car.

"Standing with, D.Dogg, Big Time, and, G Gunna, in the parking lot. Dynamite grabbed D.Dogg's arm to get his attention. "How come you didn't tell me about the syndicate?"

D.Dogg leaned against his, 64. "Because I don't think you're ready for what we about to put down."

Dynamite's cheeks turned beet red with anger. "What you sayin' D.Dogg, you don't want me to be a part of the syndicate?"

"Everything changes after tonight, Dynamite. I can't be holdin' your hand out here no more. You need to be able to stand up for yourself, to be down with the syndicate." D.Dogg warned, not sparing Dynamite any feelings.

Dynamite getting angrier by the second, put two-and-two together. "This is about them bitches jumping me isn't it? You don't think that I have the heart to handle my business, do you?"

D.Dogg had his doubts about, Dynamite, being a bona fide gangsta bitch. "Ain't no free rides, Dynamite, it's been damn near 5 months. Them bitches out here in your face every day like you ain't shit."

Dynamite pulled a wooden bat out of the back seat of, D.Dogg's car. "I'm goin' to be a part of your syndicate and I'm going' to be one of your killas."

D.Dogg looked at Dynamite dumbfounded. "What the fuck you going to do with that bat?"

"Just watch me, you and Big Time, talk too fuckin' much. Payback time, bitches!" Dynamite yelled and rushed towards Kat and Shaka, who were standing next to G., Under, and Mondo, in the parking lot. "Fuck the mob, you punk ass gutter bitches. This is the syndicate. Now what's up?" Dynamite screamed as she beat the shit out of Kat and Shaka, with her baseball bat. Amidst screams, the girls tried desperately to get away from the beating they were taking from Dynamite.

"Dynamite you lil' punk white bitch, you hit my lil' sister again with that bat, and I'm goin' to break your goddamn neck." G. warned, running towards Dynamite.

"God as my witness G., you touch Dynamite, and I'll blow your fuckin' brains out." D.Dogg ran up on G., with his 357 in his hand.

G. froze at the sight of, D.Dogg's gun, in his hand, while his heart went cold. "It's like that, D.Dogg! You pulling your strap out on me over a bitch." Not knowing what to expect from the two best friends, others more dedicated to the hood pulled out their weapons as well.

"Nigga, fuck what you going through G. This is the syndicate. Don't stop Dynamite, make them hoes bleed, bust they faces open. Teach them about fuckin with the syndicate." D.Dogg kept his gun pointed at G.'s chest.

"Where is that bitch, Young Vette, at? Tell that bitch she got hers comin' too! This is the syndicate bitch!" Dynamite screamed. While she continued to hit Kat and Shaka with her bat. "You bitches better recognized, fuck the mob, I'm the new gangsta bitch out here."

Big Time pulled Dynamite away from the two girls, who were sprawled out in the middle of the parking lot, all bloody and broken up. "Come on sis, that's enough you prove your point. You don't want to fuck around and catch a 187."

G., gave D.Dogg, a menacing stare. "You know what this means, D.Dogg?"

D.Dogg gave G., a menacing stare of his own. "It means the syndicate don't give a fuck."

"The mob don't give a fuck either, nigga." G., growled, going-tit-for tat with 'D.Dogg.

"Well then, I guess the funk season is starting early this year." Without warning, D.Dogg fired a shot into G's leg.

"Aw shit, nigga you shot me, D.Dogg." G. shouted from laying down on the ground in tremendous pain from his gunshot wound.

"I only shot you in the leg because of the love I have for you and the mob. As of now, I only have love for the syndicate. The next time G., I'm shootin' to kill," D.Dogg turned his attentions to those gathered around with guns in their hands. "Either you're with us or against us." D.Dogg got in his car along with, Big Time, Dynamite, and G Gunna.

"You should have killed me this time, D.Dogg!" G. hollered out in pain, as the trio drove away.

CHAPTER 16

The Syndicate Family

"Damn D.Dogg, you blew a hole through that nigga's leg." G Gunna laughed, still thinking about what just took place. As D.Dogg passed a bottle of bumpy face gin, around the table.

"Just followin' the rules of the game. Don't ever pull a gun on somebody unless you're goin' to use it." D.Dogg felt it necessary to defend his actions.

Dynamite still full of adrenaline from beating Kat and Shaka half to death, wasn't convinced. "The rules also say that if your goin' to shoot, shoot to kill."

D.Dogg glared at Dynamite, not liking the fact that she had just undermined him. "What the fuck you sayin' Dynamite, I should have killed the homie?"

Feeling empowered by her new status, as a bona fide gangsta bitch. Dynamite pressed on. "I'm just telling you the rules, that's all.

Besides that, punk ass nigga, ain't your homie no more, in case you forgot."

"You better check that big mouth of yours Dynamite. Remember I'm the one who gave you the game." D.Dogg pointed his index finger at Dynamite, scolding her.

"Who did D.Dogg shoot?" Jazzy, not allowed to go the meeting because of Big Time, wanted to know all the details.

Big Time took a sip of his drink. "That crazy ass nigga shot, G."

"G.? Why did you shoot, G.? I thought the two of you were best friends." Jazzy, looked around the table confused.

Big Time, pointed at Dynamite and laughed. "Yeah. Well they were best friends until Dynamite beat the shit out of his sister, Kat and that bitch, Shaka with a baseball bat."

Jazzy's eyes went buck wide with shock. "You hit them with a baseball bat, Dynamite?"

Big Time bowed his head towards Dynamite and gave a little smile. "Naw girl, what I tell you. She beat the shit out of them bitches. They goin' to need surgery."

"It's been a long time coming Jazzy. I had to get my respect." Dynamite tried to explain.

D.Dogg checked his watch. "Fuck them hoes, fuck G., and fuck the mob. Big Time, if you don't want sis involved in this, you better get her out of here. It's almost time."

Jazzy gave Big Time an accusing look. "Involved in what, Big? What's going on?"

"Something that's none of your business, so stop askin questions, and go home. I'll talk to you later." Big Time nodded his head towards the front door. Indicating that it's time for Jazzy to leave.

Jazzy sat in the chair with her arm folded. "Only if you promise to call me, after your finish doing whatever it is you're doing."

Big Time got up and walked Jazzy to the front door. "Yeah I promise. Now get out of here, we got some business to handle."

"I don't care how late it is Big, call me." Jazzy stalled for time.

Big Time opened the door for Jazzy. "I told you I'll call you. Now bounce."

Jazzy kissed Big Time affectionately. "I Love you, Big".

"I love you too." Big Time ushered Jazzy out the front door and closed it behind her.

D.Dogg, Big Time, Dynamite, and G Gunna sat in the dining room at the big round table, drinking on gin and juice. Waiting to see who, if anybody would show up. "Do you niggas think anybody else is goin' to join up with us?" G Gunna asked.

Big Time sat in the middle of the round table smoking on a cigar. "It's hard to say. A lot of niggas had their guns out. I was ready to dump on anybody that acted like they was goin' to get in it."

"Yeah Big Time, I was shocked when I saw you with that Mac .11 in your hands." D.Dogg smiled at his brother.

"I knew most of them niggas weren't goin' to like what we had to say. Plus, I know how you get down, so I came prepared for whatever," Big Time smiled back at his brother. "The one thing I did notice is that except for a handful of niggas like, Deja, Under, Chip, Mondo, Tro, Arlo, Budda, and Mac Twain, you really couldn't tell who was down with who. So yeah, I think some of them niggas will show up."

Poppa Fly, Whip, Low, Dmove, Young Tre, J.R., Worthy, Los, Mook, Ray, Pimp Cat, and Reb, where sitting throughout the house waiting for the meeting to start. Big Time stood up at the round table to get everyone's attention.

"I told everybody to be here at 8:00 O'clock. Its 8:30 now, so let's get things started. First of all, me and D.Dogg want to thank all of you niggas for coming. We know that it wasn't an easy choice for none of you to make," Big Time looked over at Dynamite, the only girl in the house. "Dynamite, pour these niggas a drink."

Dynamite looked at Big Time like he had lost his goddamn mind. "Nigga, I ain't no fucking waitress. Let these niggas pour their own fucking drinks."

"My bad sis, I don't know what I was thinking. G Gunna, pass that 5th of Gin around." Big Time smiled with embarrassment, as the room roared with laughter.

"Check this shit out," D.Dogg said, taking control of the meeting. "From here on out, anything you hear in this house stays in this house. I'm giving all of you niggas fair warning that me and Big Time is not playin'. I will kill anybody that crosses the syndicate. We got rules, and those rules will be enforced without exception. So, if any of you niggas still got any doubts about joinin' the syndicate family, I advise you to leave now. What your about to hear is privilege information for the syndicate family ears only. Nobody outside the family is ever to know our business."

Big Time looked at those gathered around inside the house and smiled. "Well since no one left, it looks like we got ourselves a family. Like D.Dogg was sayin' at the park, the syndicate is going' to be organized with some very strict rules. Breaking the rules will cost you one of three things. Money, getting kicked out of the syndicate, or your life. We running the family just like the Mafia runs they shit. Your presence here tonight is your oath.

"Countin' G Gunna, it's twelve of you niggas. That's more than enough to do what we got to do. I pretty much know all of you niggas capabilities, and what your function will be for the syndicate. All except for you, Ray. I don't know if you're goin' to be part of my hustlin' team, or if you're goin' to be one of D.Dogg's killas.

"Nigga, I'm a do both. Get my money and kill." Ray, 16, 5'9" 180 pounds, brown skinned, with a long perm. Laughed along with the others.

"Ray, no doubt you got the heart to kill. But you not a cold blooded killa like some of these other niggas in this room. Right now, we havin' some funk with them mob niggas. How far it goes, only time will tell. You're a popular nigga, Ray. All the homies got mad love for you and I know you got a lot of love for them too. But old friendships don't mean shit to me. As of now your loyalty is to the syndicate. I got way too much love for you to make you one of my killas. But if it ever came down to you havin' to squeeze the trigga on one of those mob niggas and you didn't, then I wouldn't hesitate to take you out." D.Dogg looked Ray in the eye.

Ray, a little taken back by, D.Dogg, got a little defensive. "So, what you sayin', D.Dogg? You don't think that I'm goin' to be loyal to the syndicate?

D.Dogg enjoying the feeling that his time as a boss had finally arrived, continued to set the rules for his new organized crime family. "Blood if I thought that, you wouldn't be here right now. What I'm sayin' is that you're a nice guy, with a lot of heart, and I can't use you. G Gunna, Poppa Fly, Whip, Low, and Dynamite are my killas.

"If somethin' should happen to me, Dynamite is in charge of my killa squad. The only person I trust more than Dynamite is Big Time, and he isn't a cold blooded killa either. Poppa Fly, we all know that you're the coldest killa in the house, but G Gunna is my right-hand man. He was the first to step up to the plate while the rest of you niggas sat back and watched."

"So, that means the rest of you niggas will be a part of my hustlin team. Dmove, Worthy, Mook, J.R., Ray, Pimp Cat, and Reb. Young Tre, I don't know about you. You're what 10-years-old." Big Time joked.

"Big Time, you know me, blood. I be out hustlin' niggas twice my age. Niggas just be takin' advantage of me because I'm small. If I had some killas on my team, like Poppa Fly, niggas wouldn't fuck with me." Young Tre said. Needing some muscle behind him and wanting to be a part of the syndicate family.

Big Time poured himself a shot of bumpy face. "That's the last thing you're goin' to have to worry about, Young Tre. Is nigggas takin' advantage of you and tryin' to get you for your paper. You're part of the syndicate, now. I'm goin' to give you a chance to make as much money as your young ass can handle," Big Time, looked at the others gathered around the round table. "There won't be any free rides in the Syndicate. All of you niggas are going to have to earn your keep. How much money you make all depends on how fast you move. I'm going to start all you niggas off with a kilo. All I want back is 15 G's. You can sell it whole for a quick profit or you can break it down and really get your money. Every time you drop me 15 G's, like clockwork I'll drop you another one. The faster you move, the more kilos I'll drop on you, and the faster the prices will come down. The goal is for the whole family to be on top, not just me and D.Dogg,"

"First rule for my hustlers is not to get high on your own supply. Bottom line is that if you use, then you're out of the syndicate. And if you get put out, and start spreading' family business, D.Dogg and his K-Squad, will deal with you in whatever way they feel necessary. Once a month we're goin' to have a family meetin' to check and see where everyone is at. Find out who the number one hustla in the family is. The meetin' is mandatory, that means that all you niggas better be there. If you're not there, its goin' to cost you 1 G. If your late it's going to cost you $500.00 dollars.

The money will go towards bail money, lawyers, funerals, and whatever else might come up. And just because were not down with the mob anymore, doesn't mean that we ain't still down with the South side. The South side is still the hood, make no mistake about it. But if I hear any of you niggas hollerin' out the mob, its goin' to cost you $500.00 dollars." Big Time looked over at the killas in the house. "And that goes for you niggas too."

Poppa Fly, bored with Big Time's speech to his hustlas, turned to D.Dogg. "So, what's up with us, D.Dogg? These niggas know where their money is comin' from. What about us? How do we get paid? Or do we have to kill a muthafucka first before we get our money?"

"Poppa Fly chill out nigga, and quit lookin' for a reason to kill again. But naw, blood, it ain't going to be nothin' like that. My killas are goin' to be well taken care of, believe that. As a matter of fact, here take this." D.Dogg picked up a shoe box from off the round table and counted out four thousand dollars. Giving a thousand each to Poppa Fly, G Gunna, Whip, and Low.

"That's what I'm talkin about, D.Dogg," Poppa Fly took the money and started counting it. "But what's up with Dynamite? How come you didn't give her a G.? She's just as down for the syndicate as the rest of us."

Dynamite felt a little disrespected by D.Dogg for not giving her a thousand dollars, like he did the rest of the K-Squad. "Yeah that's what I'm talkin' about, Poppa Fly. Where is my money at, D.Dogg?"

Guilt spread across D.Dogg's face. "That's the whole bundle Dynamite. I only have $300.00 dollars left. I wasn't plannin' on givin' these niggas shit. I just wanted to show them how real I am."

Dynamite gave D.Dogg her whatever look. "What kind of boss are you going to be? Can't even afford to pay your most loyal killa."

Like Big Time always says, it will be greater later. Besides you know that I'm good for it." D.Dogg said apologetically.

"Yeah daddy, I know that you're good for it. I'm not in for the money anyway. I'm in it for the love." Dynamite clinked her shot glass with D.Dogg and smiled.

CHAPTER 17

Who's The Boss

March 1986

D.Dogg and Dynamite cruised slowly down Charter Way with the top down in D.Dogg's cocaine white Mustang. With D.Dogg, smoking on a sherm soaked Newport, while Dynamite sat next to him feeling agitated. "D.Dogg, you need to hurry up with that shit. We going to be late for the concert. And roll the top up, it's not summertime yet." Dynamite rolled her eyes impatiently.

D.Dogg, ignoring Dynamite completely, continued puffing on his sherm soaked Newport. "Girl go on with that square ass shit. The concert don't start for another two hours. So, kick back. You fuckin' my high up."

Dynamite leaned her seat back and folded her arms disgusted. "You act like the Bay Area is right down the street. Plus, its Saturday night, so you know were going to catch a lot of traffic the closer we get to the City."

D.Dogg, fully loaded off the sherm, enjoying his high and his new ride, didn't appreciate Dynamite's interference. "Chill the fuck out, Dynamite. We'll be on the freeway in two minutes. Just let me finish my shit in peace. I don't want to drive to fast with the top down. The wind will make it burn to fast and fuck my high up, just like you doin' right now."

Annoyed with, D.Dogg's lack of interest in her and what she wanted, Dynamite flashed. "And put the goddamn top up!"

D.Dogg, mad at Dynamite for messing his high up, flashed back at her. "How many other 1987, cocaine white, drop top, Mustangs, do you see riding around out here on gold ones?"

Dynamite gave D.Dogg, that here we go again look. "None D.Dogg, None."

D.Dogg threw the cigarette butt out the car. "My point exactly. These muthafuckas ain't even came out yet. Nutts had this bitch custom made for me. So, stop being a bitch and let me enjoy my ride. Besides, I got a 427 Cobra Jet engine with dual holly 850 pumpers under the hood. This muthafucka will hit 180 in a straight away. As soon as I hit the freeway, I'm goin' to open this bitch up. We'll be in the City in thirty minutes."

Dynamite screwed her face up at, D.Dogg. "You don't need to try and break any sound barriers. It's not that serious. I'm not tryin' to die just to make it to some concert. You need to let me drive, since you feelin' so goddamn' good. And don't be calling me no bitch.

Seeing the frown on Dynamitc's pretty face, D.Dogg bust out laughing. "We on the freeway now you can drive on the way back. I'm high now, but I'll be fucked up on the way back."

Dynamite, for the moment forgetting about any sound barriers, more concerned with D.Dogg being high, and his state of mind. "Did you bring your strap, D.Dogg?"

D.Dogg, high and at ease driving at a high speed, looked at Dynamite like she was crazy. "You know that I never leave home without it so, why you askin' stupid ass questions?"

"Here let me have it. I don't want you doing noting crazy tonight at this concert. You know how you get off that shit. I just want to have a nice time tonight without all the drama." Dynamite put her hand out for D.Dogg to give her/his gun.

D.Dogg leaned back in his Mustang with one hand on the steering wheel and the other one resting on the door frame. Switching lanes, doing 95 mph, and feeling the wind at his face. "You bring your strap?"

"Why you asking stupid ass questions. You already know the answer." Dynamite replied smartly.

D.Dogg looked at Dynamite and laughed. "Exactly just like you already know the answer to your stupid ass question," D.Dogg, changing the subject and stopped laughing. "So how are things going for you at school?"

Dynamite, now enjoying the ride and her alone time with D.Dogg, relaxed. "It's a lot different than it was. I'm not in the background anymore, everybody knows me now. They either hate me or love me. I'm thinking about changing schools. There's way too much bullshit at Stagg. It's hard for me to focus on my school-work. My best friend Star goes to a private school, she's been trying to get me to transfer for the longest time. Star is studying to be a Lawyer too. After we graduate from college, we're goin' to start our very own law firm."

"I thought that you were going to be a lawyer for the family?" D.Dogg asked surprised.

Dynamite rocked her head to the beat of the music. "I am going to be a Lawyer for the syndicate. But I'm also goin' to have to make some money.

D.Dogg raised up the top of the Mustang. "Dynamite, we're going' to have all the money we need. Things are goin' great. That nigga, Big Time, is a smart son-of-a-bitch. He's going to be a King Pen, one day."

Dynamite reached into her purse and pulled out a joint. "I don't have any doubts about you and Big Time. The two of you make a great team and please don't question my loyalty to you or to the syndicate. Because I don't have any problem fulling my obligation to the family. But I also have an obligation to us, as your wife. I have to help prepare for our future. And having a law firm will generate a legal source of income and help keep the feds off our asses. And besides, I want to be a professional."

D.Dogg pushed in the lighter for Dynamite. "I thought you had your heart set on bein' a professional killa."

Dynamite took the lighter from D.Dogg and fired up her joint. "And what better cover could I have than to be a Lawyer. You need to wake your game up D.Dogg and stop acting like one of these game goofy niggas you always talking about. You keep smoking that shit and you're going to get left behind. All you can see is the South side. My vision for the family is world-wide."

D.Dogg turned the music down to make sure that he was being heard. "I see that Big Time's philosophy is rubbin' of on you. My getting high and my vision, is what put us in this position in the first muthafuckin' place. Ain't nobody gettin' left behind. And the next time you try to put me in a sucka's category, I'm going to check you with a back hand across that big ass mouth of yours."

Dynamite reached over and turned the tape deck back up. "I see that I struck a nerve. I'm glad that I got your attention. We have way too much to lose simply, because you want to get high and act like a goddamn fool all the time."

"Now I'm a goddamn fool," D.Dogg said mockingly. "Dynamite, you really are pushin' it, girl. That big ass mouth of yours is going to be the reason."

Dynamite jerked her head around to face D.Dogg. "Reason

for what? You slapping me? That's not going to change the facts. The truth hurts sometime, so get over it."

D.Dogg, not liking what he was hearing, picked up speed. "Just like you need to get over me getting high. Because just like you said, the truth hurts sometime."

Dynamite lean back against the seat with a look of anxiety. "What the fuck is wrong with you anyway? You had a shitty attitude all day. And you need to slow the fuck down."

D.Dogg slowed the Mustang down and turned off the music. "It's just a lot of shit going on right now with the syndicate and them mob niggas. I mean, damn Dynamite, I put in a lot of work with some of them niggas. And now Imight have to fuck around and kill a nigga that I used to be ready to die for."

Dynamite rested her hand on D.Dogg's leg. "You knew what you were up against before you and Big Time started this. So, don't let that old love that you still have prevent you from handling your business. Big Time might be the brains of the family, but you're the heart. Everybody in the syndicate is looking up to you, especially me. So, whatever you do don't ever show any weakness. And keep it gangsta at all time.'

"I done created a fuckin monster." D.Dogg and Dynamite both laughed out loud.

After the concert and from the Bay Area, D.Dogg and Dynamite parked outside of Dynamite's mom's house.

"Oh, hell yeah baby, that's what I'm talkin' about. Show daddy those oral skills." D.Dogg moaned. While Dynamite sucked his dick in the Mustang.

"You like how I suck your big black dick, daddy?" Dynamite said in her little girl voice. As she wrapped her little soft, red, lips around D.Dogg's long, hard dick.

D.Dogg leaned back in the seat with his eyes closed, ready to explode inside Dynamite's warm mouth. "I love the way you suck my dick, girl. Your mouth taste sweet just like your pussy." D.Dogg's pager went off again. Just as D.Dogg shot a load of seamen down Dynamite's throat.

"Damn what this square ass nigga want? He's been blowin' me up all fuckin' night."

Dynamite wiped her mouth off with her red bandana. "You want to go up to my room and finish? You got my pussy all wet." Dynamite smiled hopefully.

D.Dogg held up his pager in his hand, so Dynamite could see it and buttoned his pants back up. "I can't. Big Time's been blowin' me up all goddamn night. I have to go and see what's up with that nigga."

Understanding that its business before pleasure, Dynamite gave D.Dogg a peck on the cheek. "When you finish handling your business with Big Time, come back so you can handle your business with me."

D.Dogg, started up his Mustang. "I'm not making any promises. But I'll see what's up." D.Dogg said as Dynamite nodded before exited the car.

CHAPTER 18

Business Is Business

D.Dogg walked inside his duplex, where G Gunna, Poppa Fly, Whip, and Low were waiting along with Big Time. "Big Time, what the fuck is up with you, nigga? Why the fuck you been blowin' me up all goddamn night? And what the fuck is the K-Squad doin' here?" D.Dogg demanded.

Sitting at the head of the round table, Big Time looked up at D.Dogg angrily. "Why in the fuck didn't you call me back? I been blowin' you up with our emergency code all fuckin' night."

D.Dogg walked over to the round table and sat down with the others. "Dynamite was with me and you were blowin' me up. The two people that I love the most were still breathin' so, anything else could wait. So, what's up?"

Big Time, visibly upset, spoke quickly. "We got some serious problems, blood."

"What, one of the homies got arrested?" D.Dogg grabbed a bottle of Royal Crown from off the round table and poured himself a drink.

Big Time waved his hand back and forth impatiently. "Naw nigga, nothin' like that."

D.Dogg downed his drink. "What, them mob niggas trippin'?."

Big Time puffed on his Cuban cigar. "Them niggas ain't got shit to do with it. This is all syndicate business. I already told you that Reb and Pimp Cat was smokin' crack."

D.Dogg, not really interested in hearing about Reb and Pimp Cat smoking dope, started to think to himself that maybe he should have stayed with Dynamite. "Yeah, what about it?"

Big Time stood up and started pacing the room. "I should have cut them niggas loose like I was supposed to. But since they was still makin' money, I overlooked it. My bad for breakin' my own rules."

D.Dogg, tired of Big Time's stalling, yelled at him. "Fuck all that! What's the problem?"

Tell him, Whip." Big Time ordered.

Whip, sitting at the round table with his head bowed down as if he was bored, played with his two long french braids hanging down his face, spoke quietly without looking up. "I was out in the South earlier today. There was a big dice game in front of Arlow's house. A lot of them mob niggas was out there. Under, Mondo, L, Chip, Mac Twain, and Tro, to name a few. Like I said, it was hell of them fools out there."

"What the fuck that got to do with us?" D.Dogg shouted.

Whip looked up at hearing D.Dogg shout and spoke just as quietly as before. "Reb and Pimp Cat walked up high as fuck. They couldn't see me because I was in the cuts. As soon as they walked up, Reb was like, "What that S.M.G. like?" Chip said, "I thought you niggas was bangin' the syndicate? Why you hollerin' what that mob like?" Pimp Cat said, "this is the syndicate, and Reb, you need to be cool nigga." Reb was like, "Nigga, fuck the syndicate. I'm just using those sucka's for the plug, I don't give a fuck about the syndicate." And then he started runnin' his mouth like the bitch he is, and starts tellin' them niggas everything we been talkin' about in our meetings. He made us look like a bunch of clowns. I started to pop that nigga, right then and there, but it's not my call."

"What about that nigga, Pimp Cat?" D.Dogg asked taking it all in.

Whip shook his head in disappointment. "That nigga didn't say shit, D.Dogg. He was laughing at what Reb was sayin like he was enjoying what he was hearing."

With his blood boiling like a volcano about to erupt, D.Dogg pounded his fist down hard on the wooden table. "Where the fuck them niggas at now?"

"I put them bitch made muthafucka's under surveillance as soon as Whip told me what happened. They at pop's house gettin' their smoke on. Poppa Fly, is posted out front watchin' for any movement from them niggas." G Gunna reported.

"That was a smart move, G Gunna. Big Time get your boys together, and you niggas post up right here until we get back. And call Dynamite, get her over here too. K-Squad, lets bounce." D.Dogg ordered as he walked out the front door.

Back on the South side, D.Dogg pulled his Mustang into the Vista, a low-income housing complex three blocks away from his mother's house and parked his car in front of Pops apartment.

D.Dogg walked up to Poppa Fly, standing guard in front of Pop's apartment. "Poppa Fly, what's up blood? Those fools still up in there?"

Poppa Fly, leaning against his midnight black 1986 Cadillac Seville, smoking on a Newport nodded towards Pop's apartment." Yeah blood, they still up in there."

"Low, you stay outside, and don't let nobody come in. The rest of you niggas come with me." D.Dogg, G Gunna, Poppa Fly, and Whip walked into Pops house unannounced.

Reb, 18-years-old, tall, skinny, brown-skinned, youngsta, with a Jerry curl, was sitting on a little brown couch, next to Pimp Cat. A 19-year-old, medium height, medium built, youngsta, with green cat eyes. Surrounded by matches, drug paraphernalia that was laid out on a little green table in front of them. 40 ounce bottles littered the floor while little brown roaches ran around playing tag.

With a friendly smile on his face, D.Dogg walked up to the two of them. "Reb, Pimp Cat, what's up?"

Shocked and scared shitless at seeing D.Dogg and the K-Squad standing in front of them, Reb's eyes popped open wider than silver dollars. "Aw shit, D.Dogg! What's up homie? We just in here trying' to make some money."

G Gunna, frowned his face in disgust. "It's kind of hard to be makin' money, Reb when you sittin' up in here smokin' up all the profits."

"D.Dogg, what's up blood, what that mob like?" D.Dogg looked at the short, fat, old man, named Pops. "You need to get out of this crack house more Pop's. Ain't nobody in here fuckin' with the mob no more. This the syndicate old man."

Pops looked down at the floor at his black Stacy Adam shoes and shuffled his feet. "My bad, D.Dogg, I did hear somethin' about that. I guess I just forgot," Pops raised his head up and smiled. "So, whats that, syndicate like?"

"That's right Pops. get that shit right, old man," D.Dogg nodded to the others sitting around in the apartment. "What's up Trish, T-J, Bobby?"

Trish, a pretty, nicely shaped, Mexican girl, wearing an all black outfit. Was just as surprised as Reb and Pimp Cat to see the

K-Squad inside a crack house. "What you niggas doing' here? Don't none of y'all smoke crack."

"We got some syndicate business to handle with Reb and Pimp Cat. Y'all go ahead and keep smokin', don't let us fuck y'all high up. I know how that shit is." D.Dogg empathized.

Poppa Fly, finding it amusing what D.Dogg had just told Trish, busted out laughing. "D.Dogg, blood, you crazy."

Pimp Cat, recognizing the clear and present danger that he and Reb were in, tried to save himself. "I didn't say shit, D.Dogg."

"G Gunna shut that bitch ass nigga up." D.Dogg ordered, no longer pretending to be friendly. G Gunna slapped Pimp Cat hard across the face with his 40 Cal. knocking him to the ground. "Nigga, that's for bein' a bitch. Now get your coward ass up and shut the fuck up."

"You made the syndicate look like a joke today, Reb. But the joke is on you because I wasn't playin'." D.Dogg reached under his black leather coat and pulled out his 357 Mag, just as Reb made a beeline for the front door. "Get that nigga!" D.Dogg yelled.

Low held Reb in a tight head locked and walked him back into the house over to D.Dogg. With his 44 Cal pointed at the back of Reb's head. "You lookin' for this bitch ass nigga, D.Dogg?"

"Good lookin' out Low, now go post back up outside and don't let nobody in. Whip, hold that bitch nigga, so he don't run again," D.Dogg gave Poppa Fly a conspiring look. "Poppa Fly now tell everybody what happened her tonight.

Poppa Fly smiled wickedly. "My pleasure. Me, Reb, Pimp Cat, Pops, Trish, T-J, and Bobby, were all in here gettin' our smoke on. When three niggas wearing blue bandanas ran up in here, looking to rob Reb and Pimp Cat.

Pops, not liking the way this conversation was going interrupted, "Come on now, youngsta's, y'all take this shit somewhere else. I don't need this shit at my spot. I'm hot enough as it is."

"Shut the fuck up Pops." D.Dogg nodded at G Gunna. "G Gunna, help Whip hold that, nigga. I'm not tryin to chase after his punk ass no more. Go ahead Poppa Fly." D.Dogg watched in fury as Reb tried to break free of G Gunna and Whip's grip.

"Reb didn't want to give his money up and started talkin' shit, so they shot him. No, I wouldn't be able to make a positive I.D. officer. Like I said, they were all wearin' blue bandanas around their faces, Poppa Fly continued.

Reb, starting to get the feeling that his time was short, started to cry. "I'm sorry, D.Dogg. It's this crack. It's got me all fucked up. We still homies ain't we?"

"I don't have any homies, nigga. All I got is family." D.Dogg fired two shots into Reb's face, splattering blood and brains all over G Gunna and Whip.

"Oh my god. D.Dogg just killed Reb!" Trish screamed out loud. As Reb's body laid on the ground faceless and covered in blood.

D.Dogg looked down at Reb's dead body and spoke in a calm and steady voice. "G Gunna, Whip, lets bounce. Poppa Fly, make sure these muthafucka's understand the syndicate ways before the police get here."

Low, hearing the two gun shots, ran into the apartment with his 44 Cal in his hand. Seeing Reb laying in a pool of blood with Pops and Bobby kneeling down next to him. "What the fuck happened? Is that nigga dead?"

D.Dogg grabbed Low roughly by the arm. "Fuck that nigga, Low! Let's roll, blood."

CHAPTER 19

Friends, Foe, and Family

"That nigga, D.Dogg, is a fool. He don't give a fuck." Low, shouted out excitedly, as he walked into the house with D.Dogg, G Gunna, and Whip.

Big Time, hearing Low ramble on non-stop, got up from the round table where he was sitting along with Dynamite and other family members. "What the fuck is Low talkin' about?"

D.Dogg, nonchalantly, walked to the wet bar and poured himself a drink. "I smoked that nigga, Reb. That's what Low is talkin' about."

Dynamite, always down to put some work in for the family, came and stood next to D.Dogg. "What about Pimp Cat?"

D.Dogg led Dynamite by the hand back to the round table. "I just had G Gunna pistol whoop that bitch ass nigga."

Big Time looked around and noticed that Poppa Fly was

missing. "Where is, Poppa Fly?"

D.Dogg lit up a Newport. "I had the homie stay back and do some field work. Make sure that Pops and the rest of them muthafucka's make the right statements to the police."

Big Time, thinking that the worse is yet to come, Sighed deeply. "Damn nigga."

"Don't sweat it Big Time. I had to put us on the map. Let these fools know that the syndicate ain't no fuckin' joke. D.Dogg tried to reassure Big Time.

Big Time's heart went out to his brother. "You handle your business in whatever way you feel it necessary. I'm wit you, blood."

Dynamite looked up at D.Dogg with a worried look on her face. "You're going to have to find yourself a good fuckin' Lawyer, if you don't get the fuck out of Stockton."

D.Dogg downed his second shot of Tequila. "I'm not goin' no fuckin' where, Dynamite. That's the point I'm tryin' to make. That when you're organized you can get away with murder."

J.R., a 17 year old, handsome, dark brown skinned, dope dealer, and rival of Young Tre, was the best hustler in the family. Sat at the round table rolling a fat ass joint. "Dynamite is right blood. You need to raise up out of here."

D.Dogg walked over and checked the front window. "I ain't running' J.R. I'm stayin' right here.

"Los, 18, a tall, slim, brown skinned, dope dealer, known for being flashy, stood next to D.Dogg by the window. "It's not about running' D.Dogg. It's about bein' smart and stayin' low key. Until you know for sure what the fuck is goin' on."

D.Dogg patted Los on the shoulder. "Right now, Los I'm on some high power gangsta shit. I feel untouchable."

Worthy, eating on a quarter pounder with cheese. Put his two cents in. "Not even a dead muthafucka is untouchable, D.Dogg."

Dmove sat on the couch watching the news for any leads. "Worthy is right D.Dogg, ain't nobody tryin' to see you in a casket. Getting into a shootout with the police is suicide."

D.Dogg stood facing the others with all the confidence in the world. I'm not suicidal Dmove, I'm not planning on gettin' into a shootout with the cops. It's been almost twelve hours since that shit happened. If the police were comin' for me, they would have been here already. If seeing Reb, getting smoked didn't put the fear of god in Pop's, and the rest of them that was there. I know that my boy Poppa Fly, did."

Dynamite, still not convinced that D.Dogg is safe, continued to try and make her point count. "Even if Pops and the others don't talk right now, they could always make another statement later. Not only that, once the word hits the street, anyone of those cockroaches out there could drop a dime on you. For a thousand dollars, them sorry ass niggas would turn in their own mother."

"Dynamite is right, D.Dogg. Even though without an

eyewitness or a murder weapon they don't have a case. You don't want the police all up in your shit. You did get rid of the murder weapon, didn't you?" Big Time, walked over to where D.Dogg was standing.

"Of course, I got rid of the murder weapon. What the fuck you think I been doing' all this time?" D.Dogg looked at Big Time accusingly. "So, what the fuck do you want me to do, Big Time? Run away like everyone else thinks that I should?"

Big Time, feeling protective of his brother, put his arm around his shoulder. "I told you that I was with you, D.Dogg. What we're goin' to do, is that all of us are going to go out to the hood strapped down, and help Poppa Fly, put the fear of god in any would be snitches. We blood, family. We stand together and we die together. I told you that when we started this shit, ain't no turnin' back. Now let's go show these niggas how the syndicate gets down."

D.Dogg looked at Big Time with watery eyes. "I have to keep it real with you Big Time. There's been times when I wondered if we were really brothers or if mama lied to us. But by the way that you just kept it gangsta, when I really needed you to, I won't ever doubt you again."

Big Time smiled at his brother. "Don't feel bad, D.Dogg. I have some of the same thoughts all the fuckin' time."

The syndicate family posted up on the corner of 8th and Phelps. In front of the home girl Linda Fae's house. There was a dark, and lovely, beautiful looking sista, that was best friends with Winky. When D.Dogg seen his uncle, Cleptoe, walking up towards them. "Uncle Clept, what's up wit it?"

Cleptoe, the younger brother of, Winky, 22, 5'8" 185 pounds of muscle, light skinned, with a long wavy, Lord Jesus perm, a bona fide pimp, with a lot of respect in the mob. Looked around nervously. "D.Dogg, what the fuck you doin' out here? Nigga, you should be on your way to Mexico, by now. All these niggas talkin' about is what happened at Pop's house."

D.Dogg, laughed at his Uncle's Clept's nervousness. "Fuck what these niggas talkin about Uncle Clept. We out here bangin' the syndicate. You need to be down with your family, instead of out here fuckin with these Marks."

"Fuck all that shit right now, D.Dogg. You trippin' out here in the open like this. Like you don't give a fuck." Cleptoe tried to reason with his nephew.

"That's why we out here Uncle Clept. To let these niggas know that we don't give a fuck. And that they will be next if they cross game with the syndicate." D.Dogg threw up the syndicate's hand gang sign.

Cleptoe, trying with no luck to talk some sense into D.Dogg, turned to Big Time. "Big Time, I always thought like everyone else that you had good sense. What you doin' puttin' yourself on front street like this?"

"It is what it is, Uncle Clept! D.Dogg pass me the 40." Big Time, reached for the 40 Ounce of old English that D.Dogg had in his hand.

D.Dogg laughed as he passed, Big Time the 40 Ounce. "Here you go, Big Time. Fuck it, you want to hit the sherm too?"

"Naw blood, I'm cool. I ain't tryin' to get outside my body. I might start blastin' at these fools if I hit that shit. Besides, we already got enough killas in the family."

"Check Young Tre, out daddy. He out there servin' his Camero, spin those tires boy, smoke that bitch." Dynamite yelled. As Young Tre spun his dark blue Camero in 360 degree turns, in the middle of the street while everyone stopped doing what they were doing to watch the side show.

G Gunna, seeing Poppa Fly approaching, walked away from the group to meet him. "Poppa Fly, what up my nigga? What the fuck them punk police talkin about?"

Poppa Fly embraced G Gunna. "Don't even trip G Gunna. Trust me blood, ain't nobody at that house gonna say shit," Poppa Fly, pulled out a small bottle of gin from his back pocket, and took a swallow. "What the fuck you niggas doing' out here? I thought that D.Dogg would lay low for a while?"

G Gunna laughed a hearty laugh. "Nigga, D.Dogg is insane in the muthafuckin mem-brain. He don't give a fuck."

"I know that ain't my nigga Big Time over there gettin' his

drink on?" Poppa Fly laughed along with G Gunna.

"Nigga Big Time, is the one who called the shot for us to come out here." G Gunna spoke respectfully.

Poppa Fly looked around at all the mob homies hanging out on the block. "What's up with these mob niggas out here? What they talkin about?"

G Gunna put his hand on his 40 Cal that was tucked in his waist. "Nigga, all of us is strapped. Even Big Time, and he don't even like guns. So, if these niggas want it, we gonna give it to 'em."

Young Tre, park his car, and walked over to where D.Dogg and Big Time where chilling with Linda Fae and the others.

"Who taught you how to serve it like that, Young Tre?" D.Dogg slapped Young Tre playfully on the back.

"I did. If he's going' to be one of my hustla's, then his young ass has to be able to drive like a race car driver. In case he gets in a high-speed chase." Big Time spoke like a proud father.

D.Dogg glanced over Big Time's shoulders and seen Poppa Fly walking towards them. "Poppa Fly, what's up, blood?" D.Dogg and Poppa Fly embraced.

"We won't have any problems with the police. Ain't nobody in that house tryin' to meet their maker, and neither is anyone in their families. The only problems that we gonna have is in the streets." Poppa Fly, nodded towards the mob homies that were now grouped up.

"The syndicate doesn't have problems in the streets, Poppa Fly, we cause problems. Aw shit, Low is trippin." D.Dogg watched as Low, stood on top of his Pearl White Caddy. With his 44 Cal, in his hand hollering fuck the police.

"Somebody get that nigga, before he starts shootin' his gun off." Big Time ordered.

"I got him, Big Time, don't trip. Low, get your big ass down off that car, and quit trippin', boy. And put that goddamn gun away before it goes off." Dynamite hollered up at, Low.

"Fuck the police, and fuck these, niggas Dynamite! This is the syndicate." Low yelled, not moving an inch.

"Syndicate for life, Low. Now get your ass down off that goddamn car." Dynamite commanded more forcefully, as Low, got down from atop the car.

"Big Time, Suja is on the phone and he wants to talk to you!" Linda Fae yelled at Big Time.

Surprised, Big Time hollered back. "What the fuck does he want to talk to me about?"

"He wants to holler at you about all this shit that's goin' on out here!" Linda Fae yelled from the house.

Big Time, not interested in talking to the big homie Suja, hollered back at Linda Fae. "Then he should be talkin to, D.Dogg!"

Linda Fae stood in her doorway frustrated with Big Time's attitude. "He doesn't want to talk to D.Dogg. He wants to talk to you.

Just come and get the phone and show the O.G. Some respect!"

Big Time went and took the phone out of Linda Fac's hand. "O.G. Suja what's up?"

O.G. Suja a dark brown, 35-year-old, buffed out convict doing life, for putting in work for the hood, spoke directly, "Is this Big Time?"

Big Time, still uncertain why O.G. Suja wants to talk to him and not talk to D.Dogg, spoke cautiously. "Yeah this is Big Time, What's goin' on O.G?"

"That's what I'm tryin' to find out, Big Time. What the fuck is goin' on with you youngsta's." O.G. Suja snapped.

Caught off guard by O.G. Suja aggressiveness, Big Time, cleared his throat. "We just out here tryin' to handle our business O.G. That's about it."

O.G. Suja exploded at hearing Big Time saying that they were handling their business. "What! You call what D.Dogg did, handlin' your business? Look a' here lil' nigga. I been locked up since I was 18-yrs-old. And I ain't never gettin' out. For killin' a nigga that killed one of the mob homies. Now you, young niggas out there killin' each other. What part of the game is that?"

Big Time chose his words carefully not wanting to piss off O.G. Suja, anymore than he already was. "No disrespect O.G. But me and mines, we don't bang the mob no more. We bang the syndicate."

O.G. Suja, still fully active, wasn't ready to let things go so easily.

"Lil' nigga, who in the fuck you think you talkin' to? Talking' about me and mines? Lil' nigga you are mines. I heard all about you niggas puttin' together your own family. Blood, you wouldn't be shit without the mob. And the mob wouldn't be shit without me. The mob is my baby."

Big Time wanting O.G. Suja to understand that things had changed. Tried to explain. "I know how you feel O.G. But you been gone for a long time. Shit then got ugly since you left. Half these niggas out here on some snitch shit. And the other half on some soft shit. They don't even deserve to bang the mob no more. Niggas out here robbing each other, hatin' on each other. The O.G. homies from your era like, Floyd, Rainbow, L.C, Pooch, and even Al, they ain't keeping it real. If it doesn't affect them personally, then they don't give a fuck. That's why me and D.Dogg put together our own family and got organized like the mob was supposed to be when you started it.

O.G. Suja, recognizing the truth in what Big Time had to say, calmed down. "Your right Big Time, I have been gone for a long time. And I know that the homies ain't keepin' it real out there like they should. But let me give you a lil' game back. Don't under-estimate me or the mob. The only reason them niggas ain't all over you and D.Dogg is because I gave them a red light. You niggas might be sloppy out there, but up in here, behind these four walls and concrete jungle, the mob is organized. I know all about that shit that went down with you, D.Dogg, and Nutts. And how he blessed you niggas with them 20 kilos'."

Big Time, stood with the phone to his ear stunned, wondering how O.G. Suja could possibly know about the lick that he and D.Dogg had put down. "How do you know about all that, O.G.?"

O.G. Suja laughed out loud. "You niggas got a lot to learn, Big Time. Your game might be tight, but it's not deep enough yet. You niggas in way over your heads. Lil' nigga, they call me the puppet master in this muthafucka. From the way I call shots and pull people chains. That nigga, Nutts, ain't the Tycoon that you niggas think he is. I mean yeah, he's a boss, but the real Tycoon is his Uncle, Lil' Le Le. And he's here at Pelican Bay, with me, doin' all day for a hot one. I don't just call shots for the block. I call shots for the whole 2.0.9. car. Niggas like me and Lil' Le Le run the pen and the streets. Prison has its own politics and its own set of rules for our society. And it's all based on respect. You know why it took that nigga, Nutts, two weeks to pay you off?"

Big Time, fascinated with the game that O.G. Suja was lacing him with, didn't have an answer. "No."

O.G. Suja, nodded his head knowingly. "Because he had to get the O.K. from his Uncle, Lil' Le Le, and Lil' Le Le, had to get the O.K. from me. Otherwise, it would have looked like them niggas was tryin' to take over the mob, and then Stockton. It's all about respect in here, Big Time. And don't nobody in their right mind want to go to war. If them niggas would have given you that package without askin' me, I would have took it as disrespect and put a hit out on Lil' Le Le.

Big Time, feeling a little game goofy, after listening to O.G. Suja, tried to clean things up. "How come you didn't say anything to us about it? Now I feel bad that I didn't take care of you like I should have."

"The reason why I didn't tell you is because it wasn't none of your business. The only people that know is me, Lil' Le Le and Nutts. I'm from the old school, Big Time. If you don't know then you don't need to know. I wanted to see how you niggas would handle the game you was given. I watched you niggas come up from the gutter. Remember I was with your mama back in the day, before you niggas was even born. So, I know all about what you been through comin' up."

"As far as you feelin' bad for not doin' more than what you did for me. Don't trip, what you did was out of love, for me and the mob. And that says a lot about your character and the respect that you have for the game. And now that you know the real, you can pay for not knowing. As far as what's takin' place on the streets, that's on you niggas. The way I look at it, the syndicate is an extension of the mob. So, you niggas are gonna have to find a way to work this shit out between you." O.G. Suja spoke with authority. Big Time, wanting to keep the syndicate separate from the mob, protested. "Ain't nothin' to work out O.G. It is what it is."

"It is what it is out there, Big Time. In here the mob is all one. And when you lil' niggas start catchin' cases and come behind these four walls, all that syndicate bullshit is over. Because if you lil' niggas think that your gonna come up in my muthafuckin house and disrupt what I put together, then you got me, and the game fucked up." O.G. Suja continued to lace Big Time on the game.

"Trust me O.G. We wouldn't come in there tryin' to change nothin' that you put together. We would respect the O.G.'s call." Big Time felt a twinge of guilt knowing that D.Dogg wouldn't like what he had just said.

"You make sure that crazy ass brother of yours respects it too. And don't forget Big Time, I hold the keys to the syndicate future. So, if you had any ideas of Nutts having your back against the mob, then you made another big mistake in underestimating me. You niggas are on your own against the mob."

O.G. Suja, continued to lace Big Time, with more game.

"It wasn't even like that O.G." Big Time reassured O.G. Suja.

"However, it was doesn't matter. I'm just tellin' you how it is. Hand Linda Fae back the phone my time is up. I'll get back at you when I can. Tell your mama, I said thanks for the package and that I send my love. Alright then Big Time, you stay up, I'm out, one luv." O.G. Suja finished his conversation with Big Time.

"Foe'sho, O.G. One luv, blood." Big Time had a look of relief, as he gave the phone back to Linda Fae. Glad to be finished with his conversation with O.G. Suja.

Big Time left the house and went back outside with D.Dogg and the others. "So, what's up with the O.G.? What did he have to say?" D.Dogg grilled, Big Time.

"The O.G. is straight blood," Big Time looked over at all the mob homies that were grouped up, watching them. "I'll get at you later about what he had to say. All you need to know is that he isn't against us."

D.Dogg, high off the sherm, and feeling untouchable, took what Big Time had to say to heart. "So, what you sayin', nigga? That the O.G. is bangin' the syndicate now?"

Big Time shook his head disapprovingly. "Come on now, D.Dogg. I know you not that fucked up. The O.G. is the mob. He ain't tryin to go against the grain.

D.Dogg followed Big Time's eyes to the group of mob homies staring at them. "What the fuck? I thought you said that he wasn't against us?"

"As far as the O.G. is concerned the syndicate is still a part of the mob. That's why he isn't against us. Big Time clarified knowing that it was useless to talk to D.Dogg when he was high.

D.Dogg spit in the direction of the mob homics. "The O.G. got shit twisted if he thinks that I'm still part of the mob. You should have let me holla at him. I would have told him what was up."

Big Time started to get a little impatient with D.Dogg. "Believe me D.Dogg, the O.G. already knows everything. He knew all about what went down in Oakland with us and Nutts. He knew all about the 20 kilos' we got and the two weeks it took us to get it. He knew that and a lot of other shit that we didn't know."

"How the fuck did he know about all that? And what else did he know that we didn't know?" D.Dogg tried to focus on what Big Time had just told him.

Big Time got closer to D.Dogg's ear, to make sure that he could hear what he had to say. "Bottom line D.Dogg, the syndicate ain't shit in the pen. And if we ever get locked up, the O.G. strongly advises us not to bang the syndicate or he will be against us."

"Well then, he's going' to have to be against us then because we bangin' syndicate, no matter where in the fuck we at. And who ever doesn't like it, fuck'em. That nigga ain't callin' no shots for the syndicate!" D.Dogg shouted at Big Time, feeling disrespected by the O.G.

"I'll holla at you about what's real later. I'm not tryin' to go there with you right now. Just trust me, the O.G. is a lot more organized than we thought." Big Time warned.

G Gunna tapped D.Dogg on his shoulder to get his attention, as Deja, Under, Mondo, Chip, Tro, Arlow, Budda, and, Mac Twain, came walking up. "Check this shit out D.Dogg."

"D.Dogg,that was some foul shit you did. Takin' out the homie Reb, like that. And now you niggas out here acting like its nothin'." Deja frowned at D.Dogg.

"We ain't actin' Deja. And why you up in syndicate business anyway?" D.Dogg glared back at Deja, feeling the tension in the air. More mob homies came and stood around Deja and the others. Cleptoe stood next to his nephew, as the rest of the syndicate family gathered around D.Dogg.

"Whatever goes on out South is mob business. The only reason why you niggas still out here is because of the O.G. Suja. If it was up to me, you niggas would have been gone a long time ago." Deja threatened.

D.Dogg, ready for whatever, wouldn't back down. "The syndicate isn't up under the O.G. So, don't let that be the reason that you niggas don't handle your business."

"Rather that's true or not, only time will tell. But the fact remains that we still respect the O.G.'s call. But just so you know, that after tonight, the mob belongs to me. The O.G. gave me the keys to the streets. So, from here on out ain't no more passes for you niggas. The only reason we ain't ridin' for the homie Reb, is because he chose to be a part of the syndicate. But make no mistake about it, if you niggas touch one of the mob homie's, let alone kill on of 'em. We gun'n foe' you niggas.

D.Dogg looked at Deja with a cocky smile on his face. "You mob niggas might outnumber us, but believe y'all ain't ready for it."

Big Time, not wanting things to escalate into something more serious than it already was, stepped up. "Say Deja, all these threats not necessary, blood. We still got love for the mob. We just doing things our own way.

Mondo stepped in front of Deja. "Big Time, you ole, bitch ass nigga. I better not ever hear the mob come out of your mouth again. If I do, I'm goin' to knock your square ass out and piss on you."

Big Time squared up with Mondo. "Nigga, you got me fucked up. I never did like your weak ass anyway. We can go head up right now. The only one who's goin' to get pissed on is you."

"What's up then, nigga? We can handle it." Mondo balled his fist up.

"Nigga, you touch my brother, and I'll have you pissing out blood. And that goes for the rest of you niggas too. If y'all don't back the fuck up and let us through." Dynamite held her chrome .38, firmly in her right hand.

Deja stepped up to Dynamite, with no regards to the chrome .38 that she was holding. "You niggas heard Dynamite. Back the fuck up and let these niggas through. And Dynamite, when you get tired of playin' with lil' boys, come my way and I'll show you how a real gangsta gets down." Deja turned his attention to D.Dogg. "I see you still haven't learned how to put your bitch in check. You better teach her how to stay in a bitch's place. If she ever pulls a gun out on me again, I'm goin' to have her lil' fine ass pushin' up daisies. Just like I would a nigga."

D.Dogg led the syndicate family through the group of mob homies. "Gangstas do what they want to, sucka's do what they can."

CHAPTER 20

Laugh Now, Cry Later

July 4th, 1986

Dynamite lounged in her back-yard sipping on a strawberry margarita, smiling, as she watches her guests splash water on each other in her mother's swimming pool. D.Dogg stared across the small glass round table at Dynamite. Mesmerized by her beauty. At 18 yrs old, 5'5", short, thick, sexy, beautiful green soulful eyes, and high maintenance like her mother. Sitting with her legs crossed, her gold ankle bracelet, and matching toe ring only added to her pretty pedicured feet, and red painted toenails. D.Dogg's eyes ran up and down Dynamite's sexy, toned, perfectly tanned legs. All the way up to her little skimpy, red bikini bottom. He couldn't help, but to think how Dynamite had matured into a bad bitch.

"So how does it feel to be 18-years-old Dynamite?" D.Dogg asked. His shinning bald head glowing in the sunlight and shirtless.

D.Dogg wore a long pair of baggy shorts that hung off his ass, a gold rope, laced with diamonds, and a 3" solid gold 'syndicate' medallion hung around his neck.

Dynamite flashed her beautiful smile at D.Dogg, and flung her shinning, curly, blonde hair, over her shoulder. "It feels the same way it did yesterday, except for this fabulous party." Dynamite spread her arms wide apart indicating her surroundings.

D.Dogg took a drink of some exotic Vodka that he had never even heard of. "Yeah, Gail went all out on this party. She really needs to stop spoilin' you so much. Look at all this shit. She got you a live band and a D.J., a caterer all the way from the City. Talkin' about, Ebony's is the best caterer in Northern Cali. Shit, I could have put some ribs and steaks on the grill with some burgers, a little potato salad, macaroni and cheese, some corn on the cob, and hooked it up better than this. Half this shit they got, I don't even know what the fuck it is."

Dynamite covered her eyes with a pair of black RayBan sunglasses. "You only turn 18 once. So, stop being so difficult. Besides, I don't see you complainin' about the wet bar that you keep running to every 10 minutes."

D.Dogg finished off his Vodka. "Don't get me wrong. Being a spoiled lil' rich girl does have its advantages. I'm just surprised that Gail would even get you a wet bar. She has enough alcohol here to open up her own liquor store."

Dynamite picked up a bottle of Sunscreen from off the little glass table. "She knew what kind of niggas were coming. And that if there wasn't any alcohol here, that you niggas would go out and get your own. Here, rub some sunscreen on my back."

D.Dogg took the bottle of sunscreen from Dynamite and rubbed her back with it. "And that's what she did do, is hook it up. She's got all kinds of fancy named top shelf shit up in here." After rubbing Dynamite's back with Sunscreen, D.Dogg reached into his pocket and pulled out a little box. And handed it to Dynamite. "Happy Birthday."

Dynamite snatched the little box from D.Dogg's hand. "Daddy, what is it?"

Not wanting to give anything away, D.Dogg wore a poker face. "Open it and find out."

Dynamite opened the box and looked inside. "Ow wow. It's so beautiful. Thank you! I love it daddy and I love you." Dynamite held the 3.5 Carrot, princess cut, diamond ring, with her eye's and mouth wide open.

D.Dogg sat next to Dynamite with a big smile on his face. "You better like it, because it's also your engagement ring."

"No daddy, that's not fair. I want two different presents." Dynamite pouted.

"Damn girl, for 15 G's, you better act like its two presents. You really are a spoiled lil' girl, ain't you?" D.Dogg shook his head.

Dynamite put her ring on her finger and held it up to the sunlight. "That's right daddy. And you better get used to it. Because this time next year, I'm going to be your spoiled lil' wife. And its goin' to be your job to see that I stay spoiled. I want it all." Dynamite reminded D.Dogg. "But since this is such a beautiful ring, I'm goin' to let it be my engagement ring, and you can buy me a birthday present later." Dynamite ordered with a smirk.

"Oh, you're goin' to let it be your engagement ring. I heard the fuck out of that one." D.Dogg laughed as Dynamite got up out of her seat and stood in between his legs wrapping her arms around his neck.

"I love you so much daddy." Dynamite spoke in her softest little girl voice ever.

D.Dogg took both of his hands and squeezed Dynamite's sexy ass. "I love you too, but you better stop with all that spoiled lil' girl shit. Unless you want to get fucked right here, right now, in front of everybody. Seeing you in that lil' skimpy, ass bikini, got me horny as fuck. My dick is harder than penitentiary steel right now."

Dynamite smiled seductively, and put her hand down D.Dogg's shorts. "Damn daddy, you do want to fuck me, don't you? I ain't never seen your dick this hard."

"Aw shit come on now, Dynamite. You got all these people around here. Now ain't the time to be playin' around. D.Dogg moaned. As Dynamite caressed his dick with her little soft hands.

Dynamite, enjoying D.Dogg's discomfort, was all smiles. "What's wrong daddy, the gangsta can't handle a lil' teasing."

D.Dogg looked at Dynamite with lustful eyes. "Not unless you want to put on a freak show for everybody."

Dynamite bent down and nibbled on, D.Dogg's ear. "So, you do like my teasing."

"I never said I didn't like it. I just can't handle it. Mmm, Goddamn." D.Dogg grunted.

"How about this daddy. Can you handle this?" Dynamite reached inside D.Dogg's shorts and pulled his dick all the way out and started massaging his balls.

"Woo shit. You doin' way too much Dynamite. You going to fuck around and bring that salvage beast out in me and get your birthday dick a lot sooner than you expected." D.Dogg warned, using all is super-human strength not to take Dynamite right then and there.

"Oh, so now you just gonna be Mr. Man and take the pussy?" Dynamite squeezed D.Dogg's balls even harder and started stroking his dick even faster.

D.Dogg's dick was sticking straight up in the air. "I can't take what's already mine.

Dynamite's best friend Star walked up. An 18-year old, standing 5'7", red boned, short red hair with a Holly Berry cut, and reddish brown eyes. Star was a dime, with a radiant smile, and a body to die for. She was dressed in a little, sexy, orange, two-piece bikini.

Star walked up on D.Dogg and Dynamite in their little private alcove. "Damn D.Dogg, I didn't know you was packing like that." Star laughed out loud.

"One of Dynamite's well-kept secrets." D.Dogg, mad for the interruption, put his dick back in his pants.

"What the fuck you doin' lookin' at my man's dick anyway bitch?" Dynamite laughed.

"I couldn't help but to see it sticking up like it was a flagpole. If you don't want anyone looking at it, you shouldn't have it on public display like that." Star gave D.Dogg a disapproving look.

"Star, you got me fucked up with that flagpole shit. I'm a Gorilla, my shit is King Kong." D.Dogg boasted

Star rubbed D.Dogg on his bald head. "Well excuse the fuck out of me. My bad, King Kong."

Dynamite held her diamond ring out for Star to see. "Bitch get off my man's dick. And come look at the diamond ring he bought me. See how it sparkles in the sunlight?"

"Damn D.Dogg, I'm impressed, it's beautiful. I didn't know that you had something like this in you. You have some very good taste." Star held Dynamite's hand admiring her ring.

D.Dogg looked at Star real close while he sipped his drink. "I'm glad that you approve of the ring Star. Like you, I like the finer things in life. I have a strong want for high quality and things that are beautiful."

Star blushed for a split second. Then smiled at D.Dogg. "Dynamite is a lucky girl."

"I'm the one who's lucky Star," D.Dogg gave Dynamite a kiss on the cheek. And started to walk away. "I'm about to bounce over to where the homies are."

"Ciao daddy." Dynamite waved goodbye with her diamond ring sparkling in the sunlight.

"Yeah ciao D.Dogg, and make sure that you keep that Gorilla locked in his cage. He's too big to be roaming around free. We wouldn't want him to hurt anyone." Star teased.

"I'll do my best to keep him in his cage, Star. But you know sometimes he has a mind of his own and when he gets that way, he becomes uncontrollable." D.Dogg flirted back with Star.

"Nigga, I'm the only bitch that has the key to that cage. I wish some dumb bitch would make the mistake and fuck my man. And let me find out about it. Because first, I would kill her disrespectful ass. And then I would kill your stupid ass for gettin' caught." Dynamite gave D.Dogg and Star a warning look. D.Dogg nodded at Dynamite to ease her mind about fucking her friend and then head towards the homies.

D.Dogg walked up to the syndicate family lounging by the wet bar. Smoking weed, drinking, and checking out all the pretty girls in and around the pool. "Don't you niggas ever get tired of smokin' weed. That's what sucka's do, smoke weed all muthafuckin' day."

Big Time laughed as he puffed on his joint. "Nigga, you just mad that you promised Dynamite that you wouldn't get high off that shit."

J.R. rolled up a king size joint. "I guess that I'm a sucka then. Because I'm gona keep gettin' blowed."

"Pass that shit Big Time, fuck what D.Dogg talkin' about." Dmove took the joint from Big Time and took a big chocking hit.

"You got me fucked up D.Dogg, I ain't no sucka, I'm a hustla." Young Tre gave a goofy smile with his eyes blood shot red and half closed.

"Call it whatever you want to, Young Tre," D.Dogg looked into the pool where Worthy and Los were playing with two pretty girls. "Who are them bitches in the pool with the homies?"

J.R. nodded his head towards the swimming pool. "The one with Los, her name is Candy, and the one with Worthy, her name is Chocolate. They some strippers. They bumped them hoes down in Sacramento the other night when we went to the racetrack."

"Strippers! Damn J.R. what's up with you? I know they got some potnas. How come you didn't get hooked up? Your game that weak?" D.Dogg laughed along with the others.

J.R. puffed on his king size joint. "Come on now, D.Dogg

you know better than that blood, my game is air tight. Shit it was five of them hoes, in the same section as us watching the races. I lost 3 G's at the track. After that, I wasn't really feelin' them hoes."

Mook, a short, overweight, 18-year old, short, with a long french Indian braid, hanging down his back. He was never one to be left out when pussy was the topic of the conversation, so he joined in the ribbing of J.R. "Don't let losin' your paper be the reason that you didn't bump one of them hoes. You was just scared, nigga."

"Scared! Mook, you got me fucked up. You ol'alcoholic, trick ass is the one who is scared to get at a bitch. If you didn't sell dope you wouldn't get no pussy. Them hoes you be fuckin' ain't fuckin you, they fuckin your pockets." J.R. snapped.

Poppa Fly, lusting after Dynamite's preppie girlfriend's lounging around in skimpy bikini's, got tired of hearing J.R. and Mook bitch about nothing. "Man, fuck that shit you niggas talkin' about. Look at all these bad ass bitches out here. Does all these hoes go to the private school that Dynamite goes to?" Poppa Fly let out a small whistle. "Damn I'm goin' to have to get back into school."

Mook took a drink of Tequila. "Blood these hoes, ain't ghetto fabulous like them hoes you used to fuckin' with. These hoes is all college bound. They ain't fuckin' with niggas like us from the hood."

Dmove went and stood next to Poppa Fly. "Poppa Fly tell that trick ass nigga to speak for his self. These square ass bitches ain't all that. Ain't no bitch unattainable. All you got to have is game."

"I feel you Dmove. Mook you got me fucked up. I'm a fly boy nigga. That lil' fine ass, white, bitch, Veronica, been givin' me game all day. I'm about to go bump that hoe." Poppa Fly gave Dmove daps.

"That's right Poppa Fly go bump that hoe. And tell her Dmove sent you." Dmove laughed.

Mook look at Dmove with a frown on his face. "Dmove, how come you settin' the homie up? You know good and damn well ain't none of these prissy hoes fuckin' with us.

Dmove pulled out a money clip full of money. "Us! Mook, you got me, and the game fucked up. You givin' these prissy ass hoes way too much credit. Just because you lackin' in your mackin' doesn't mean that mine ain't crackin'. I got a G. that says I can bump the baddest bitch up in this muthafucka."

"Nigga, your game ain't flawless, you act like you Super Fly or somebody." Mook had his doubts about Dmove pimping abilities.

Dmove gave Mook a look of disgust. "Come on now Mook, I know that your trick ass ain't tryin' to question my pimpin'. The only reason you even get pussy without payin' for it is because of me. If I didn't send you my throwaways, you'd go broke."

Young Tre, high as a kite, had his doubts about Dmove pimping abilities too. "Damn Dmove, why you on the homie like that. I know that you got game. But it ain't flawless. You can't just bump any bitch you want at any given time."

Dmove smiled his handsome, lady killer, smile. "I see that you then joined, Mook's, trick, cheerleading squad, Young Tre. I'm gonna teach you about going against the grain. Any of you other sucka's want to jump on the trick squad bandwagon. Just drop it on the table."

G Gunna took a sip of his drink and smiled. "Ain't nobody a trick, nigga. I just don't believe that you can do it."

Dmove puffed on the joint that he's been holding onto. "I see you then joined the trick squad too, huh G Gunna."

Big Time reached in his pocket and pulled out a wad full of $100.00 bills. "Fuck it Dmove, we all on the trick squad, blood. Put your paper up nigga and we get to pick the bitch."

Dmove dropped $1,000.00 dollars down on the table. "Yeah, Big Time, you clowns get to pick the bitch. Now, you niggas patch up and come together like booty cheeks. And it drop it on the table."

The syndicate family, all through their money on the table matching Dmove.

"How about that bitch Chocolate out there with Worthy? That black ass, bitch, is badder than a muthafucka." Young Tre grabbed his dick to make his point.

"That black ass bitch ain't all that Young Tre. Check out that light skinned bitch, with all that ass in that white two-piece out there getting here freak on." G Gunna pointed to the young woman out on the dance floor.

Big Time grabbed G Gunna around the shoulders excitedly.

"G Gunna that bitch is cool boy. But check out baby, steppin' out the pool. Now that's your winner."

J.R. fired up another joint. "Yeah, Big Time that's Stephanie, I'm with you. I was tryin' to holla at her earlier. That bitch is dangerous."

All eyes turned to the very pretty, Indian, and black girl, climbing out of the swimming pool, dripping wet. Looking like a model, in a Victoria Secret magazine, in her sexy, yellow, two-piece bikini.

Dmove puffed on his Endo joint and smiled at the beautiful Stephanie. "Damn that bitch is bad. It looks like Big Time and J.R. picked a winner.

D.Dogg held up his hand. "Wait a minute. That bitch Stephanie is fine as fuck, no doubt. But she ain't the baddest bitch at the party. Check out that bitch, Star, over there with Dynamite. Now that's your winner."

Mook patted D.Dogg excitedly on the back. "Oh wee, how in the fuck we missed that one. That bitch Star is fine."

G Gunna put his hand over his heart. "Goddamn y'all, I'm in love. Star is bad as fuck. She gets my vote."

D.Dogg laughed out loud. "Get that shit right then, G Gunna.

What about you Young Tre?"

Young Tre rubbed his chin in deep thought. "Man, I don't know. Both them hoes is fine. But Star's body is bangin' a lil' harder than Stephanie's."

J.R. gave Star a second look. "Shit, I'm in love too, G Gunna. Stephanie is a bad bitch Big Time but Star, is a star."

D.Dogg gave J.R. daps, "Welcome home J.R."

"You niggas is blind. Y'all then let that dope fuck up y'all vision. That bitch, Star ain't got shit on Stephanie." Big Time said. Angry that the others didn't agree with him.

Dmove smiled at the others confidently. "Fuck it Big Time, don't even trip. After I bump this bitch, Star. I'll knock that bitch, Stephanie for you. But I'm glad that you niggas picked a real winner. Because that bitch Stephanie was going to be way too easy anyway. This bitch Star, is going to be a little more difficult."

Mook poured himself another shot of Brandy. "Don't be tryin' to back out now super mac."

"Back out! You got me fucked up. Mook you ol'trick ass nigga. I'm gonna teach you along with the rest of these sucka's, about testin' my pimpin'." Dmove walked over to where Dynamite and Star were chilling under the big willow tree along with Sweet Ass, and Teayana, admiring her ring.

"You niggas think Dmove is going to bump that bitch, Star?" Young Tre asked no one in particular.

Big Time made himself another drink. "Say D.Dogg did you hear about that shit that jumped off last night? With the mob and them East side crip, niggas?"

D.Dogg sipped on his Vodka, mad that he promised Dynamite that he wouldn't get high." Dynamite was sayin' somethin' about it last night, but I wasn't really payin' attention. So, what happened?"

"Them crip niggas ran up in Steele Bill's, house last night, and laid him down. Tied up his wife and Chip's lil' sister Niki. They tortured the homie right in front of his family." Big Time turned serious.

D.Dogg, sat his shot glass down, and gave Big Time his full attention. "Dynamite didn't tell me all that. Why in the fuck didn't Steele Bill just give them the money?"

Big Time shook his head angrily. "Blood, he did give them the money. Them crab, ass niggas, tortured him after the fact."

"Fuck! That's some coward ass shit. Luckily, they didn't kill everybody in the house." D.Dogg's mood turned dark. After hearing about his O.G. Potna, Steele Bill. Big Time, knowing how close that D.Dogg was to Steele Bill, wanted to calm him down. "Chip, Under, Mondo, Tro, Budda, Arlo, and Mac Twain, went through the East side and lit them fools up after they found out about it. Since then, it's been on sight. They been blastin' at each other all night."

D.Dogg paced back and forth. "It's about time them niggas

show some heart. They should of killed them, niggas. I ain't feelin'
these crip niggas doin' the O.G. like that. I don't give a fuck about
Chip or the rest of them mob, niggas. But Steele Bill, is a real solid
ass nigga. He always keeps it gangsta with me."

Big Time, recognizing the insane look on D.Dogg's face for
what it was worth, tried to talk some sense into him. "I know how
you feel, D.Dogg. But that's on them niggas. It ain't got nothin' to do
with the syndicate."

"It's just in my blood. I don't feel comfortable knowing that
them crip niggas are comin' through the hood, gettin' off. And I'm
not gettin' off back." D.Dogg said always ready to put in some work
on the enemy.

G Gunna, high ass a kite, off the Endo weed, that he's been
forced to smoke due to D,Dogg's promise to Dynamite, that there
would be no sherm smoking at her birthday party, felt D.Dogg's pain
in wanting to put some work in. "I don't like it anymore than you do,
D.Dogg. But the bottom line is that they wouldn't have our backs
either. So just save all that shit for when it's on us, blood," G Gunna
smiled like the devil. "We all know it's just a matter of time before
somethin' jump's off between us and them crip niggas."

D.Dogg, not ready to accept things as they were, protested.
"Yeah, I feel what you sayin', G Gunna. But its goin' to be hard not
gettin' at them fools."

"No regrets, D.Dogg ain't nobody said it was goin' to be

easy. And anyway, you got some other shit that you need to be thinking about. G. is in Y.A. fat mouthin' like a muthafucka. Talking about how he goin' be at you when he gets out." Big Time said changing the subject.

D.Dogg gave a little wry, smile. "I wouldn't expect anything less from that nigga."

"Well just so you know, his violation is almost up." Big Time put D.Dogg up on game.

D.Dogg poured himself another shot of Vodka. "Damn, I really ain't lookin' forward to seein' that nigga. I would really hate to have to kill, G."

G Gunna sat up straight in his lounge chair and frowned at D.Dogg. "What the fuck is that supposed to mean? You goin' soft, blood. Fuck that nigga. He had his chance to be a part of this. Ain't no regrets. If he got any problems when he gets out then I'm the answer. Because believe me I won't hesitate to pull the trigga on that, nigga."

"G Gunna, I got mad love for you, blood. And I know how you feel about the syndicate, so I'm goin' to overlook that soft comment. But if you can't understand why I'm not lookin' forward to killin' a nigga, that I used to call my brother, then I guess you're a harder nigga than me, G Gunna. Me and G., put in a lot of work together. Out of all the homies I really thought that G. was goin' to be the first one to hook up with me and Big Time. We always used to talk about how the mob wasn't organized,"

D.Dogg let out a small laugh. "I mean shit, I'm the one who shot that fool and G. got sent to Y.A. in the first place. That snitch ass nigga I shot, only knew G., he didn't know me. The police knew that G. wasn't the shooter. But since he wouldn't give me up, he did the time for it. Did two years for me, and now he's doin' a violation because I shot him. Now that's some crazy ass shit if you asked me. D.Dogg watched as Dynamite mingled by the pool with some more of her friends showing off her diamond ring.

G Gunna stood up and put his arm around, D.Dogg's shoulder. "All that shit was a long time ago, D.Dogg. G. don't feel that way about you no more. That nigga is talkin' about he goin' to kill you. So, if you want to reminisce that's on you blood. But don't regret havin' to kill that fool. Because one day, me and you goin' to reminisce about how that fool wasn't shit for goin' against the syndicate family."

D.Dogg shook his head disappointingly. "G Gunna, I sure am glad you're on our side, because you're a cold ass, nigga." D.Dogg yelled at Dynamite to come dance with him.

Dynamite smiled brightly and walked over with D.Dogg hand in hand over to the designated dance area. "Slow dancing in public what's gotten into you?" Dynamite whispered in D.Dogg's ear.

D.Dogg. heavy hearted with a lot of pain inside, held

Dynamite even closer. "Do I need a reason to dance with my girl?"

Dynamite wrapped her arms around D.Dogg's neck and grinded her body up against his. "Of course, you don't need a reason. It's just not like you, that's all."

"I love you, Dynamite." D.Dogg whispered, into Dynamite's ear.

"I love you too, daddy." Dynamite whispered back to D.Dogg.

"What you out there doin' D.Dogg tryin to slow dance?" Dmove yelled as he walked back to where the syndicate family was waiting for him.

D.Dogg held Dynamite tight in his arms. "I'm out here mindin' my own, and you need to do the same."

"Who are you supposed to be the ghetto love machine? Nigga, I thought you was gangsta." Dmove continued with his ribbing of D.Dogg. While the rest of the family started to laugh.

"Dmove, you better watch your mouth, blood." D.Dogg yelled at Dmove, not liking that the joke was on him at the moment.

"Aw shit I done hit a nerve." Dmove, laughed.

Dynamite held D.Dogg's face in her hands and looked him in the eyes. "Don't pay them clowns no mind daddy."

Big Time pushed Dmove playfully to get his attention. "Damn what that nigga D.Dogg is out there doin'? Did you bump that bitch, Star, or not?"

Dmove took a joint that was tucked behind his ear and fired it up. "She gave a nigga a little game. But like I said that bitch, Star is a hard knock. In the time that's goin' to take to bump that bitch, I could knock three or four different hoes. So do the math niggas. Because I don't have the time or the patience to put that kind of work in. My interest in the bitch ain't that fuckin' strong."

Big Time picked up the money up off the table and started counting it. "So basically, you didn't bump the bitch?"

"Excuse me Big Time, I apologize. I forgot I was dealin' with a bunch of tricks. I know that it's hard for you niggas to understand but try to pay attention and keep up. I already told you that I didn't bump the bitch." Dmove smiled devious at his friends.

Big Time divided the money with the others. "Call me a trick all you want as long as you pay for it."

"Yeah thanks Super Mac, I told you that your game wasn't all that." Mook laughed.

Dmove, knowing that his reputation of mac'n' on hoes is on the line, defended his mac game.

"Mook, you slow and playin', catch up just like the rest of these sucka's. My game is immaculate and my pimpin' is legendary."

"I can't tell, Dmove. You couldn't bump that bitch Star and you had money riding on it. That ain't pimp shit, that's sucka shit. Young Tre laughed along with the others.

"I'm disappointed in you Young Tre, I thought that you had more faith in your boy. Never underestimate a real nigga and never count a pimp out. Game is to be sold and not told, lil' nigga. So, consider this a free lesson and respect pimpin' when it's in your presence." Dmove called out to Stephanie to come here. And shocking everyone, Stephanie walks over and puts her hand in Dmove's back pocket. "Charm tell these sucka's what's up. Dmove smiled, posing like a pimp with his arms folded across his chest.

Charm smiled at the others. "Dmove, that's what's up."

"Oh shit, what the fuck." Young Tre, shouted. With his mouth gaped open. Not believing what he was seeing.

"Not what the fuck, Young Tre, it's called pimpin' at its finest. Somethin' you sucka's don't know nothin' about. Never trust a bitch with a sexy ass and a pretty smile. She'll cross you every time. Charm is my bitch, I told her to tell you niggas that her name was Stephanie. I was goin' to charge you niggas a G. to get up on game. But since D.Dogg put that bitch, Star in the game. I wanted to see if she was down to do a lil work. All women got a lil hoe up in them. They just need the right nigga to bring it out of 'em." Dmove, laced Young Tre.

With renewed faith in Dmove, and wanting to be a pimp just like him, Young Tre confessed. "Blood, I'm never goin' to question your pimpin' again.

Dmove, in full pimp mode, continued to lace Young Tre.

"Pimpin' ain't easy, Young Tre but it's necessary. Pimpin' and hoes is the best thang goin' lil' nigga. Pimps up, hoes down, punks in the trunk, bitches in the back seat rollin' down the street makin' my ends meet. Rain, sleet, or snow them hoes goin' bring me my dough."

Mook, eyeing Charm closely, not believing that she's a hoe, confronted Dmove. "So, what you sayin' Dmove, that we can fuck Charm if we pay you."

Dmove, standing 5'11" 190 pounds, darker than 2:00 O'clock in the morning, lady killer smile. Bedroom physique, always well groomed, and an immaculate dresser. Self-proclaimed pretty boy, with the game of the devil himself. At age 18, Dmove, is a bona fide pimp. "Nigga unlike you, I don't work with feelings. All this bitch can do for me is break tricks like you. It's pimp or die on mine."

"Blood, you know I don't have no problem payin' for some ass. So how much is it goin' to cost me to fuck, Charm." Mook pulled out his wallet and smiled. Ready to pay whatever the price of pussy was going for.

G Gunna staring hard at Charm standing there in her tiny, yellow bikini, with her ass cheeks hanging out. Yeah OK, Dmove, you big pimpin', blood. I got a lil' extra change to spend, so what's up."

Big Time grabbed Charm by the hand and pulled her to him. "Fuck what Young Tre and that nigga Mook goin' through. I'm the one who picked her, so I'm goin' first."

Young Tre looked at Charm and grabbed his dick. "Fuck that shit, big homie. Just because you picked her don't mean you get to go first."

Dmove puffed on his joint and smiled at his friends. "Calm down, Young Tre, we goin' to have an auction. And whichever one of you niggas bid the highest for the pussy gets to go first, and on down the line."

Big Time pulled out his wad of $100.00 dollar bills. "Where the fuck we goin' to take her. Because I'm doubling anyone of these niggas bids.

Dmove laughed and slapped Big Time on the back. "Don't trip Big Time, I stray ready to get deep in a tricks pockets. I got a spot all ready.

"Yeah nigga, because we can't go to my spot. Jazzy is over there in bed with a summer cold." Big Time led Charm by the hand out through the back yard.

"Where the fuck you niggas goin'. And what the fuck y'all doin' with Stephanie?" D.Dogg questioned the syndicate family as they passed by him and Dynamite, dancing.

"A pimp is going to get paid. And these tricks are goin' to get laid." Dmove had a big smile on his face.

Young Tre, pumped up off the game that Dmove, just put down. Shouted at D.Dogg. "Blood, this bitch name ain't even

Stephanie her name is Charm. She's Dmove's hoe. That niggas been playin' us the whole time. And now we about to go and run a train on her. I bet the homies, Whip and Low, are going to be mad that they didn't come."

D.Dogg smiled and let out a little laugh. "Is that lil' nigga serious? Y'all about to go and pay Dmove to fuck home girl."

"Yeah that lil' nigga serious. What the fuck you thought, I told you that my pimpin' is legendary." Dmove said with no pun intended.

"Big Time, you ought to be ashamed of yourself. Jazzy is at home sick and you out here about to fuck some hoe." Dynamite shook her head disapprovingly.

Big Time froze in his tracks. "You ain't goin' to say nothin', are you sis?"

"I wouldn't do, or say anything that would help tear you and Jazzy apart."

"Thanks sis." Big Time answered feeling a little guilty.

D.Dogg, mad that he can't go with his friends, tried to play it off. "All you niggas is a bunch of tricks."

"Nigga I bet you wouldn't be sayin' that if Dynamite wasn't standin' next to you!`'" Mook shouted at D.Dogg.

"Nigga fuck you, Mook. I don't pay for pussy." D.Dogg shouted back. Mad that Mook had put him on the spot in front of, Dynamite.

Dynamite, found it funny that D.Dogg was embarrassed. "Would you have gone with them if I wasn't with you?"

D.Dogg, still mad that he had to stay behind, spoke sharply, "I told you I ain't no trick. I don't pay for pussy."

"Yeah right. You'll tell me anything." Dynamite teased.

D.Dogg grabbed Dynamite's by her ass. "The only pussy I'm payin' for is yours."

Dynamite wrapped her arms around D.Dogg's neck and smiled. "That's what you better say."

Later that night D.Dogg, Dynamite, and Gail, chilling under the stars laid back on lounge chairs. "Thanks for the party mom it was great." Dynamite smiled at her mother.

Gail, enjoying the fresh summer breeze, and the company of her daughter, and soon to be son in law. Smiled back at Dynamite. "Your welcome baby. I'm glad that you had a good birthday."

"Gail, how come you weren't at the party? Where you been all day?" D.Dogg asked, feeling more and more like Gail's son.

Gail laughed her Motherly laugh at D.Dogg's intrusion. "I didn't realize that you were so nosy, Derek. But if you must know, I went out with some of my girlfriends. I didn't want you kids feeling uncomfortable by having like I was some mean chaperone. Besides, standing next to all those teenage girls in their little bikinis would have made me feel like an old lady.

"That's unbelievable, Gail. I seen you in a bikini before and it's not like I was checking you out or anything, but a person, especially a man, would have to be blind not to notice that you got it goin' on," D.Dogg smiled at Gail.

"My point is, that if anything those teenage girls you so worried about they the ones who should be embarrassed."

"Wow Derek. Thanks for the compliment. I'm glad to know that you think I still got it going on," Gail, smiled fondly at, D.Dogg. "And Derek, I appreciate all the nice gifts that you and your brother have given me. But you don't have to buy me anything else. You already more than quadrupled what I loaned you."

D.Dogg lounged with his hands resting comfortably behind his head. "That's nothin' Gail. We owe you a lot more than what we gave you. Without you, the syndicate family wouldn't be where it is today."

Gail sat up in her lounge chair and took D.Dogg by the hand. "Listen to me carefully Derek because I'm very serious. I don't know and I don't want to know where the syndicate family is. It wasn't my intentions to help you put your gang together. All I wanted to do was to help a little boy that needed some help. I'm disappointed that you took the money I gave you and bought drugs with it. I should have known better, but I was the naive one.

What's done is done we can't turn back the clock. But had I known how serious you were about being a gangster. I would have done everything in my power to keep Michelle away from you. Even if it met sending her to live with her Father. I love my daughter unconditionally and I love you as if you were my own son. And there's nothing that I wouldn't do for either of you. But I didn't raise my daughter to be a gangster. I raised her to be a regular person. Go to college, get a job, get married, have some kids, and be happy. Not to be fighting in the streets, selling drugs, and lord only knows what else."

D.Dogg felt guilty, by what Gail had to say. "I told you when I first met you Gail that I was a gangsta. My bad, for getting, Dynamite involved in this criminal lifestyle."

Gail cut D.Dogg off. "I'm not blaming you Derek. Michelle is a very smart girl with a strong mind. She's doing exactly what she wants to do. And you're right Derek, you did tell me that you were a gangster. My bad for not believing you." Gail smiled reminiscing to herself. "All I could see was this little handsome boy trying hard to be brave. I'm not ever going to approve of the criminal lifestyle that the two of you are choosing to live. But it's also not right for me to judge anyone." "I will always be here for the both of you if and when you should ever need me. I know firsthand how hard and how cold the streets are. And the things people do in order to survive.

Derek, I'm depending on you to protect my daughter like you promised me you would. And Michelle, I expect you to be a good wife and a real woman to the man that you're choosing to marry.

Dynamite with tears running down her face went to Gail and gave her a hug. "I love you so much mom."

"I know you do Dynamite. And I love you so much too baby," Gail cried. And with tears in her eyes, reached out to D.Dogg. "What are you doing D.Dogg waiting for an invitation? Come here and give me a hug unless that's something gangstas not supposed to do."

D.Dogg gave Gail a hug. "Gangstas do what they want to do, Gail."

"I know they do son. And I love you for who you are." Gail kissed D.Dogg on his cheek.

"I love you to, Gail." D.Dogg said back to Gail with all sincerity.

CHAPTER 21
Young Ballers

Big Time, sat on his brand new black and Grey, Ninja motorcycle smoking a joint in front of the Vista gym. "Man, I can't believe that we just let them niggas beat us like that."

Dmove, J.R., Worthy, Young Tre, Los, and Mook, all posted up at Ninja's after the basketball game they just had with the 10th and Oak Boys; another crew of young dope dealers and rivals of Big Time family of hustlers.

"Worthy, kept lettin' that nigga, Pole, drive right pass him like he wasn't even there," Los turned his attention to Dmove. "Dmove, let me get one of those bottles of Budweiser." Dmove tossed Los a Budweiser.

"Shit, Mook couldn't buy a basket. That nigga was throwin' up so many bricks I thought he was tryin' to build a house." Laughed J.R. Smoking on a joint he had dangling from his lips.

Young Tre popped the top off from his bottle of Budweiser. "That's what the fuck I be talkin' about. What's so goddamn funny? That's what's wrong with you no hustlin' ass niggas. We just lost 5 G's to those weak ass niggas and y'all out here actin' like it ain't nothin."

"It ain't shit lil' nigga. What the fuck you doin' trippin' off a lil' change for anyway. You out here pushin' weight faster than them fools at McDonald's is pushin' hamburgers. While the rest of these niggas, is movin' slower than that dumb ass nigga, drivin' that old white bitch, Ms. Daisy around all muthafuckin' day." Big Time scolded Young Tre.

"You know that it ain't the money, Big Time. Like you said its nothin' to a boss, it's just the principal. I be hustlin' way too hard to just give it away, like we just did." Young Tre, idolizing Big Time and not wanting to get on his
bad side defended himself.

Smokin' on his Endo joint, Los laughed out loud. "Hold on a minute, Big Time. Young Tre ain't the only nigga in the family that be getting his money. The rest of us is getting paid too. The only reason that lil' nigga be goin' so hard 24-7, nonstop is because he ain't gettin' no pussy yet." Laughs rang out around the little small circle of friends. With everyone thinking it funny, the rumor, that Young Tre wasn't getting no pussy.

Young Tre, aware of the rumors that he wasn't getting no

pussy, wanted to set the record straight. "You niggas, don't need to worry about my dick. I get all the pussy I need and want, while I'm out on my grind. But unlike most of you niggas, I love my money, I don't love them hoes." -----STOP HERE------

"Don't take things so personally, Young Tre. These niggas just givin' you a hard time, because you the baby of the family and the number one hustla." Big Time spoke like a proud Father.

Dmove, standing next to his red and black Ninja puffing on his Endo joint, walked over to, Young Tre and put his arm around his shoulder. "Yeah calm down lil' nigga. You already know that it's money over bitches on mine. So, fuck them gold diggin hoes and keep gettin' your money."

"Yeah nigga because I'm on you cousin. You might be going 24-7 nonstop. But I'm pushin' weight like Mr. Universe, so if you ever get sidetracked, by some lil' cutie on your dick. I'm goin' to take your spot as the number one hustla in the family." Young Tre's older cousin J.R. warned.

Young Tre pulled out a wad full of $100.00 dollar bills. "Cousin, I ain't worried about none of that shit. I wouldn't give a fuck if I started layin' up for weeks at a time, fuckin' with these hoes. You niggas still wouldn't be able to out hustle me. I hustle harder than the muthafuckin' ants crawling around on the ground all day hustlin' for food."

"Lil' nigga put your money back in your pocket and stop

being flashy. Ain't nobody in the family hurtin' for money." Big Time frowned.

Mook took a swallow of his Budweiser and changed the subject to what was really on his mind. "Say Big Time, you know that we put all those fliers out advertising this ass shakin' contest at Cutie Pie, today. So, if we're goin' to go through with it we need to do it movin'. I need to take a shower and get fitted. Since I'm goin' to be one of the judges, I got to be lookin' right and smelling right."

"Yeah, I know that today is the day of the Big Booty Ass Shakin' contest. We get there when we get there. I'm givin' out a thousand dollars to the winner and a hundred dollars to any bitch that gets up on the table and shakes her ass with no shame. So, trust me blood, them hoes won't be goin' anywhere anytime soon. We got all the time we need family. This is our show," Big Time revved his engine up. "Give me a couple of hours to sex Jazzy up real good, so she won't be trippin on a bunch of half-naked bitches shakin' their asses in my face." Big Time popped a wheely as he took off from in front of the gym. With the rest of the syndicate family, following suit.

"Boy, its hoes out here in this muthafucka today. Cutie Pie, is representin' its name sake to the fullest." J.R. shouted excitedly. Standing next to Big Time watching all the females dressed to impress in their latest hoe wear. Mingling all around, amongst the players, and hustlers, shooting dice, and smoking weed waiting for the contest to start.

Worthy walked up to Big Time with Scoob by his side. A tall, muscular, light skinned, dope dealer, with a long wild afro and one eye, sipping on some Hennessy. "Say Big Time, when you goin' to put these hoes on display. My nigga, Scoob, is waitin' on me to handle some business. I ain't tryin' to hold him up, but I also ain't tryin' to miss these nasty freaks shake their assess either."

Young Tre, within ear shot of the trio, overheard their conversation, and butted in. "That's just what in the fuck I be talkin' about. No hustle ass niggas. Blood, you need to get your priorities straight, fuck these low budget gold diggin', nasty ass bitches, lookin' for a quick come up. Its money over bitches, nigga. What's stoppin' Scoob from findin' another plug?'

"You niggas always findin' somethin' to argue about. Niggas with money shouldn't act like this. The reason Scoob ain't goin' to find another plug is because we got the best prices and the best dope around. The money ain't goin' nowhere, Young Tre. These other niggas are just holdin' on to it until we decide to pick it up. Ain't that right Scoob," Big Time smiled at Scoob who smiled back in agreement.

"So, don't trip family because right now we about to watch these nasty freaks, get nasty, for us. I was tryin' to wait on D.Dogg and the K-Squad but it ain't no tellin' where in the fuck they at. J.R., go ahead and get this muthafucka started." Big Time nodded to J.R.

who was sitting in his black Chevy Blazer, parked on the grass next to the concrete table that the girls would be dancing on, organizing his music.

J.R. adjusted the music so that he could be heard over the crowd of people that were gathered around waiting for the contest to start. "Alright everybody back the fuck up and make some room! Give the ladies some room to do their thing. Cakes, you up first, so get your fine ass up on the table and show our three judges what you workin' with!" Cakes dressed in a red Betty Boop T-shirt and a tight pair of acid wash jeans, fitting tight across her big round ass, smiled at Big Time, Dmove, and Mook, who were judging the contest.

Whodini's "I'm a hoe, you know I'm a hoe", blasted from J.R.'s Chevy Blazer. Cake's, stood on top of the table, dancing with no shame, bending over and touching her toes, while bouncing her luscious ass high up off the table. To the delight of the crowd and the three judges.

J.R. turned the music down on his stereo. "Alright Cakes, that was a great show, a true exhibitionist. Next up we got Beanka." Beanka one of Big Time's girlfriends. Dressed in a pair of black spandex top and bottom. Showing off her luscious curves. Climbed on top of the table and backed that ass up, in front of all three of the judge's faces. Twirling her ass around and around with her hands on the ground in a doggy style position. The three judges sat with big smiles on their faces for the next two hours judging the contest. As one would be stripper after another got up on the little concrete table and danced with no shame. Trying to out due the other to win the $1000.00 prize money.

Big Time, Dmove, and Mook, sat inside J.R.'s Chevy Blazer, smoking weed, trying to decide which girl should win the prize money. "I don't know man it's too close for me to call. Tae, Tae always gets my dick hard. But Beanka's lil sexy, chocolate ass, had it standin' to attention when she was up there doin' her thang." Big Time let out a cloud of Endo smoke.

Dmove, refilled his weed pipe. "You know me, I really don't give a fuck which one of these hoes win the money. I'm just out here lookin' for some new work."

Mook, always plotting on some new pussy, decided to make his play. "It's like this blood. Money ain't a thing to me. I'll put the prize money up myself. But check game, that lil' bad ass freaky bitch, Fae. I been wanting to fuck her since the 10th grade. So, I say that we make her the winner, and tell her that she has to come with me to get paid." Big Time and Dmove both choked on the weed, from laughing so hard.

"Mook you a super trick." Dmove, shook his head disgustedly, and took another hit off his weed pipe.

"It's your money, nigga, if you want to spend it all on pussy, that's on your dumb ass." Big Time laughed. As the three judges stepped out of the Blazer, high as fuck. To a crowd of young women, waiting eagerly to see who would win the $1000.00 prize money.

Mook took the microphone from, J.R. "Check it out ladies we picked our winner. It was a hard decision because all of you deserve to win," Mook took a deep breath. "Fae, you're the winner." A lot of cussing and boos could be heard throughout the angry crowd of people. As boyfriends alike were hoping that their girl would be the one who won the prize money.

Fae was more than happy to go along with Mook to collect her $1000.00. While the other girls in the contest grudgingly accepted their $100.00.

CHAPTER 22

Folsom Lake

1986

Labor Day Weekend,

Dynamite stood on the dock in her powder blue bikini showing off her sexy curves. The rest of the P.P.G. who were dressed in sexy bikinis of their own. Stood with her looking out at Folsom Lake's clear blue water. While the syndicate family stood watching, D.Dogg and Big Time revved the engines on their jet skis and prepared to race.

"I got a hundred on my nigga D.Dogg!" Yelled G Gunna. He and his best friend, Young Tre, stood next to each other in the picnic area.

"Nigga bet D.Dogg so fucked up he'll be lucky if he don't fall off the goddamn jet ski." Young Tre laughed as he shouted back at G Gunna and passed him a bottle of Hennessy.

"Alright, time is up y'all been revvin' up them engines for the last fifteen minutes. What the fuck are you waitin' for?" Dynamite yelled out to a laughing D.Dogg and Big Time.

"We waitin' on you white girl, set us off!" Big Time yelled back at Dynamite.

"I got your white girl, nigga! On three, ready? 1..2..3!" Dynamite shouted.

D.Dogg and Big Time sped off across the lake leaving the syndicate family and the P.P.G. shouting in hysteria. Rounding the turning bend, Big Time moves ahead of a determined D.Dogg.

"It's over now! Dmove shouted. Standing next to Mook while smoking on a fat joint.

"It ain't over until the fat bitch snags. And I don't see no fat bitches." Poppa Fly stated factually. Posturing in his big white chef's hat leaving no doubt as to who oversaw the grill.

"Fat bitch or not, this shit is over!" Low laughed standing next to Poppa Fly while sipping on some Remy."

Jazzy, wearing a sexy little black bikini, jumped up and down ecstatically as Big Time crossed the finish line first. The rest of the P.P.G. joined in the cheering.

"Nigga, you cheated. You jumped the gun." D.Dogg protested.

"Blood don't tell me you gonna start actin' like a bitch in front of all these females." Big Time laughed as he sat on his jet ski facing his brother.

D.Dogg shot up from his jet ski. "Nigga I got your bitch!" He yelled grinning as he dove into Big Time causing both to splash in the water.

Whip, Worthy, and Ray pulled up respectfully on their jet skis near the tousling twins. "You niggas is crazy!" Whip shouted at D.Dogg and Big Time and shook his head disgustedly. He sped off following his friends who were chasing after Hot Sauce, Rie, and Shorty.

Star, wearing a revealing beige bikini that perfectly offset her cinnamon colored skin, eased up next to D.Dogg who had taken over the grill from a drunk Poppa Fly. "I was rooting for you to win."

D.Dogg smiled lustfully at Star checking her out from head to toe. "Sorry I disappointed you."

Star reached up and adjusted the chef hat that D.Dogg was now wearing. "Who said that I was disappointed?" Feeling the heat coming off of Star's body, from standing so close to him, D.Dogg begin to get an erection. "Is there somethin' you wanted Star."

Star smiled seductively at D.Dogg and whispered in his ear. "What's wrong D.Dogg, does the gorilla want out of his cage."

"Bitch what the fuck you doin' all up on my man." Dynamite questioned walking up from behind the two of them.

"I was just telling D.Dogg how I like his Bar-B-Que better than I like Poppa Fly's Bar-B-Que." Star said, without missing a beat.

Dynamite gave Star a warning look. "Yeah, well bitch you don't have to be all up on him to do that."

"Bitch quit trippin' ain't nobody interested in your man." Star waved her hand dismissively and wisely walked away.

"Punk rock bitch got a lot of nerves," Dynamite spoke out loud to herself before turning her attention to D.Dogg.

"Big Time wants you to know he's down by the water. Said that he has something important to tell us." Dynamite informed D.Dogg.

"This nigga is takin' this boss shit a little too far. Think he can order me around." D.Dogg smiled with a hard dick. Glad that Dynamite has forgotten about Star for now.

Dynamite laughed playfully and grabbed D.Dogg by the hand. Come on I want to hear what's so important that he can't tell me unless your there."

D.Dogg and Dynamite walked over to where Big Time and Jazzy were waiting in a secluded area. "I'm glad that the two of you finally decided to bless us with your presence." Big Time teased.

"I only been gone for five minutes Big Time, so save the speech and just tell us what's so goddamn important." Dynamite insisted.

"Patience, patience sis, good things come to those who wait," Big Time held onto Jazzy's hand with a big cool aide smile on his face. "Jazzy is pregnant we're going to have a baby.

Dynamite rushed over to Jazzy and gave her a big hug. "Congratulations Jazzy, I'm so happy for you and Big Time.

D.Dogg laughed out loud. "Ain't this a bitch, I'm goin' to be an Uncle! It's time to celebrate!"

"Not yet D.Dogg. We want to keep it to ourselves for a while. Jazzy doesn't want all the attention and to tell you the truth, neither do I." Big Time rested his hand on D.Dogg's shoulder.

"Yeah D.Dogg. We just wanted to share the good news with you and Dynamite. I hope you respect our decision to keep it to ourselves for a while." Jazzy looked D.Dogg in his eyes.

"Come on now sis do you even got to ask. Of course, I'll respect you and Big Time's privacy." D.Dogg gave Jazzy a hug.

"Big Time, I'm so happy for you. I can't believe your about to be a Father." Dynamite said giving Big Time a hug.

"Well, you better believe it because you and D.Dogg are going to be the God parents." Big Time laughed, pulling out two Cuban Cigars and giving D.Dogg one.

"God parents? I'm not even used to the idea of being an Uncle yet." D.Dogg laughed.

Big Time turned serious. "D.Dogg, I know that we don't always see eye to eye and that we both got our own opinions on what it means to be a man. I might have my doubts about how you handle your business out on the streets. But, I don't have any doubts about your heart and the love that you have for your family. God forbid if anything should happen to me or even worse somethin' should happen to Jazzy. I don't have any doubts about who I want to raise my kid. That bein' you and Dynamite.

D.Dogg looked at Big Time respectfully. "Thank you Big Time. That means a lot to me comin' from you. I don't have any doubts about you either. You're going to make a great Father."

The brothers looked at each other, both with proud stares before joining the rest of the Syndicate family.

CHAPTER 23

There's A Devil in the Ghetto

October 31st, 1986

Friday 9:00 A.M.

D.Dogg and Big Time sat inside of Denny's having breakfast. They were mourning the death of their friend, Pretty Boy L., who was recently killed by the East side crips. Big Time took a bite of his Belgian Waffle. "Are you goin' to the homie's funeral?"

D.Dogg played with the French Toast in his plate and hesitated before answering. "Yeah, I'm goin'. That's some fucked up shit, Them crab niggas killed the homie. L was a real nigga, a true mobster. He wasn't on some weak shit like a lot of these niggas still lucky to be alive."

I know exactly how you feel D.Dogg. The homie L was as real as they come. At times like these I wish that I was still from the mob. I feel like puttin' some work in." Big Time threw his fork down in frustration.

"Blood don't even trip, me, Dynamite, and thc K-Squad picked up the homie's L's, lil' brother, Mac Twain, and went through the East side and lit them fools up like it was the 4th of July. We put it down for the homie. We might not be from the mob no more, but we still from the South side. Them crabs don't give a fuck about us; we targets just like them mob niggas." D.Dogg answered still emotionally charged from putting in work last night.

Big Time picked up a piece of bacon from off his plate. "You should have called me. I would have like to let them niggas know that it was us, and not the mob that was puttin' in work for the homie. Pretty Boy L was my nigga."

D.Dogg sipped on his cup of strong black coffee and smiled proudly. Don't sweat it Big Time. Them niggas out East know that it was the syndicate family dumpin' on them last night, we made sure of that."

Big Time still not satisfied wanted revenge. "Yeah that's all good. But the next time the K-Squad goes through the East and start dumpin' I'm goin' with you."

D.Dogg always ready to put in some work smiled at his brother. "Shit I don't have a problem with that. Me and you can go through right now and handle our business."

Big Time took a drink of his Orange juice and let out a small laugh. "I said I wanted to put some work in. I didn't say that I wanted to go on a suicide mission."

D.Dogg wanting to put some work in with his brother tried to be rational. "Life is a suicide mission we were born to die."

"Maybe, but I'm not tryin' to rush mine," Big Time leaned forward and lowered his voice." But check this shit out. G. and Mondo called me earlier."

D.Dogg, already on edge behind the homie L getting killed, turned his anger loose on Big Time. "What the fuck they calllin' you for?"

Big Time already knowing how D.Dogg felt about G. and Mondo tried to explain. "They tryin' to get a deal on some kilos'. Ever since Steele Bill got laid down by them crip niggas. Chip then jacked the prices up sky high and they say Fat Juan talkin' about it's a drought. So he ain't showin' nobody no love."

D.Dogg, full of rage, slapped his hand down hard on the table. "Fuck them niggas Big Time, let them muthafuckas starve to death. They don't give a fuck about you, they just playin you."

"Quit makin' this shit so personal D.Dogg. Business is business and bullshit is bullshit. This is a way for us to make some money and be at peace with them niggas at the same time." Big Time spoke quickly hoping for the best while trying to sell D.Dogg the idea.

D.Dogg jumped out of his seat making a scene. Blood fuck peace! Don't think that just because I put some work in for the homie

L, that I give a fuck about the rest of them niggas.

"Sit down blood! You got all these people up in here ear hustlin' all up in our business. You can't be exposin' game like that D.Dogg. If they don't know then they don't need to know." Big Time using the wisdom of O.G. Suja to try and calm D.Dogg down.

D.Dogg, respecting Big Time's insight, sat back down. "I don't give a fuck about shit right now blood. You slippin' even talkin' to them niggas."

Big Time convinced that D.Dogg feels the same way he does about the mob. Mistakenly confessed his own beliefs. "Come on now D.Dogg, you know that deep down inside we're still apart of the mob."

"Nigga, the homie L getting killed don' fucked you up. I'm syndicate foe' life and so are you blood. Ain't no lookin' back Big Time, especially when you're mourning a loved one. There's too many feelings involved. Just don't fuck with them niggas." D.Dogg demanded. "I'll holla at you later, I'm about to bounce up out of here. Poison's lil' sexy ass keeps blowin' me up, wantin' me to smash them guts for her," D.Dogg chuckled. "Tell sis I send my love and that if she needs anything to let me know." D.Dogg and Big Time stood up getting ready to leave.

Big Time left a tip on the table. "Yeah I'll tell her. But what you doin' hookin' up with Poison? I thought that you and Dynamite were goin' to Star's Halloween party tonight?"

"You know how I do it boy. I fuck and duck. I'll be in and out the pussy long before the party starts," D.Dogg laughed and gave his brother a hug. "I love you boy."

"I love you too, nigga." Big Time answered as the two brothers walked out of Denny's and went their separate ways.

Friday October 31st 8:00 P.M.

D.Dogg and Dynamite were chilling in Gail's house getting ready for Star's Halloween party, at the Union Hall.

Dynamite stood in the mirror checking out her sexy Louie Vuitton Vampire costume; a short black leather skirt, matching short black leather coat, black lace stockings, and a pair of black Louie Vuitton high heeled boots. She also had a pair of pearl white fang teeth in her mouth, a short and red silk cape that hung around her neck. Dynamite was looking beautiful and sexy as ever.

D.Dogg stood behind her in his black tailored made Armani suit. A pair of white fangs hung down his mouth and a long black silk cape hung around his neck.

"So how do I look daddy?" Dynamite spun around so D.Dogg could see her full costume.

D.Dogg spread his arms open wide. "You're my finest creation lil' one. Come to me so I can suck your blood."

Dynamite laughed humorously. "I don't think so Dracula. That's how I got this way in the first place.

D.Dogg smiled showing off his perfect white teeth along with his fangs. "So how do I look?"

"I think you're the most handsome Dracula ever." Dynamite walked into D.Dogg outstretched arms and kissed him long and hard.

"You got two choices either we can make love, or you can come outside with me so I can get my mind right." D.Dogg smiled knowingly.

"Your mind isn't going to ever be right you keep smokin' that shit. How come you can't just smoke weed like everybody else." Dynamite whined as she followed D.Dogg down the stairs.

"We can always have sex." D.Dogg stopped dead in his tracks on the stairs.

"Yeah right, we start havin' sex and we won't be goin' to no Halloween party." Dynamite pushed D.Dogg forward.

"That wouldn't be a bad thing, would it?" D.Dogg opened the front door and stepped outside.

"No, it wouldn't be a bad thing, but I want to go to the party. We can always fuck afterward," Dynamite stepped outside with D.Dogg and closed the door behind her. "And just so you know, I decided that I'm not going to a Major University like I had planned. I'm going to stay right here in Stockton and go to U.O.P."

D.Dogg, starting to feel the effects of the sherm, was surprised by Dynamite's announcement. "U.O.P. Fuck U.O.P. I thought you wanted to go to Stanford like your mother did. She already pulled a lot of strings and made a lot of moves to get you in."

"Yeah, I know, but that was then, and this is now. With all the shit goin' on with the family, I want to stay close in case I'm needed." Dynamite's pretty green eyes glowed intently under the moonlight. D.Dogg, taken back by Dynamite's sexiness, laughed out loud without really meaning to. "I'm sure the family will be alright without you for a lil' while."

Dynamite folded her arms like a stubborn child. "That's probably true, but I'm still not gonna want to be away from you right after were married. Besides U.O.P. is a good school academically, plus Star is goin' there. So, stop tryin' to get rid of me because I'm not going anywhere."

"Hey whatever girl. I really don't give a fuck what school you go to. I was just wondering. Come on, let's get the fuck out of here." D.Dogg said to high to argue.

Friday October 31st 11:00 P.M

Big Time pulled up inside the old rail yard station in his new 1986 dark brown Cadillac. Listening to 'Color of Success' by Morris Day in the tape deck. When he spotted G. and Mondo standing next to G.'s white Monte Carlo. Seeing his two old friends, Big Time drove up to where the two were standing and turned his engine off.

G. walked up to the driver side of the Cadillac and looked in. "Damn nigga what took you so long? I thought you were gonna fake on your boy."

Big Time looked up at G. With his eyes on Mondo who was standing next to him. "Ain't shit fake about me, G. I'm here so what's up."

G. gave Big Time a friendly smile. "My bad blood, I understand that we haven't been as close as we used to be. But hopefully after tonight that will all change, and we can get back to how things were before all this bad blood started between me and D.Dogg," G. gave Big Time daps through the open window. "So now that we got all that out of the way did you bring the four kilos'?"

Big Time relaxed some, glad to be talking business and not personal issues. "What the fuck you think nigga? That I came all the way out here, in the middle of the night, just to see your ugly ass faces? Of course, I got the package, you got the money?"

Mondo stepped up and looked inside Big Time's Cadillac. "You out here by yourself blood? Where is D.Dogg and the rest of your boys at?"

Big Time, noticing the menacing look in Mondo's eyes, tried to hide his fear. "They told me not to fuck with you niggas. They don't understand business like I do." G. and Mondo glanced around and then pulled their guns out from behind their waist and snatched Big Time out of the car. "You should have listened to your people

Big Time. Mondo check that nigga for a weapon." G. ordered as he took the four kilos' of cocaine that Big Time had stuffed inside a green duffel bag.

Mondo pushed Big Time up against the car and patted him down roughly. "This bitch ass nigga ain't strapped blood."

G. walked back to his Monte Carlo and motioned for Big Time to follow him. "Come here Big Time I want you to see somethin'."

Big Time stood his ground stalling for time searching for a way out. "What part of the game is this G.? We used to be like family."

Mondo shoved Big Time hard in the back. "You heard the homie nigga get movin'."

G. gave Big Time a wicked look. "Family? What family? You and D.Dogg betrayed the family when you started the syndicate."

Big Time staggered up next to G. and looked in the trunk. "What the fuck!" Big Time yelled not believing what he was seeing. King lay face down in the trunk of the car hog tied, ass hole naked with a sock stuffed in his mouth.

What the fuck you thought Big Time. That this was a game that you could talk your way out of." G. reached down and pulled King up out of the trunk by the rope that he was tied up with. Then he dropped him on the ground before pulling his sock out of his mouth.

"Big Time, what is this all about? Why you niggas doing this?" Said a terrified King, shocked to see Big Time with G. and Mondo.

Mondo reached down and slapped King hard across the face with his gun. "Nigga don't talk unless I tell you to or I'm goin' to cut your tongue out your fuckin mouth." Mondo pulled out a big hunting knife from his waist.

"Just be cool homie and try not to panic. These weak niggas got me jacked just like they got you." Big Time reassured his friend that he wasn't a part of this.

G. glared down at King. "Did you here that shit Mondo? Big Time called this crip nigga his homie. And this the nigga that killed the homie L."

"That's what this is all about? I promise you G. I didn't have shit to do with L getting killed." King with tears running down his face tried in vain to plead his case.

Mondo reached down and slapped King across the face again with his gun. "Nigga I told you to keep your fuckin' mouth shut."

"What the fuck is this all about G.? You know damn well King didn't have shit to do with the homie L getting killed. If you niggas want the dope just take it."

"The only thing I know Big Time is that you show this crip nigga more love then you show us. The word on the street is that you two niggas put a plan together to wipe out the mob and take over Stockton. So, tonight me and Mondo is about to send a message to whoever, that the mob runs Stockton and is not to be fucked with." G. looked down at King who was crying and bleeding from the mouth.

Big Time, feeling that things were about to get ugly, started hearing voices in his head. He could hear D.Dogg telling him not to fuck with these niggas and his mama telling him never to show weakness to your enemies. Dynamite's voice boomed in his head promising revenge on anyone that hurt her brother. He could hear the syndicate family cheering him on as he was fucking Charm. After out bidding them for the right to go first. He could hear the sweet-sounding voice of his girlfriend Jazzy, telling him how much she loved him and how he was going to make a wonderful Father. A wave of peace flowed through Big Time's body as he thought of his unborn child and those he loved. Which strengthen his resolve to face the clear and present danger he was now facing without fear.

G. pointed his gun at Big Time's head and nodded at Mondo. Mondo took his hunting knife and knelled down next to defenseless King. "G. please don't kill me. I got more money and more dope you can have it all." King cried, trying disparately to save his life.

Mondo, cold and heartless and without any feelings, grabbed King by his Jerry Curl and pulled his head back. "I told your punk ass to stay quite." Mondo growled before taking his big hunting knife and cutting King's throat. Big Time stood in complete shock at seeing King choking on his own blood with his eyes popping out his head and his mouth wide open.

"I can't believe this nigga still tryin' to talk. I told you nigga to shut the fuck up." Mondo smiled down menacing at King and in one quick motion, reached down with his hunting knife and cut off King's dick and stuck it in his mouth, before shooting him in the stomach." Suck dick and die slow muthafucka."

Big Time, accepting his fate and full of hate, looked down at his dead friend and spit in Mondo's face. "I always knew that you were a coward ass nigga. You didn't have to do the homie like that."

Mondo put his gun to Big Time's temple. "You need to be worryin' about how I'm goin' to make you suffer instead of tripping' off some dead ass crip."

Big Time refusing to beg for his life looked at G. "G. I know you niggas are goin' to kill me. But don't let this fagot ass nigga cut my shit off."

G. thought of his old friend D.Dogg and looked at Big Time, regretting already what he had to do. "You turned out to have a lot more heart than what I gave you credit for Big Time. You got my word ain't nobody goin' to cut your shit off. From the cradle to the casket, you was steady mobbin'."

"Nigga fuck the mob and fuck you. This is the syndicate family foe' life. Remember me as a boss and bury me as an O.G.

Nigga!" Big Time spat in G.'s face and knelled down on the ground next to his friend King with no regrets. G. pressed his 44 Cal to the back of Big Time's head and squeezed the trigger, killing him execution style. "Pay Big Time for his dope, Mondo. It wasn't the money that got the homie killed. It was his love for the game that got him killed. Big Time, a rich ass youngsta, who died way too early in the game before he had a chance to fully become the boss that he was made to be. R.I.P. my nigga, see you at the crossroads." G. said with a heavy heart and keeping it gangsta knowing that things were far from over. As he watched Mondo dump a bag full of money over Big Time's dead body.

CHAPTER 24

Sunshine

January 12th, 1999 2 months later

Sunshine walked into Syndicate's hospital room with a dozen roses and a bottle of Hennessy and kissed him on the cheek. "Happy Birthday Daddy."

Syndicate sat up in his hospital bed and watched as Sunshine arranged the flowers she had just bought. "What's so happy about it unless you call turnin' 31, and bein' stuck in a punk ass hospital happy? So how is everything at the liquor store?"

Sunshine fixed Syndicate a drink and sat on the bed next to him. "Krystal has everything runnin' smoothly its business as usual."

Syndicate took the drink from Sunshine. "I still can't believe that I was in a coma for 47 days."

"You can believe whatever you want to believe daddy, we're all just thankful to have you back with us." Sunshine smiled and patted Syndicate's hand. "Sugga said that you can go home in a week so quit stressin' so much."

Syndicate swallowed his drink in one gulp and put his cup for Sunshine to refill it. "I'm not stressin' Sunshine, I'm just restless. I can't sleep good knowing that the muthafuckas who's responsible for me being here is still out there."

Sunshine, happy to have her Father back, refilled his cup. "Dynamite is furious at G Gunna and the rest of the family for not findin' them niggas yet. She even told Nutts that he could go and fuck himself when he told her to let the K-Squad go home and to just let his people handle it."

Syndicate laughed out loud. "Nutts told me how Dynamite ain't tryin' to hear shit except where them niggas at."

"I thought with you comin' out of your coma she would calm down. But fuck, it's like she's even more intense now than she was when you were in a coma." Sunshine felt helpless in dealing with Dynamite.

Syndicate, understanding Dynamite's mentality, took up for his wife. "Dynamite feels that she let me down by not getting them niggas in a week like she promised me when I first got shot. That's why she's riding down so hard on everybody, especially the K-Squad.

Knowing that she's her daddy's one and only weak spot, Sunshine wasn't ready to give up on the K-Squad. "I love Dynamite more than I do my own mother. But that bitch is crazy! She told G Gunna and the rest of the K-Squad, not to come back to Stockton until they killed whoever was responsible for you gettin' shot. And that was over a month and a half ago. Nutts had to damn near force her to let some of his people come down here to help out."

Syndicate took another shot of Hennessy. "Nutts is a real boss. He's been in the game a long time. He understands what it means to be at war."

"Well, I'm glad you feel that way. Because he also said that when you get out of the hospital, you're goin' to start ridin' with bodyguards rather you like it or not." Sunshine smiled knowing how her father felt about having bodyguards.

Syndicate thought of Nutts and smiled. "Nutts must be getting old if he thinks that I'm ridin' with bodyguards. Either that or the nigga thinks that he's my father," Syndicate winked at Sunshine. "Besides I already have a bodyguard."

Sunshine frowned at Syndicate. "Just because smokin' that shit makes you feel untouchable doesn't mean that it's true."

"That's not what I was talkin' about as a matter of fact, I'm through with that shit. No, I was talkin' about you Sunshine. I didn't mentioned it to you before, but I'm very proud of you by the way you handle yourself under pressure. A lot of niggas wouldn't have had the heart to do what you did. I see a lot of me in you. I can't help but to think about how things would have been different. If I had been there for you when you were growing up," Syndicate smiled despite himself. "Dynamite would have spoiled you like the lil' rich girl that she is, and I would have done everything in my power to keep you out and away from the game."

"We would have had you in a little private school. Maybe joined the soccer team, or maybe gymnastics, or even cheerleading, or whatever it is that normal little girls like doin'. We would have raised you like a normal little girl with hopes and dreams that you wouldn't become like us. I apologize for movin' way too fast and not seein' what was right in front of my eyes. My bad, the game god has his own unique way of blessing his own. You will always be daddy's lil' girl but the game god is the one who raised you not me." D.Dogg expressed and for the first time feeling uneasy about the game, before snapping in the gangsta boss that he is.

"You're as much a part of this game as I am Sunshine, and I won't ever again force you to go against the grain. It's all or nothing with me Sunshine. There is no middle ground. I'm married to the game for better or for worse, until death do us part," Syndicate gave Sunshine a conspirator smile. "Truth be told Sunshine, if I had been around from the beginning you would have been miserable. You have the heart and the blood of a gangsta runnin' through your veins."

"Nothin' can't change what is, you're the person the game god raised you to be. So, stay true to it and have no regrets, because it is what it is. I love you more than anything or anyone in this whole fuckin' world. And I can't think of anyone that I would rather have as a bodyguard. Welcome to the syndicate family, Sunshine you made the K-Squad."

Sunshine, dreaming of being a part of the syndicate family way before she even knew that Syndicate was her Father, beamed with delight at hearing the news that she made the K-Squad. "Ow wow daddy, are you serious? Thank you so much and I promise you I won't let you down."

Syndicate sat up in his hospital bed and observed Sunshine. "Just remember Sunshine, always respect and protect the family's interest. But most of all, always keep it gangsta no matter what."

Sunshine reached over and gave her father a big hug. "Keeping it gangsta, is all I know how to do."

Dynamite and Sugga walked into the hospital room with Birthday balloons and party hats. "Happy Birthday daddy." Dynamite walked over and kissed Syndicate on the lips.

Sugga smiled at Sunshine and gave her a hug. "Hello Sunshine and how is our patient? You taking good care of him?"

Sunshine returned Sugga's hug. "It's more like the other way around. So, what's up with you Sugga?"

"Oh, nothing much I just came in for a minute to check on your father and see how he's doing," Sugga playfully pulled on Syndicate's mustache and kissed him on the lips. "Hey baby what's up? How's the Birthday boy doing?'

"How I'm doin? How does it look like I'm doin'? I'm still waitin' for you to sign the papers, so I can get the fuck up out of here." Syndicate, heavily spoiled by the three women in the room, had a temper tantrum.

Sugga smiled affectionately showing off her beautiful white teeth. "Oh, there, there now, it's going to be alright. You'll be able to come home real soon," Sugga patted Syndicate on the hand. Then turned serious. "You only been out of your coma for a week. We still have to monitor you closely and make sure that there aren't any more complications. You lost an awful lot of blood we had to give you multiple blood transfusions. Plus, there's still a bullet lodged in your back that we can't take out. And on top of all that, you can't even walk without support. You're going to have to just deal with being a little uncomfortable for a little while longer. So, stop crying like a big ass baby." Sugga ordered.

Syndicate grabbed his dick. "I got your big baby right here."

Sugga smiled shaking her head in disbelief. "You're bad daddy."

"How am I supposed to feel? I been laid up in the hospital for over two months now. I'm ready to lay up with you and Dynamite under some silk sheets handlin my business. And the sooner you sign my release papers, the faster we can make it happen."

"Trust me baby, you're way too weak to handle what me and

Dynamite have in store for you. Coming home too soon could prove to be fatal. Even at your best you would have your hands full trying to keep up with the two of us. Plus, after all I did to help keep you alive, I'm not about to have you die on us now." Sugga squeezed Syndicate's hand.

Syndicate looked at the two beautiful women in his life. "Your right Sugga, maybe I'm not ready to handle what you and Dynamite have in store for a nigga. But at least, I'll be able to watch you and Dynamite put on a show for me. That's a lot more than what I'm getting right now." Syndicate smiled seductively at Sugga and the a Dynamite.

Dynamite smiled down at Syndicate resting in his hospital bed. "Slow down daddy our love ain't goin' nowhere. Like Sugga said, it's just way too early for all that right now. And in the famous words of my big brother Big Time, it will be greater later." Dynamite turned her attentions to Sunshine who was enjoying the show. "So what was that shit you was talkin' about it bein' in your blood and all that? What's in your blood?"

"Bein' a gangsta, daddy made me a part of the K-Squad." Sunshine announced proudly.

Dynamite looked at Syndicate like he was out of his mind. "Mama is always the last one to know.", Dynamite said in disbelief.

"If you have somethin' to say Dynamite then just say it. Don't start bittin' your tongue now." Syndicate attitude turned sour at having his judgment being questioned.

Dynamite stood facing Syndicate defiantly and mad as hell. "This has a lot more to do with just syndicate family business and you know it. Sunshine is my daughter too, you know. And I don't like that you made a decision this important about Sunshine, and about us without discussing it with me first."

Syndicate pissed that Dynamite is second guessing him snapped. "So, what the fuck you sayin' Dynamite? That you don't want Sunshine to be a part of the family business?"

Dynamite looked at Sunshine with all the love and warmth a mother could ever give her child. "Sunshine has been the biggest part of our family's business ever since she came into our lives. I just think that the K-Squad is a little extreme. You didn't see her at the hospital after you got shot. She was a very scared and frighten little girl. I'm not questioning her heart, because she does have the heart of a gangsta," Dynamite smiled at Sunshine. "And like she said it's in her blood. But she doesn't have the stomach for it, Syndicate. The K-Squad are some cold blooded killas with no exceptions. And to involve Sunshine with the ugly side of the family's business right now would be a big mistake. It could really fuck her up mentally or worse, get her killed." Dynamite stared hard at Syndicate hoping that she made her point.

Sugga, not liking the idea of Sunshine becoming one of Syndicate's killers any more than Dynamite, let go of his hand while frowning down at him. "Dynamite is right Syndicate! She's still a young girl with her whole life ahead of her. What we should be discussing is what college she's going to be attending. Not this madness that were discussing now."

Sunshine, respectful of Sugga's feeling for the game, spoke softly. "The syndicate is my life, Sugga. All I ever wanted to do was to be a part of the syndicate family.

Sugga brushed Sunshine's cheek with her fingertips. "Sweetheart like Dynamite said. You're already the biggest part of this family. Nothing you do or don't do will ever change that. You don't have to prove yourself to your father or anybody else as far as that goes."

Dynamite, always respectful and true to the game, tried to compromise with Syndicate. "Why don't you just let her take over the dope game and see how she does with that? I think that would be a much better fit for her to serve the family's interest. And a way for her to learn the game at its highest level without having to get her hands bloody."

Sugga exhaled letting out her frustration. "All this talk about killing people and selling drugs is really beyond me. If it were up to me, Sunshine would have her young ass in school somewhere getting a real education. But Dynamite is right Syndicate, there isn't any logical reason for you to want to put your little girl's life on the line just because she has the heart for it."

Syndicate, growing tired of having to defend his actions, looked over at Sunshine. "Sunshine's life is always gonna be on the line, no matter what she does or where she goes. She's always goin' to have a big fuckin' target on her back. Just based on who she is. Just like you and Dynamite have targets on ya'll backs. But it's her life so it's her choice. She's a gangsta in my book, so she can do whatever the fuck she wants to do."

"Daddy you always tell me to keep it gangsta at all times no matter what. All my life I wanted to be on top. And get my revenge on them niggas that raped me and tried to turn me out to be some broken down hoe. For years, I hated you daddy, for leaving me all on my own. I blamed you for what was happening to me and I wanted you to hurt like I was hurting. So, I allowed myself to be taken advantage of because I always made myself believe that you loved me and wouldn't approve of what I was doing. When I used to see you come through the hood and look at how all the other niggas respected you. I used to tell myself that's how I was gonna be when I grow up. You were my hero Syndicate, long before I even knew that you were my father," Sunshine smiled at Syndicate. "And you're still my hero today daddy. But like you said the game raised me. I will always be your lil' girl, but I'm Dynamite's baby, and she's my mama. Whom I love more than any other woman on this earth. So, I'm going to keep it gangsta and do what Dynamite wants because I would be disrespecting the game if I didn't." Sunshine locked eyes with Syndicate with no regrets.

Syndicate broke the long stare with his daughter and smiled at Dynamite, who was standing close by Sunshine's side. "Even now you're still that spoiled lil' rich girl. You just got to have your way all the fuckin' time."

Dynamite smiled mischievously back at Syndicate. "I wouldn't be gangsta if I didn't, now would I daddy?"

CHAPTER 25
K-Squad

Friday October 31st, 1986 2:09 A.M.

Star's Halloween party at the Union Hall was jumping. Loud music could be heard throughout. Little orange and black ribbons were tacked around the walls, along with paper witches, ghost, and goblins. Crowds of people were out on the dance floor dressed in their best costumes dancing to the beat.

Star, who made a sexy little devil, wore a devil's tail, a short little red mini skirt, a tight-fitting red blouse tied in a knot at the waist showing off her perfect abs. She also wore, a pair of sexy red lingerie stockings and a pair of red high heel pumps that completed the costume. Star was looking every bit like the devil's daughter out on the dance floor with D.Dogg. Dancing to George Clinton's "Atomic Dog".

When Dynamite ran up to them with a weird look on her face

and yanked D.Dogg ruffly by the arm. "Daddy we got to go right now!" Dynamite shouted over the loud music.

Caught off guard by Dynamite's odd behavior, D.Dogg shouted back at her. "What the fuck is you talkin' about? They haven't even picked the winner for the best costume yet."

Star, feeling tipsy and a little horny, rubbed up against Dynamite with her hands high in the air. "Yeah bitch, why you want to leave so early. And why you look like someone just died."

Unable to control her emotions any longer, Dynamite fell to the ground on her knees covering her face as her green eyes filled with tears. Star, concerned with her best friend, got down on the floor with Dynamite and held her in her arms. Crying uncontrollably, Dynamite looked up at D.Dogg as the others out on the dance floor gathered around to see what was going on.

"Big Time is dead, daddy. They killed him." Dynamite whispered from the floor.

D.Doggg, full of rage at hearing that his brother was dead, reached down and snatched Dynamite up off the ground by her throat. "Bitch! What the fuck did you just say?"

Star, fearing for Dynamite's life with D.Dogg chocking her the way he was, jumped up and very gently put her hand over his and pried it away from around Dynamite's neck. "You're going to kill her D.Dogg let her go so she can talk."

Dynamite, breathing heavily and short of breath with tears

running down her pretty face, took her hand and touched D.Dogg softly on the side of his face. "Winky just called me a minute ago. She said that someone killed Big Time. "Hearing the news that his brother was killed, D.Dog's heart instantly turned stone cold. "Where is my mama?"

A quick rush of fear passed through Dynamite as she looked into D.Dogg's soul less eyes. "She's at St. Joseph's Hospital with Big Time." D.Dogg ran out of the Union Hall with nothing but murder and revenge on his mind.

"Mama what the fuck happened?" D.Dogg shouted as he rushed into the hospital morgue, where Winky was waiting for him.

"Someone killed Big, baby. They shot him in the back of the head," Winky cried, with tears rolling down her face. "They killed his friend King too."

D.Dogg, with water in his eyes, walked over to Winky and put his arms around her." It's gonna be OK mama, them niggas goin' to pay for this." D.Dogg refused to let a tear drop. As he tried to make some sense out of Big Time and King's death. "What the fuck was Big Time doin' with King?"

"I don't know. But whoever did this is a sick son-of-a-bitch. They cut King from ear to ear and then cut his dick off and stuck it in his mouth, before shooting him in the stomach." Winky said full of anger as she started to regain her composer.

"It doesn't make any goddamn sense. What the fuck was Big

Time doin' with King?' D.Dogg shouted still not accepting the fact that Big Time was dead.

Winky wiped the tears from her grieving face with the back of her sleeve. "That's not all baby. Big Time's body was covered with blood money, over thirty thousand dollars."

"Thirty thousand dollars? It's on mama, this shit here is personal. There isn't a goddam thing I can do for Big Time right here. I got to go." D.Dogg breathed heavily fighting back the tears.

G Gunna and Poppa Fly came running into the morgue. "Blood we just heard. Aw man tell me it ain't true. Winky tell me my nigga Big Time ain't dead." G Gunna, already knowing the answer, gave Winky a big hug.

Winky, unable to control herself, broke down and started crying again. "Big is gone G Gunna, Someone killed my baby.

Fuck!" Poppa Fly yelled. As he slammed a lamp down on the floor shattering it to pieces.

D.Dogg held Winky close to him. "Mama page Uncle Clept and tell him to get off the block. I'm about to go through there and let them niggas have it."

Winky looked at D.Dogg intently. Wanting him to kill whoever was responsible for killing Big Time. "Don't worry about your Uncle Clept he already knows what's up. Just go and handle your business and get them muthafuckas."

D.Dogg locked eyes with Dynamite, G Gunna, and Poppa

Fly. "Let's ride."

Dynamite sat behind the wheel of D.Dogg's cocaine white custom made Mustang. Gripping her pearl white .38 resting comfortably over her lap smashing through the hood with D.Dogg seated next to her checking the rounds in his .357 Mag. G Gunna right on Dynamite's tail in his Burgundy Cadillac with his left hand on the steering wheel and his right hand clutching his .40 Cal. Poppa Fly, with two red bandanas, tied around his wrist. A .50 Cal in one hand and a Mac .10 with a 30 round extended clip in the other one, sat in the passenger seat.

Mob niggas were hanging out on the block selling drugs and gang banging. When Dynamite, driving slowly, made a right on Spring St. coming off Phelps. To the surprise of those hanging out on the block. D.Dogg twisted his body over the hood of the Mustang and start letting loose with his .357 Mag yelling this is the syndicate the whole time.

Dynamite, following D.Dogg's lead, pointed her .38 out the window and started shooting at anything moving. Mob homies accustomed to rival gangs doing drive bye's, took positions behind park cars and trees. With some of the more dedicated soldiers standing tall through it all returned D.Dogg's and Dynamite's gunfire.

G Gunna, right behind Dynamite, immediately started unloading with his .40 Cal. at anybody in eyesight. Poppa Fly, hanging out the window, getting off with his Mac .10 with mob homics shootings back at the two slow moving cars. Poppa Fly jumped out of the car and yelled," This is for Big Time!" as he stared getting off with his .50 Cal in the middle of the street.

"That nigga Poppa Fly is crazy!" Yelled a mob homie clutching a sawed-off pump as he started to run away.

Poppa Fly, out of rounds, jumped back in the slow-moving car and loaded back up the two guns. Dynamite smashed off down the block to Scribner St. and made a right crossing over 8th St. headed into the Vista with G Gunna right behind her.

D.Dogg banged his hand hard on the dashboard. "G. and Mondo, them two niggas going to die tonight. Hit Volleny St. G. got a spot over there."

Dynamite, pumped up and full of adrenaline, drove through the Vista at a high speed stopping on Volleny St. in front of one of G.'s crack houses. G Gunna pulled up behind Dynamite and jumped out his car along with Poppa Fly. Joining D.Dogg and Dynamite out in the middle of the street who were still dressed in their Halloween costumes reloading their weapons.

"Blood, we got to keep it movin' D.Dogg. Them mob niggas and the police not goin' to be far away." G Gunna spoke quickly, scanning the dark streets while holding his .40 Cal

D.Dogg stood in the middle of the street holding his .357 Mag. "D.Dogg is dead G Gunna. From now on, my name is

Syndicate."

Two cars rounded the corner driving fast. Syndicate and the others clutched their weapons ready to fire. Recognizing the two cars, the syndicate family relaxed. Low and Whip rode in the first car with Dmove, Young Tre, and Mook riding in the second car.

"Blood we heard what happened to Big Time. That's some fucked up shit. We were posted on the Scrib Block, in front of mom's house, when we heard a lot of gunshots around the corner. Then you niggas came smashin' through, so we jumped in our cars and gave chase. Was that you niggas doin' all that dumpin'? Low stood in the middle of the street with his .44 Cal in his hand.

Syndicate walked towards G.'s crack house. "Ain't no time for talkin' right now. Whoever is strapped come with me and hurry the fuck up!" Without another word the syndicate family with guns drawn followed closely behind Syndicate.

Doc, a tall, muscular, dark skinned, youngster with a short perm. Wild Wild, a short little, red skinned youngster with a big mouth and Money, a light skinned, fat youngster, with short braids in his hair all walked out of the apartment when they noticed the syndicate family walking towards the front door.

Doc laughing, trying hard to hide his fear spoke first. "D.Dogg what's up blood? Trick or treat is over nigga, what the fuck you doin' still dressed up?"

Syndicate took his .357 Mag and hit Doc hard across the

face. Knocking him down to the ground. Syndicate continued to beat Doc to unconsciousness, beating him repeatedly over his head without mercy.

"My name is Syndicate, nigga. D.Dogg is dead and the next time you call me D.Dogg you're goin' to be dead." Syndicate yelled to a now disfigured Doc laid out on the ground covered in blood.

Dynamite held her gun pointed at Money. "Where the fuck is G. and Mondo?"

Money put his hands up in surrender not wanting any part of what was going on. "I haven't seen anyone of them niggas in a couple of days."

"You tell them niggas that the syndicate family got a message for them. Burn this muthafucka down family!" Dynamite shouted.

G Gunna, Young Tre, and Low, ran inside the small apt. and began lighting curtains on fire, blankets, trash, and whatever else would burn easily.

"You niggas hurry the fuck up! We got to get up out of here!" Syndicate yelled from outside the crack house.

"Syndicate we got to move blood. Nosy ass neighbors are starting to come outside." Dmove warned. G Gunna, young Tre, and Low, ran out of G.'s crack house after setting it on fire.

"I hear sirens daddy we got to go!" Dynamite yelled to Syndicate.

Wild Wild, confused as to what was going on, mistakenly yelled to Syndicate. "D.Dogg why you niggas doin' this?"

"Blood didn't my folks just say to call him Syndicate from now on?" Poppa Fly took his .50 Cal and shot Wild Wild right square in his eye knocking his brains out of his head.

Whip, standing next to Wild Wild when Poppa Fly shot him, looked disgustedly at all the brain matter and blood that was all over his face and body. "Aw shit blood you blew that nigga brains out."

Money, not waiting to be victim number three, took off faster than a Cheetah. "Somebody get that nigga!" Dynamite yelled. While shooting her .38 in Money's direction.

Poppa Fly, not wanting Money to get away, took off after him in hot pursuit. "Fuck that nigga Poppa Fly, let him go we got to get the fuck up out of here!" Syndicate hollered out to Poppa Fly, who continued to chase Money with his .50 Cal in his hand, but was unable to stop Poppa Fly. Syndicate and the rest of the family jumped in their cars and sped off seconds before the police arrived.

CHAPTER 26

The Game Is Ugly

Gail sipped on her early morning coffee surfing through channels on the television. Looking for any news on Big Time's murder. While Syndicate and Dynamite sat stone face on the sofa, still dressed in their Halloween costumes.

"Lord have mercy. What is this world coming to? I can't believe some of the things that people do. Big Time was sucha' good kid. He didn't deserve to die at such a young age. All this killing just doesn't make any sense to me. This used to be a real quiet little town. Now there's just as much violence here as it is in the big cities." Gail set down her remote control on the coffee table.

Syndicate, still wired from the family's early morning activities, spoke openly to Gail. "Get used to it Gail, because there ain't goin' to be no peace on the streets for a long time."

Gail looked at Syndicate and Dynamite with a worried look

on her face. "You might be right, Derek. I saw on the news earlier that someone was killed out by your mother's house early this morning. The neighbor's reported that they heard a lot of gun shots moments before a gang of young people drove up to the crime scene and got out of their vehicles carrying weapons. Said on the news that they got into a confrontation with the victims. Where one was killed and another was seriously injured. It was also reported that before the suspects left the crime scene, they set the victims apartment on fire. Witnesses also said that two of the suspects, a man and a woman, were dressed up like vampires. The two of you wouldn't know anything about that, would you?"

"Why you askin' questions that you already know the answer to Gail?" The phone started to ring before Gail could answer Syndicate's question.

"Dynamite picked up the phone. "Hello! Yeah, just a second. It's for you, daddy. It's G Gunna." Dynamite gave Syndicate the phone.

Hearing that it was G Gunna on the phone, Syndicate became instantly more alert. "G Gunna, what's up?" Syndicate spoke into the phone.

"Syndicate, the police, they got Poppa Fly." A disappointed G Gunna answered from the other line.

"Fuck! What happened?" Syndicate shouted, concerned for Poppa Fly and wanting details.

"They saw Poppa Fly chasing that nigga Money with his .50 Cal in his hand. They let the dogs out on him. He said that he stashed the gun under somebody's house. They charging the homie with two murders and attempted murder on that nigga Doc, plus arson." G Gunna spoke calmly as if it was just business as usual.

"Two? What you talkin' about two murders?" Syndicate yelled into the phone, wondering how Poppa Fly could have two murder cases.

"Poppa Fly told me that he tried to hit a high ass fence, but lost his grip and fell off. The K-9 was all over him when he hit the ground. He picked up a brick and started bashin' one of the K-9's head in, killing him. The only reason the police didn't shoot he says is, because the other two K-9's were still attackin' him. He just called me a minute ago, from the hospital. The fucked-up part about it is, the police fucked him up worse than what the dogs did. Mook's mama is his nurse. She slid him a phone and let him make a call." G Gunna waited patiently for Syndicate to reply.

Syndicate, concerned for one of his killers, was looking ahead for a way out for Poppa Fly. "Has anybody identified Poppa Fly at the crime scene?"

"All he knows right now is what he's charged with." G Gunna answered calmly not having anymore information to give Syndicate.

Syndicate's heart, full of pain and hate, was ice cold. "Tell all the homies to stay on their P's and Q's. And to stay strapped up. It's on sight with them niggas G., Mondo and whoever is down with them."

"Yeah foe' sho Syndicate. You know we stay ready to get it crackin'. You stay up to my nigga and stay strong blood one love." G Gunna spoke quickly finish with his conversation.

"One love family," Syndicate gave the phone back to Dynamite. Then leaned back on the sofa with his eyes close. "The police they got Poppa Fly."

"Oh, shit Syndicate what happened." Dynamite asked shocked to hear that Poppa Fly had been arrested.

Syndicate sat back up and looked at Dynamite. "They seen him chasin' that nigga money with his .50 Cal and let the K-9 loose on him."

Dynamite heart starts to beat faster. "Oh, my god that's not good. Did they shoot him."

Syndicate shook his head with a grim look on his face. "No, they didn't shoot him. But between the K-9's attacking him and the police beating his ass he's pretty fucked up."

"Yeah well at least they didn't kill him." Dynamite sighs grateful that the police didn't kill Poppa Fly.

Syndicate, aware that Gail is watching the two of them closely, continued to speak freely. "Yeah, that's a good thing, but with all the charges they got against my nigga, they might fuck around and try to give my nigga the death penalty. Especially if that nigga Doc fuck's around and die."

Dynamite looked at Syndicate surprised. "If Doc dies, what does that have to do with Poppa Fly."

Syndicate shook his head back and forth knowing once again that Poppa Fly was in deep shit. "They charged Poppa Fly with everything that happen last night. Plus, that nigga killed one of the K-9's that was chasin' after him. So that's another murder that he's charged with."

Dynamite looked at Syndicate with a blank stare on her face. "What the fuck did he do, shoot one of the dogs."

Syndicate let out a little smile slide across his face. "Naw, he got rid of the gun when he was running'. He bashed in one of the K-9's head with a brick."

Dynamite let out a little laugh herself glad that Poppa Fly killed one of the police dogs.

"Yeah my nigga Poppa Fly is a cold blooded killa." Syndicate laugh admiringly.

Gail sat staring at Syndicate and Dynamite intensively, sitting on the sofa in their vampire costumes. "It sounds like the two of you were busy last night."

Syndicate stared back into Gail's penetrating blue eyes. "It is what it is Gail. Them niggas killed Big Time and we goin' to kill them."

Gail was looking distraught while trying to talk some sense into Syndicate and Dynamite. "It's not going to bring Big Time back. All it's going to do is get you into trouble like your friend Poppa Fly, or worse yet get yourselves killed."

"I was born into trouble Gail. Just like I was born to die in it." Syndicate spoke without a second thought.

"The life of a real gangsta ain't never easy mama. We both knew that the job was dangerous when we took it." Dynamite added feeling like a bona fide gangsta bitch.

Gail gave Syndicate an exhausted and defeated look. "So, what are you going to do know Derek?"

Syndicate didn't have any doubts or any regrets about what he was about to do. "First, I'm goin' to find my boy Poppa Fly a good Lawyer. After that, I'm goin' to put my brother to rest like the real boss he was. Then I'm goin' to go on a mad manhunt for G. and Mondo."

Gail nodded her head in understanding realizing for the first time that Syndicate and Dynamite are really gangsters. And that things would never be the same again. "I guess there's nothing left for us to talk about. It seems to me as if you already have your mind made up about what you're going to do. So, the only thing that's left for me to do is to go down to the county jail and see if there's anything I can do for your friend Poppa Fly."

Syndicate let out a sigh of relief, grateful that Poppa Fly was getting Gail as his Lawyer. "Thanks Gail that's some real gangsta shit."

Gail got up from her seat without smiling. "For you maybe, but for me Derek, it's called unconditional love."

CHAPTER 27
Syndicate

1986 November 5th

After the funeral, everyone gathered at Syndicate and Big Time's duplex. Playing cards, smoking weed, drinking, listening to music and reminiscing about Big Time. Syndicate, high off the liquor and sherm that he's been using to help numb the pain, sat at the round table smoking a Cuban Cigar and playing poker with Nutts, Winky, G Gunna, Dmove, and Worthy. Dynamite stood behind Syndicate massaging his neck and shoulders.

Dmove puffed on his Endo joint and bobbed his head to the music as he dealt out the cards. "My nigga Big Time was a ghetto celebrity. Mt. Calvary was packed wall to wall with people showing their respect. A lot of them I didn't even recognize."

"Blood did you see all them hoes up in there goin' crazy over my nigga? I knew that Big Time had hoes, but I didn't know that he was doin' it like that. I bet twenty." Worthy threw a $20.00 bill down on round table.

Dynamite, still angry over the whole scene, stopped massaging D.Dogg's neck. "I felt like shooting' them punk rock bitches showin' off like Big Time was there man, disrespecting Jazzy like that. She was so upset she had her mother take her home right after the funeral. She didn't want to go to the cemetery afterward or come over here and hang out with us. But them sorry ass hoes wasn't the only ones I was watchin'. I had my eyes on all them mob niggas at the funeral too. Just in case they tried somethin'."

G Gunna puffed on his Cuban Cigar and tossed his $20.00 on the round table. "I call your twenty nigga. You didn't have nothin' to worry about Dynamite. I put the word out on the street that any mob nigga, or any other gang member that wanted to come and pay their respect was goin' to be searched comin' in. Low, Whip, and Nutts people had all them niggas under surveillance. "Oh Shelia" by Ready for the World played over the stereo. "Dynamite turn that shut up! That was Big's favorite song. I call your twenty and raise you twenty. Dmove, pass the joint." Winky tossed $40.00 dollars down on the round table and took the Endo joint from Dmove.

Nutts took a shot of Hennessy and puffed on his Cuban Cigar. "Any word on them two niggas that took out Big Time? I call your forty Winky." Nutts tossed his $40.00 down on the round table.

Syndicate, high off the sherm in deep mourning unable to suffocate the pain he was feeling, took a puff off his Cuban Cigar. "I told the family to lay low until after Big Time's funeral. We haven't been kickin' in any doors tryin' to find them niggas. So, the answer to your question is naw blood. Ain't nobody seen or heard from them niggas since Halloween night. But please believe me Nutts after tonight it's on. And when they do finally poke their heads up the syndicate family is goin' to be right there to chop the muthafucka's off. Y'all too rich for me I fold."

Dmove took a shot of Hennessy. "So, what they talkin' about with the homie Poppa Fly. How many cards y'all want."

Dynamite stood next to Syndicate exhaling Endo smoke through her nose. "His court date is this Friday at 9:00 A.M. My mother said that she wouldn't know anything until after the preliminary hearing."

Worthy's adrenaline was pumping feeling the effects of the weed and liquor he's been consuming. "Blood you niggas was on one. Y'all put it down for the homie. First, y'all went through the hood and let them niggas have it out on the block. Then y'all went to G.'s crack house and handled y'all business some more. Shit y'all even burnt the muthafuckin' house down. I wish I could have been there. Let me get two cards."

G Gunna, high off the sherm, turned up a 40-ounce bottle of Old English. "I wish them two punk ass niggas G. and Mondo would have been there. Blood I can't wait to catch up with them two niggas. It doesn't even really matter anymore if they killed Big Time or not. I'm goin' to kill them niggas just based on. Give me three cards."

Winky sat at the round table with tears in her eyes. "If only Big would have listened to you. When you told him not to fuck with them two sorry ass niggas he would still be alive today. Give me one card."

Nutts scanned those sitting around the round table. "You know that it's not just business with us Syndicate, we're family blood. And you know as well as I do that this shit is far from over. King's people are going to be out for revenge on anybody and everybody and you still have them mob niggas to deal with. With Poppa Fly gone, you one shooter short. My point is I got a gang of killas on the payroll. All you have to do is say the word. I'll let them loose all over this town until G. and Mondo's dead bodies show up. Let me get four cards."

Syndicate, feeling like an untouchable in mourning, smiled at his friend. "That's one love Nutts, but this is syndicate business. Not only that I'm not tryin' to start a war between my O.G. Suja and your Uncle Lil' Le Le because in the end, that would start a war between me and you."

Nutts looked at Syndicate respectfully. "I respect you for being loyal to Suja. Just like I'm loyal to my Uncle Lil' Le Le. You have a lot more game and understanding than what I gave you credit

288

for. I always thought that you were just a hot headed youngsta who liked to get high and shoot people. I'm glad to see that Big Time wasn't the only one with some brains. Just remember two very important things. One, my Uncle Lil' Le Le and Suja are living in a completely different world than the one we live in. The second thing is that the only two people that can start a war between me and you is me and you. So, you handle this shit however you want to. It's your call. Just remember that I'm here for you in full force, if you ever need me. And fuck whoever disagrees with it." Nutts poured himself another shot of Hennessy. Taking Big Time's death hard and wanting revenge on whoever was responsible.

Syndicate tapped his glass with Nutts. "I feel you Nutts I feel you.

Looking out the window and smoking on a Newport, Los called out to Syndicate. "Syndicate you better come check this shit out we got company blood."

Syndicate walked to the window and looked outside. Three Caddy's full of mob homies had just pulled up in front of the house. In the first Caddy was Under, Chip, Deja and Clept. Riding in the second Caddy was Tro, Arlo, Budda, and Mac Twain. In the third Caddy was Coon Dogg, Jerrod, Grim, and Huey.

Syndicate grabbed Big Time's Mac .11 with the 30-round extended clip. "What the fuck these niggas want," Syndicate, cursed angrily, as he walked outside to face the mob. With the rest of the syndicate family right behind him with their guns drawn. "Uncle Clept what the fuck is wrong with you comin' to my spot three carloads deep with these niggas."

Syndicate's Uncle, Clept, trapped in the middle of blood and loyalty wanted to squash any all rumors before they got started. "They just want to holla at you. If it was anything more than that I would be over there with you."

Syndicate held Big Time's Mac .11 in his right hand and smoked on a Newport with his left hand. "So, what the fuck you niggas want to talk to me about?"

The O.G. Homie, Coon Dogg, stepped forward. "Like your Uncle Clept just said, we didn't come here to start any funk D.Dogg."

Syndicate let out a little laugh and smiled. "Nigga you startin' funk right now Coon Dogg. It ain't no secret that I changed my name to Syndicate. The last nigga that called me D.Dogg ain't with us no more and the nigga before that probably wishes he was dead.

Coon Dogg laughed out sarcastically. "Yeah we know all about what happened to the homies the other night. That was some fucked up shit. But I'm not them, I'm Coon Dogg. I'm the one who put you on lil' nigga and gave you the name D.Dogg. You need to start rep respecting the O.G.'s."

"Nigga you got a lot of nerve talkin' about rep respecting the

O.G.'s. A nigga's rep don't mean shit to me. Syndicate smiled as the devil danced in his eyes. "But the only reason you still standin' Coon Dogg is because I do respect the O.G.'s. The real one's anyway, like Suja. But make no mistake about it O.G. If you disrespect me again by callin' me D.Dogg, I'll chop your muthafuckin head off and that goes for the rest of you niggas too."

Deja stood next to Coon Dogg trying hard to control his temper. "Check this out blood. We really don't give a fuck what your name is. If you want to be called Syndicate so muthafuckin' what. You really need to chill the fuck out with all that high power talkin' you doin'. You niggas ain't the only ones with guns. And like the O.G. homie Coon Dogg just said, we came here to try and squash the bullshit, not add to it."

Syndicate played with the trigger of his Mac .11, itching to squeeze it. "What the fuck you talkin' about squashin' it? My brother is dead nigga. So, until G. and Mondo is dead or I'm dead, these streets is goin' to be just like the Middle East. Fuck Peace!"

Under, leaning against his smoked Grey Caddy with his arms folded across his chest and a 9-millimeter Glock tucked showing in his waist, walked up to Syndicate. We not talkin' about squasin' it with G. and Mondo. Killin' Big Time like that was some real fucked up shit. Once upon a time we were all like brothers. Now we out here killing each other like we never knew one another. Me and you are on the same level Syndicate."

"The O.G.'s not the ones that's puttin' in work these days. It's youngstas like us that's keeping the block fired up." Under shook his head. "I'm just sayin' blood goddamn. All of us grew up together right here in the same hood. It hurts that you niggas disowned the mob like you did. But there has to be a better solution than us killing each other. The homie L is gone, Big Time is gone, Wild Wild is gone that's three homies in a matter of days. Plus, we can't forget about the homie Reb. That shit that went down on the block Halloween night. With you niggas comin' through the hood and gettin' off like that. Then goin' to G.'s spot and handlin' your business the way you did. It's regrettable, but under the circumstances it's understandable."

"Mac Twain told us how he went with you K-Squad niggas through the East side and put some work in for the homie L. That was one love on you nigga's part. Point is Syndicate that we decided to wash our hands on them two niggas G. and Mondo. So, whatever happens between you and them niggas is on y'all niggas. The mob is goin' to be on the sidelines rootin' for nobody. And like the O.G. Homie Suja said, we all from the same hood rather we like it or not."

Syndicate put his arm around Dynamite who was standing next to him with her .38 in her hand. O.G. Suja is right about us bein' from the same hood. But that doesn't mean that we're from the same gang. I'm from the syndicate and this is my family," Syndicate nodded his head towards the syndicate family that was standing around him ready for whatever. "But as long as you niggas keep your word and stay on the sidelines while we handle our business with them two niggas, G. and Mondo. The funk between us is over as of now."

Syndicate and Under gave each other daps signaling an end to any funk between the two gangs. "That's it then blood all that shit is squashed between us. And tell that nigga Poppa Fly ain't nobody coming to court to testify against him. We already got at Doc and Money and warned them niggas to keep it gangsta. Fuck the police." Under threw up the mob's gang sign. Feeling like homies again the syndicate family and the mob gave each other daps.

"Do you think them niggas really meant that shit? Or were they just spying for G. and Mondo." Dynamite asked Syndicate, as the three carloads of mob homies smashed out.

Syndicate grabbed a hold of Dynamite's hand as they walked back towards the house. "I've known them niggas all my life. So, I seriously doubt if they were tryin' to play me. They already know where I'm at wit it. But if I'm wrong, I'm goin' to take Nutts up on his offer and kill all them niggas."

CHAPTER 28

Star

Friday November 21st 10:30 P.M.

Star knocked on Syndicate's front door dressed in a pair of tight-fitting Guess Jeans, glued to her well-rounded hips and ass as if it were a part of her fabulous looking body. Wearing a little Guess denim jacket worn open and her black t-shirt tucked in at the waist with her high heeled black leather boots. Star was looking and feeling like a real dime piece. "Who is it?" Syndicate yelled. While sitting down at his round table counting drug money. He was dressed in a pair of long black, baggy shorts, and a pair of black corduroy house shoes with no shirt on revealing his many gang tattoos. Now that Big Time was gone, Syndicate took over the family's drug trade. Pissed off from being interrupted from what he was doing, Syndicate grabbed Big Time's Mac .11 from off the round table and walked to the front door and looked in the peep hole.

Surprised to see that it was Star on the other side, Syndicate smiled and opened the door. "Girl what you doin' out here in the hood at this time of the night all by yourself?"

Star smiled and brushed pass Syndicate. "I told Dynamite I would keep my eye on you while she was visiting her father in L.A. to make sure you didn't get into any trouble."

Making sure that the door was locked, Syndicate walked back to the round table and placed the Mac .11 next to the money. "I don't think this is what she had in mind," Syndicate smiled as he watched Star closely as she made herself comfortable sitting on a bar stool. "You want a shot of Hennessy Star?" Syndicate went to the bar and fixed him and Star a drink.

"Thank you," Star said taking the shot glass from Syndicate. "You have a nice place hear Syndicate. My feet are killing me is it OK if I take these boots off?"

"By all means make yourself comfortable," Unable to hide his lust, Syndicate's dick started to bulge from underneath his baggy pants. "You still haven't told me how your goin' to keep me out of trouble."

Star finished her shot of Hennessy and flashed Syndicate a gorgeous smile. "That all depends."

Syndicate laughed out loud and fixed Star another drink. "And what the fuck is that supposed to mean?"

Star walked up to Syndicate boldly and took the shot glass

out of his hand. Tipped on her pretty red painted toes. Placed her free hand on his chest and whispered in his ear. "It means that I want to help break your gorilla out of his cage. As long as it doesn't cause either of us any trouble later."

Syndicate's dick throbbed uncontrollable with desire for Star as she leaned up against him. "Only trouble we goin' to have in this muthafucka is gettin' these tight ass jeans off that big sexy ass of yours. Syndicate swiftly snatched off Star's denim jacket and t-shirt and sucked hungrily on her tender young breast. Star, turned on by Syndicate's impulsive behavior, wrapped her arms around his neck and held his head firmly in place. Enjoying the way that Syndicate was making her feel; kissing and sucking on her little nipples.

Syndicate, wanting to fuck Star since he first met her, began unbuttoning her jeans with Olympic speed. Syndicate licked his lips as Star stepped out of her blue panties. Dick hard as a brick, Syndicate easily slipped out of his baggy short pants and boxers in one quick motion.

Star blushed at seeing Syndicate's big black dick standing up like a soldier at full attention from wanting her; unable to control his lust any longer. Syndicate picked Star up by her sexy round ass, and ruffly pinned her against the wall. Star, too filled with excitement to complain, locked her legs tightly around Syndicate's waist as he drove his dick hard and deep inside of her.

Syndicate uncompromisingly penetrated in and out of Star's

little, tight pussy. Star lovin' every minute of Syndicate's hostile takeover of her young body. Closed her eyes tightly. "Oh, goddamn Syndicate, fuck me nigga, Oh, goddamn yes, we gonna get in trouble." Star cried out.

Syndicate, turned on by Star's antics, drove his dick harder and deeper into Star's sweet sugar walls. "You lovin' this big gangsta dick ain't you bitch." Syndicate turned Star around bending her over in a doggy style position. Grabbing a Handful of Star's short red hair. Syndicate hit it from behind with his balls slapping up against her big red ass.

Star screamed out in fulfillment making little fuck faces. Backing her ass up in rhythm with Syndicate's big dick going in and out of her. "Oh, god yes, right there, Syndicate, don't stop, don't stop, goddamn yes, fuck this pussy, you big dick nigga." Star pushed back into Syndicate as hard as she could grinding her ass up against his hard body.

"Oh, hell yeah Star. I been wantin' to beat this pussy up for a long time." Syndicate full of lust continued to dick Star down.

"Oh, goddamn yes, beat the pussy up Syndicate, beat it up." Star moaned as she came hard all over Syndicate's dick.

Syndicate, appreciating the fact that he's finally got his dick inside of fine ass Star, wanted to make the most of it. "Turn around and open your mouth Star. I'm about to nut and I want you to swallow the babies. Syndicate quickly pulled his dick out of Star's sweet pussy and put it in her sweet mouth. Using both of his hands, he grabbed Star by the back of the head and faced fucked her like she was a prostitute.

"That's what the fuck I'm talkin' about Star. Show your love for a gangsta and suck this muthafucka." Star took Syndicate's dick all the way down her throat. Syndicate let out a loud unknown animal noise before shooting a giant load of semen down Star's throat.

Sitting up on her knees, Star smiled up at Syndicate. "The gangsta's penis is clean of all it's babies." Star laughed as she finished up Syndicate's dick and balls with a hot tongue bath.

"Go and get me a wet face towel." Syndicate ordered, done with Star and wanting to get back to counting his drug money.

Star, startled by Syndicate's sudden rudeness, got up off her knees and reluctantly went to the bathroom to get Syndicate a face towel. "So how was it Syndicate? Was it good to you?" Star stood directly in front of Syndicate, butt ass naked, with a face towel in her hand.

Syndicate snatched the face towel out of Star's hand, wiped his dick and balls off and gave it back to her. "Was it good to me? Bitch you already know what time it is. I fuck and duck. So, save all that romantic shit for them square ass niggas you be fuckin' wit." Syndicate put his boxers and short pants back on and walked over to the round table. Sat back down took a swallow of his 40 Ounce and started back counting his drug money.

Star, offended by Syndicate's rude behavior, begin putting her clothes back on. "Damn Syndicate, I didn't ask you if you loved me. I just asked if you liked it nigga."

Syndicate refused to make eye contact with Star. "You served your purpose. You kept me out of trouble. But I got to finish counting this money, so I'll holla at you later."

Star walked up to Syndicate and rubbed him playfully on his bald head. "Why you got to be so hard Syndicate? "

Syndicate, not interested in how Star was feeling, replied without looking up. "I only got feelings for one girl Star and her name is Dynamite. So, don't get shit twisted, because it is what it is."

"I don't have shit twisted, because I already know what it is. I wasn't trying to compete with Dynamite. I just wanted to fuck. So, fuck you. And I know that you liked it just as much as I did. Even if you won't admit it." Star turned around and marched out without looking back. Holding her head up high like the dime piece she was.

CHAPTER 29

Nowhere To Hide

1:30 A.M. That same night

Syndicate sat at the round table with a drink in his hand thinking about Big Time. When the phone rang disturbing his thoughts. "Yeah who this?"

"Syndicate what's up blood. It's me O.Z. I got some news for you." O.Z. spoke hurriedly from the other line.

"I'm not interested in any crackhead deals that you tryin' to hustle off on me nigga." Syndicate not in any mood for O.Z.'s scheming bullshit.

O.Z. feeling disrespected, yelled angrily into the phone, "Nigga fuck you! I ain't callin' about no crackhead shit! This is some family shit! I'm out here in Boss Track and I just seen that nigga Mondo ride by with that bitch Poison!"

Syndicate jumped to attention at hearing Mondo's name.

"What the fuck you just say blood? Mondo and Poison? Are you sure it was them?" Syndicate shouted back in the phone not believing that Poison would be riding in the same car with his brother's killer.

"Blood this shit is way too serious for me not to be sure about it." O.Z. spoke quickly making his point.

Syndicate, fuming, gripped the phone tightly. "Poison that lil gold diggin' bitch. She done sold her fuckin soul to the devil riding in the car with that nigga. Im'a kill that hoe too." Anxious to get off the phone with O.Z., Syndicate shift gears in the conversation. "I'll have somethin' for you later blood. Right now, I'm about to go and hunt this nigga down."

O.Z.'s heart went out to Syndicate. "You don't owe me shit blood, we family. If I had been strapped, I would have shot that nigga myself." "That's one love O.Z. Don't trip on it blood I'm on this nigga." Syndicate hung up the phone with O.Z and immediately begin blowing up Poison's pager.

Poison was a medium height, light skinned, pretty face, small waist and big ass, long red dyed hair, and sexy as hell. She pulled up into the parking lot with Mondo at the 2 for 1 motel out in Boss Track with her pager going off. "Who the fuck is that blowin' you up like the world is comin' to an end!" Mondo yelled. Irritated by the constant beeping of Poison's pager.

Poison pulled the pager down from the sun visor. Seeing

Syndicate's number come across the little screen, Poison's heart skipped a beat. True to the game and fast on her feet, Poison recovered quickly. "It's my brother."

Mondo took a drink of his 40 Ounce. "What the fuck's wrong with that lil' nigga?'

Poison pulled her black Honda Accord in front of the cheap motel room and let Mondo out of the car. "I'm goin' to drive over to the pay phone and call him back, since there's no phone in these cheap ass rooms. It must be important by the way he keeps blowin' me up."

Mondo slammed the car door shut. "Just hurry the fuck up and tell that nigga I said to quit cock blockin'!!"

Poison pulled up next to the pay phone in front of the motel office. Nervously she got out of the car and dialed Syndicate's number. "Poison!" Syndicate yelled into the phone after picking it up on the first ring.

"Damn nigga why, you yellin' at me, and why you blowin' a bitch up?" Poison spoke quickly trying unsuccessfully to sound normal.

"Bitch don't play games. I'm not even goin' to ask you why, hoe. But if you don't tell me where that nigga Mondo is. Your own family won't be able to recognize you at your funeral bitch!" Syndicate yelled into the phone.

Hearing the venom in Syndicate's words, Poison's knees

became weak and her legs started to tremble with fear. "We're out in Boss Track over on Lincoln St., at the 2 for 1 motel room number 8."

With murder on his mind, Syndicate gripped the phone in a powerful death grip. "Keep it gangsta then bitch and make sure that nigga doesn't leave the spot. If he does or if you try to warn him and set me up, I'll kill everybody in Your goddamn family bitch including your dog."

Poison, terrified for her family and mad at herself for getting caught up in some gangsta shit that has nothing to do with her, decided to play it smart. "I promise you Syndicate that I'm not going to tell Mondo or anyone else a goddamn thing. Just please don't kill me or my family."

Syndicate full of hate, isn't in the mood to be trusting Poison, but at the same time he didn't have any other options. "Just make sure you keep that bitch ass nigga slippin' until we get there."

Poison, deep in the game, as she has accepted her fate for what it is. "Fuck it! If it's goin' down, then let's get it over with. You niggas just hurry the fuck up."

"Don't worry about us bitch. You just keep it game tight for me and keep that nigga immobile." Syndicate hung up the phone with Poison and called the K-Squad.

Syndicate, G Gunna, and Low sat at the round table checking their guns when Whip walked into the room. "Syndicate what's up blood. Where in the fuck is that nigga hiding at? Let's go smoke that punk muthafucka. What are we waiting for?"

Syndicate downed a shot of Hennessy. "We just been sittin' here waiting on you to show up. That bitch Poison got that nigga held up at the 2 for 1 motel out in Boss Track."

Whip downed a quick shot of Hennessy. "I'm here now so let's go and get that nigga."

"Let's ride then blood." Syndicate grabbed his fully automatic Mac.11 from off the round table and walked out the front door.

With the rest of the K-Squad following close behind wearing red bandanas tied around their heads and faces. The K-Squad smashed down the street in Killa mode in G Gunna all black 1972 four door Caddy.

Back at the motel, "Oh, hell yeah Poison. I heard you had some cool oral skills but damn." Mondo laid flat on his back butt ass naked smoking on a joint as Poison, wearing only a pair of pink panties, laid on her stomach with her feet dangling over the edge of the little bed sucking on Mondo' dick.

When the K-Squad kicked in the front door of the motel room with their guns drawn, Poison quickly jumped up off the bed, grabbed her clothes, and ran out the front door in her pink panties.

Mondo, realizing that Poison had set him up, thought twice about going for his gun that was on the floor. Syndicate smiled wickedly at Mondo's discomfort at being caught with his pants down. "Never trust a bitch with a big ass and a pretty smile. They'll cross you every time." G Gunna close the door."

Mondo's heart, filled with fear, at the sight of Syndicate and the K-Squad. "It wasn't me Syndicate. I killed that crab nigga King, but I didn't kill Big Time. I told G. not to kill the homie, but he said he wasn't leavin' any eye-witnesses." Mondo rambled on trying desperately to talk his way out of his immediate death.

Syndicate's heart went out to Big Time's memory. "Put this bitch ass nigga in the trunk." Syndicate's Mac .11 shook uncontrollably in his hand from itching to kill Mondo.

Low pointed his .44 Cal. at Mondo's head. "Get the fuck up nigga and wrap that sheet around you." Mondo wrapped the sheet around him and started walking slowly towards the front door.

"If that nigga does anything stupid, kill him." Syndicate ordered.

Gunna had the Caddy backed up in front of the motel room with the trunk already open. When Mondo and Low walked out of the Motel room followed by Syndicate and Whip. Low hit Mondo in the back of the head with his gun then shoved him in the trunk. "Get your bitch ass in the trunk nigga. Low slammed the trunk close and rushed into G Gunna's waiting Caddy with the rest of the K-Squad.

G Gunna smashed out the Motel parking lot fish tailing. "So, where we dumpin' this nigga off at." G Gunna asked Syndicate.

Syndicate lit a Newport. "Take this nigga to Whiskey's Slue. We about to take this nigga on a fishing trip way out in the middle of nowhere. So, nobody can hear his screams when I torture his ass. My grandfather used to take me and Big Time out there when we were kids. It's the perfect place to dump this nigga off at."

G Gunna smiled at the thought of killing Mondo and leaving him way out in Whiskey's Slue's famous river, known for turning up dead bodies.

"Damn blood its pit black out here blood I can't see shit." Low grumbled while looking out the back window.

Whip sat uneasily in the back seat next to Low. As G Gunna sped down the dark and narrow rode. "Blood! You need to slow the fuck down. You keep speedin' around these curves you goin' to fuck around and go over one of these cliffs."

G Gunna, doing 50 mph. Looked back at Whip in the rear-view mirror. "Whip you ol' scary ass nigga. I got this blood."

Syndicate, not trusting G Gunna's driving anymore than Whip and Low, yelled over to G Gunna from the passenger seat. "We far enough from the streets pull this muthafucka over anywhere!"

G Gunna pulled over to the side of the rode next to the water and turned the engine off. The K-Squad, with guns in hand, got out and walked to the back of the Caddy. G Gunna took his keys and opened the trunk to find Mondo wrapped up in a sheet and curled up in a fetal position.

Syndicate lit another Newport and headed down the hill to the water bank. "Get that nigga out of the trunk and bring his punk ass down here."

Whip pointed his double barrel sawed off shot gun at Mondo who was curled up in the trunk. "You heard Syndicate nigga, get your bitch ass out of the trunk."

Mondo, blinded by the night, climbed out of the trunk wearily with a sheet wrapped around his body. "Where the fuck we at."

Low laughed and pointed his .44 Cal. at Mondo pushing him forward down the hill. "We goin' shark fishin' nigga and you the bait."

Syndicate squatting down looking out at the river smoking on his Newport with his Mac .11 in his hand mourning Big Time til he heard Mondo and the K-Squad approaching. "If you have any hopes of leavin' here alive, I strongly advise you to tell me the truth about what happened Halloween night." Syndicate spoke without moving.

Mondo looked around nervously at the K-Squad unsure of his whereabouts and looking for a way out. Mondo spoke quickly knowing that his life was on the line. "I already told you Syndicate, I didn't kill Big Time. G. killed the homie."

Syndicate tossed his cigarette in the water. Then turned around and faced Mondo. "Then why in the fuck didn't you kill G. for killin' the homie?"

Mondo feeling the pressure that his time was running out panicked and rushed towards Syndicate. "I'm'a kill you, nigga!"

Syndicate ready for whatever raised his Mac .11 and shot Mondo's right knee off. Mondo fell to the ground in tremendous pain. Holding on to a knee that wasn't there anymore, Syndicate kicked Mondo hard where his knee used to be with no regard to the pain that he was suffering. "I'm only goin' to ask you one more time blood. What happened Halloween night?"

Mondo, laying naked on the ground in state of shock from his gunshot wound, came clean about what happened Halloween night. Praying that Syndicate would have mercy on him for not killing Big Time.

Tears fell from Syndicate's eyes hearing how Big Time went out like a young boss. And knowing for certain that his old friend killed his brother. Syndicate walked up to G Gunna who was also in an unforgiving mood, after hearing how Big Time died. "G Gunna give me the knife." G Gunna gave Syndicate a hunting knife. Syndicate stared down at Mondo cold and heartless. "So, you like to cut muthafuckas up before you kill them huh, Mondo? Hog-tie this nigga in his sheet."

Mondo did his best despite his gunshot wound to fight off

Whip and Low as they struggled to hog-tie him. Syndicate stood over a naked Mondo hog-tied in his motel sheet with the hunting knife in his hand. Desperate to save his life, Mondo, pleaded his case. "I told G. not to kill the homie. You know how G. is, that nigga is crazy." Mondo, feeling death getting closer by the second, begin talking faster. "Come on blood. All I did was kill that crip nigga King, whose homies killed, the homie L. You goin' to kill me for that?"

Without answering, Syndicate kicked Mondo in the head knocking him over to his side. Then took the hunting knife and stuck it in Mondo's ass as far as it would go. Filled with hate, Syndicate drove the hunting knife back and forth inside of Mondo's blood-soaked asshole. Mondo cried out in pain as Syndicate ripped his asshole apart. "I want everybody to know that you died a bitch with no manhood left in you. This is for King you fagot." Syndicate took the hunting knife and chopped off Mondo's dick. Mondo yelled out in agony at the pain he was suffering. Tired of hearing Mondo's screams, Syndicate took his red bandana from off his head and tied it around Mondo's mouth.

"And this is for Big Time." Syndicate spoke silently to himself. Taking the hunting knife, he carved "You're Next G." in Mondo's back. Before cutting his throat from ear to ear with the blood-stained hunting knife. G Gunna walked up and looked down at the almost dead Mondo. And without any warning shot him three times in the head with his .40 Cal.

"Dump that nigga's body in the water," Syndicate ordered. Low and Whip picked up Mondo's dead body and threw him into Whiskey's Slue. "You're next G." Syndicate spoke into the night. As he walked back up the hill with the K-Squad before smashing out in G Gunna's black Caddy.

CHAPTER 30

Fuck The Rules

Leaning down low in his cocaine white Mustang, cruising down the street with the top down blasting 'It's Called Survival' by Grandmaster Flash in the tape deck, Syndicate gripped the steering wheel with his right hand while resting his left hand on the door frame. He was wearing a red hooded sweatshirt over his bald head, black 501 jeans, and a pair of red Fila shoes.

Dynamite in the passenger side, dressed the same, with a picture of in loving memory of Big Time on the front and back of her red sweatshirt. It's been over a month since you niggas killed Mondo and that nigga G. still hasn't been spotted. I say it's time we quit playin' with this nigga and get serious and force him out from whatever rock he's hiding under." Dynamite's green eyes blood shot red from the Endo weed she's been smoking.

Syndicate, comfortable in his own little private thoughts and tired of hearing Dynamite bitch about not being able to find G., Tried to pacify her. "We been hittin' all that nigga spots on a regular basis. It's just a matter of time before we catch up with him."

Dynamite leaned back in her seat fuming. Regretting the fact that she wasn't with the K-Squad when they killed Mondo. "That's some gay shit and you know it. For all we know that nigga could be out of state some fuckin' where. We just wasting our time hittin' all his known kick it spots."

Syndicate, frustrated with this old conversation, turned the music down so that he could hear Dynamite better. "So, what the fuck do you suggest that we do?"

Dynamite sat up in her seat and smiled deviously. "I suggest that we hit the right spot." Dynamite explained making it all sound so simple.

Syndicate rolled his eyes knowing that Dynamite expected him to ask the question. "And where the fuck is that Dynamite?"

The smile left Dynamite's pretty face and turned into a serious frown. "His mama's house."

Syndicate shook his head in disbelief. "What the fuck! You can't be serious. You that game goofy that you think that nigga is hidin' out at his mama's house?"

Dynamite took a long drag off her joint. "I'm far from game goofy baby. And no, I don't think that he's hidin' out at his mama's house. But I bet she knows where he is."

Syndicate gave Dynamite a peculiar look. And wondered to himself what ever happened to that sweet little girl he use to know. "What the fuck you sayin' Dynamite. You want to run up in that nigga mama's house and force her to tell us where he's at?"

"Why the fuck not?" Dynamite snapped.

"Why the fuck not? Because G.'s mama ain't got shit to do with this." Syndicate snapped back. "Plus, she's a real sweet lady. She was always nice to me and treated me like I was her son." Syndicate said as and after thought.

Dynamite's heart filled with rage at the thought of Syndicate having sympathy for G. and his mama. "Fuck that old bitch. Blood is thicker than water. Lil' Big Time ain't never goin' to have his daddy around. So, if I can't kill G.'s punk ass I'm goin' to kill those closest to him startin' with his mama. Like you said this shit is personal. So, fuck that nigga and his mama." Dynamite turned the music back up signaling that she was done with the conversation. Syndicate, amused by Dynamite's animated performance, started to laugh. "You got the mouth for it no doubt, but do you have the heart for it."

Dynamite took out her black murder one shades from the glove box and put them on. "I'm startin' to wonder if you still have the heart for it."

Syndicate nodded his head at Dynamite respectfully. "From the cradle to the casket."

Syndicate called an emergency meeting at his house for the syndicate family later on that night. "So, what's the word on the street?" Syndicate looked around at the rest of the family gathered around the house, smoking weed and taking Tequila shots.

"The word on the street is that the mob killed King. So, it's on sight as usual with them East side niggas and them mob niggas. As for us and the mob? So far, they stayin' true to their word and stayin up out of our business," J.R. let out a little whistle. "The block is on fire though blood. The police been raiding damn near every day since they found Mondo's body floating in Whiskey's Slue. They jacking up everybody, tryin' to get some answers to all these murders that's takin' place." J.R., the unofficial spokesman for the family confirmed.

Syndicate sat next to Dynamite at the big Oak round table. "Yeah, I'm already knowin' that things are hot right now. The punk police had me and Gail down at the station grillin' me for about three hours straight last week. They were hittin' me up with questions from all angles. From the syndicate family bein' organized to all these unsolved murders takin' place."

"They brought up that shit that went down on Halloween night with Poppa Fly. Gail was all over them muthafuckas. They don't have shit on the homie; no fingerprints, no murder weapon, nothin'. Technically they can't even place Poppa Fly at the murder scene without an eyewitness. Not only that, the police fucked up when they didn't read the homie his Miranda rights. Gail said that alone could get the case thrown out. They brought up that shit that went down with Reb and that nigga Mondo. Talking about how they heard that I was the one responsible for their deaths. Which Gail made clear it, that was all hear say."

Dynamite slammed her shot of Tequila down her throat and banged her shot glass down hard on the round table. "Alright everybody check this shit out. We already know that the block is hot. So, let's cut out the bullshit and get to the point as to why this meeting was called. To talk about how we goin' to force this nigga G., to come out from whatever rock he's hidin' under."

G Gunna stood next to the round table drinking on a 40 Ounce of Old English. "I hear you talkin' Dynamite, but you ain't sayin' nothin'."

Dynamite looked at G Gunna and the others with murderous vengeful eyes. "What I'm sayin' is that we're goin' to grab G.'s mama and force him out of his hidin' place."

Worthy whistled out loud not liking the idea of grabbing G.'s mother. "And what if that doesn't work?"

Dynamite with a straight face looked at Worthy. "Then I'm goin' to kill her."

The room went silent upon hearing how Dynamite wanted to snatch G.'s mother and threatening to kill her. Everyone knew in their hearts, all having mothers of their own, that a nigga's mama was untouchable. Even gangsters had their limits.

Syndicate, fully aware of the unspoken code in the hood, noticed the concern on the faces of those around him, spoke up in Dynamite's defense. "Still water runs deep blood. I'm tired of playin' with this nigga."

Los coughed, chocking on the joint that he was smoking. Shocked that they were even discussing something as crazy as this. "Goddamn Syndicate you can't just kill the nigga's mama."

"You must got me fucked up with yourself Los. I can do whatever the fuck I want to do. But since you're so worried about that nigga's mama getting hurt, you're more than welcome to go up in the house with Dynamite and make her talk." Syndicate challenged.

Los smiled at Syndicate trying to make light of the fact that he was scared. "Shit come on now Syndicate, you know that shit ain't me. Besides, she knows who I am."

"Scary ass nigga. What the fuck you talkin' about she knows who you are. The only muthafucka that she doesn't know in this room is Dynamite." Syndicate snapped. Mad at Los for being scared and for what he took as being disloyal to the family.

"Quit scarin' the homie Syndicate. I'll go up in the house with Dynamite and make that bitch talk. Like you said blood, it's time to stop playin' games with this nigga." G Gunna feeling it his duty to protect the family and wanting to save Los of anymore embarrassment, volunteered to go up in the house with Dynamite.

Mook sigh's a sign of relief glad that the tension between Los and Syndicate is over, since G Gunna volunteered to go with Dynamite. "So, what about that bitch Kat. What if she's at the house?" Mook asked. Glad that his heart wasn't questioned.

Ray laughed. "Shit, I bet Dynamite is wishin' that bitch is there."

"If she is there then she's a dead bitch." Dynamite warned with no fun intended.

"That bitch Kat lives with her baby's daddy and their three kids. So, it's highly unlikely that's she's goin' to be at her mother's house, especially while she's at work. Which is when I want the two of you to break in and lay low until she gets home from work." Syndicate took charge of the operation.

G Gunna nodded his head in agreement. "That sounds a lot better than havin' to kick the door in. Even though we're not that close, she is my Aunt. I would hate to give her a heart attack."

"Yeah and that's what we don't want, anything happenin' to that nigga's mama. So, Dynamite make sure that you cover your face up. I don't want you lookin' for a reason to kill her." Syndicate gave Dynamite a warning look to let her know that he was serious about her not killing G.'s mother.

Dynamite returned Syndicate's glare challenging his authority. "If she talks then she'll live. And if she doesn't then she'll die. It's as simple as that boss."

Syndicate shook his head in disgust with Dynamite's wanting to kill G.'s mother. "She works the swing shift at Del Monte. That's 2:00 to 10:00 P.M. So, make sure that the two of you are inside the house before she gets off work tomorrow night. Whip you and Low, go and take Winky to a safe house until all this shit is over. I'm not tryin' to make the same mistake that G. made by not protecting his mama."

CHAPTER 31

The Game Is Deep

Dynamite and G Gunna waited impatiently inside G.'s mother's house with all the lights out. G Gunna sat on the leather couch with his .40 Cal laying beside him. "Damn where in the fuck is this bitch at? It's going on 11:00 O'clock.", sounding agitated.

Dynamite stood at the window peaking out of the curtains, wearing a black ski mask pulled over her face and her .38 tucked in the waist of her jeans. "G Gunna, just chill the fuck out and be quiet. I see a car pulling into the driveway now, it has to be her." Dynamite whispered as her heart begin beating faster, eager for some action.

G Gunna grabbed his gun from off the couch and ran to the window. "It's her! Wait until she gets inside and close the door before you do anything." G Gunna pulled his black ski mask over his face.

G.'s mother, a pretty, overweight Mexican lady with long

black hair. She was wearing her Del Monte uniform. After walking into the house and locking the door behind her, she was caught off guard when G Gunna suddenly turned on the lights.

"Don't move bitch!" Dynamite whispered from behind her black ski mask with her gun pointed at G.'s mother's head.

Blinded by the light for a quick second before realizing that a young white girl was pointing a gun at her. G.'s mother let out a loud scream. Dynamite, full of hatred, grabbed the older woman by her hair and jammed the .38 inside her mouth forcing her down to the floor. "You better shut the fuck up bitch. If you scream one more fuckin' time, I'll blow you're fuckin' brains out."

G Gunna leaned down and tapped Dynamite on her shoulder. "Take the gun out of her mouth. She's not goin' to scream anymore, isn't that right Ms. Torres." Looking at G Gunna and remembering that D.Dogg warned not to kill her, Dynamite took the gun out of Ms. Torres' mouth.

"Oh god, sweet mother of Jesus. Please take whatever you want and get out. You don't have to kill me." Ms. Torres cried. as she wiped the blood off her mouth with the back of her sleeve.

G Gunna politely helped Ms. Torres up off the ground and sat down next to her on the couch. "We're not here to rob you Ms. Torres. We're her lookin' for your son, G."

Ms. Torres gave G Gunna a guarded look. "He's not here. I haven't seen him in weeks."

"Listen very carefully The only reason that I'm here is to try and save your life. Because if you don't convince me that your tellin' me the truth," G Gunna pointed at Dynamite. "You see that girl over there," Ms. Torres nodded her head in Dynamite's direction. "She's goin' to kill you." G Gunna warned.

Ms. Torres, full of anguish, looked up at Dynamite. "Holy Mother of Jesus. Why on god's green earth would you want to kill me? What wrong have I done to you to make you want to do something so evil?"

Dynamite pointed her .38 at Ms. Torres head and yelled. "Bitch shut the fuck up and save the speech for someone who really gives a fuck, because I don't! If you don't want to die, I strongly suggest that you tell me where your punk ass son, G. is hidin' at!"

Ms. Torres found her resolve and looked at Dynamite directly. Hating the young white girl that had the gun pointed at her head. "I already told you, I haven't seen my son in weeks."

G Gunna sitting on the couch next to Ms. Torres. Reached up and placed his hand on top of Dynamite's .38 indicating for her to stop pointing it at Ms. Torres head. "This isn't about you Ms. Torres or anything that you done. It's about G. and what he's done. You're from the hood just like me. So, I shouldn't have to spell it out to you. But your son G. crossed the game and now where here to make him pay for it."

Dynamite frowned impatiently at G Gunna through her black

ski mask. "Look at here bitch. Times up. Plain and simple, your son is a dead man. And if you don't tell us where he is right fuckin' now, you're goin' to buried right next to him."

"She's right Ms. Torres. I understand that you want to stay loyal to your son. But your son needs to be loyal to you. Gettin' yourself killed, which you undoubtedly will, if you don't tell us where your son is hiding. And it won't save your G. We're goin' to find him eventually and when we do, we're goin' to kill him." G Gunna spoke truthfully trying hard to save G.'s mother's life.

Ms. Torres took a deep breath. "Why do the two of you want to kill my son?", she asked.

G Gunna let out a small chuckle. "If I told you that Ms. Torres then I would have to kill you myself. But since that's not why I'm here, I'll tell you what I'm goin' to do. I'll make a deal with you. You give me a phone number where I can reach your son and I promise that no one in this room will kill you." G Gunna looked at Dynamite who was fuming through her black ski mask.

Ms. Torres spirit picked up at the idea of not having to tell where her son G. was hiding. "You promise that's all I have to do in order for this crazy ass white girl not to kill me?"

"I promise you MS Torres, you give us a righteous phone number and nothin' will happen to you." G Gunna eyed Dynamite through his black ski mask, willing her to be cool.

Ms. Torres feeling a lot better about her circumstances

decided to press her luck. "Will you promise not to kill my son too?"

"Right now, Ms. Torres my only concern is tryin' to save your life and you're makin' that very difficult." G Gunna nodded towards Dynamite standing like an executioner, holding her .38 in front of her with her arms crossed. "She's really goin' to kill you if you don't give us that phone number right this minute."

Ms. Torres looked up at Dynamite with distaste. "What kind of girl are you?"

Dynamite spoke calmly without moving from her stance. "I'm a gangsta bitch. Now give us the goddamn phone number."

Ms. Torres grunted unfriendly at Dynamite. "916-209-4150. There you have your number, so can you please leave now."

"In a minute Ms. Torres. But thank you for the phone number," G Gunna spoke in a friendly business tone as he picked up the phone and called Syndicate. "Blood we didn't get the address, but we got a phone number. The bitch ass nigga is hidin' out in Sacramento."

Syndicate's blood boiled with rage knowing that he was getting close to revenging Big Time's death. "Sacramento! Ain't that a bitch. Give me the number."

"916-209-4150 that's the number she gave me." G Gunna looked over at Ms. Torres praying to god that she gave him the right number.

"Is she still breathin'?" Syndicate asked praying to himself that Ms. Torres is still alive.

G Gunna looked over at Dynamite not liking the look on her face. "Yeah she's still with us, but for how long I don't know. Your girl didn't like the deal that I made to get the phone number and you know how unpredictable she is."

Tell Dynamite to come back to the house and get that nigga's mama to the spot. And stay there until I call you." Syndicate breathed a little easier hearing that Ms. Torres was still alive.

"One love blood and keep it gangsta nigga." G Gunna answered before hanging up the phone.

CHAPTER 32

The Heart Of A Gangsta

Syndicate had G. on the telephone when Dynamite walked into the house. "That's right nigga I got the number from your mama. And if you don't want her to be pushin' up daisy's you better hit the freeway movin' right muthafuckin now."

"What the fuck you sayin' blood that you gonna kill my mama? My mama don't have nothin' to do with this. This funk is between me and you." G. tried to reason with Syndicate in hopes of saving his mother.

"Fuck ya feelings nigga. You should have thought about that before you killed Big Time." Syndicate felt nothin', but hate for his one-upon-a-time best friend.

"So, this is what its comes to huh D.Dogg? You goin' to kill my mother if I don't come back?" G. asked already knowing the answer to his questions.

"You got one-hour nigga. Your mama's life is in your hands now. And in case you haven't heard the name is Syndicate. D.Dogg died when you killed Big Time." Syndicate spoke without any regrets.

"Nigga I don't give a fuck what them other niggas call you. You always gonna be D.Dogg to me," G. hesitated for a second. "Say D.Dogg I know that shit that went down on Halloween was some foul shit. But for the life of me, I didn't want to have to kill Big Time. I just didn't see any other way out. As far as you holdin' my mama hostage that's some fucked up shit. I would never involve Winky in any of our shit." G. regretted that he had killed Big Time and put his mother in harm's way.

"Ain't no love nigga. You got one hour to meet me at the rail yard and make sure you come by yourself. If you don't, your mama's goin' to die." Syndicate looked over at Dynamite who nodded her head affirmatively.

"So as long as I come by myself, my mama lives. No matter how gangsta I go out." G. putting everything on the table.

"You got my word as a gangsta. You come by yourself no matter how it turns out, your mama lives." Syndicate spoke from his heart.

Almost an hour later, Syndicate stood out in the open as the K-Squad positioned themselves around empty box cars waiting on any would-be shooters.

Then G. pulled into the old rail yard in his white Monte Carlo, smoking on a sherm-soaked Newport, and playing "Friends" by Whodini in the tape desk. G. couldn't help reminiscing to himself about how things used to be with an A.K. assault rifle next to him in the passenger seat.

From his car, G. looked at Syndicate. "D.Dogg, you want to hit this shit blood. For ol'time sake." G. held up the sherm-soaked Newport so Syndicate could see it.

"Naw blood I'm straight. You bring anybody with you." Syndicate stood 10 yards away with his Mac 11 in his hand.

G. threw the sherm soaked Newport out the window. "What? So your bitch ass would have an excuse to kill my mama? Naw nigga, it's just me and my lil' friend." G. said and then dove out of the passenger side of the Monte Carlo with his A.K.47 assault rifle in his arms. He was rolling on the ground like he was a Navy seal letting off rounds. Syndicated dove behind an empty box car for cover.

Using his car as a shield with bullets flying all around him from Syndicate's Mac.11, and the K-Squad's small arsenal, G. lay flat on his stomach letting off round after round. His A.K. 47 assault rifle knocked holes in the empty box cars.

Syndicate and the K-squad caught off guard by G.'s relentless suicidal assault, repositioned themselves to come up behind him. "I'm the closest." Dynamite yelled as she took off running. Syndicate pointed towards G.'s back side.

"I knew G. was a gangsta, but goddamn. This nigga got heart like Poppa Fly." G Gunna yelled over the gunfire to Syndicate one box car over.

Syndicate checked his clip. "G. is goin' all out blood. He knows that he's dying tonight." Syndicate yelled back before letting off a few rounds trying to provide Dynamite some cover.

G., feeling like Custard at his last stand, made his way to his feet and leaned over his Monte Carlo continuing to let off rounds from his A.K. "Why you niggas hidin' like little bitches. Y'all been lookin' for me, so now you found me."

"Damn how many rounds this nigga got." Dynamite, breathing heavily, spoke to herself as she came up behind G. with her .38 in her hand.

G., high off the sherm and only focused on one thing and that is to kill Syndicate, never knew what hit him as Dynamite crept up on him and put two bullet holes in the back of his head with her .38

"When you get there tell them a white gangsta bitch named, Dynamite sent you." Dynamite stood over G.'s dead body emotionless.

Syndicate came and stood next to Dynamite with his Mac .11 in his hand. "Now that was some gangsta shit." Dynamite looked up at Syndicate as the rest of the K-Squad gathered around. "I'm going to always keep it gangsta foe' you daddy."

CHAPTER 33

A Teenage Love

May 1987

6 months later

Syndicate and Dynamite sat in the back of their black stretch limousine sipping on champagne on their way to Dynamite's High School prom. Dressed in his black Tuxedo, Syndicate raised his champagne glass to Dynamite. "Here's to the most beautiful girl in the world."

Dynamite, wearing a black Peter Som gown, tapped her champagne glass with Syndicate's, as her princess-cut, 3.5 caret diamond ring osparkled. Here's to the most handsome gangsta in the world." Dynamite gave Syndicate her deadly smile as the two young gangsters gave each other a toast.

Syndicate eyed Dynamite lustfully as he sipped his Champagne amazed at how sweet and innocent, she looked in her prom dress. "It's been four years since we started this gangsta shit Dynamite. Since then, I've watched you grow up from a spoiled, little, rich, white girl into the seductive, sexy, beautiful gangsta bitch you are today." Syndicate confessed proudly.

"Niggas in the game thought I was crazy when I first brought you to the hood and introduced you as a gangsta bitch. They was like nigga, what you need to do is put that lil' white bitch out on the track, Because she ain't got enough heart to be a gangsta. I used to want to shoot them niggas on the spot from disrespecting me like that. I understand where they was comin' from. How could a lil' square white girl survive in a black man's game unless she's a hoe." Dynamite gave Syndicate a menacing gangsta bitch grin as he continued.

"I tried to tell them to give you a little time to get your feet wet and soaked up the game. And that if you couldn't handle it, I'd put a stop to it. The bitches were worse than the niggas. That's why I was so hard on you to handle your business when them hoes jumped you. A lot of the sistas wasn't feeling me putting you on like I did." Syndicate let out a small laugh. "They be tryin' to be on some high-power black movement shit talkin' like we from the Deep South or New York. I had to explain to'em that we from killa Cali and we ride to a different beat out here. So, get the fuck away from me with all that racist bullshit."

Dynamite looked at Syndicate teasingly. "Whatever."

"I'm just keepin' it gangsta. It's a different story now though baby and you deep in the game. Ain't a goddamn thing anybody can do to stop it. I made you and you make me better baby. We in this shit from the cradle to the casket until death do us part."

Dynamite put her arms around Syndicate and smiled innocently. "I love you so much daddy."

The black stretch limousine drove slowly through the school parking lot coming to a stop in front of the V. House, (short for victory). "Damn look at all these limousines and fancy ass cars parked out here. Shit if I didn't know better, I would think we just pulled up at the Grammy's." Syndicate joked as the chauffeur opened the limousine door for the two of them to exit.

Dynamite smiled and grabbed Syndicate by the hand. "Welcome to the silver spoon society. If you thought I was a spoiled lil' rich kid, wait 'til you meet some of these assholes. Listening to some of these dumb ass rich bitches talk makes me want to strangle them. And the boys, wow, don't let me get started on them. A bunch of pricks that I would love to shove my gun down their throats and watch 'em shit on themselves."

Both Syndicate and Dynamite laughed at her jokes, as they walked down the red carpet. "Hate it or love it, money makes the world go round." Syndicate smiled as he stepped off the red carpet and walked into the auditorium. Different color Crystal balls hung from the ceiling with trip lights bouncing off the walls throughout the auditorium. Two large tables of Hors d'oeuvres with a big Crystal bowl of spiked fruit punch sitting on each one. The table was next a giant purple banner that read on the left side, that read: "Welcome to Golden Valley High 1987 High School Prom."

DJ Davey D had his equipment set up on stage playing "Super Freak" by Rick James. Syndicate laughed out loud as he watched the rich kids out on the dance floor trying to keep up with the beat. "I see that even the silver spoon society like to get their freak on." Syndicate joked

Dynamite took Syndicate by the hand excited to finally be able to show her boyfriend off to her classmates. "Come on, Syndicate let's go get us some punch and find us a table."

"Fuck! I should've never let you talk me into not gettin' high. I need to get my mind right. It looks like it's going to be a slow night. I hope that one of these squares spiked the punch." Syndicate smiled as he looked around the auditorium at the young men wearing their Tuxedo's and the young women wearing their finest evening Gowns.

Frank, a tall, handsome, dark skinned jock walked up to Syndicate and Dynamite as they were getting some punch. "Hey, Michelle, what's up? I thought you said that you weren't coming to the prom?"

Dynamite smiled rudely at Frank. "I didn't say that I wasn't comin' Frank. I said I wasn't comin' with you."

Frank looked Syndicate up and down trying to size him up.

"And who is this dude supposed to be, your boyfriend or some-body?" Frank asked trying to sound tough.

Dynamite smiled and squeezed Syndicate's hand signaling for him to be cool. "Who Syndicate! No, he's not my boyfriend Frank. He's my daddy. Daddy this is Frank and Frank this is Syndicate." Dynamite announced Syndicate's presence like he was the President of the United States.

Frank gave Syndicate a disapproving look and grunted. "Syndicate? What kind of name is that?"

Syndicate busted out laughing. "I guess this is one of them niggas you was talkin' about earlier, huh Dynamite?" Syndicate stopped laughing and faced Frank. "Blood, I strongly advise you to go and play some basketball or whatever sport it is that you play. You really ain't tryin' to fuck wit me. I play wit guns nigga and I hate jocks." Frank stood speechless scared to death.

"I thought I told you I had me a gangsta nigga Frank?" Dynamite waved her hand at Frank dismissively and smiled as she walked away hand in hand with Syndicate.

Syndicate sat at the table with Dynamite bouncing his head to the rhythm of the music being played by DJ Davey D. A tall, white kid, with long blonde hair. "That white boy is up their jamming.'"

Dynamite's green eyes lit up when she smiled. "That's DJ Davey D. He's pretty cool for a square white boy." Dynamite spoke while tapping her feet to the beat of the music.

Syndicate laughed out loud. "Ain't that a bitch. Look who's talkin', the lil' square white princess herself."

Dynamite rolled her eyes at Syndicate. "I might be a lil' white girl, but I'm far from a square, baby. I'm game-tight plus I'm fine. So, don't get shit twisted."

Syndicate grabbed Dynamite by her hand. "Chill with the ugly ass faces lil' white girl. I don't have shit twisted. Come on, let's show these squares how gangsta's boogie and turn this muthafucka out."

The dance floor was jammed packed with kids dancing to Rob Bass 'I'm Not Internationally Known'. Syndicate stood in front of Dynamite with his hands high in the air moving from side to side smiling. Watching Dynamite go wild holding her hands on her small hips and shaking her ass bouncing it up off the ground.

The other students begin taking notice of the little white girl they only knew as Michelle. Dancing with no shame along with the black kid that look like a gangsta. "Alright Michelle you and your friend look pretty good out there dancing to something fast. Let's see what kind of moves the two of you can make to something slow. "DJ Davey D yelled at Syndicate and Dynamite while he put on Marvin Gaye's, "Sexual Healing".

Dynamite smiled into Syndicate's handsome face and wrapped her arms around his neck pulling him close to her. "They're playin' our song."

"Who needs a song when the whole world belongs to us." Syndicate kissed Dynamite long and hard on the mouth oblivious to everyone around them. After the few more dances, Syndicate lead Dynamite back to their table.

Erin, a lil' sexy looking white girl and good friend of Dynamite's. walked up to Syndicate and Dynamite's table. Along with Star and their two dates, "Damn Dynamite! I didn't know you could dance like that." Erin laughed.

Dynamite smiled at her good friend. "I have a good teacher."

J.D., a tall, dark skinned kid with ambitions on being the next District Attorney was standing next to Star. While Chris, a big goofy, friendly white kid, and next in line to take over his family's big retail business stood next to Erin.

Syndicate smiled at the two boys. "You niggas goin' to sit down or you waitin' on an invitation?"

Star, looking very elegant in her prom dress, rolled her eyes. "Don't nobody need an invitation from you. They were just being polite like how a gentleman is supposed to be. Something you obvious don't know anything about." J.D. Pulled out Star's chair for her to sit down. "J.D. Meet Syndicate and Syndicate meet J.D."

A very serious looking J.D. stuck his hand out for Syndicate to shake it. "Glad to meet you Syndicate."

Syndicate smiled at J.D. and slapped his hand. "Yeah foe'

sho my nigga."

Erin smiled up at her boyfriend Chris who was sitting next to her. "Syndicate this is my boyfriend, Chris. And Chris this is Dynamite's boyfriend, Syndicate."

Chris smiled his big friendly smile at Syndicate. "Hey, Syndicate, what's up dude?"

Syndicate smiled respectfully at the big goofy white kid. "What's goin' on Chris?" Syndicate laughed as he playfully tapped the back of his fingers with the back of Chris fingers three times from across the table.

Erin laughed at Syndicate and Chris touching fingers. "What is that some kind of secret handshake for boys?"

"It's not a secret Erin. It's just some playboy shit." Chris laughed as he tapped his fingers with Syndicate three more times.

J.D. inhaled and exhaled as if bored with the little show of comradely between the two new friends. "It's not called playboy shit Chris. It's called player shit."

"Actually, it's called pimp shit." Dynamite snapped, not liking J.D. anymore than Syndicate did.

"So, Syndicate where do you go to High School?" J.D. asked sounding uptight when he spoke.

Syndicate looked at J.D. and smiled mischievously. "I graduated from sidewalk high. I'm now enrolled in Gangsta University with a Master's Degree in Game." Everyone at the table laughed, except for J.D. Syndicate, enjoying the ribbing, continued to play with J.D. "So, what about you J.D.? What are your plans after graduation?"

"I have a full scholarship to attend Georgetown University." J.D. announced proudly.

"Oh wow! That's great good for you, J.D. So, what's your Major?" Syndicate smiled sounding interested in what J.D. was saying.

"Criminal Law. I want to be the District Attorney of Stockton one day." J.D. answered sincerely.

Syndicate, secretly wanting to shoot J.D. for what he thought was a bad career move. "Imagine that? Go figure. Who would have thought? We have a lot in common J.D. I'm interested in criminal law myself." Syndicate smiled trying hard to hide his distaste for J.D.

"So, what about you Chris? What are your plans after graduation?" Dynamite butted in wanting to change the direction of the conversation. Knowing how strongly Syndicate feels about black men becoming police officers.

My Father wants me to go to Duke University like he did. But I decided to go to U.S.C. to be with Erin." Erin giggled and kissed Chris on his cheek.

Dynamite smiled at her two friends. "That's really sweet of you Chris, choosing to be close to Erin instead of following your father's wishes."

A big goofy smile spread across Chris's face. "Don't give me too much credit. The Trojan's have a much better football team and I want the chance to play for a national championship one day."

Syndicate laughed out loud. "That's right Chris! Keep it real!"

"What about you Star? Have you decided on a college yet?" Erin asked.

Star held her breath preparing for the criticism she was going to get from J.D. "Me and Dynamite decided to stay right here and go to U.O.P."

J.D. looked disgustedly at Star. "U.O.P.? For Christ sake Star you can't be serious? You're the school's Valedictorian number 1 in your class. You can go to any college in the country. Why would you want to waste it on a nothing ass school like U.O.P?"

Star gave J.D. a very ugly look. "You're not my boyfriend J.D. So, I don't owe you any explanations. And besides, me and Dynamite are going to have a blast. Star gave Dynamite a high five.

Mr. Powell, the school Principal, a distinguished looking white man, stepped up to the microphone as everyone gathered around the stage to listen. "Ladies and Gentleman, may I please have your attention? As you all know, it's that time of the evening to announce our 1987 Golden Valley Prom King and Queen. And as you all should know, we do things a little different at Golden Valley.

338

We judge couples not individuals, which makes our school so special. Remember there are no losers here, because you're all so beautiful. So without further a-due, this year's winner for Prom King and Queen are…Derek and Michelle!"

Mr. Powell announce excitedly into the microphone. Syndicate and Dynamite cheered and applauded just as loud as everyone else not recognizing their real names.

Chris looked at Syndicate and Dynamite unbelievable. "OK, ok, that's cool. But it would be nice if the two of you would stop clapping and go get your crowns. So that the rest of us losers can stop clapping for you." Chris laughed as he ushered the winners forward.

Dynamite grabbed Syndicate by the arm overwhelmed with emotion. "Oh, my god! I can't believe it! We won Syndicate. We're the King and Queen of the Prom."

Syndicate laughed at the irony of it as he walked with Dynamite through the crowd. "Yeah we won ain't that a bitch. I'm the King of the squares."

"Step right on up here," Mr. Powell spoke over the roar of the crowd as Syndicate and Dynamite made there way up on the stage. "Let's hear it again for our Golden Valley 1987 Prom King and Queen." The students applauded their approval as Mr. Powell placed the King and Queen crowns on top of a smiling Syndicate and Dynamite's head.

DJ Davey D walked up to a laughing Syndicate and Dynamite as if he were a court Jester. "Excuse me sire, your Royal highness, of what song do you request it of me. So, that you may lead our most beautiful and graceful Queen Michelle out to dance for all to glorify in her beauty."

Syndicate, enjoying the moment of a normal teenager and wanting Dynamite to feel the same way, if only for one night, decided to play along with DJ Davey D. "Forever My Lady by Jodeci. Fool."

DJ Davey D bowed his head preparing to leave. "Excellent choice Sire," DJ Davey D turned and faced the crowd. "Alright you peasants make room for the King and Queen." DJ Davey D limped over to his turn table and put on Syndicate's request. With the other kids gathered around in a circle watching, King Derek and Queen Michelle danced as if the only thing that mattered was the here and now. She held on to Syndicate and he returned Dynamite's affection.

After the Prom and still on cloud-9, Syndicate and Dynamite sipped on champagne while riding in the back of the limousine. "So, my Queen did you have a good time?" Syndicate smiled playfully.

"I had a fabulous time my King, and thank you for entertaining me with your presence." Dynamite smiled back at Syndicate and started busting up laughing.

"Girl cut that square shit out." Syndicate said with a straight face trying hard to keep from laughing.

Dynamite hit Syndicate on his leg. "Don't try and act all hard now. You were enjoying that square shit a minute ago."

Unable to hold back any longer Syndicate let out a hearty laugh. "Imagine that, I'm the prom King. Who would have thought that shit?. The King of the squares." Syndicate said and then busted out laughing again.

Dynamite squeezed Syndicate's hand affectionately. "I guess that makes you the King of both worlds, since you're already the King of the gangstas."

Syndicate pulled Dynamite close to him. "And, you my lil' sexy gangsta bitch, is the Queen of all gangsta bitches."

Dynamite looked intently into Syndicate's deep black eyes. "I guess what they say is true then, that gangsta rule the world." The two young gangstas tapped their champagne glasses in agreement.

CHAPTER 34

Respect The Game

Syndicate, Dynamite, and Young Tre were hanging out at the mall arcade, playing video games, when Under, Chip, Tro and Arlo walked up on them. "Syndicate what's up blood? What you doin' down here in the arcade playin' video games?" Under looked over at Dynamite, who was eyeing him and the others closely.

Syndicate continued to press on the video game buttons and spoke without looking up. "It's Young Tre's birthday so me and Dynamite takin' him on a shoppin' spree. He started fat mouthin' about he could beat me in Mario Brother's, so I brought him down here so I could whoop his young ass."

Young Tre pushed on the buttons as fast as is hands would allow. "Blood you crazy. You ain't whoopin' nobody's ass. I'm smashin' you fool."

"So, what you niggas up to?" Syndicate spoke without missing a move on the Mario's Brother's game.

"We just up here passin' time, tryin' to bump a bitch." Chip answered as he watched the young girls walk by. Arlo and Tro begin playing the Sprint racing video game next to where Syndicate and Young Tre were playing Mario's Brother's.

"Syndicate we heard that you were turnin' your duplex into a gamblin' shack?" Under lit a Newport despite the fact that it was no smoking in the mall arcade.

"Fuck!" Syndicate shouted. Angry that Young Tre had just killed his last man and beat him in Mario's Brothers. "Yeah you heard right. I just bought a big ass pool table and put it in the middle of the house. Plus, we got the big round table to play cards on. So, you niggas bring your paper tonight because it's goin' to be 24-7 gangsta party.

Under took a drag off his Newport. "I also heard a rumor that you and Dynamite were getting married?"

Syndicate turned around and faced Under and Chip. "That ain't no rumor, me and Dynamite about to tie the knot. That's the main reason why I'm about to turn my spot into a gamblin' shack. It's time for a nigga to upgrade his environment." Syndicate glanced at Dynamite standing next to Young Tre. "Me and Dynamite, we been checkin' out some houses in Quail Lakes."

Under eyed Syndicate suspiciously. "Quail Lakes? "The

game must be treatin' you great nigga, because those some million-dollar homes they got out there."

Syndicate recognized the doubt in Under's voice. "It is what it is. The game god blesses those of us who want it the most."

Under looked over at Dynamite and thought twice about asking if the rumor about her killing G. was true or not. "It's all good homeboy! And congratulations on the wedding. You and Dynamite, y'all two of a kind. The perfect soul mates."

"That's one love blood," Syndicate and Under gave one another daps. "So, what's up? You niggas comin' through tonight?"

Chip laughed out loud. "Yeah, we'll be there. Just make sure that you niggas bring enough money."

Young Tre pulled out his bankroll. "Blood what the fuck you talkin' about make sure we bring enough money? The syndicate family has enough money to sink a battleship."

Chip pulled out his own bankroll. "Just make sure you niggas bring that chicken feed money with you tonight. I can use it for my expensive weed habit." Chip and Under gave each other daps.

"Laugh now and cry later nigga. The only way you goin' to get high off this money is from inhaling my Endo smoke that I'm goin' to be blowin' in your face. While I'm takin' you nigga's money." Young Tre and Dynamite, thinking it funny, gave each other a high five.

"Why you so quite Dynamite." Syndicate asked as they were leaving the arcade.

Dynamite twisted her face up in disgust. "I don't trust them niggas. Especially Under and that lil' sneaky punk ass nigga Chip."

"Girl quit trippin' those niggas don't want no problems. Under might be a lot of things, but I know for a fact that he ain't no snitch. So, if he had a problem with the way we handled our business, he would've handled it in the streets. And keep the police up out of it like a real gangsta is supposed to." Syndicate held Dynamite's hand as they walked through the mall, not really giving a fuck what anybody else thought about what he did as a gangsta.

Dynamite broke free from Syndicate's hand. "You can believe whatever you want to believe Syndicate. But I still don't trust them niggas," Dynamite grabbed Young Tre by the hand and headed for the department stores. "Come on Young Tre, let's get you fitted for your birthday."

Syndicate being the gangsta he is, didn't go after Dynamite. Besides he knew it wouldn't do any good. Her mind was made up.

Beside if 'em niggas was going to try something, Syndicate to respond to the situation as he always does, like a gangsta.

CHAPTER 35
Y.G's to O.G's

"Shoot a hundred and bet a hundred." Young Tre yelled at those gathered around the pool table.

Chip threw two hundred dollars down on the pool table. "Nigga drop it on the table. I'm goin' to teach you about fuckin' with a bona fide hustla."

Young Tre dropped his two hundred dollars down on the pool table. "Nigga you ain't the only bona fide hustla at this table. I was born into the game just like you. Only I earned my stripes the old fashion way."

"Bet my boy hit for a hundred." Worthy shouted.

"Bet nigga drop it." Tro shouted back as Young Tre rolled the dice out of a cup across the pool table stopping on the number four.

"What you do wit it, nigga?" Chip shouted at Young Tre.

"Nigga bet two hundred." Young Tre shouted back as both he and Chip threw down two hundred dollars on top of the pool table.

"If it ain't Ace Tray in the doe, then nigga I don't want it," Young Tre stood shaking the dice in the cup grandstanding before throwing them across the table. Stopping on the numbers 1 and 3.

"Ace Tray in the doe blood, just like I called it! What the fuck you niggas thought? That y'all was just goin' to come up in our spot and win our money?" Young Tre looked at Chip and the rest of the mob homies as he picked up his winnings.

Under grabbed the dice from off the pool table, after Young Tre crapped out. "Shoot a hundred!" Under shouted as he tossed a hundred dollars down on the table.

"Shoot blood!" Ray shouted back at Under. Before throwing a hundred dollars down on the table.

Syndicate, wanting to get in on the action, yelled over at Chip, "What your daddy hit for Chip?"

Chip threw down three hundred dollars. "Bet he hit for three hundred nigga!"

Syndicate tossed down three hundred dollars on the table. "Bet nigga!"

Under rolled the dice out of the cup across the pool table. Stopping on the number 8.

Chip tossed down three hundred dollars more on the table.

"8 nigga, that's the block. Bet my boy mob for three hundred!"

Syndicate threw three hundred more dollars down on the table. "Nigga I don't give a fuck about y'all block number! This is the syndicate family nigga!"

Under threw the dice out of the little cup across the table stopping on the number 6. "6 and 8 runnin' mates nigga!" Under shouted as he threw the dice out again stopping on the number 7.

Dynamite, Star, Erin, Sweet Ass, and Teayana sat at the round table taking Tequila shots while playing cards. "So, Dynamite when is the big wedding going to be?" Star asked as she dealt out the cards.

Dynamite took a shot of Tequila. "Sometime in August we're not sure yet. It all depends on when my father can get away from work."

"So, is it going to be a big church wedding or are you guys planning on eloping?" Erin smiled as she fired up the joint she's been holding.

"Shit they better not elope, I want to be there to catch the bouquet." Sweet Ass teased.

Teayana took a shot of Tequila. "Bitch if you think catching a bride's bouquet is going to make Clept want to get married, then you must really be drunk."

Dynamite laughed. "We're not eloping or getting married in a church. We already decided to get married at my mother's house."

"How many brides maids are you going to have?" Star smiled innocently.

"Bitch you don't need to worry, no one is going to take your spot. But no, actually I would like for all of you to be my bridesmaids and of course Jazzy." Dynamite's green eyes brighten with expectation.

Erin, high off the weed and tipsy off the Tequila shots, felt comfortable in her new surroundings. "I would consider it an honor to be one of your bridesmaids Dynamite."

"Bitch, you know that I'm there. Anything else would be uncivilized." Sweet Ass busted out laughing.

"Dynamite what kind of question is that bitch? We home girls, Hell yeah I want to be one of your bridesmaids." Teayana fired up another joint.

"Dynamite you already know how I feel about being one of your bridesmaids. We been talking about our weddings since the 6th grade." Star took a puff of the joint she had been holding in her hand.

Erin smiled mischievously and took another shot of Tequila. "Dynamite, who is that over there shaking the dice?"

"That's one sneaky lil' bastard that you need to stay far away from." Dynamite pointed her finger at Erin warningly. While the other girls at the table laughed.

Chip tossed down six hundred dollars down on the pool table. "I'm about to put the Syndicate family out of business. Shoot three and bet three!" Chip shouted while smoking on his fat Endo joint.

"Nigga you'll have a better chance at breakin' Las Vegas than you do at breakin' us!" Young Tre shouted back at Chip, as he tossed down his six hundred dollars down on the pool table.

Mac Twain waved a hundred dollars in his hand. "Bet my boy hit for a hundred."

"Nigga bet!" yelled Los, as he threw down his hundred dollars.

Chip rolled the dice out of the small cup stopping on the number 7. Chip laughed as he picked up his money off the pool table. "I told you Young Tre, I want all you got including your new birthday outfit!"

Syndicate threw down six hundred dollars on top of the pool table. "Nigga quit fat mouthin', you ain't did shit!"

Chip laughed as he tossed down his six hundred dollars down on the pool table. "Oh, you didn't like the way I just lashed your lil' homie, huh Syndicate? I'm goin' to lash you the same way nigga! Just like you were a Hebrew slave!"

Under held Chip's arm to keep him from shooting the dice. "Hold on a minute Chip. I need to get my bet on with these suckas before you shoot. Bet my boy hit for two hundred!"

Mook threw down his own two hundred dollars next to Under's. "Nigga bet!"

Chip rolled the dice out of the cup across the table stopping on the number 11. Under laughed out loud along with the rest of his mob homies. "That's right Chip, that's what I'm talkin' about lash these niggas.

Syndicate, not liking the fact that the mob homies is laughing at the syndicate family, shouted angrily at Chip. "Nigga shot twelve hundred. That is if you got any heart."

Chip let out a wicked laugh. "Blood you don't believe that fat meat is greasy do you?" Both Syndicate and Chip threw down twelve hundred on top of the pool table. As the rest of the gamblers made their bets.

Chip rolled the dice out of the cup across the pool table stopping on the number 7. "That's right Chip lash these niggas and show them what that mob like!" Under yelled as the mob homies picked up their winnings.

Chip gave Syndicate a big-headed look. "You better stick to bein' a gangsta Syndicate and do what you do best. Because you out of your league tryin' to out hustle me." Chip looked at his mob homies and laughed while holding two handfuls of money. "You niggas ready to go smoke? Syndicate just made a twelve-hundred-dollar donation. The mob homies threw up gang signs as they walked out of the gambling shack laughing.

"How much paper you lose tonight Syndicate." G Gunna asked as he sat around the round table with members of the syndicate family, getting high and listening to music.

Syndicate poured himself a shot of Hennessy. "I lost about 3 G's."

G Gunna's girlfriend, Tosha, sitting on top of his lap frowned at Syndicate. "Damn Syndicate that's a lot of goddamn money to be losing'"

"It's nothin' to a giant Tosha. Money comes and goes, loyalty and family last forever." Syndicate raised his shot glass in a toast to the rest of the syndicate family.

Dynamite, high off the weed and drink, was feeling the love in the room and even more love for Syndicate. "It doesn't get no more real than that daddy." Dynamite tapped her shot glass with Syndicate's.

Low highly intoxicated off the sherm was feeling the absence of his homeboy Poppa Fly. "So, what's up with my nigga Poppa Fly? Ain't nobody heard nothin' yet?

Syndicate himself, also highly intoxicated, poured himself another drink. "Gail said that she's workin' to get Poppa Fly a bail hearing. But she doubts very seriously that the judge will give the homie a bail. She said they offered Poppa Fly 60 years to life."

Whip's blood boiled with rage hearing about the deal they offered his homeboy Poppa Fly. "What the fuck kind of deal is that."

Dynamite, feeling the weed and Tequila shots, had a worried look on her face. "My mom said that if Poppa Fly is found guilty on all the charges, that they could give him the death penalty. Their hoping that he will be scared of the death penalty and accept a deal for life in prison." Dynamite, wondered to herself, if they would give her the death penalty one day for killing G.

Dmove' eyes where blood shot red from all the weed, he had been smoking. "Scared! They got my nigga Poppa Fly fucked up. I know my nigga ain't about to take no crazy ass deal like that?"

"Gail told me they have a weak ass case against the homie especially with no eyewitness. She said the homie has a 50-50 chance at winning at trial." Syndicate hoped like hell that Gail knew what she was talking about and could get Poppa Fly off.

Dynamite, recognizing the doubt in Syndicate's voice, spoke up. "My mother is a great trial Lawyer. She wouldn't allow Poppa Fly to go to trial if she didn't think she could win."

Dmove sat at the round table puffing on his Endo joint thinking about how to approach the family. "I ran into King's Uncle, Dino, the other day in traffic. He told me that he heard a rumor that Dynamite took out G. for killing Big Time and King." Dmove exhaled the Endo smoke before he continued with what he had to say. "He also told me that he heard that the syndicate took out Mondo for the same reason."

Dynamite quickly became alarmed then angry that Dino had somehow learned about family business. "And what did you say."

A big smile covered Dmove's face. "I told him the next time

he hears somebody startin' rumors to shoot to kill." Dynamite's, stone cold face, cracked into a small smile. As the rest of the syndicate family started to laugh in uncontrollable laughter.

CHAPTER 36
Sugga

Syndicate and Nutts sat inside 'The Game' on the third level V.I.P. section, an exclusive nightclub in San Francisco known for attracting underground Kingpins, mob bosses, and the country's biggest pimps.

Nutts puffed on his Cuban Cigar and smiled like a proud father. "Syndicate this is your night youngsta. A week from today you're going to be a married man. So tonight, I'm going to see to it that you have an overdose on pussy. Because once your young ass is married, it's all over with. Threw with pussy at the ripe old age of 19 now, that's a goddamn shame." Nutts laughed as he watched the pretty, red boned girl, dressed in a sexy cat woman costume winding and grinding seductively on top of Syndicate's lap.

Syndicate sipped on his champagne enjoying the show being put on by the stripper. "Just because I'm getting married, old man doesn't mean that I'm through with pussy."

Nutts stopped laughing long enough to get the attention of the pretty cocktail waitress dressed in her tight fitting red and black bunny outfit. "Nigga Dynamite told me that if your dick even acts like it wants to get hard from looking at another bitch after y'all married, that she's goin' to chop that muthafucka off."

"Well then I guess that she's goin' to have to chop this muthafucka off then, because I'm hard than a muthafucka right now." Syndicate smiled at the stripper while taking in his new surroundings. Crystal glass tables with little black telephones sitting on top of them could be seen throughout the third level V.I.P. section. Strippers gave private lap dances. Some danced in cages. While others made love to the pole standing in the middle of the room.

Nutts leaned back in his seat. "I'm just sayin' Syndicate, Dynamite ain't naive as she likes to act. She knows you be out fuckin' with hoes. And I promise you that if you don't cut that shit out, it's going to come back and bite you in the ass one day," Nutts raised his hands in surrender. "I know that you ain't tryin' to hear me. But I'm just keeping it gangsta out of my love for you and Dynamite."

"Goddamn nigga, if you keep on preachin' like you doin' right now, Dynamite isn't going to have to chop my dick off. You doin' a real good job of killin' it right now with all that square ass shit you talkin' about." Syndicate laughed out loud as the stripper continued on with her lap dance. "Damn blood, your wife, Daphane must have your old ass pussy whipped. I guess that you forgot that gangstas do whatever the fuck they want to do."

"I'm just tellin' you to be careful Syndicate. You might not be able to tell by lookin' at Dynamite. But that pretty lil', innocent looking white girl that your about to marry, is a gangsta just as much as you and me. And she feels the same way that you do. That she can do whatever the fuck she wants to do." Nutts took a more serious tone with Syndicate.

"Goddamn blood why you keep preaching to me about Dynamite? I raised that girl. That's my gangsta bitch and she does whatever the fuck I tell her to do. Which is exactly what she wants to do. Make no mistake about it. Me and Dynamite is tight like Fred and Wilma Flintstone. She ain't goin' nowhere and neither am I. So, lighten up on that shit old man," Syndicate reached around the stripper and refilled Nutts champagne glass. "And I thought you were goin' to help me overdose in some pussy tonight." Syndicate said, smirking at Nutts.

Nutts puffed on his Cuban Cigar as he looked at all the strippers dancing throughout the nightclub. "You're right young blood. This is your bachelor party. So, go ahead and pick out 3 or 4 of these bad ass, half naked strippers and we can take them back to my room at the Marriott. They can put on a private lil' show for us."

Nutts gave a mischievous smile at Synidcate.

Syndicate had his eyes glued to a pretty, honey-colored sista, with long reddish-brown hair, and gray Siamese cat eyes. She was wearing a Chanel skirt and a plain matching top. Syndicate starred at her, as she sat across the room with two other friends. "Man, I ain't no trick Nutts. I ain't tryin' to pay for no pussy."

Nutts handed the stripper $300.00 dollars after she finished giving Syndicate his lap dance. "What the fuck you mean, you ain't no trick? You got a lot to learn Syndicate. Every real nigga buys pussy one way or the other. What the fuck you think you was doin' when you bought Dynamite that $15,000 diamond ring? Anyway, why you worried about it? Ain't nothin' comin' out of your pocket."

The stripper smiled seductively at Syndicate as she notices him staring at the pretty girl across the room. "I hope you enjoyed your lap dance Syndicate. And Nutts is right. It ain't trickin' if it's yours. So, if you really tryin' to die in some sweet, tight pussy tonight like you say you are, I got that killa pussy that niggas kill and die for."

Syndicate let out a small laugh as he took another lustful look at the pretty stripper, dressed in the sexy little cat woman costume. "I can't imagine you havin' anything but some killa pussy. My dick is still harder than a muthafucka. But tonight, I'm on some other shit." Syndicate took another look at the pretty young woman across the room. "But if I ever get back up in 'The Game', I'll be sure to holla at you."

"I'll be waiting here patiently for you to get back up in 'The Game' and when you do, I'm going to take real good care of you. All you have to do is ask for Destiny." Destiny bent down and kissed Syndicate on the cheek and walked away without looking back.

"Do you know any of them Nutts?" Syndicate sipped on his champagne.

Nutts, dressed in God Father fashion, puffed on his Cuban Cigar. "Yeah I know all three of'em. They some high-class hoes that some pimp got out lookin' for tricks like you." Nutts laughed out loud. "Trust me youngsta, you'll save a lot of money and have a lot more fun by just grabbin' 3 or 4 of these strippers, like Destiny. Those some high-class hookers over there boy, they going to cost you diamond rings, vacations, and new cars."

Syndicate sat in a daze by the magnificence of the young woman's pure beauty sitting across the room. "If those ladies over there are hookers then we in the wrong profession."

"Only one way to find out," Nutts signaled for the cute little Mexican cocktail waitress who was passing by the table.

"Excuse me beautiful can you please tell me the number of the table over there in the back? Where the three young ladies are sitting." Nutts nodded towards where the three young ladies were seated.

"Sure, that's table number 23. Is there anything else that I can do for you sir?" The cute little cocktail waitress asked in her heavy accented English.

Nutts pulled a $100.00 bill out of his gold money clip and gave it to the cocktail waitress dressed in her tight fitting black and red bunny costume. "No that's it. Thank you, senorita."

"Thank you, sir. If you need anything else please just call the bar and ask for me. My name is Angelica." Angelica smiled flirtatiously as she tucked the $100.00 bill inside her bunny outfit.

Nutts slid the phone across to the table to Syndicate. "So, what are you waiting for instructions? Pick up the goddamn phone and invite them over to the table."

Syndicate slid the phone back across the table to Nutts. "That's what old corny white muthafucka's in the movies do. Gangstas step up to the plate." Syndicate stood up and walked over to where the three young women were sitting.

"Pardon me beautiful sista. I don't mean to alarm you, but I believe you have somethin' of extreme value of mine in your possession." Syndicate whispered in the young woman's ear.

"Excuse me?! " The young woman laughed as she pulled back from the handsome man staring down at her.

Syndicate smiled innocently and place his hand over his heart. "My heart! From the moment, I first laid my eyes on you. It's like my heart jumped out of my body and landed at your feet. Now I was hoping that you and your two lovely friends would join me and my good friend at our table. So, as I might be able steal your precious heart away from you as you have undoubtedly stolen mine away from me." Syndicate pointed to where Nutts was puffing on his Cuban Cigar with a big smile on his face.

The young woman looked Syndicate up and down, dressed in his tailor-made Armani suit and Rolex watch. "Maybe I should stay right here and keep your heart held hostage for ransom." The young woman responded while her two friends laughed.

Syndicate accepting the challenge smiled confidently. "By all means beautiful. You should always do what's in your best interest."

The young woman smiled at Syndicate showing off her perfect white teeth. "I see. And what did you say that your name was?"

Syndicate looked pass the young woman's pretty gray Siamese cat eyes down to her soul. "My real name is Derek. But everyone calls me Syndicate."

The young woman eyed Syndicate closely. "Syndicate, Mmm, I like it."

Syndicate was shocked of being so relieved that this fabulous looking young woman approved of his street name. "That's cool that you like the name Syndicate. Now tell me what name could possibly fit someone as fine as you?"

The woman blushed. "My name is Lynette. But everyone

calls me Sugga short for Brown Sugga."

A big smile spread across Syndicate's handsome face. "Brown Sugga! I like it."

"My Father gave it to me the day I was born. Said that I was his little Brown Sugga."

Syndicate gave Sugga a warm friendly smile. "Father knows best." Syndicate tone became more serious. "So Sugga now that we got all that out of the way. Will you and your two friends please come with me over to my table? So, that I don't have to face my good friend all alone."

"I think a little embarrassment would do your priceless heart and your big ego a lot of good," Sugga smiled at Syndicate as the other two women started laughing. "Just kidding with you Syndicate. We would be happy to join you and your friend at your table."

Syndicate walked over to where Nutts was sitting puffing on his Cuban Cigar, along with Sugga and her two friends. "Goddamn youngsta! What took you so long? I was starting to get worried about you." Nutts looked over the three beautiful women more closely.

Syndicate held onto Sugga's hand. "Nutts this here is Sugga and Sugga this here is Nutts."

Sugga smiled at Nutts. "Hello Nutts. Glad to meet you."

Nutts smiled back at Sugga still believing the three women were high paid hookers. "Please, please, the pleasure is all mine.

And who are these two beautiful ladies that you have with you?"

Sugga smiled at her two friends just as Syndicate pulled her chair out for her to sit down. "This one here, her name is Shantay," Sugga nodded in the direction of Shantay. A very attractive, professional looking, light skinned sista. Shantay was sexy with a well-toned, hard body, black hair, black eyes, and with the smile of an angel.

"And this one here, her name is Tiki." Sugga nodded in the direction of her other friend. A beautiful dark skinned, professional looking sista, with a body banging harder than the strippers. Unlike her other two friends, Tiki had a wild look in her eyes, like an untamed cheetah.

Angelica brought another bottle of champagne to the table that Syndicate had ordered, as everyone continued to get acquainted with one another. "Champagne? Wow! What's the occasion?" Sugga teased.

Syndicate smiled a devilish smile at Angelica before giving her a $100.00 bill. "I'm getting married next week. So, this is my last night out on the town as a free man. Syndicate spoke with ease as he poured everyone a glass of champagne.

Sugga smiled respectfully at Syndicate for his honesty. "Congratulations."

Syndicate nodded his head. "Thank you."

"Wow Syndicate. Congratulations." Tiki smiled a little

uncomfortable for her friend Sugga.

"So, who's the lucky girl?" Shantay blurted out thinking to herself that whoever the girl was, she must be a hell of a woman for Syndicate to admit to Sugga that he was getting married. Especially, after that smooth ass line he just dropped on her.

Syndicate looked into Sugga's gray Siamese cat eyes knowing in his heart that his life would never be the same again. "Her name is Michelle. But everyone calls her Dynamite."

Sugga laughed good hearted. "Syndicate and Dynamite. That's unique. Sounds like the two of you were made for each other."

Nutts poured everyone another round of champagne. "They were made for one another, alright. Just like the devil was made for hell." Nutts laughed.

Shantay laughed along with Nutts as she sipped her champagne. "You're nothing like what the papers and the media makes you out to be. They make you sound like some evil spirited monster."

"Only believe half of the shit you can see and don't believe none of the shit you hear, Shantay." Nutts said thinking to himself that these hookers don' hit the jackpot, seeing the way Syndicate was carrying on behind Sugga.

Syndicate, full of life, leaned back and sipped on his champagne. "So where are you ladies from?"

"We're all from the City!" Tiki blurted out overly excited to be in the presence of the notorious Nutts.

Syndicate puffed on his Cuban Cigar and smiled for no apparent reason. "Oh Ok! So you ladies are all from San Francisco?"

"Yes, and this is our last night out together. Kinda like a coming out party. We just recently graduated from Stanford college and after this weekend, we're all off to conquer our very own different parts of the world. We always wanted to come here to 'The Game' and check it out for ourselves. To see if it lived up to its reputation of being a high-class underworld nightclub." Sugga smiled at her two friends. "The thing is, we were always too chicken to come inside. So, since this was our last opportunity to explore the underworld at its highest level before becoming professional women, we decided to throw all that caution to the wind, and just enjoy the moment." Sugga put her hands over her head and danced along to the music. Shantay and Tiki joined in on the dancing putting their hands high over their heads along with Sugga.

Nutts took a sip of his champagne and smiled at the three women. Respecting the pimp that had these three-bad ass hoes so well-trained, to milk a trick for all he was worth. "Believe me Sugga when I tell you it's official. You three lovely ladies are most definitely professional."

Syndicate picked up his Champagne glass and eyed Sugga more closely. He started to have his doubts of his own about the beautiful woman with the gray Siamese cat eyes, sitting down next to him. "So, tell me Sugga what's your profession?"

"I'm a Doctor, the same as Shantay and Tiki." Sugga answered.

Nutts let out a loud laugh. "P.H.D.'s! Imagine the fuck out of that one! Who would have thought?" Nutts laughing non-stop, prepared to pay whatever it took for him and Syndicate to get fucked and sucked by these professional head Doctors.

"You don't look old enough to be a Doctor." Syndicate answered finding it hard to believe that Sugga's a Doctor.

"I'm a very exceptional student or how would you say it Syndicate? I'm very game gifted. I graduated high school when I was 16 and I'll be 25 on my next birthday, so you do the math." Sugga smiled and sipped her champagne, fully aware of what Syndicate is thinking.

Syndicate smiled back at Sugga content with letting things be as they are for the moment. "I'll leave the math problems for the exceptional students. How about goin' down to the second level where it's a lil' less exotic and dance with me."

"I would love to." Sugga took Syndicate's offered hand as she stood up from the table.

"Nutts, will you please entertain Dr. Shantay and Dr. Tiki while I take Dr. Lynette down to the second level to get better acquainted with her?" Syndicate had a big boyish grin on his face.

"Yeah, yeah, Syndicate. You go right ahead and take Dr.

Lynette wherever you want to. And don't worry about Dr. Shantay and Dr. Tiki, I'm sure that I have enough for both of them to operate on." Nutts cracked up laughing.

Syndicate held Sugga closely, smelling the sweet scent of Channel perfume, as he whispered in her ear. "I was worried there for a minute."

Sugga felt the warmth of Syndicate's body as he held her close out on the dance floor. "Worried about what? That I was a prostitute?" Sugga smiled into Syndicate's strong black eyes and wondered what someone so young and so sweet could possibly have in common with someone like Nutts.

"I can't lie, it did cross my mind." Confessed Syndicate.

"Why would that bother you? Isn't that why you came to 'The Game' tonight? To have one more run at it before you get married next week?" Sugga found herself being more attracted to Syndicate then she had anticipated.

"I didn't come down here to pay any woman to have sex with me. That's not my style." Syndicate answered a little defensively.

"So, what's your style?" Sugga smiled disarmingly at Syndicate not meaning to offend him.

"My style is to keep it gangsta no matter what. Even if it kills me." Syndicate came clean with Sugga not wanting to give her any false impressions about himself.

Sugga smiled not exactly sure of what to make out of the

comment that Syndicate just made. "I see."

Syndicate held Sugga close. "Do you Sugga. Do you really see me?"

"I only see what you want me to see Syndicate." Sugga smiled. Taking Syndicate by the hand and leading him back to their table.

"Would the two of you like to order something from the bar?" Asked the chocolate, sexy-looking cocktail waitress who was dressed in her red and black bunny outfit.

"I'll have a beautiful just like you, Isora. No, make that two." Syndicate flirted with the cocktail waitress while reading her name tag.

"Two beauties for the gentleman. And what would the beautiful lady like this evening?" Isora smiled at Syndicate and Sugga suggestively.

Sugga gave Isora a friendly smile. "Oh, just a diet coke please."

"Two beauties and a diet coke. Coming right up." Isora smiled and winked back at Sugga.

"So, what's in a beautiful?" Sugga asked as Isora returned with their drinks.

Syndicate looked deep into Sugga's eyes. "You and a whole lot of Brown Sugga." Syndicate smiled at a blushing Sugga, as he reached into his pocket and gave Isora a $100.00.

"Oh wow! Thank you sir! If any of you need anything, please don't hesitate to call and ask for me." Isora smiled suggestively, before switching her sexy ass back and forth as she walked away.

"A big tipper? I'm impressed." Sugga smiled approvingly towards Syndicate.

"It's nothin' to a giant Sugga." Syndicate boasted. Finishing off his drink in one big gulp.

"It's not good to change from one drink to another. I hope you're not the designated driver tonight?" Sugga spoke good naturally.

"No, I don't think that I would qualify for that job." Syndicate said seriously as he finished off his second beautiful.

Sugga smiled brightly at Syndicate, fascinated with the young man who was sitting in front of her. "So how old are you Syndicate? And what's your relationship with Nutts."

Syndicate laughed out humorously as he searched for another cocktail waitress. "Damn Sugga. I thought you told me that you were a Doctor? It sounds to me like your workin' for the Feds. I'm going to have to search you for a wire before I answer those questions."

"No, I don't work for the Feds and I'm not trying to investigate you. It's just that you have the advantage over me, because I don't know anything about you, except that you're getting married next week." Sugga spoke lighthearted.

"I'm 19-years-old and I'm from Stockton. Nutts is my role model and mentor." Syndicate laughed as he put a mouth full of peanuts in his mouth.

Sugga looked at Syndicate with concern. "So, what are you saying Syndicate, that you're a gangster?"

Syndicate stopped one of the pretty cocktail waitresses passing the table and ordered another beautiful. "You're the one who's the exceptional student, so figure it out."

"The security guards warned us at the door that there's nothing but game up in here and a lot of smooth talkers. I put up my wall and thought that I was mentally prepared for any fast-talking player that approached me. But you were pretty smooth by the way you slid through the cracks in my armor and peaked my interest. Impressive, I applaud you for having more game than anyone I ever had the pleasure of talking to." Sugga clapped her hands together mockingly.

"First of all, Sugga get it right. I'm not a player as you say. I'm a gangsta and the only game I ever ran on you was that I kept it real at all times. No matter what because that's what a real nigga do." Syndicate spoke from his heart.

Sugga looked at Syndicate with a frustrated look on her beautiful face. "So what? You telling me all that bullshit about your heart jumping out of your body wasn't game or just another pick up line?"

Syndicate leaned in closer to Sugga. "I'm not the kinda' man that relies on luck. Any man that needs to rely on pick-up lines is clueless and gameless. I always come straight from the heart. Rather you accept it or reject it, hate it or love it, you're goin' to respect it. I'm going' to let you know where I'm at all times. That way it won't ever be a misunderstanding between the two of us. Point being, that's why I told you that I was getting married next week." Syndicate relaxed a little bit, taking for granted that Sugga knew exactly what he was talking about.

"Exactly. So why you tell me that your heart jumped out of your body and landed at my feet if it weren't true? Unless of course you were just trying to test your mac game out on me?" Sugga tapped her foot on the ground anxiously waiting to see what Syndicate would say next.

"For someone who claims to be an exceptional student and a doctor no less, you sure don't pay attention and listen to what someone is tellin' you. The only game I have is the truth. My love for you has no boundaries. From the moment I first seen you smile that beautiful smile of yours, I knew that you were the one for me. Love at first sight, isn't something that I believed in until now. I would go to the end of the earth to prove to you that my love is true." Syndicate spoke with a lot of sincerity.

Sugga smiled in spite of herself, impressed with Syndicate's game. "How can you sit here and say that you love me and you're about to get married in a week."

Syndicate held Sugga by her hand. "To know me is to love me Sugga. My heart is a lot bigger than the average man. Me and Dynamite are soul-mates and nothin' will ever compete against that. We're one and the same. When you see me, you see her and vice versa. I would never have told you that I love you if I didn't think that Dynamite would approve of you or that you would approve of Dynamite."

"What are you saying Syndicate? You want me to do a threesome with you and Dynamite? And what even makes you think that I go that route? Sugga smiled enjoying the conversation.

Syndicate shook his head stubbornly. "What I'm talking about is a lot more than a threesome, Sugga. Dynamite is bisexual and I'm lookin' for someone that compliments us. And until now, I didn't think that I could love another woman other than Dynamite."

"I don't know Syndicate. That's a lot to consider. I mean I had a lesbian experience or two in college." Sugga smiled nervously. "But to be in a committed relationship with a woman and her husband, is not what I had in mind."

"Like I said, I'm not your average man." Syndicate smiled proudly. "All I'm askin' you to do is meet to Dynamite and see if the two of you have the same kind of chemistry that the two of us have."

Sugga, respecting Syndicate's honesty, decided to give him a few style points. "You want me to meet Dynamite and that's it?"

"That's it." Syndicate whispered holding his breath.

Sugga took a deep breath. "Ok I'll meet her. But I'm not making any promises other than that."

Syndicate kissed Sugga passionately on the lips. "That's all I'm askin' you to do."

Shantay and Tiki sat on the opposite sides of Nutts, sipping on champagne, and laughing when Syndicate and Sugga came walking up from the second level. "Well, well, look who's here I see that the two of you finally decided to resurface." S;aid a smiling Tiki.

"It doesn't look like we been missed too much." Sugga laughed. Surprised to see her two friends sitting so up close to Nutts.

"Guess what Sugga? Nutts thought that we were all some high-class hookers, working for some pimp." Shantay laughed uncontrollably clearly affected by all the champagne she's been drinking.

Sugga rolled her eyes up at Syndicate who stood next to her smiling. "So, I heard."

Nutts, sitting with his arms spread stretched out around both Shantay and Tiki, started to laugh. "It seems that I was wrong about these three lovely ladies Syndicate. They really are who they say they are. And why are the two of you still standing there like statues? Have a seat, have a seat." Nutts nodded his head motioning for Syndicate and Sugga to sit down.

"I'm sorry Nutts. But it's getting late and I'm the designated driver to get these two wino's home. So, we really are going to have to leave now." Sugga gave her two friends a firm look. "Come on you two. Say your good byes and let's get out of here."

"Damn that shit Sugga. You and Syndicate sit your asses down. Nutts said, refusing Suggas intentions to leave. "I'll have my chauffeur drive you ladies anywhere you need to go. So please sit down and finished enjoying the evening with us." Nutts urged again, not quite ready to part ways with the two young doctors.

"That's very sweet of you Nutts, but I'm afraid not. We really have to go now." Sugga look over at her two friends living it up with Nutts.

"Sugga is right Nutts. I had a great time, but it really is time for us to get going." Tiki kissed Nutts on his cheek.

"I guess that means I'm out voted. I had a great time too Nutts, I've never been out with a gangster before. It was a totally entertaining experience. Thank you so much for being a real gentleman." Shantay kissed Nutts on his other cheek and got up from the table.

Syndicate kissed Sugga tenderly. "I'll call you in a couple of weeks."

"I'm looking forward to meeting Dynamite." Sugga smiled mischievously.

"I'm sure that she's goin' to feel the same way as we do."

Syndicate smiled hopefully as the two of them kissed again.

"Ok now Sugga, you're the one who's rushing us to leave so let's go." Shantay fussed good humorously.

"Ok, Ok let's go. It was nice meeting you Nutts." Sugga gave Nutts a warm friendly smile.

Nutts leaned back in his seat and puffed on his Cuban Cigar. "Oh, I'm sure that were going to meet again Sugga. You ladies take care and drive safely."

"Nice meeting you Syndicate." Shantay smiled.

"Like wise." Tiki assured Syndicate.

"The pleasure was all mine ladies." Syndicate smiled at the three ladies as they walked towards the elevator.

Nutts slapped Syndicate playfully in the back of the head. "I can't wait to meet Dynamite. What the fuck was that all about?"

Syndicate puffed on his Cuban Cigar and leaned forward putting his arm around his mentor's shoulder. "Law of Attraction my nigga. Law of Attraction at it's finest. You better get up on it," Syndicate let out a big laugh. "Come on old man, let's grab a handful of these strippers and bounce back to the room so we can get served like some gangsta's is supposed to."

Nutts couldn't help but to think about Big Time and wish that he was there with them, enjoying the moment. "I thought that you were way to cool to fuck off some blood money on some pussy."

Syndicate laughed at his good friend Nutts, while pouring

them both another glass of champagne. "I thought that you knew Nutts. A married man is the biggest trick in the game."

"Trick or treat youngsta. It all depends on how you look at it." Nutts spoke the real as the two gangstas tapped their champagne glasses

CHAPTER 37

The Wedding

August 26, 1987

Rosa, the maid smiled brightly as she walked into Gail's enormous bedroom unannounced "The groom sent me up here to check on Michelle. He told me to tell you that if you don't hurry up and get your ass outside, he was going to break tradition and come up in here and get you." Dynamite stood in front of the huge mirror glowing. She was wearing only her white laced panties and bra, surrounded by her five bridesmaids, along with Gail and Winky.

"You tell that crazy boy that if he even steps a foot inside this house, it's going to be the last house that he sees." Gail replied in a very uncompromising motherly voice. As she stood behind Dynamite brushing her daughter's hair.

"I'll make sure that your future son-in-law gets the message." Rosa smiled and exited the room.

"I'm so happy for you Dynamite." Jazzy cried while holding her son, lil' Big Time, in her arms.

Dynamite, with tears in her eyes, turned around and gave Jazzy a big hug. "Thank you Jazzy. I'm so happy you're here, I love you so much." Dynamite kissed lil' Big Time on top of his little head. "And I love you to Lil' Big Time."

Gail smiled in appreciation of the two girls' friendship. "Alright you two, that's enough of that. I spent all morning doing Dynamite's makeup and I'm not trying to have it ruined before she gets married. Come on Dynamite let me get you zipped up."

"Oh, my god I can't believe that I'm actually getting married today!" Dynamite continued to cry.

Star gave Dynamite a tissue to wipe her tears away. "It's too late now to be getting cold feet girl. Your about to be a married woman, in less than an hour."

Dynamite started laughing to fight back the tears. "I'm not getting cold feet I'm crying, because I'm so happy. Syndicate is everything that I ever wanted in a man. I'm just so overwhelmed with joy that I can't stop crying."

Tears started to take form in Winky's eyes. "It's ok Dynamite. Even gangsta's cry sometime. Come here and give me a hug." The two gangsta bitches embraced, in a hug full of love and warmth.

"I won't ever disrespect you Winky, by bringing disgrace to

the family's name in anyway." Dynamite spoke out of respect for Winky.

"Dynamite, that's the last thing I'm worried about. You're the best thing to happen to this family in a long time. And I know that you're going to make Syndicate a wonderful wife. It's that hardheaded son of mine that I'm worried about. Which is why I'm going to go outside and make sure that he doesn't bring his ass up here." Winky took little Big Time from Jazzy and walked out. She left the room, leaving Dynamite, Gail, and here bridesmaids cracking up laughing.

Alright ladies, the five of you go on outside and make sure everything is in order, while I get Dynamite's face all cleaned up. Oh and send Dr. Michael up here. Tell him, his daughter is almost ready to be given away." Gail wiped the tears from her own eyes as she gave the bridesmaids their instructions.

"Ow wow, I'm so excited and happy for you Dynamite." Erin cried along with the other bridesmaids hugging and kissing Dynamite on the cheek, before leaving her alone with her mother.

Minutes later…"Knock! Knock!" Dr. Michael, a tall, lean, handsome man with salt and pepper hair, strongly knocked on the door.

"Daddy!" Dynamite's green eyes sparkled at the sight of her father.

"Michelle, my baby! Look how beautiful you look. You look

just like your mother did on her wedding day." Dr. Michael held Dynamite by her slender shoulders, while looking down into her soft green eyes.

"Thank you, daddy. It means a lot to me for you to say that." Dynamite smiled looking up to her father.

"So, Michael, tell me, what do you think about Derek?" Gail asked apprehensively.

"Well, he most certainly is a very brave hearted young man. A lot more than just a roughneck like you described him to be Gail," Dr. Michael smiled accusingly at Gail. "But be that as it may, I can also see that Derek is very much in love with our daughter. Any reservations that I may have about Derek marrying Michelle wouldn't be fair to him, because I'm extremely bias and over-protective when it comes to Michelle." "I don't think any man is good enough for her. I love Michelle unconditionally or should I say Dynamite," Dr. Michael smiled at Dynamite. "And I'm trusting that she knows exactly what kind of man it is that she's marrying." Dr. Michael turned to Dynamite and gave her a very serious, fatherly look.

"I know exactly what kind of man Syndicate is daddy, and I love him for it. Just like he knows exactly what kind of woman I am. I couldn't be happier with anything in this world, than to be Syndicate's wife." Dynamite held her breath, feeling like a little girl wanting her Father's acceptance.

Dr. Michael's stern face broke into a wide smile. "As long as you're happy baby, then I'm happy." Dynamite and her father embraced in a long hug.

Gail exited the room, as Dynamite and Dr. Michael continued their father-daughter talk. Gail took her seat next to Winky as the musician begin playing, "Here Come's the Bride" on the Grand piano. The bridesmaids made their way down the aisle, while Syndicate stood at the alter, looking Debonair in his black Tuxedo. G Gunna, Whip, Low, Dmove, and Young Tre were standing close by, dressed in their white Tuxedos.

Dynamite, looking elegant in her white wedding dress, wrapped her arm around her father's, as the minster gave them the que to walk down the aisle. With her head held up high and smiling brightly. Dynamite gracefully made her way up to the alter and took her position next to Syndicate.

"Ladies and gentlemen, we are gathered here today to join Derek and Michelle in holy matrimony. If anyone here has any objections as to why these two should not be joined together, please let them speak now or forever hold their peace," The grey-haired minster stood in front of Syndicate and Dynamite with an open bible in his hand speaking to the crowd.

"With no objections from the well-wishers, the minister continued. "Please let us continue." The minster turned to face Syndicate and Dynamite. "It's been brought to my attention that the two of you have written your own wedding vows for each other. Is that, correct?" The bride and groom nodded their heads in agreement. "By all means, Michelle, as always, ladies first."

"Actually, we decided not to write anything down on paper. We didn't want to start our marriage off by picking up bad habits." The guest erupted into a wild laughter at hearing Dynamite's joke. Dynamite looked into Syndicate's deep, black eyes as the crowd settled back down. "There aren't any words that the human mind could understand or express to you how deep my love is. Syndicate, you are my heart, my mind, my body, my soul and my whole being. You are my King, Syndicate. I promise you in front of God and everyone concerned that I will always be loyal and faithful to you and only you. Not even in death will my love for you ever die." Tears filled Dynamite's beautiful green eyes as her heart became overwhelmed with joy.

Syndicate reached out and cupped Dynamite's soft hands inside his own. "My beautiful Dynamite. I love you more than my own life. To have you as my wife is a dream come true. There's nothing I wouldn't do for you to make you happy. To say that I would lay down my life for you is too simple. For you my weakness, I would kill. I promise in front of God and all that we love, I will always keep it gangsta foe' you, no matter what."

The minister smiled at Syndicate and Dynamite. "That was truly heart felt. The rings please." G Gunna and Jazzy gave

Syndicate and Dynamite their wedding rings. Smiling like they were on cloud nine, Syndicate and Dynamite placed the rings on each other fingers.

"Now, with the power invested in me I know pronounce you husband and wife." The minster announced proudly. Syndicate and Dynamite kissed for the first time as husband and wife. While the photographers and guest alike took pictures.

"Excuse me son. But I believe the first dance with the bride goes to the father." Dr. Michael smiled favorably at Syndicate as he took Dynamite by the hand and led her into a dance.

Following Dr. Michael's lead, Syndicate bowed gracefully in front of Gail. "May I have this dance Madam?"

Gail laughed naturally while accepting Syndicate's outstretched hand. "My. what a gentleman. Of course you may."

Syndicate and Gail joined Dynamite and Dr. Michael in the designated dance area, surrounded by all the well-wishers, cheering them on. With the song coming to an end, Syndicate walked up to Dr. Michael, and tapped him on the shoulder. "Excuse me sir, but I believe the next dance is mine."

Dynamite's green eyes lit up with joy as Syndicate took her by the hand and led her off into their first dance as husband and wife. Syndicate held Dynamite close in his arms as the two of them danced the night away. "It's just like I dreamed it would be Syndicate. I'm the luckiest and happiest girl in the world. This is the best day of my life."

"It's only the best day, because tomorrow isn't here yet." Syndicate winked at his new bride informing her that the best is yet to come.

Dynamite's grandmother, Jessie May, a short, attractive, feisty old lady, who had a little too much to drink, yelled out to Syndicate and Dynamite who were still out on the dance floor enjoying their moment in the sun.

"Alright you two. That's enough of that shit! You been out there dancing for forty-five minutes. Some of us old people can't stay up as long as we used to. I want a piece of that fancy looking wedding cake, before I turn in for the night."

Dynamite smiled over at her grandmother. "I'm sorry grandma, I wasn't paying any attention to the time."

Dr. Michael, all too familiar with his ex-mother-in-law's inappropriate behavior, spoke up. "It's all that liquor that you been consuming, that's making you sleepy Jessie May. Now leave the kids alone and let them enjoy their wedding day."

"If I wanted your opinion Dr. Asshole, I would have asked for it." Jessie May flipped Dr. Michael off as a way of showing him what her opinion was of him.

Syndicate laughed out loud enjoying the scene being put on by his new in-laws. "Come on Jessie May let's go and cut the cake, so you can turn in for the night, if you want to." Syndicate and Jessie

May walked arm and arm over to the cake.

"Shit boy, I'm not tired. I'm trying to do you a favor and help you get the hell out of here. I know you can't wait to get up in that hot little white snatch, that your new wife has waiting for you." Jessie May gave Syndicate a knowing look. "Grandma!" Dynamite giggled embarrassed.

"What! Shit Syndicate knows that I'm telling the truth. Just like I know you can't wait to have that big black piece of meat inside of you. That shit about all black men having big dicks might be a myth, but I had one by the name of Randolph. Child let me tell you, that man's dick was so big, I damn near fainted every time he put it inside of me. I guess that's why my father always told me never to have sex with a black man. He must have known that he would take that big black dick of his and take out all his ancestor's pain and frustration deep inside of me. Which to tell you the truth, isn't such a bad thing if you know what I mean." Jessie May gave a sly wink to Dynamite and laughed.

Everyone gathered around watching as Dynamite and Syndicate cut their wedding cake, and spoon fed each other. "Aw shit Dynamite you trippin' girl." Syndicate laughed as Dynamite smeared cake all over his face.

"Come on Syndicate, I know you not going to let her get away with that. You better show her who the boss is now before it's too late." Dynamite's cousin Kim said. A pretty girl, with blonde hair and blue eyes.

Syndicate took his piece of cake and smeared Dynamite's face with it. "Oh, believe me, she know who the boss is." Syndicate laughed as the crowd cheered him on.

Winky, feeling good off the weed and champagne, raised her champagne glass high in the air. "Everyone fill up your champagne glasses. I want to propose a toast! After all the glasses were filled, Winky started her toast. "To Syndicate and Dynamite. Never have I met two people that were a more perfect fit for each other, than the two of you. May the love that the two of you share today only grow stronger and stronger as the years pass by."

"My turn, my turn!" Jazzy tipsy off the champagne, raised her glass in the air. "To my brother and sister. May the two of you cherish each and every moment that you have together. And in the words of my beloved Big. It will only get greater later." G Gunna, highly intoxicated, raised his shot glasses in the air. "To Syndicate and Dynamite. The modern-day Bonnie and Clyde. May the two of you always be ready to ride or die for each other. And may your gangsta love, go down in history as the greatest love story of all time."

"To the youngstas Syndicate and Dynamite. Be true to the game and the game will be true to you. When the game god brings together two of his finest as he's done today, any of us true to it can see it and respect it for the blessing that it truly is. There is no greater gift that anyone can ever give than the gift of love. Which is why we are all blessed to be here today. To witness the gift of love that the two of you have given to one another. Forever is not a dream, it's a reality if you believe it. Loyalty, honesty, respect and trust is all part of love for any marriage. At the end of the night, no matter what the day may bring, remember who the person is that's lying in the bed next to you. What that person means to you. To Syndicate and Dynamite may the two of you raise a family, have many grand kids, grow old and fat together. Retire to Miami like the real gangsta's that you are." Nutts, who cherished his role as the Godfather, raised his champagne glass in honor of the newlyweds.

Syndicate stood proudly next to Dynamite holding her hand amongst all their guest. "Say Listen up everybody. We would really like to thank all of you for helping us make our wedding day, a day for us to remember for the rest of our lives. But the time has come for me and my beautiful wife to make our exit. We have a very early flight to catch in the mornin', thanks to my father-in-law Dr. Michael. We are grateful for the two-week honeymoon trip in Hawaii, that he gave us as our wedding gift. So, all of you please continue to enjoy yourselves and do what you do. As for me and Dynamite, we have a room waiting for us at the Hilton to rest up until the mornin'."

"Yeah right. Rest up my ass! You and that little wife of yours is going to be 10 toes up and 10 toes down." Jessie May teased.

"Mother if you don't stop." Gail laughed.

"Stop what! Shit everybody in here knows what they're going to go and do. It ain't no goddamn secret. It's their wedding day for Christ sake." Jessie May waved her hand intolerantly, in response to Gail's rebuke.

"Yeah go ahead and get your money, my nigga. We ain't mad at you." Dmove joked. As the crowd begin cheering and throwing rice at the newlyweds, while they ran out from the back yard into a waiting black limousine.

CHAPTER 38

Daddy's Lil Girl

Dynamite stood in front of the hotel room with her hands folded like a spoiled little brat. "You're supposed to carry me over the threshold Syndicate."

Syndicate shook his head in disbelief and laughed. "Come on now girl, you trippin'. That's only when you first enter your own house. Not a hotel room."

Dynamite stubbornly stood her ground. "I don't care Syndicate. I'm not goin' inside unless you carry me in."

Syndicate bent down and swept Dynamite off her feet in one fast motion and held her in his arms. "Forever the spoiled lil' rich girl. You should have made that one of your wedding vows. I vow to be a spoiled lil' brat for the rest of my life, and drive Syndicate crazy."

The two newlyweds laugh as Syndicate carried Dynamite

inside. "May I be of any more service to the two of you?" The bellhop asked as he sat their luggage down inside the hotel room.

"Naw man, we cool. Just make sure that they give us that eight o'clock wake-up call in the mornin'." Syndicate sat Dynamite down on the fancy looking bed and reached into his pocket and gave the bellhop a $100.00 bill.

"Thank you, sir, and don't you worry about that wake-up call, I'll take care of it personally. I hope the two of you have a pleasurable evening," The bellhop bowed his head in Dynamite's direction. "And may I say sir you, have a very beautiful wife."

"Rather you may or may not say it? You already said it, so it must be cool." Syndicate and Dynamite laughed as the bellhop closed the door behind him.

Syndicate picked up a card sitting next to a chilled bottle of champagne and two glasses. "Check this out!" Syndicate yelled out to Dynamite. "It's a card and a bottle of champagne from your mother.

Dynamite walked confidently out of the bedroom and back into the front room, wearing the sexy lingerie that Jazzy bought for her, and wrapped her arms around Syndicate's neck. Syndicate, taken by Dynamite's half naked appearance, smiled approvingly. "Goddamn girl. You must be tryin' to stay here for the whole two weeks. Comin' out here lookin' like a Victoria's Secret's model."

Dynamite smiled naughtily at Syndicate before taking the

card out of his hand. "Let's see what mommy has to say. Dear Mr. and Mrs. Gaines, tonight is the first night of the rest of your lives. So, take your time, have a glass of champagne, and savor the moment. Love mom."

Syndicate took a break from admiring Dynamite magnificent looking body and poured the two of them a glass of champagne. "Damn! Gail keeps it gangsta at all times."

Dynamite accepted a glass of champagne from Syndicate. "It almost sounds like she's tryin' to give us instructions on how to make love." Dynamite teased half jokingly and half serious.

"Gail's just bein' Gail. She already knows that I got this. I'm the only instructor you're ever goin' to need or want." The two newlyweds tapped champagne glasses. "To us."

With a devilish grin on his face, Syndicate took the champagne glass out of Dynamite's hand, and kissed her gently on her sweet soft lips. Dynamite responded by putting her arms around Syndicate's neck, closing her eyes and hungrily explored Syndicate's open mouth with her tongue.

Syndicate picked Dynamite up off her feet and carried her back into the bedroom and gently laid her down on the king size bed. Syndicate stood over Dynamite's half naked body, looking down at her in complete silence, and thrilled at how beautiful his new wife was looking in her sexy new lingerie. "Damn girl, my perfect vision of you at this very moment, didn't do you any justice. You're more beautiful today, here and now, than you ever were in my mind." Syndicate took his time taking off his Tuxedo, while not once taking his eyes off his beautiful young wife. "You're the most beautiful woman I ever known Dynamite. You look so young and innocent lying there, that I'm almost afraid to touch you."

"You don't have to be afraid of touchin' me Syndicate, but you better be afraid of not touching me." Dynamite smiled as she opened her arms for Syndicate to come to her.

Syndicate laughed as he crawled on top of the king size bed on his hands and knees. Kissing Dynamite from her cute little toes, all the way up her sexy legs. Pausing only for a second to take off Dynamite's black panties. "I said that I was almost afraid to touch you. I didn't say that I was scared. So, don't get it twisted baby girl."

Syndicate smiled mischievously at Dynamite before burying his face inside of her sweet, tight, pink, pussy. Dynamite moaned in ecstasy as Syndicate masterfully teased her young pussy with his tongue. "Mmm Syndicate, my husband." Dynamite moaned.

"Damn girl, your pussy taste sweet. Like cotton candy." Syndicate raised his head up from licking on Dynamite's little sweet pussy.

Dynamite looked Syndicate in his deep black eyes. "Mmm damn daddy, that felt good. Why you stop?" Dynamite pouted.

"Don't even trip, baby girl. That was only a preview of my love. The best is still yet to come." Syndicate gently slid his finger inside Dynamite's tight pussy at the same time as he kissed her passionately on the mouth.

Dynamite, overdosing on pleasure, bit down on her bottom lip, and moaned. "Mmm daddy, my husband. I love you so much." Dynamite's little pink nipples stood firm and erect as Syndicate sucked on her soft white breast. Taking his finger out of Dynamite's sweet young pussy Syndicate buried his face back in between Dynamite's sexy, white, creamy thighs.

"Mmm…oh god daddy. You got skills like a lesbian lover. I can't stop cumming." Dynamite's radiant green eyes rolled in the back of her head as she held on to Syndicate's shinny bald head with both her hands.

"I'm just keeping it gangsta foe' you." Syndicate smirked. Pulling himself up from sucking on Dynamite's little pink pussy and sitting back on his knees stroking his big black dick.

"Come give it to me daddy," Dynamite reached up and pulled Syndicate on top of her. "Mmm! Syndicate. stop teasin' me and give me what I want." Dynamite moaned into Syndicate's ear. While he stroked her pussy with the head of his dick in a nice slow motion.

Gaining momentum, Syndicate stroked Dynamite's pussy faster and faster, long dicking her with his strokes. He pushed her legs behind her head. Bent down and slapped her wet pussy with his big tongue. Before sticking his dick back inside her. "Goddamn this pussy is good," Syndicate groaned.

"It's your pussy daddy. You can have it, however or whenever you want." Dynamite panted. As she spread her legs farther apart so Syndicate could get deeper inside of her.

Sweat dripped off Syndicate's face. As he fucked his new wife for all he was worth. "Goddamn Dynamite, the pussy is to fuckin' good. I'm about to bust." Syndicate warned.

"No, not yet. Pull out. I want to take you in my mouth." Dynamite breathed heavily.

"Your wish is my command." Syndicate smiled. Before taking his big black dick and putting it into Dynamite' mouth.

Licking on his balls and dick at the same time. Dynamite deep throated Syndicate nice and slow. "Oh, hell yeah, Dynamite I love the way you suck my dick."

Syndicate, ready to bust, grabbed Dynamite by the back of her head. "That's it baby, do it the way daddy really likes it." Syndicate moaned as he exploded a load of seamen down Dynamite's throat. And like a true gangsta bitch Dynamite swallowed all of it.

CHAPTER 39

From The Bottom To The Top

Passengers, please fasten your seat belts and prepare for takeoff. The Captain spoke over the intercom of the plane as it started down the runway. Dynamite held onto Syndicate's hand as the two of them sat in the first-class section of the Southwest Airlines 747 Jet Passenger plane.

"Hello, is there anything I can get for the two of you?" Asked the pretty blonde-haired stewardess, smiling down at the two newlyweds.

Syndicate looked up at the friendly stewardess noticing her name tag. "Yeah Cheryl, I would like some orange juice please."

"Not a problem sir. And is there anything I can get for the glowing young lady sitting next to you?" Cheryl smiled in Dynamite's direction.

"Yes, may I please have a cup of coffee?" Dynamite smiled

back at Cheryl.

"Not a problem and would you like cream and sugar with that?" Cheryl continued to smile.

"No thank you. I like mine black." Dynamite winked at Cheryl. "I heard that girlfriend I like mine the same way." Cheryl winked back at Dynamite then walked away.

Dynamite grabbed hold of Syndicate's arm and leaned into him. "Oh Syndicate, I have never been so happy in all my life. If I'm dreaming, please don't ever wake me up."

Syndicate looked tenderly into Dynamite's green eyes. "This ain't no dream baby girl when your married to a real gangsta. Anything and everything is possible. Look at us, way up here in the sky, riding on cloud nine together chasing the stars. We doin' it the way it's supposed to be done. Who would have imagined we would live to see this day become a reality?"

Dynamite threw her arms around Syndicate's neck. "I always believed in us, Syndicate, and I always will." Syndicate kissed Dynamite affectionately, as they "searched for the stars together".

"Passengers, may I please have your attention. We'll be landing in Maui's International Airport in approximately 10 minutes. Will you please fasten your seat belts and prepare for landing? Thank you for flying Southwest Airlines. The Captain's voice coming from over the intercom, woke Syndicate and Dynamite up from their peaceful sleeping.

"My god Syndicate. Look, it's so beautiful." Dynamite opened her eyes to see Hawaii's beautiful island surrounded by the Pacific Ocean.

"Now I see why everyone wants to come to Hawaii. It looks like paradise." Syndicate, excited by the beauty of Hawaii, smiled like a little kid as he looked passed Dynamite at the deep blue sea.

Syndicate laughed while he stood next to Dynamite, with both of them wearing tourist Lai around their necks, waiting to pick up their luggage. "Goddamn they weren't bullshitin' about this bein' an International Airport. They got every race of people in the world up in here. I think I just seen a couple of aliens walk by."

Dynamite, feeling on top of the world, laughed along with Syndicate. "Be nice Syndicate. This is our honeymoon," Dynamite noticed their luggage coming around the conveyor belt. "Oh, good. Here comes our luggage."

"Damn Dynamite! What the fuck you got up in these suit-cases?" Syndicate complained as he lifted Dynamite's heavy suitcases off the conveyer belt.

"How are you supposed to protect me from the bad guys if you can't even pick up a lil' luggage?" Dynamite teased.

"I ain't no muthafuckin' muscle man, baby girl. I'm a gangsta. Besides, these lil' punk ass suitcases you talkin' about weighs more than a 100 pounds apiece. All my Mac .11 weighs is 8 pounds, fully loaded. So, as long as I can pick up my gun I won't have any problems puttin' a nigga's dick in the dirt, if he gets out of line."

Syndicate grabbed hold of Dynamite's two suitcases and stormed off as Dynamite smiled proudly at her husband. The newlyweds walked out of the terminal and into the beautiful sunlit city of Maui. Palm trees could be seen lined up and down the streets. Natives and tourists walked down the busy metropolitan sidewalks, wearing big Hawaiian shirts, and traditional Lai around their necks.

Syndicate and Dynamics scanned the streets, while cars zoomed around the many buildings throughout the city. A taxi driver parked in front of the airport and desperately waiting for any possible customer, jumped out of his taxi at the sight of Syndicate and Dynamite, looking like lost tourist.

"Looking for a taxi?" Asked the taxi driver. Already knowing the answer, he reached for the two suitcases that Syndicate was carrying. Gratefully, Syndicate released the luggage to the taxi driver.

"How did you know that we were lookin' for a taxi?" Syndicate asked while the taxi driver put their luggage in the trunk.

"I been doing this for a long time now son. So where are we off to?" The taxi driver asked all business like.

"Take us to the Kaanapali Beach Hotel." Dynamite beamed from the back of the taxicab taking it all in.

"Kaanapali Beach Hotel? That's a very exclusive hotel young lady." The cab driver looked suspiciously at Syndicate and

Dynamite through his rear-view mirror.

"She didn't ask you what you thought of it. She told you where she wanted to go." Syndicate feeling disrespected by the cab driver racist remarks. Responded defensively.

"No need to get hostile young man. I was only trying to be helpful." The cabbie waved his hand up in the air as a way of apology.

Dynamite, noticing the mood change and not wanting Syndicate to lose his temper, laughed good naturally. "It's OK, no harm, no foul. You didn't know that we were a very exclusive couple." The cabbie relieved that all was forgiven for his stupidity, did his best to repair any damage that his big mouth might have caused him from getting a big tip. "So, have the two of you been to Hawaii before?" The cabbie asked as he drove slowly through the city streets. He also, pointed out the different tourist spots to the newlyweds.

"I was here a long time ago with my parents when I was just a kid. All I can remember is playing with my mother and father out on the beach. Now, I'm all grown up and on my honeymoon. So, I'm sure that I'll have alot more special memories this time around." Dynamite had a big smile over her face.

"So, the two of you are here on your honeymoon? Congratulations! I hope that your stay here in Maui is a memorable one for the two of you." The cabbie said thoughtfully. Still hoping for a big tip as he continued through the busy streets talking about the rich tradition of Maui and Hawaii in general.

CHAPTER 40

Gangsta's Paradise

"Damn this is a big ass hotel," Syndicate stood outside the cab next to Dynamite looking up into the sky at the tall Kaanapali Beach Hotel. Syndicate reached into his pocket and pulled out a $50.00 dollar bill and gave it to the cab driver. "Keep the change."

The cabbie quickly put the money inside his pocket. "Thank you, sir, and I hope that the two of you have a pleasant stay here in Maui."

Dynamite smiled into the sky looking up at the Kaanapali. "I hope that you're not scared of heights daddy. My father reserved the penthouse honeymoon suite for us and it's on the top floor."

"You got it all wrong baby girl. I'm not afraid of heights. I'm afraid of being stuck on the bottom." Syndicate slapped Dynamite playfully on the butt at the same time the bellhop placed their luggage on the little carry on cart.

The manager, a tall, well groomed, handsome white man whose name tag read Joshua, smiled happily at Syndicate and Dynamite, who were standing in front of his desk. "Good afternoon and welcome to the Kaanapali. How may I help you?"

"We're Mr. and Mrs. Gaines and we have a reservation." Dynamite said proudly. Happy to be using her married name for the first time.

"That's fantastic. That will save us both a lot of time and paperwork. Just let me check through the reservation log to see what room we have the two of you in." Joshua flipped through the reservation log. "Gaines, Gaines, aw yes! Here we go. Oh, good I see that we have newlyweds visiting with us, and with great taste I might add. The Penthouse honeymoon suite is one of our most luxurious suites'. It doesn't get any better than that." Joshua snapped his fingers at thee bellhop. "Peter, will you please show our newlyweds to their honeymoon suite?"

Peter, a short man with a head that looked too big for his body, and no neck, nodded grudgingly towards Joshua. "Yes boss! Follow me please!" Peter steered the cart carrying Syndicate's and Dynamite's luggage through the lobby towards the elevator.

"Ow wow Syndicate! This is fabulous!" Dynamite looked around in awe at the dream-like honeymoon suite, as the two of them walked inside. I didn't expect it to be so big." Dynamite smiled sweetly at her Syndicate.

The beautifully decorated suite had soft red, wall to wall carpet lined the floor. In the corner fitted diagonally on the left side of the suite, was a shiny black brick original fireplace. Off to the right of the fireplace, sat a beautiful custom- made jacuzzi, designed to look like a giant rose. There was a big Crystal chandelier hanging from the ceiling and a dining room table set for two sitting directly underneath. The fully stocked wet bar sat against the far wall on the right side of the room, and a beautiful two-piece ivory sofa and love seat sat in the middle of the room. The master bedroom, was a giant size heart shaped bed with red silk sheets.

"Would you like for me to put your luggage inside the bedroom or would this be OK?" The bellhop stood inside the suite waiting impatiently for Syndicate and Dynamite to make up their minds."

"No, they're good right where they're at. You served your purpose, you can leave now." Syndicate gave the bellhop a $10.00 bill and slammed the door in his face.

Dynamite laughed and put her arms around Syndicate. "Why were you so rude to the little man daddy."

"Syndicate's mind flashed back to his and Dynamite's lovemaking the night before and pulled her close to him. "He reminded me of this sucka I know." Plus, he had a fucked-up attitude."

Dynamite's green eyes danced with joy. "He didn't have an

attitude daddy. You were just being mean."

Syndicate squeezed Dynamite's ass with both hands and held on tightly. "He was a sucka and bein' around suckas make me mean."

"Well, I don't see any suckas around right now, so there's no need for you to be mean Mr. Gaines." The two young newlyweds smiled at one another and without any spoken words begin kissing each other with great urgency. Syndicate, still holding onto Dynamite's ass, picked her up and carried her into the bedroom. Laying her down lovingly on the big heart shape bed making love to her all through the wee hours of the night and throughout the day.

The next day, Dynamite sat in the passenger seat of the black Jaguar, wearing her brand-new black, two-piece bikini with her hair flying in the wind, while looking out at the ocean. "Maui is so beautiful and to think it only took us four days to finally make it outside to see it." Dynamite gave Syndicate a naughty lil' girl look. "Damn daddy, you sure do look sexy driving that Jag with the top down and no shirt on."

Syndicate leaned back with one hand on the steering wheel and laughed approvingly. "Well, if I'm sexy baby girl, then you're sexier than a muthafucka. Sitting over there looking like one of those Bay Watch girls. You know if it were up to me, we could have just stayed back at the Kaanapali and fucked for the whole two weeks that we're goin' to be here."

Dynamite squeezed Syndicate's hand. "I wouldn't like anything more than to make love to you all day, everyday Syndicate. But this is our honeymoon and I want to enjoy it to the fullest, before we have to get back to the Syndicate and family business." Dynamite smiled and turned back around to face the ocean whilie marveling in its beauty.

"Shit my bad, I thought us fuckin' out on the balcony of the penthouse overlooking the city, sipping on champagne was enjoying our honeymoon to the fullest." Syndicate grabbed his dick visualizing about the last four days.

"You're right daddy. You are bad." Dynamite teased. Biting down on her bottom lip and moaning as if she were having an orgasm.

Feeling great about his prowess, watching Dynamite moaning and carrying on as she was. Syndicate stuck out his chest. "Girl, you knew that I was a bad boy when we first met. So, don't act surprised now.'

Dynamite smiled fondly at Syndicate. "I'm not surprised Syndicate. Gangsta life is the only life for me."

Syndicate, enjoying the peace and serenity around him, laid stretched out on his back on top of a blanket with his hands resting comfortably behind his shinny, bald head. While Dynamite sat with her legs folded under her body feeding him lady finger grapes. "Now this is what I'm talkin' about, baby girl. Yeah, this is the life for me.

No gunshots or shootouts, no enemies to worry about, and no drug deals to stress over. Shit I might fuck around and just stay chillin' right here in Maui. I mean, look around you, Dynamite a nigga would have to be really crazy to want to go back to the hood after experiencing something like this."

Dynamite fed Syndicate another lady finger grape. "I'm goin' to have to stop finger feeding' you these grapes. You call me spoiled. Look at you all laid back like you some big ole pimp. Talking' that nonsense about not wanting to go back home."

Syndicate laid on his back looking up at Dynamite. "It's not nonsense baby girl. Shit ain't the same without Big Time around. I want something more than what I'm getting from off the streets."

Dynamite, not accustomed to hearing Syndicate talk like that, was startled. "So, what are you tryin' to say daddy? That you don't want to be a gangsta anymore."

Seeing the worried look on Dynamite's face, Syndicate sat up straight and held Dynamite in his arms. "There you go, baby girl actin' like that square ass white girl you claim not to be. I'm gangsta foe' life make no mistake about it. But I'm also a real nigga, my game covers every aspect of the word. Chillin' here like this shows me how much I been missing out on, just hanging out on the block all day. It's time we take our business and our family to a higher level."

Relieved to hear that Syndicate hasn't found religion and that he's only trying to expand his game, Dynamite relaxed. "Oh, I see. You're one of those multitasking game gifted niggas that's seldomly seen, but always heard."

"Ha ha funny. Go ahead and try to get your clown on lil' funny lookin' white girl. I ain't mad at you. Just remember that game is what separates the real from the fake." Syndicate laid back down appreciating the fact that he could chop up some boss game with his wife and not be misunderstood.

Dynamite playfully threw the grapes in Syndicate's face. "I got your funny lookin' white girl."

Syndicate reached up and pulled Dynamite down on top of him. "Calm down killa."

Dynamite buried her face into Syndicate's chest. "You calm down." The Syndicate jumped up, still holding on to Dynamite's hand and headed towards the ocean blue.

Holding her hand tightly and pulling her along, Syndicate led Dynamite farther out into the ocean's incoming waves. "Come on now girl, quit bein' a punk!"

Dynamite's screams went unheard as a big waved washed over them. "Fuck this shit Syndicate! You can call me a punk all you want. I'm goin' back to dry land. I'm not trying to get caught up in one of these currents and be pulled out to sea." Dynamite yelled as she stormed off back towards the beach. Pissed off at herself for letting Syndicate talk her in to going out so far.

"What's wrong baby girl? I know you not goin' to just let these waves punk you like that?" Syndicate stood facing the incoming waves with his hands resting on his hips in his pimp posture, daring the waves to touch him. And without any regards to Syndicate's prowess, the fast-moving waves ran right through him sending him tumbling over backwards.

Later that night, Syndicate and Dynamite sat down Indian style in a large circle sipping on a sweet tasting native drink out of a coconut. "Damn this is some good shit! I wonder what the fuck they got up in here" Syndicate asked Dynamite while the two of them enjoyed the traditional Luau that was being hosted by the natives.

Using her straw, Dynamite sipped on her sweet tasting drink. "I don't have a clue as to what they put in here, but you're right daddy, this is some good shit." No sooner than the words left Dynamite's mouth, a muscular, mostly naked, Hawaiian hula dancer came up to Dynamite doing a hula dance with his arms stretched out in front of him signaling for Dynamite to join him.

Dynamite cheeks turned beet red with embarrassment as she pleaded with the hula dancer. "No please don't pick me," Turning to Syndicate for help she covered her face with her hands. "Make him go away."

Syndicate laughed along with everyone else sitting around the large circle cheering for Dynamite to get up and dance. "Don't look at me, you're on your own kid."

The hula dancer took Dynamite by her trembling hands and led her out to the middle of the circle. Syndicate hysterical at seeing his new bride doing thee hula dance, wasn't prepared for the little sexy half naked hula dancer approaching him. Shaking her hips in miniature little circles with her hands held out in front of Syndicate for him to join her.

"Aw naw, I'm good." Syndicate laughed as he put his hand up in protest.

"A real gangsta is always a gentleman, so what are you daddy?" Dynamite yelled over at Syndicate. As she stood in the middle of the circle shaking her hips putting on a show with the male hula dancer.

"I don' told you time after time about testin' my gangster-ism." Syndicate jumped up and put his arms out on both sides of the little hula dancer and started shaking his hips in little tiny circles to the laughter of the crowd and Dynamite. The little sexy hula dancer smiled at Syndicate and guided him to the middle of the circle, then passed him off to Dynamite. The two of them joined the natives and the rest of the couples in the hula dance.

The two newlyweds continued to join in on the other traditional festivities until the early morning hours.

CHAPTER 41

The World Belongs To Us

Syndicate and Dynamite sat naked in the Jacuzzi sipping on champagne. Dynamite, high off of life and feeling her prowess, tapped her champagne glass with Syndicate's. "To us! May we always keep it gangsta."

"Even if it kills us baby, even if it kills us." Syndicate replied. The two young newlyweds locked eyes and turned up their champagne glasses to complete the toast.

"These last two weeks have been the best days of my life." Dynamite smiled.

"This is only the beginning Dynamite. Our love was made to last forever." Syndicate couldn't help but to notice Dynamite's little pink nipples poking out just above the water in the Jacuzzi.

"I'm not talkin' about us Syndicate. I'm talkin' about this unbelievable dream that we been living here in Hawaii. From the late-night walks on the beach ending with our making love in the sand alongside the ocean. Even the bird watching that I had to bribe you into doing with me, is something that I will never forget" Dynamite giggled out loud, remembering how she had to give Syndicate a blow job while he watched the birds in order for him to go.

"Even hiking up the side of that old burnt-out volcano that you wanted to climb was fun. The only bad thing about it was that it was to many people up there for us to make our own hot lava like we had planned. All that plus the extravagant restaurants that we visited; it's just been so unreal." Dynamite smiled a little sadly in spite of herself. Not so eager to get back to the streets as she was only a couple of days ago.

"Yeah, I feel you baby girl. It's a much different world than the one we come from." Syndicate looked around the room marveling at his surroundings.

"I know one thing, when we buy our house. if it doesn't come with a Jacuzzi we're goin' to most defiantly have one put in." Dynamite said holding her glass out for Syndicate to refill it.

"This Jacuzzi is nice, but you know what I'm goin' to miss the most? All those Luau's. The natives really know how to throw a party." Laughing at his on remarks Syndicate squeezed Dynamite's little hard nipples.

Dynamite slapped Syndicate's hand away. "All you goin' to

miss is all those half naked pretty girls dancing all provocative around you."

Syndicate stood in front of Dynamite massaging her soft white breast peaking out just above the water. "Why would I miss them other girls when I got you? You're sexier than all of them put together," Syndicate looked lustfully into Dynamite's green eyes. "Especially when you put your hands over your head and start movin' your hips in those tiny circles. You had a nigga wantin' to fuck so bad, I was about ready to take you right then and there in front of everybody. I bet we could make a million dollars if we made a sex video of you dancing like a naughty lil' hula girl."

Dynamite grabbed hold of Syndicate's hard dick poking out from underneath the water. "And I would bet a million dollars to a coconut that you would make a cameo appearance."

Syndicate leaned back against the Jacuzzi wall. "What's with that weird ass look on your face? Why you lookin' at me like that?"

Dynamite pressed her wet naked body up close against Syndicate's chest and wrapped her arms around his neck. "I was just thinking of the cute lil' boy that you were when I first met you and how much you grown, and yet still remain the same."

Syndicate wrapped his arms around Dynamite's soft naked body and pulled her in close. "Money's not supposed to change you Dynamite. It only changes the way people think about you."

Dynamite looked intently into Syndicate's eyes. "Rather we

had a million dollars or eatin' out of a garbage can my, my love for you would be the same. I fell in love with you for who you are on the inside. Your heart is so genuine and I'm so in love with you. I'm proud of you for being the man that you are."

Syndicate bent down and kissed Dynamite on the top of her forehead. "I'm proud of you too baby girl. You proved everyone wrong who doubted you. No one believed that you had the heart to be a gangsta bitch. As it turns out you have a lot more heart than the average nigga hangin' out on the block. My bad for underestimating you Dynamite. And I promise you baby girl that I would be on death row from tryin' to get it before I ever see you eatin' out of a garbage can."

"And that's why I love you so much daddy. Because I would be on death row in a cell right next to yours before I would ever see you do without." Dynamite forced her tongue inside Syndicate's mouth as if it were the last kiss she would ever get. Using her small lips and tongue as a weapon against Syndicate's self-control.

Dynamite licked and kissed on Syndicate's chest at the same time reaching down with her little soft hands and squeezing on his big throbbing black dick "Um Mmm! You like that don't you daddy." Dynamite teased while holding Syndicate's testicles hostage by massaging them with her delicate little fingers.

"You show me a gangsta that doesn't like getting his balls massaged on and I'll show you a gangsta with no balls." Syndicate moaned out loud.

Dynamite smiled sweetly at Syndicate before squatting down in the Jacuzzi and taking him in her mouth. Syndicate, wanting to get the full enjoyment of Dynamite's deadly oral skills, lifted himself up and sat on the edge of the Jacuzzi so, that she would have more leverage to work with. "Goddam girl where did you learn how to suck dick so muthafuckin' good."

Dynamite rested her arms across Syndicate's open legs and stroke his dick and smiled naughtily. "If I told you that I would have to kill you."

Syndicate pushed Dynamite's head back down over his dick. "Either that or I'll have to kill you," Dynamite licked up and down on Syndicate's dick at the same time curling his balls up inside her little sweet tongue. Syndicate watched helplessly as his dick went in and out of Dynamite's sweet tasting mouth. "You can finish polishing it off later, but right now I want to fuck."

Syndicate kissed Dynamite possessively on the mouth and turned her around in the Jacuzzi, Penning her sexy little body back up against the wall. Dynamite full of excitement, wrapped her legs around Syndicate's waist in a tight vise like grip.

Syndicate full of passion took hold of his dick and like a guided missile penetrated deep inside of Dynamite's eagerly waiting pussy. Dynamite, breathing heavily, held on tightly as Syndicate fucked her harder and harder. "Oh, god yes, fuck me daddy, fuck me good nigga, write your name in it!"

Syndicate fought hard to maintain his self-control. "Damn girl this pussy is sweet. You keep moaning in my ear like that I'm goin' to bust way to fast."

"Ah, mmm, yeah, ah, mmm, ah, oh goddam Syndicate you big dick nigga. You love this lil' sweet white pussy don't you daddy?" Dynamite moaned in Syndicate's ear right before she had another orgasm.

Syndicate groaned with delight as he shot a fat load of seamen into Dynamite's hot pussy. "Ahh shit yeah!
Damn Dynamite, pussy that goddamn good has to be illegal."
"Naw nigga, that big black dick of yours is the one that should be illegal. Dynamite laughed.

"Without a doubt baby girl without a doubt." Syndicate playfully kissed Dynamite on the top of her nose and walked up the little stairs out of the Jacuzzi. Seizing the moment, Dynamite ran behind Syndicate and slapped him hard on the back of his bare ass. "Ouch! Alright Dynamite, it's on! You want to play huh?" Syndicate smiled mischievously at Dynamite and took off chasing her around the big honeymoon suite.

Dynamite out of breath and laughing her ass off, stood bent over holding her stomach with one hand and trying to fight off Syndicate with the other one. "No, no, ok, I'm sorry! I'm sorry!"

Syndicate stood in front of Dynamite backed up against the

kitchen wall. "Aw naw fuck that! Don't be sorry now!" Using both his hands Syndicate reached around and popped Dynamite hard across each one of her ass cheeks. Leaving two big red handprints on the back of her sexy white ass.

"Oh, no that's not fair Syndicate. I only hit you once." Dynamite stood with her back against the kitchen wall, laughing and rubbing her hands fast across her ass. Trying to take the sting away from Syndicate spanking her.

"Cry me a river girl. Life isn't fair. I'm goin' to teach you about fuckin' with me." Syndicate stood arrogantly in front of Dynamite with his hands on his hips and his dick swinging freely.

"Boy shut up! I'll play with you whenever and wherever I want to." Dynamite stood boldly in front of Syndicate and play fully slapped him in the face daring him to slapped her back.

Syndicate laughed lighthearted and smiled. "You lil' white bitch."

Dynamite looking like a playboy centerfold smiled back at Syndicate. "Yeah that's right and you love this lil' white bitch, don't you nigga?"

"I wouldn't be here if I didn't love you Dynamite." Unable to resist the devil's temptation standing in front of him any longer. Syndicate scooped Dynamite up off her feet in one fast motion and carried her over to the big heart shape bed. Where they made love continuously until the break of dawn.

On their flight home, Syndicate sat next to Dynamite with a worried look on his face. Not wanting to spoil the mood that she was in and not quite sure how to tell her what was on his mind.

Picking up on Syndicate's uneasiness, Dynamite squeezed his hand and smiled. "What's wrong daddy? Why are you so quiet?"

Syndicate, thinking quickly inside his own mind, shifted gears and smiled happily. "Ain't nothin' wrong. I was just thinkin' about the surprise I got waitin' for you when we get home."

Hearing the word surprise, Dynamite became instantly excited. "A surprise, what kind of surprise."

Choosing his words carefully, Syndicate exhaled. "I have someone that I want you to meet."

Dynamite's pretty face turned into an ugly face. "That's the surprise? You have someone you want me to meet. What's up with that? Who the fuck is it, Janet Jackson or somebody?"

Syndicate let out a little chuckle in spite of himself. "Close! But no. I found that special someone that we been searchin' for to compliment us and make us more complete."

Irritated that Syndicate would even think about another woman on their honeymoon no less, snatched her hand away from his. "Damn, I guess my pussy wasn't good enough for you. Here we are still on our honeymoon and already you trying to bring another bitch into our bedroom."

Syndicate, feeling like the cat that ate the canary, tried to wiggle his way out of a tight spot. "Hold on a minute baby girl and pump your brakes. This isn't just about me. It's about us, and who we are as a couple. We been talkin' about this day for years. But if for whatever reason you don' had a change of heart, all you have to do is say the word and I'll make her go away." Syndicate held his breath hoping like hell Dynamite didn't have a change of heart.

"My heart is still the same, I just didn't expect you to bring it up on our honeymoon that's all." Dynamite pouted.

Syndicate, thankful to the game god that Dynamite didn't have a change of heart. And not wanting to hurt his wife, started talking fast. "It's no hurry at all baby girl. It's just a meet and greet to see if there's any chemistry between the two of you. If it isn't then she's out of our lives as simple as that."

Dynamite, fully over the shock, wanted details. "It better not be some bitch you don' already fucked."

Back in control Syndicate relaxed. "Come on girl, I wouldn't disrespect you like that. If she doesn't mean anything to you then she doesn't mean shit to me either."

Dynamite's green eyes turned murderous. "If she isn't a part of me and fucks my husband, then she's a dead bitch."

Syndicate, well aware of Dynamite's temper, didn't want things to get out of his control. "Trust me Dynamite it's all good. If she wasn't worth it then I wouldn't be tryin' to bring her to our table."

Dynamite gave Syndicate a bi-curious look. "What's her

name?"

Syndicate smiled gratefully glad to see that Dynamite was back to keeping it gangsta. "Sugga. Her name is Sugga. Short for Brown Sugga.

Chapter 42

Two Dimes

Dynamite had a big frown on her face as she sat next to Syndicate inside the bar at the Marriott, sipping on some Remy, and waiting on Sugga to arrive. "Who in the fuck this bitch thank she is the Queen B or some fuckin' body? She got me fucked up, sittin' up in here like I'm some punk rock bitch."

Syndicate squeezed Dynamite affectionately on her knee. "Girl kick back and chill out. Trust me, it's all good I promise you."

Dynamite slammed her shot of Remy down her throat and slammed her shot glass down on the table. "I'm givin' this punk bitch five more minutes then we out. And I wouldn't give a fuck if you turned into Perry Mason's punk ass, you still wouldn't be able to defend this bitch to me. She got us sittin' here lookin' like a couple of desperate horny ass swingers."

Sugga stepped inside the hotel bar looking like 'Seduction the Sex Goddess' in her black Prada strapless dress, hugging tightly to her sensual curves, and luscious body. The patrons in the crowded bar both male and female stop doing what they were doing and took notice of the stunning black woman. Holding her little chic handbag in her hand, Sugga spotted Syndicate and Dynamite in a corner table.

A smiling Sugga walked towards them as Tony, Tone Toni's "It Never Rains In Southern California" played on the juke box. Seeing Sugga, Syndicate's face brightens as he stood up and waved her over. Dynamite grudgingly admired Sugga from a distance admitting only to herself that Sugga was a bad bitch,

"I'm sorry that I'm late, the city's traffic is horrendous this time of the day." Sugga smiled apologetically as she gave Syndicate a big friendly hug.

"Don't trip off nothin' Sugga. It's all good," Syndicate assured Sugga while holding onto her hand facing Dynamite. "Say baby, this is Sugga. Sugga this is my wife Dynamite." Syndicate, feeling the tension between the two beautiful women prayed to the game god to work out the details.

"Glad to finally get the chance to meet you Dynamite." Sugga smiled showing off her perfect white teeth and looking into Dynamite's curious green eyes. Sugga admired the glow coming from the pretty white girl dressed in the low-cut Marisa Kenson sundress, with black heels showing off her well-toned, tanned legs.

Sugga expecting a hard core looking gangsta bitch. Wasn't prepared for this sweet, innocent looking young woman sitting in front of her. "The pleasure is all mine." Dynamite, still not trusting Sugga, answered defensively with a half smile and a noticeable attitude.

Syndicate smiled at the two women trying to lighten up the mood. Poured some Remy into each of their glasses. "Alright then! Now that we're all acquainted, let's have us a little toast. To us, may there always be one."

"To us." Dynamite smiled self-assured looking straight into Syndicate's eyes. The three of them raised their shot glasses and tapped them together in acceptance of Dynamite's unspoken message. As to who had the final say in this arrangement if there was going to be one.

"So how was the honeymoon?" Inquired Sugga, breaking the silence as Syndicate refilled there shot glasses.

Dynamite smiled. Remembering their honeymoon and allowing her to temporary forget any animosity that she may have felt towards Sugga only moments ago. "Oh, it was fantastic we had a great time. Hawaii is so beautiful. Have you ever been Sugga?"

Sugga smiled gracefully at Dynamite. "No not yet unfortunately. I have made it one of my goals to visit there one of these days."

"Oh, my god Sugga, Hawaii is so beautiful! You really need to go and see it for yourself. We stayed at this fancy hotel called the Kaanapali. My father reserved the honeymoon penthouse suite as our wedding gift. Our room was so fuckin' big. It felt like we were celebrities! We even had our own fuckin' Jacuzzi. Everyone was so friendly and the Luau's were great! The beaches and the water were breath taking. Everything was just so peaceful and serene. The whole experience was just so exotic like a dream come true." Dynamite described anxiously.

"It all sounds so wonderful. I feel like I was on your honeymoon with you." Sugga reached over and touched Dynamite gently on the hand.

Syndicate, noticing the change in the atmosphere, was happy to see that the game god was working out the details. "All well shit. We goin' to have to do somethin' about that now, aren't we Dynamite? We can't be having Sugga missing out on all the fun."

Dynamite, starting to take a new interest in Sugga, gave her a warm smile. "Yeah Sugga, Syndicate is right. We do need to get you down to Hawaii, so that you can see how beautiful it is."

Sugga returned Dynamite's warm smile with one of her own. "I'll be looking forward to it."

"So Sugga tell me, how does it feel to be a doctor?" Dynamite asked with a genuine interest in the beautiful woman sitting across from her.

Sugga let out a small laugh. "Let's not get ahead of ourselves Dynamite. I just recently started my Internship at San Francisco General. So as of right now, I'm really not allowed to do anything except to observe and assist."

Dynamite smiling face turned into an ugly frowned. "That doesn't sound like any fun to me."

Sugga smiled sweetly at Dynamite. "This is what I went to school for. Being an intern is all part of the big picture. I didn't want to become a doctor so that I could have fun. I wanted to become a doctor so that I could help people." Sugga pointed a finger at Dynamite and laughed. "You just wait and see all the bullshit you're going to have to go through after you graduate."

"A lawyer fresh out of college and starting off with a new law firm, is treated a lot worse than an intern, and for a longer period of time, I might add. So, before you pass judgment on me sweetie, let's wait and see how much fun you'll be having to doing all the research and field work. Especially, while your law firm and its partner's pockets get fat off of all your hard labor." Sugga smiled affectionately at Dynamite at the same time Syndicate refilled the two ladies shot glasses.

"Shit you got me twisted Sugga I ain't working for no goddamn body. Me and my girl, Star, are going to start our own law firm. I'm the only boss that I'm ever going to answer to."

Sugga clapped her hands approvingly. "A very independent

woman, we need more women like you Dynamite." Dynamite and Sugga clapped their shot glasses together in a united womanhood moment. Followed by uncontrollable laughter.

Being the only man at the table, Syndicate felt it his duty to stand up for the real niggas of the world. "You know I'm all for this independent woman movement that the two of you are representing, but there's limits on this shit you know. I wouldn't give a fuck how bossy you get Dynamite. I'll always be that nigga you answer to."

Dynamite wrapped her arms around Syndicate. "Don't ever get it twisted daddy. Without you, there wouldn't be a me. You will always and forever be the boss of me."

"Wow Syndicate I didn't realize that you were such a big baby." Sugga teased.

Syndicate stared into Sugga's gray Siamese cat eyes. "If you plan on stickin' around you better get used to it."

"Damn daddy. Lighten up some, boss. Sugga was just teasing you." Dynamite slapped Syndicate playfully on his leg.

Sugga took a sip of her Remy. "Yeah lighten up some, boss I was only teasing," Sugga gave Syndicate a disarming smile. "I didn't mean to strike a nerve."

Syndicate, satisfied that his point had been made, thanked the game god for allowing Dynamite and Sugga to like each other. "It's nothin' Sugga I don't trip on small shit. I'm just glad to see that you and Dynamite are getting comfortable with one another.

Sugga smiled at Dynamite. "I would also like for us to be friends Dynamite. That is if you don't have any problems with it?

Dynamite sat next to Syndicate watching Sugga closely and raised her shot glass in the air. "We're more than friends Sugga, we're family." Sugga, fully aware of the code of the streets that the two gangstas live by, tapped her shot glass with Dynamite's.

Syndicate smiled approvingly at the two beautiful, sexy, woman in his life. "Welcome to the family Sugga."

CHAPTER 43

Money And The Power

Summer 1994 7 years later

Saturday afternoon

Syndicate lounged inside his new seven-bedroom million-dollar home with Sugga; watching the volleyball game between Stanford and U.O.P. on their big 52-inch screen television. "Are you comin' with me and Dynamite to Poppa Fly's welcome home party?"

Sugga leaned forward and set her Garfield coffee mug down on top of the Crystal glass coffee table. "Why you would even ask me a stupid question like that Syndicate? You already know how I feel about you and Dynamite's criminal behavior."

Sugga dressed comfortably in her black sweatpants and red T-shirt leaned back on the sofa and tucked her feet underneath her. Enjoying her day off from St. Joesph's Hospital.

Syndicate dressed in a pair of black baggy Fubu jeans, a

crispy white T-shirt and a pair of black and white Adidas. Jumped up off the sofa excitedly and started pacing the floor. His 14k 3" solid gold rope and diamond 'Syndicate' medallion swung freely around his neck.

"Damn I can't believe this shit. My nigga Poppa Fly is on his way home right now as we speak. Gail put the smash down on the D.A. Winning his appeal based on the fact that the police didn't read him his Miranda rights when they arrested him. It's been 8 long years that Poppa Fly been locked up." Syndicate checked the time on his new Presidential Rolex watch that Dynamite and Sugga had recently bought for him. "Where the fuck is Young Tre at? That lil' nigga should have been got at me." Syndicate pulled out his cell phone and dialed Young Tre's number.

"Syndicate what's up blood!" Young Tre yelled into his cell phone while riding in his new black 5.0 Mustang along with Ray and Los, smoking on a blunt, and sipping on some Hennessy.

Syndicate playfully pulled on Sugga's pretty little, glossy painted, French tipped toes. While he held his cell phone up to his ear. "What's up wit Ty Bud and them Oak Park niggas? Did they drop off that 70G's like they were supposed, to?"

Sugga, fully engrossed in the volleyball game, slapped Syndicate's hand. "Stop pulling on my toes."

Young Tre, proud to be the number one hustler in the family, leaned back in his Mustang and puffed on his blunt. "You know Ty

Bud and them Sacramento niggas always keep it gangsta, I dropped them off 5 more. I got a buck fifty for you whenever you ready."

Syndicate stood looking out of his window admiring his cars. A brand new black Escalade, a cocaine white Mercedes Benz, a two-seat black Jag, and a candy apple red customized Porsche. "Bring it on by the house when you can and drop it off. If I'm not here leave it with Sugga."

"So, what time is the homie supposed to touch down?" Young Tre asked, anxious to see Poppa Fly again after so many years.

"I don't know. They had the homie way down by the Arizona border in Cincinnal. It took G Gunna, Whip, and Low about nine hours to get down there yesterday. They hit me about 10 o'clock this morning and said they should be here about 8 o'clock tonight. It's about 4 right now, so they should be here in a few hours."

Young Tre, feeling like a million dollars riding around with his family, spotted a little cutie pie that he's been trying to catch up with speed by in her green Camry. "Say Syndicate, let me holla at you later blood. This lil' breezy, that's been on my radar, just shot pass me."

Syndicate laughed out loud thinking how proud Big Time would have been of Young Tre. "Don't let a piece of pussy keep you away from the homie's comin' home party tonight lil' nigga."

Young Tre riding low in his Mustang followed behind the

cutie pie in the green Camry. "Never that Syndicate. You got me mixed up with that trick ass nigga Mook. It's money over bitches on mine."

Syndicate pulled on Sugga's big toe. "Just make sure it stays that way. One love Young Tre. I'll catch up with you later," Syndicate hung up his cell phone. "Here comes your girlfriend." Syndicate laughed at Sugga.

Sugga sat up on her knees on the sofa and looked out the window to see Dynamite driving up. "Don't be jealous."

Hair blowing in the wind and a pair of black Ray Ban sunglasses covering her green eyes. Dynamite pulled up in the driveway looking like a superstar with the top down in her black BMW, wearing a tight-fitting pair of designer jeans, black leather boots, and black tank top tuck in at the waist showing off her well-shaped, athletic-looking body.

Syndicate held the door open for Dynamite, blocking her path. "Shit never that Sugga, I wouldn't have it any other way."

Dynamite walked up to Syndicate and kissed him on the cheek. "Why you standing there blocking the door looking all silly?"

Sugga smiled at Dynamite who sat down next to her on the sofa. "He's just being stupid as usual."

Dynamite sat her keys down on the Crystal coffee table. "Who's winning the game."

Sugga gave Dynamite a disgusted look. "U.O.P. won the

first match, if you could believe that."

Dynamite smiled proudly. "That's right U.O.P. Whoop Stanford's ass."

Syndicate flopped himself down on the love seat with one leg on the floor and the other one resting comfortably over the side. "So, what's up with moms? Is she comin' to Poppa Fly's comin' home party?

Dynamite smiled to herself remembering the conversation she had with her mother. "I'm afraid she's not going to be able to make it. She said the last thing she needed was to get caught up in a raid hanging out with a bunch of criminals."

"My nigga Poppa Fly is going to be disappointed. Gail is his M.V.P. Without her, he would've probably be on death row."

Sugga, disgusted by Syndicate's arrogance and also his ignorance, angrily pressed the off button on the remote control turning off the television. "Well, if he feels that strongly about it Syndicate. Maybe he should just take her out to lunch at a nice restaurant like a normal person would do, to show their appreciation. Instead of parading her around in front of a bunch of gangsta's like she was his trophy."

Syndicate sat up straight. "Come on now Sugga, you puttin' way too much on it. All my nigga tryin' to do is show his love for Gail for helping him wiggle out of a bad situation."

Dynamite playfully hit Sugga with one of the small pillows

sitting on the sofa. "Damn Sugga, you know that I love you. But I'll be so fuckin' glad when you get over this square ass shit. Quit being so naive and wake your game up. Ain't no body thinking no dumb shit like that but you. Everyone in the family knows that mom is family. Besides being normal is for suckas."

Sugga playfully hit Dynamite back with the pillow. "For someone who claims to be so sharp, you really are slow Dynamite. It's the suckas that's doing all the hard time not the squares. So, I'm sorry sweetie, but I'm afraid that you have things a little twisted as usual." Sugga leaned back on the sofa and smiled confident that she had made her point.

"Hmm, a square ass bitch like you would believe some weak shit like that. But just for the record sweetie, the only reason why most real niggas is locked up is because some so-called normal square ass bitch like yourself, snitched them off." Dynamite smiled back at Sugga knowing from experience that her good friend and lover wouldn't let it go that easy.

"I honestly didn't know what game goofy was until I met you Dynamite. The only way a square bitch like me could ever snitch on a so-called real bitch like you, is if her dumb ass stayed true to formed. And committed her crime in front of me." Sugga laughed kindheartedly.

"Is that so? Well thanks for the warning square. The next time I commit a felony, I'll make sure there aren't any suckas like you around." Dynamite laughed out loud at the same time throwing one of the small pillows at Sugga.

Syndicate stood in front of Dynamite and Sugga. Y'all need to save all that foreplay for later, right now I need to make some boss moves. So what's up Dynamite, you want to bend some corners with me in the Beamer? Or are you going to stay here and play with your girlfriend."

Dynamite picked her keys up off the coffee table and laughed. "Boss moves my ass nigga. All you want to do is get your drink on and use me as your chauffeur."

"Girl quit talkin' shit and let's bounce. I want to go and side on these niggas before we hit the club tonight."

Dynamite stood in front of the door with her keys in her hand. "Are you sure that you don't want to go to the club with us tonight Sugga?"

Sugga picked up a novel by Mya Angelo from off the coffee table. "Yes, I'm sure. You two gangstas go ahead and have your little gangsta party. I'm going to stay right here at home where it's safe with my feet tucked under me and read my little square ass book."

Dynamite stared lustfully at her exotic-looking girlfriend. "Well, if you change your mind later on tonight, just give me a ring, and I'll come back for you."

Sugga waved her hand shooing Dynamite out the door. "Don't you be worrying about me girlfriend. I promise you that I won't be changing my mind anytime soon."

CHAPTER 44

Ain't No Shame In The Game

Syndicate leaned back in the passenger seat of Dynamite's BMW, smoking on a sherm soaked Newport as they cruised through the neighborhood with the top down. "This is the best part of the summer, when the sun is going down, and it's a nice lil' breeze out. This is what that nigga Fresh Prince was talkin' about in his song."

"Yeah it was over 100 degrees earlier. It's still hot, but I see you're not the only one who's feeling the summer buzz. Look at all these niggas hanging out on the block." Dynamite laughed as she drove down Phelp's on her way to up to Cutie Pie Park. "Everybody and their mama is out here tryin' to cool off."

Dynamite pulled into the little cul-de-sac parking lot, full of illegally parked cars, and blasting music. Criminal activity was taken for granted while socializing couples and friends lounged around on blankets, underneath the shade trees in the small park.

Dynamite parked her car next to Dmove's black Lexus. "There goes that lil' bad ass girl again, dancing for them old ass niggas like she's a stripper." Dynamite looked with disgust at the pretty young girl rubbing up against two grown men in a small corner of the park.

"Them niggas need to be shot getting off on a lil' girl like that." Syndicate glared angrily at the two young men as he stepped out of the Beamer.

"All shit! Niggas better watch out! You know what they say? When the sun goes down, gangstas come out to play." Dmove laughed. High, off the weed, enjoying the summer buzz along with Mook.

"What you niggas up to?" Dynamite asked.

"We just hangin' tough. Waiting on the homie Poppa Fly to touch down, so we can do it big, feel me? What y'all up to?" Mook took a sip of his Hennessy."

Syndicate picked up one of the little plastic cups sitting on top of Dmove's Lexus. "We ain't doin' shit, just bendin' some corners. We waiting on the homie Poppa Fly to touch down, too. Let me get a shot of Hennessy blood."

Dmove poured Syndicate a shot of Hennessy. "You want a shot Dynamite?"

Dynamite leaned back against Dmove's Lexus observing her

surroundings. "Naw I'm cool Dmove. I got to keep my head tight in case things get rowdy tonight."

"Say blood, who's lil' girl is that over there rubbing up against them niggas?" Syndicate nodded towards the young girl with the long curly hair, dancing provocative in front of the two young men. Dmove looked at Syndicate accusingly. "Nigga don't play dumb. You know good and goddamn well who her father is."

"What the fuck you talkin' about nigga? How in the fuck am I supposed to know who her father is?" Syndicate shouted defensively.

"Blood! All I'm sayin is open your goddamn eyes a little bit and take a real good look at her." All eyes turned to the young girl.

Syndicate was momentarily shocked to see how much the little girl resembled him. "So, what's that supposed to mean nigga? All black people look alike?"

Dmove, still believing that Syndicate knew that he was the father and just not claiming the little girl, started laughing. "Blood save that, we all look alike shit for them white folks the next time you in a police lineup. I don't look like none of you ugly ass niggas. Syndicate don't tell me you didn't know that Kat was her mother."

Syndicate took a deep breath trying to get his thoughts together. "Blood I haven't talked to that bitch Kat since the 9th grade. The last thing I'm tryin' to know is who in the fuck her kids are."

Dynamite, famous for picking up on game fast, had a strong urge to kill Kat. "I always thought that lil' girl looked like you daddy and now I know why.

Syndicate nervously begin calculating in his head how many years it's been since he had sex with Kat. "Hey y'all need to slow y'all row for a minute and stop jumpin' to conclusions. For one we don't even know how old the little girl is. And two, it was a lot of niggas running' up in Kat back then, just like it is now."

Mook laughed out loud and poured himself another shot of Hennessy. "Yeah that bitch has 3 different kids by 3 different niggas. Ain't no tellin' who that lil' girl's father is."

Fuming with the thoughts of Kat keeping Syndicate's baby girl away from him, Dynamite exploded. "It ain't no goddamn secret that Kat is a sorry ass hoe and a punk rock bitch. But it's only one way to get to the bottom of this." Dynamite stormed off towards the young girl dancing with Syndicate close behind.

Dynamite walked up to the young girl dancing with the two young men and snatched her roughly by the arm. "Damn Dynamite what's up gangsta?" Said G.Man, a dark skinned young man known for his shady dealings.

"Nigga shut the fuck up if you want to keep breathin' and that goes for the rest of you niggas too." Syndicate spoke to the small crowd of people gathering around to see some action.

"Let go of me! What's wrong with you?" The young girl

shouted. As she tried to pull away from Dynamite.

"Do you know who I am?" Dynamite shouted in the young girl's face.

"Everybody knows who you are. You're Dynamite and that's Syndicate. So, what!" The young girl said in defiance and wanting to show Dynamite how tough she is.

Syndicate, feeling up with emotions that he never felt before at the possibility that this young girl might be his daughter, asked the question. "What's your name little girl?"

"Sunshine. And just because I'm young doesn't mean that I'm a little girl, so stop calling me one." Sunshine said starting to feel a little uneasiness as to why the neighborhood's two most famous gangsta's were taking an interest in her.

"You're absolutely right Sunshine. You're not a little girl. You're still a baby. So, tell us how old you are?" Dynamite added the fact that Kat was a sorry ass mother for another reason to kill her.

"I'm almost 13-years-old." Sunshine stood in front of Dynamite showing off her fast growing, well developing young red boned body. Looking and sounding a lot older than 13-years-old, dressed in her hoochie mama cutoff jeans, cut off black T-shirt, and a pair of black sandals. Her long curly brown hair bounced off her shoulders.

Syndicate looked thoughtfully at the young girl. "Ain't that a bitch. You're out here running' around wild like this and you're not even 13-years-old yet?" Syndicate looked over at Dynamite who was already doing the math in her head.

"Where is your mama?" Dynamite asked impatiently, ready to confront Kool Kat.

"My mama? I don't know, but probably at home. Why you askin?" Sunshine still confused by the sudden interest of the two gangsta's. Looked wearily in Dynamite's direction.

Dynamite walked the short distance to her Beamer and held the door open for Sunshine. "That's my business. Now get your young ass in the car. We're going to have us a little talk with your mother."

Sunshine reluctantly climbed into the back of the Beamer. "My mama ain't goin' to talk to you Dynamite. She said that you was the one who killed my Uncle G.

Syndicate shook his head disappointingly, not surprised that Sunshine would know who killed her Uncle G. "You let us worry about that Sunshine."

Dynamite was full of rage as she sped down Phelp's St. on her way to the Vista Housing Projects. "Kat is a sorry ass punk bitch for not telling you Syndicate."

Syndicate noticed the weird looks they were getting from the niggas hanging out on the block. As they sped by at the same time, Sunshine started to feel a little paranoid and angry that Dynamite called her mother a bitch. "For not tellin' Syndicate what? What didn't my mama tell you?" Sunshine yelled from the back seat.

Syndicate turned around and faced Sunshine. "That I'm your father."

Sunshine, at a loss for words, looked at Syndicate distrustfully. "My father? Are you serious? What part of the game is this?"

"It's the part of the game that you find out the truth about your father and that your mama is ass punk bitch. "Dynamite whispered to herself full of hate as she pulled up in front of Kat's apartment.

"Aw hell naw! What in the fuck is my baby doing in the car with you two muthafuckas?" Kat jumped up from her seat on the front steps. Where she was smoking a joint with her boyfriend, Mad Ass Boop. "Get the fuck out of that car right fuckin' now Sunshine! That's the white bitch that killed your Uncle G. And that punk ass nigga standin' next to her is the nigga that told her to do it!" Kat yelled hysterically. As Syndicate, Dynamite, and Sunshine got out of the Beamer. Dynamite walked up to Kat like the Queen Gangsta bitch she is. "Bitch, I strongly advise you to shut the fuck up and stop spreading rumors before your sorry ass comes up missing." Dynamite turned to face Sunshine. "What your scantless ass mama didn't tell you is that someone killed your Uncle G., because his punk ass killed your Uncle Big Time."

Kat, feeling trapped and refusing to back down, prepared herself for the worst as she stepped to Dynamite. "Look whose spreading rumors now you, punk rock white bitch. And what the fuck you talkin' about Big Time is Sunshine's uncle?"

Syndicate, in his respect for the dead and not wanting to relive any painful memories, stood between the two women who were both out for revenge. "Bitch save all the drama for your mama because the joke is up. We didn't come here to talk about Big Time and G. You know exactly why we're here. So, stop playin' dumb bitch." Syndicate stared down Kat.

Sunshine stood next to Syndicate dumbfounded with the possibility that Syndicate could be her father. "So, is it true mama? Is Syndicate my father?" Sunshine prayed to the game god that it be true.

Kat, fuming, snatched Sunshine by her shirt and yelled into her face. "Who in the fuck told you that Syndicate was your father?"

Sunshine had tears in her eyes as she came to understand the truth about her family's dark past. "So, it's true then, huh mama? Syndicate is my father?"

"Yeah, it's true. He's sorry ass is your daddy.". Kat admitted grudgingly.

Sunshine relieved and angry at the same time, yelled at her mother. "Why in the fuck didn't you tell him that I was his daughter? Huh mama? Tell me why? God, I hate you!"

Kat pointed hatefully at Dynamite. "I didn't tell him because of that punk rock white bitch right there. If it wasn't for her snotty, little Ms. wanna be gangsta bitch ass, me and your daddy would still be together. So I didn't want her fake white ass to be a part of your life. That's why I didn't tell his punk ass."

Dynamite reached around Syndicate and hit Kat on the soft part of her chin knocking her to the ground. "You stupid bitch, if it wasn't for you, Sunshine wouldn't be out on the streets now doing all shit she's been doing."

Kat made it back to her feet and squared off with Dynamite. "It's on now bitch. I been waiting a long time to whoop on you."

Dynamite tossed her Ray Ban's on the ground. "I sure in the fuck can't tell bitch. I ain't hard to find."

As if on que the two-women charged towards each other. Swinging wildly Kat hit Dynamite in the face causing her to stumble backwards.

"Aw hell naw bitch. You don' fucked up now!" Dynamite grabbed a hold of Kool Kat's hair and yanked her head back and pounded her face repeatedly to a bloody mess.

Syndicate wrapped his arm around Dynamite's waist and pulled her away from Kat. "Let that punk bitch go Dynamite! That's not why we're here!"

Kat struggled to break free of Boop's hold. "It ain't over bitch. Boop let me go!" Kat yelled at her boyfriend.

"Yeah it's over with bitch. Sunshine get in the car. I'm takin' you home with me and Dynamite From now on, your goin' to live with us." Syndicate wrestled with Dynamite to get her in the car.

Kat fought desperately to break out of Boop's tight grip. "Sunshine, you better not get in that goddamn car! Syndicate you and that white bitch ain't takin' my daughter no fuckin' where!"

Syndicate with the look of a menace turned towards Boop as he closed Dynamite's door. "Boop if that punk bitch gets loose, I'm goin' to take it real personal."

Sunshine sat in the back of the Beamer with her head spinning in different directions. "What about all my clothes and stuff?"

Dynamite, still full of anger, flashed on Sunshine. "Anything that you left behind needs to be burned and that goes for that hoe wear outfit you got on now. I'm not going for any of that bullshit in my house."

CHAPTER 45

The Game Don't Stop

Sugga smiled a look of surprise to see Dynamite and Syndicate back so soon. "Damn it looks like the two of you bought out the mall." Sugga nodded towards all the shopping bags that the three of them were holding. "What happened to those boss moves you had to make and who is this pretty young girl standing here, looking like a fashion model for a designer jean commercial?

Syndicate dropped the shopping bags he was holding on the floor. "Sunshine this is Sugga. Sugga this is Sunshine, my daughter."

Hearing Syndicate say what was clear by looking at the little girl dressed in Gucci from head to toe. Sugga instantly became more attentive to the situation. "Your daughter? Oh wow!

"Yeah, that's right you heard me. Sunshine is my daughter and don't be giving me that dead beat dad look. I just found out myself a couple of hours ago.

Sugga, still not convinced that Syndicate is telling the truth, tapped the spot on the sofa next to her for Sunshine to sit down. "Come and sit down next to me baby, while your daddy and Dynamite explains what is going on."

Sunshine. feeling a little uncomfortable, not knowing the relationship between the three grown-ups, sat down wearily. "Thank you."

Sugga, fully aware of Sunshine's discomfort, put her arm around the young girl's shoulders and pulled her in close. "Thanks, isn't necessary Sunshine. We're all family here," Sugga looked at Syndicate and Dynamite. "Well?"

Dynamite poured herself a shot of Hennessy from the bar. "You remember that bitch Kat I told you about awhile back? The one who's brother killed Syndicate's brother Big Time?"

Sugga sat with her arm around Sunshine waiting patiently. "Yes, I remember. And?"

Dynamite downed her shot of Hennessy clearly upset. "Kat is Sunshine's mother. She's been keeping it a secret from Syndicate for the last 13 years."

Sugga looked thoughtfully at Syndicate and Dynamite, afraid to ask the next question, and knowing how ruthless her two lovers could be. "Wow, that's terrible! So, how did her little secret become known to the two of you?"

Dynamite smiled like a proud parent. "How we found out isn't important. What's important is that Syndicate's little girl is home where she belongs."

Sugga gave Sunshine a big friendly hug. "Wow that's great, now Syndicate and his little girl are reunited after all these years. I did notice the strong resemblance in the two of them when she walked inside the house and figured that they were related. But it never even crossed my mind that they might be father and daughter."

Syndicate and Sunshine sat outside in the backyard with their feet dangling in the swimming pool. "You have the advantage over me Sunshine. You know who I am, but I don't know anything about you." Syndicate lifted Sunshine's head up with his finger. "Things are going to be a lot different for you now Sunshine. All that running around acting all wild and shit is over. I don't want to ever see you disrespecting yourself ever again. What ever happened in the past is in the past. You got a fresh start now and a new look on life."

Sunshine smiled at Syndicate. "Is it ok if I call you daddy?"

Syndicate felt as if his heart would break in two as he heard the words. "Whatever you're comfortable with calling me is fine with me Sunshine."

Sunshine, mesmerized by her father, broke into a wide grin. "All of this is so unbelievable to me. Syndicate the biggest and baddest gangsta in the hood is really my father."

A wave of guilt shot through Syndicate at the thought of Sunshine suffering due to his selfish ambitions of being a gangsta. "None of that means shit to me Sunshine. If I could take it all back and be with you I would do it in a heartbeat."

Sunshine twisted her face up in a frown. "Fuck that square shit daddy. We ain't givin' nothin' back."

Syndicate smiled despite himself. "Hasn't anyone ever told you that little girls shouldn't talk like that?"

Sunshine's big black eyes stared confusingly at Syndicate. "I'm sorry daddy, but you talkin' about givin' all this back," Sunshine spread her arms wide indicating the enormous house. "Just doesn't make any sense to me."

Syndicate smiled at his young daughter. "It's nothin' to a giant Sunshine, you'll get used to it. In a few months, you'll be complaining about your room being too small for all your stuff."

"I doubt that very seriously daddy." Sunshine looked up to see Sugga approaching with a cell phone in her hand.

"I hate to interrupt you and Sunshine's conversation. But there's someone on your cell phone that insist on talking to you." Sugga smiled at Syndicate as she held the cell phone out to him.

"Tell whoever it is to call me back tomorrow, because right now I'm spendin' some overdue quality time with my daughter."

Sugga relayed the message to the caller on the cell phone. "It's your friend Poppa Fly on the phone. He said that if you don't get your ass on the phone right now, he's going to come over here and whoop your ass right in front of you're little girl." Sugga laughed, not use to hearing Syndicate's friends stand up to him.

"Shit I got so caught up chillin' with Sunshine that I forgot all about Poppa Fly's comin' home party." Syndicate laughed. "Give me the phone."

Sugga gave Syndicate his cell phone. "Poppa Fly what's up my nigga?"

"You! Me, and the family blood. That's what's up nigga!" Poppa Fly yelled while sitting inside the Notorious Elk's club famous for its gang violence and numerous murders. Along with his girlfriend Shy and the rest of the syndicate family.

Syndicate, hearing the loud music playing in the background over the phone, checked his Rolex Watch. "My bad blood for not being there with you to help you celebrate your freedom, but I'm sure that you heard by now that I just found out that I have a little girl?"

Poppa Fly's heart went out to his old friend. "Yeah, the family already put me up on game. That bitch, Kat, is a cold hoe for keeping your little girl away from you."

Syndicate fought to contain his anger as he looked over at Sunshine. "Yeah, blood this shit here is crazy. That punk bitch. Kat is way out of pocket. She's lucky I don't just blow her fuckin' brains out."

Poppa Fly's girlfriend, Shy sat on his lap as he sipped on his drink. "I feel your pain my nigga. She's with her daddy now, so don't even trip, it's all good. So, go ahead and put her young ass to sleep and come kick it with your folks. I Haven't seen you niggas since my trial ended."

Syndicate's toned turned serious. "Not comin' to see you was your choice."

Poppa Fly finished his drink before responding. "Don't take it for more than it's worth Syndicate. I appreciate everything that you and Dynamite did for me and my family while I was gone. And it's still my choice for you and Dynamite never to have to see the inside of a prison. Fuck all that square ass shit though nigga. I'm out now. So, give your lil' girl some milk and cookies. tuck her young ass in bed and come holla at your folks! The Elk's is crackin' blood!"

Syndicate smiled over at Sunshine. "Blood Sunshine isn't your average little girl. The last thing she's tryin' to do right now is go to sleep. So, I'm just going to have to catch up with you in the morning. Besides I'm lounging in short pants with my feet dangling in the swimming' pool."

"You and Dynamite go ahead and go out with your friends. Don't worry about Sunshine she'll be here when you get back." Syndicate looked up at Sugga, who was leaning down over his back with her arm wrapped around his neck.

Syndicate stood up from where he was sitting. "Let me get

back at you in a minute Poppa Fly. I got your number locked in my phone."

"Nigga save all that call me back shit for them suckas. Having money don' turned you soft nigga. If you and Dynamite not down here in the next 30 minutes. I'm bringing the whole Elk's club to your front door! Crips and all!" Poppa Fly yelled into his phone.

Syndicate gave Sugga back his cell phone. "Let me holla at Sunshine for a minute Sugga."

Sunshine, wise beyond her years, stood next to Syndicate. "It's ok daddy. I know that you have to go. I might be young, but I'm not new to the game. I heard of your friend Poppa Fly and how he killed someone for calling you D.Dogg after you told him not to call you by that name anymore."

Syndicate shook his head and laughed. Impressed as well as curious as to how this little girl knew so much about him. "First thing that you need to know is that all I have to do is stay black and die. Everything else is optional," Syndicate tousled Sunshine's hair. "And where in the world are you getting all this information about me?"

Sunshine smiled proudly at her father. "Like you just said daddy, I'm not your average little girl. I come from the South side of town just like you and I pay close attention to my surroundings. Speaking of which, when are you going to tell me who Sugga is?"

Syndicate roared in laughter. "Aw shit! Just what we needed

another Winky."

"Winky? I know who Winky is." Sunshine bragged.

Syndicate smiled at his young daughter. Not surprised that she knew who Winky was. "Is that right? Well, I'll bet you a $100.00 to a box of dunkin doughnuts that you didn't know that she was your grandmother.

Sunshine stood in shock with the news that the infamous Winky is her grandmother. "Winky is my grandmother? Damn that's deep!"

Syndicate laughed out loud. "I thought that would get your attention. And as far as Sugga goes," Syndicate looked up to the night sky as if in deep thought. "Me, Dynamite, and Sugga are all in a relationship together. We all share the same bed. And that's all you need to know for now."

Sunshine smiled as she took hold of Syndicate's hand. "Damn daddy I knew that you were a gangsta. But I had no idea that you were a big ole pimp, too." Syndicate and Sunshine shared a good laugh as they walked hand in hand into the house.

CHAPTER 46

Gangstas Make The World Go Round

Friends, foe and family alike, danced to the underground music blasting out of the gigantic 20" speakers. Out on the miniature dance floor, young women in short skirts and tight jeans were shaking their asses and popping their pussy with no shame.

While the niggas who were dancing with them threw up gang signs high in the air. Boss playas mingled at the bar chopping up boss game while they hollered at the ladies passing by. While the gangsta's chilled at their tables getting their drink on.

A very drunk Poppa Fly sat at one of the four small tables, inside the jam-packed Elk's club that the syndicate family had rearranged into one big table, so that they could all be seated together.

"Blood I'm missing Big Time a lot more now that I'm out, than I did when I was locked up."

"Wait until you see his son Lil' Big Time. That nigga is the spittin' image of his Father. I need to call Jazzy and tell her to bring him over so he can spend some time with his cousin." Syndicate, highly intoxicated and feeling Big Time's absence, put his arm around Poppa Fly.

"Big Time is still with us nigga. When you see me, you see Big Time as long as I'm breathing his memory will live through me." G Gunna, high off sherm and liquor, sat across from Syndicate and Poppa Fly.

"I'm with you on that one family. Big Time's memory won't ever die, my nigga is always right her with us." Poppa Fly, stood up and raised his glass to the sky. "To my nigga Big Time severely missed, but never forgotten," Poppa Fly swallowed his shot of Hennessy in one big gulp and sat back down. "I would spend the rest of my life in the pen if I could just see my boy one more time and tell him from the cradle to the casket, the game don't stop.

Dynamite, sitting next to Syndicate, smiled at Poppa Fly. "I think that you need to slow down on all that drinking your doin' Poppa Fly. You're so drunk, if you haven't already sexed up Shy like you should have, you might not be able to get it up later." Dynamite teased. As the rest of the syndicate family laughed unmercifully at Poppa Fly obvious embarrassment.

Poppa Fly raised his middle finger at Dynamite and gave her a very unpleasant stare. "Fuck you Dynamite and why you worried about my dick. The only dick you should be worried about is that nigga sitting next to you."

Dynamite covered her mouth mockingly. "Oh, poor baby, did I embarrass you Poppa Fly. I'm sorry I didn't mean to hurt the big baby's feelings." Dynamite laughed at the same time she reached over and patted Poppa Fly on the side of his face.

Syndicate, glad to have Poppa Fly back, joined in on the teasing. "Damn Poppa Fly! Most niggas I know come home out the pen harder than they were when they went in. It looks like the pen had the opposite effect on you."

Poppa Fly, not used to being disrespected without repercussions, stood up and started unbuttoning his pants. "You niggas got me fucked up. Here you niggas so worried about my dick you must want to see the muthafucka."

Dmove, puffing on his blunt exhaled the Endo smoke. "Blood you need to sit your drunk ass down. Ain't none of us tryin' to see your dick nigga."

Shy, sitting next to Poppa Fly and laughing her ass off, pulled Poppa Fly by the arm. "Poppa Fly you better not pull your dick out. They were just playing with you."

Being away for 8 long years Poppa Fly was uncomfortable with having his family make fun of him. "You niggas must of forgot I ain't no muthafuckin' joke on the streets or in the pen. You niggas can't just be talkin' to me any kind of way."

Young Tre recognizing Poppa Fly's discomfort reached in his pocket and pulled out a big fat wad of $100.00 dollar bills. "Here nigga. This is for you blood," Young Tre tossed the wad of $100.00 dollar bills over to Poppa Fly. "You not in the pen no more, big homie. We all family here, so you don't have to prove your manhood to us. Everybody sitting around this table already know that you ain't no muthafuckin' joke. We just happy to have you back out here with us. So, chill the fuck out and get used to livin' again. This is us blood." Young Tre looked in both directions acknowledging the rest of the syndicate family sitting around the table.

Poppa Fly held the wad of money out in front of him and nodded his head respectfully at Young Tre. "I see that you not that little boy who was looking for protection when I left. I didn't think that you had it in you like that Young Tre. Big Time would have been proud of you."

Young Tre broke out in a wide grin. Glad to have earned Poppa Fly's respect. "It's all a part of growing up big homie. It's all a part of growing up."

"So, Syndicate now that you're a daddy, are you going to change your evil ways?" Shy laughed. Glad that the tension around the table has eased up.

Syndicate sipped on his Hennessy enjoying the night out with his family. "Yeah, I was thinking about getting a job at the post office and becoming a mail man. At least that way I would always have paper." Syndicate laughed loudly amused by his own joke.

Los sitting at the other end of the table drunk and smoking weed heavily. Yelled out to Syndicate. "Nigga don't tell me you gonna start workin' for the Feds?"

Syndicate fought to contain his temper. Not liking the fact that everyone was now laughing, because the joke was on him. "Nigga if you ever see me working for the Feds, Popeye is a punk." Syndicate, feeling vindicated, joined in on the laughing.

Dynamite, ruthless as ever, wasn't ready to let it go that easy. "You better watch what you say daddy before someone gets the wrong idea. Everyone knows that Popeye wasn't shit without his spinach. Bluto used to beat the shit out of him everyday. Not only that. He was a sucka for a little skinny white bitch. So, I don't think it's wise for you to compare yourself to Popeye."

Listening to everybody's laughing from Dynamite's teasing and high off the sherm and alcohol. Syndicate's level of rage jumped instantly from 1 all the way to 10. "Check this out bitch and this goes for the rest of you niggas too. I don't eat no goddamn spinach and I don't fight niggas, I smoke'em," Syndicate turned towards Dynamite and gave her a frightening look. "And the only bitch I could ever be accused of being a sucka for is you. And who also better know that I will chop her muthafuckin' head off if she ever mistakes me for one."

The table grew silent realizing that Syndicate wasn't playing with his wife. Dynamite also noticing that Syndicate was in a dark space, inhaled and chose her words carefully. "I was only playing with you Syndicate. I wouldn't ever intentionally disrespect you."

Shy, seizing the moment to break the silence surrounding the table, jumped up from her seat and grabbed Syndicate by his arm. As Easy E's "Boyz in the Hood" blasted over the speakers. "Come and dance with me Syndicate, they jammin'. and Poppa Fly is too drunk. He can barely stand up."

Syndicate looked around the club watching as everyone made a mad dash for the small dance floor. "It's not polite to turn down a lady when she asks you to dance." Dynamite smiled playfully at Syndicate who hesitated to get up.

Syndicate eyed Dynamite carefully. "I never said that I was polite. Come on Shy. I'll dance with you." Reluctantly, Syndicate stood up and walked with Shy through the crowded club over to the small dance floor.

"If this nigga bumps into me one more time without sayin' excuse me, I'm going to have his head." Syndicate growled at Shy at the same time he mean mugged the young man dancing next to them.

Shy smiled at Syndicate trying to defuse the situation before it turned ugly. "This little dance floor is crowded as hell Syndicate. I don't think he's doing it on purpose."

Syndicate looked over at the young man dancing next to him.

"I wouldn't give a fuck how crowded it is in this bitch. Niggas better start rep respecting a nigga up in this muthafucka."

The young man frowned back at Syndicate. "You talkin' to me?"

Syndicate squared off with the other young man. "You the only muthafucka up in here that's bumpin' into a nigga." Syndicate challenged. As seven more of the young man's friends gathered around.

"Nigga I don't know who in the fuck you supposed to be. But you got me fucked up ole country ass nigga. I ain't one of these Valley niggas that respects you. Nigga I'm Leland fool and this the Bay, South Richmond Gangstas in the house tonight." Leland stood fearlessly toe to toe with Syndicate. As mob homies out on the dance floor gathered around Syndicate ready for whatever.

"Blood is that Syndicate over there trippin' with those out of town niggas?" G Gunna stood up from the back of the club to try and get a better look.

"What the fuck!" Poppa Fly yelled before jumping on top of the tables and running towards Syndicate as if he hasn't had a drink all night. The rest of the syndicate family following close behind pushed and shoved their way through the crowded club to make it over to Syndicate.

Syndicate caught a glimpse of Poppa Fly charging across the tables like a big wild Gorilla. "Nigga fuck what you talkin' about and fuck South Richmond. I'm Syndicate nigga and this is the syndicate's house." Syndicate reacting swiftly grabbed a half empty 5th of gin bottle from off a nearby table and smashed it across Leland's forehead knocking him down to one knee.

Poppa Fly leaped off the table kicking one of the South Richmond Gangstas in the face sending him flying into the arms of Mac Twain. Ready for whatever, Mac Twain picked up the South Richmond Gangsta and slammed him down to the ground.

Chip and Arlo, standing on point next to Mac Twain, repeatedly kicked the South Richmond Gangsta down on the floor as a riot erupted inside the small club.

Innocent bystanders and gangstas not directly involved in the riot scrambled around the rioters towards the exit trying to make it out the club without becoming a victim. Leland, back on his feet and going toe to toe with Syndicate, exchanging hard blows to the head and face. At the same time the East Side Crips always out for blood against their rivals joined forces with the South Richmond Gangstas.

Low, up for the challenge, knocked out two crips that foolishly ran up on him. Dmove, Mook and Young Tre stood in a fierce battle against four South Richmond Gangstas and two crips. Worthy, Los, Ray, and Under, noticing the disadvantage that Dmove, Mook, and Young Tre we're up against, made their way through the riot to help their three friends. G Gunna, feeling it his personal responsibility to protect Syndicate, jumped in the fight against Leland who was putting up a valiant effort against the two killers.

Whip, not interested in fighting, opened fired with his 44 Cal. shooting a South Richmond Gangsta in his left shoulder spinning him around and knocking him off his feet. Screams could be heard throughout the club while bullets with no names attached to them shot out in search of any would be targets. Gangstas from all sides scrambled their way outside as the riot inside the club quickly escalated into a gun fight outside the club.

Dynamite and Poppa Fly stood side by side outside the club exchanging gunfire with a carload of South Richmond Gangstas. Riddling their car with bullets as they sped off from the club. Hearing police sirens approaching fast, the shooters put their gun battle on hold and raced for their cars that only seconds ago they were using as shields. Burning rubber up out of the parking lot to escape arrest, the gangstas let off a few more rounds at each other as a reminder that the gun fight was far from over."

The syndicate family and the mob homies involved in the fight at the club sat around inside Syndicate's gambling shack drinking and smoking weed trying to calm down after all the excitement.

Young Tre sat at the round table shaking a pair of dice and holding a blunt puffed hard on the weed and exhaled the smoke through his nose. "Blood who was them outta town niggas fighting with them crip niggas?"

"Thcm niggas was from South Richmond, that nigga I busted across the head said his name was Leland." Syndicate sat on a small couch next to Dynamite sipping on some Hennessy.

G Gunna, sitting next to J.R. at the round table, poured himself another drink. "For what it's worth them niggas had heart. That nigga Leland is a salvage. G Gunna laughed out of respect. Always acknowledging the real in a nigga even if he is from the other side.

Dmove looked at his self in the mirror on the wall disgustedly. Mad to see that his handsome face was swollen. "I wouldn't give a fuck how much heart them niggas got. I'm going to have at them niggas for fuckin' my face up like this."

Poppa Fly sat on the couch across from Syndicate and Dynamite with his girlfriend Shy. "Muthafuckas was getting off somethin' decent tonight. I see niggas still with the business, it almost feels like I never left."

Dynamite sipped on her drink. "Them East side niggas are going to get their hats brought to'em. Getting up in our business like that."

Whip, fully loaded off the sherm, leaned back in his rocking chair with his eyes closed and his 44 Cal. laying across his lap. Fuck them crab ass niggas. I was tryin' to get at them niggas more than I was them South Richmond niggas.

Chip stood arrogantly at the pool table shaking a pair of dice in a small cup. "Say blood, fuck them niggas for now. What y'all need to do is come over here and try to win some of this paper."

"So, what they hit foe' nigga. That fat ass mouth of yours is gonna cost you Chip." Young Tre shouted.

Syndicate stood up from the couch along with Dynamite. "Say Poppa Fly, I'm about to raise up out of here family. I got to get up early in the morning and look after my little girl. I hope that you enjoyed your homecomin' party." Syndicate laughed at the irony of his own joke.

Poppa Fly stood up from his seat on the couch to face Syndicate. "Best party I ever had nigga."

Syndicate nodded his head in agreement before the two old friends embraced out of love and respect for one another.

Dynamite gave Poppa Fly a warm hug. "See you tomorrow Poppa Fly."

Poppa Fly laughed out loud. "I don't know about all that Dynamite. After tonight I might have to go incognito for a couple of months, just chill out with my girl, and make me a couple of babies. Hangin' out with the family is hazardous to my health."

"That's the last thing we need is a bunch of little Poppa Fly babies running around acting like they daddy, not givin' a fuck." Dynamite teased.

Poppa Fly smiled at Dynamite. "Don't you be worrying

about me and mine's boss lady. What you need to be worryin' about is that lil' bad ass girl that you and Syndicate got waiting for you at home."

CHAPTER 47

It's In The Blood

A very animated Syndicate walked through the front door of his mother's house unannounced, with Dynamite and Sunshine by his side. "O.Z. What's up blood? Where my mama at?"

O.Z. sat in on the little red couch drinking a bottle of Budweiser, watching the baseball game between the Oakland A's and the San Francisco Giant's on the big screen T.V., that Syndicate had bought for his mother.

"She's in the room. Winky, your crazy ass son and his crazy ass wife is here." O.Z. yelled across the room.

A big smile spread across Winky's dark and lovely face as she walked out of her room. "My, my, if it isn't the King and Queen of the South side. And what do I owe the pleasure of you two coming down to the hood, where us common folks live?" Winky gave Syndicate and Dynamite both a big warm hug.

"Winky you really need to go on with all that punk shit. We been trying to get you out of this house for years. You're the one who wants to stay here in the hood, talking about you don't want to leave, because of all the sentimental value and shit." Dynamite fired back at Winky with no pun intended.

Ignoring Dynamite, Winky looked over at Sunshine puzzled. "Sunshine, is that you girl?"

Syndicate's face turned into a frown of confusion. "You know Sunshine mama?"

Winky, still confused herself, looked at Syndicate impatiently. "I know her name. I had to chase her young ass off the block a couple of times, but that's about it."

Dynamite gave Winky and accusing look. "Do you know who Sunshine's mother is Winky."

Remembering her own fucked up childhood a very angry expression spread across Winky's face. "I have no idea who her mother is. But if I did, I wouldn't hesitate to put my foot deep off in her ass. I know that I wasn't the best mother to Syndicate and Big, but I'd be damned if I would have allowed any little girl of mine to run the streets the way Sunshine does. And who ever her punk ass daddy is, somebody needs to fill his sorry ass up with bullet holes for allowing this to happen."

Sunshine giggled to herself enjoying the show being put on by Winky, on her behalf. Syndicate rested his hands on Winky's shoulders. "You might as well get your gun and start dumpin' then mama. Because I'm Sunshine's daddy." Syndicate announced proudly.

Flabbergasted, Winky covered her mouth to try to keep from laughing. "Boy, you ain't making no goddamn sense. Please don't tell me you don' fucked around and smoked some of that crazy ass shit? And now you think that little Sunshine is your daughter?"

Dynamite, thinking it's funny as hell that Winky believes Syndicate is high, laughed uncontrollably until tears ran down her face. At the same time, Syndicate feeling a little disrespected by Winky's comments, laughed it off. "Come on now mama, you puttin' way too much on it. A nigga ain't even high and even if I was, I wouldn't be trippin' that goddamn hard."

"Well if you ain't high then I must be, because I'm missing something here." Winky smiled at Sunshine.

Syndicate inhaled and exhaled slowly. "You ain't high mama and you ain't missin' nothin'. You know that bitch Kat?" Syndicate hesitated.

"Yeah, and so what." Winky fussed.

"Well, she's Sunshine's mama and she just told me last night that I was Sunshine's daddy. So now Sunshine is stayin' with us." Syndicate smiled thinking, "All's well that ends well."

"Fuck that punk rock ass bitch! She didn't come forward with the information voluntarily. We found out on a fluke." Dynamite exploded.

Winky fumed inside as her blood boiled with hate for Kat. "Ain't that about a bitch! I heard the fuck out of that. You mean to tell me, that bitch been keeping Sunshine away from her family for all these years?"

Sunshine laughed, not used to anyone fussing over here. "I feel you grandma. Ain't that some shit."

Winky smiled at Sunshine and opened her arms wide for her to come to here. "Girl and don't you be callin' me grandma. That shit makes me sound like some old ass lady. You can call me Winky, just like everyone else. Now come and give me a hug."

O.Z. looked back and forth between Syndicate, Sunshine, and Winky. "Damn I never really tripped on it before, but Sunshine looks just like you guys."

A shock wave of guilt ran through Winky's heart. "I always knew there was something special about you. That made me want to protect you when I would see you out on the block being fast and shit. But for the life of me, I had no idea that you were Syndicate's daughter. Yet, here you are now standing here looking just like your daddy, with those juicy lips and big nose," Winky wiped her tears away with the back of her hand. "It's a goddamn, shame I didn't even recognize my own granddaughter!"

Seeing the pain in Winky's eyes Sunshine's young heart went out to her grandmother. "Please don't feel bad grandma for not recognizing me. It's not your fault. You had no reason to believe that I was your granddaughter."

Dynamite smiled to herself thinking that it's cute how Sunshine isn't afraid to call Winky grandma even after Winky warned her not to. "It looks like you don' met your match grandma." Dynamite teased Winky.

Winky put her hand under Sunshine's chin and raised her head up. "I'm glad to see that you have your father's heart. The blood of a gangsta runs deep in our family. Make sure that you always respect it."

Sunshine, well aware of Winky's reputation of being a bona fide gangsta bitch, didn't need to be told twice what was meant by her grandmother's choice of words. "Believe me grandma, now that I know who my real family is, I won't ever disrespect myself or my blood again."

"I'm glad that you understand me Sunshine, because if I ever see or hear about you acting like a hoe again, I'm going to beat you like you were a runaway slave." Winky gave Sunshine her menacing look.

Syndicate walked up to Winky and put his arm around her shoulder, and pulled her close. You don't have to worry about none of that weak ass shit mama. Me and Sunshine don' already had a long talk, and all that old shit was put to rest last night."

Dynamite, knowing her mother-in-law all too well, spoke

quickly. "I already don' whooped on that punk bitch Kat, so you don't have to lose any sleep for wanting to do somethin' to her."

With murder on her mind, Winky growled. "Whoopin' her scant-less ass isn't exactly what I had in mind."

Syndicate, determined not to let the day pass without letting everyone know that Sunshine is his daughter, checked the time on his Rolex watch. "Say mama, we goin' to have to do this another time. I'm about to make some boss moves. Its time these niggas out here started paying homage to Sunshine." Syndicate kissed Winky on her cheek.

"I understand. You go ahead and do whatever it is you feel that you need to do," Winky held Sunshine by her hand. "I'll come by the house later on this week, so that we can have our own little heart to heart, and get to know each other."

Sunshine smiled at Winky and gave her a big hug. "I'll like that a lot grandma."

Sunshine rode in the back of Dynamite's Beamer feeling on top of the world. "Wow! This is totally fuckin' insane. My family tree is full of gangstas, killas and drug dealas. I'm going to be a gangsta bitch, like Dynamite and grandma."

Dynamite smiled to herself as she drove down 8 St. remembering the conversation, she had with Syndicate years ago. "At least you didn't ask permission, that puts you way ahead of me."

Syndicate looked at Sunshine through the rear-view mirror

with a heavy heart. "I'm not so sure that wanting to be a gangsta is such a good idea. Being a gangsta is a very dangerous job. And not only that, a real gangsta respects the O.G.s that came before them. And what that means, in your case young lady, is that you're going to have to learn how to watch your mouth."

Guilt spread across Sunshine's young face. "I'm sorry daddy. I wasn't trying to be disrespectful."

Dynamite frowned at Syndicate, understanding of his not wanting Sunshine to be caught up in the game. But at the same time, recognizing game when it was in her face. "I don't ever again want to here you say that you're sorry Sunshine, for anything that you say or do. And Syndicate, you really need to wake up and smell the coffee, because it is what it is. The sooner you embrace it the sooner you'll respect it."

CHAPTER 48

Krystal

Syndicate tapped Dynamite on the leg then nodded his head in the direction of a group of young Fly girls, walking down the street. "Pull up and pick up Krystal. I need to holla at her."

Dynamite pulled up next to Krystal and her two friends. A very, pretty, light skinned shorty, dressed to impress in her designer jeans outfit, complete with all the jewelry, and accessories that Sunshine now enjoyed having.

Sunshine wrinkled her nose in a jealous fit. "Why you pickin' her up?"

Hearing the jealously in Sunshine's voice, Syndicate laughed. "Because Krystal is my lil Potna. And I want the two of you to be friends."

Krystal walked up to the passenger side of the Beamer, while her two friends stood back respectfully. "Hey Syndicate, what's up?"

Krystal frowned at the sight of Sunshine even though grudgingly impressed with her new fly girl look. "What y'all doin' with that lil' stank hoe in the car?"

Infuriated, Sunshine jumped up in the back seat, ready to jump out of the car on top of Krystal. "You ole ugly stuck up bitch! You got a lot of nerve callin' me a stank hoe. You punk rock bitch!"

Dynamite, close to losing her temper, reached back and pulled Sunshine back down to her seat. "Girl, if you don't sit your ass down and get your dirty ass shoes off of my leather seats, you're going to have a lot more to worry about than what Krystal is talkin' about." Dynamite turned to Krystal. "Krystal, if you don't shut your big fuckin' mouth right now and get in the goddamn car, it's going to get ugly out here."

Syndicate, finding the whole thing amusing, opened the door for Krystal to get in. Krystal looked back at her two friends and gave up the fly girl gang sign before hoping into the back seat of the Beamer, next to Sunshine.

Syndicate turned around and faced the two teenage girls. "Alright check this shit out. I don't know what the problem is between the two of you and quite honestly, I really don't care. But whatever it is as of right now, its squashed." Syndicate eyed the two girls closely as Dynamite cruised through the neighborhood.

Krystal sat in the corner of the back seat as far away from Sunshine as she possibly could with her arms folded tightly over her heaving breast. "Why do the two of you even care about this little stank hoe anyway?"

Sunshine raised up in her seat like a King Cobra ready to strike. "Listen here you weak bitch, that's the last goddamn time you going to disrespect me. You do it again and I wouldn't give a fuck what Dynamite or my daddy does to me! I'm goin' to beat your muthafuckin' ass!"

A look of anguish spread across Krystal's pretty face. "Your daddy?"

Seeing the hurt look on Krystal, Sunshine rubbed it in. "Yeah, you heard me right bitch! Syndicate is my daddy so get used to it!"

Krystal's ears burned with hate from trying to block out what she was hearing. "Please Syndicate don't tell me that this little stank hoe is your daughter?"

Syndicate smiled at his young potna Krystal. "It's true Krystal. Sunshine is my daughter, I barley found out about it yesterday. I know what you're thinkin'. But whatever Sunshine was doin' before yesterday is dead to me. She's my daughter and I love her unconditionally," And Sunshine, Krystal her is my lil' crime potna, who I got mad love for. We go way back. Years ago, when she was a little girl, she was playing in the back room of her grandfather's apartment. I had to go over there and handle some business, and I didn't think to check the back rooms to see if anyone was there."

"My boy Poppa Fly told me she seen the whole thing and was traumatized. I had a long talk with her afterwards and took her under my wing. To this day, she never said a word about it to nobody. So, I want the two of you to respect the game and respect each other, because you're both part of the same family."

Krystal, knowing enough about Syndicate not to ever go against him, let her guard down and soften up some. "You're the one who needs to respect the game Syndicate, and let me get my hustle on like you promised."

Syndicate relaxed comfortably in his seat. Gratefully for the change in the conversation. "Girl, you still on that shit? Why you in such a big hurry to take penitentiary chances. You already got everything a young dope dealer could want except for a car."

Krystal leaned forward and wrapped her arms around Syndicate's neck. "That's right Syndicate and don't you forget, you promised me a new car for my 16th birthday.

Syndicate laughed out loud. "I haven't forgot. You still got what, 6 months until your birthday?"

Krystal smiled triumphantly at Sunshine. "More like 4 ½ months, thank you very much."

Dynamite pulled into the old neighborhood car wash located in between Cutie Pie Park and the Vista housing project. Playas stood next to their shinny cars, blasting their music, and attracting the attention of the Cutie Pie's riding by. At the same time, dope fiends scrambled around with little buckets filled with car cleaning supplies, trying to out hustle one another for customers. A big dice game was taking place at the back of the car wash, next to the brick wall."

"If you don't get you driver's license, the only kind of car you're going to be driving is a hot wheel." Dynamite laughed.

Krystal threw herself back against the seat pouting. "That's messed up Dynamite."

Sunshine rolled her eyes at Krystal. "Unbelievable! Why don't you just get your license?"

Syndicate nodded his head in acknowledgment to some niggas in the parking lot and turned around to face Sunshine and Krystal. "Because she doesn't know how to drive yet, that's why."

Sunshine laughed out of shock more than she did mockingly. "Damn Krystal! You about to be 16-years-old and you still don't know how to drive? I learned how to drive when I was barley 10."

CHAPTER 49
Untouchables

Syndicate's cousin, Junior, a neighborhood crackhead, ran up to Dynamite's Beamer with his bucket full of towels, rags and Armor All, just as she was raising the top up. "Cousin, cousin!" Junior shouted. Letting the other crackheads and winos know that Syndicate and Dynamite was family, and for them to back off. "Dynamite let me wash the Beamer for you cousin."

Dynamite smiled at the sight of Junior. "Hey Junior! What's up cousin?"

Junior opened the car door for Dynamite and smiled flirtatiously. "Dynamite why would someone as fine as you, marry someone as ugly as my cousin Syndicate? Shit you could have got with me with all the money you got."

Dynamite reached back inside the Beamer and grabbed handful of quarters from out of one of the little compartments. Then she handed them to Junior. "Junior you need to go on with all them crack pipe dreams of yours. And don't think just because we're family that the job is automatically gonna go to you all the time. Family or not, if you do a half-ass rush job like you did last week, not only are you not getting paid, but I'm going to stop fuckin' with you." Dynamite reached back into the Beamer and took out two $20.00 dollar bills and gave them to Junior.

Junior hurried up and put the money in his pocket, then smiled his toothless grin. "I got you cousin Don't even worry about it. I'm' ma have you lookin' like you just left the showroom floor."

Syndicate walked up to Junior and slapped him playfully on the back. "Nigga you better take care of my wife's car or I'm going to break your crack pipe."

Junior laughed at Syndicate's joke, proud that his young cousin is the man. "Nigga you break my crack pipe and I'm goin' to tell your wife about that fat ass bitch you was with the other night."

Sunshine stood next to Syndicate laughing. "You see this nigga here Sunshine?" Syndicate nodded towards Junior. "This here is your cousin Junior. The family wino."

Junior took a long hard swallow from his tall can of Old English while he fed the machine quarters. "How is this pretty young girl my cousin?

Syndicate smiled like a proud father. "She's your cousin,

because she's my daughter nigga."

With no sense of time or thought as to why he hasn't seen Sunshine with Syndicate before. Junior smiled showing off his two front teeth. "How did someone as ugly as you have a fine ass daughter like this?"

"I got that pimp juice nigga! Somethin' your old ass wouldn't know nothin' about." Syndicate laughed as he held on to Sunshine's hand and left cousin Junior to his business.

Dynamite suddenly looked around uncertain and then frantically searched her pockets. "Shit! I forgot my cigarettes at home."

Syndicate teasingly pulled out a pack of Newport's from his back pocket and lit one up. "Don't look at me. You know how we get down. I'm not supporting your bad habits." Syndicate laughed as he strolled to the back of the car wash, and over to the big dice game.

Dynamite pissed off at Syndicate for not giving her a cigarette and knowing better than to get loud with her husband in public, flipped him off behind his back. "Fuck, I need a cigarette." Sunshine Could you and Krystal run across the street to Segorines and get me a pack of Newport's? I'm not tryin' to leave Junior alone with my car." Sunshine and Krystal both giggled at Dynamite's predicament and headed across the street.

Young dedicated mob homies, Porky, Dink, and Jeff stood around the car wash's phone booth, smoking blunts, and chopping up game. When Sunshine and Krystal walked back by on their way from the grocery store, Porky looking for some action stepped out in front of the two girl's path. "Sunshine, what you supposed to be a fly girl now? Who's dick you don' sucked to get fitted like that?"

Dink look over at Krystal with a smirk on his face. "And what you doin' hangin' out with Sunshine? I didn't know that dick pleasing Democrats hung out with dick teasing Republicans."

"What, you mean to tell me your fagot ass daddy and your gold diggin' ass mama didn't hook back up yet?" Krystal clapped back at Dink.

"You know what you need Krystal? A big fat dick in your mouth. Someone needs to teach you how to be a Democrat like young Sunshine here." Dink laughed at his own joke.

"Ain't that right Sunshine? Why don't you tell your new girlfriend who taught you how to suck dick like a Democrat?" Porky eyed Sunshine lustfully.

Sunshine, unlike usual of letting the insult go as if she didn't care, felt it was her duty as Syndicate's daughter to stand up for herself. "Nigga you call what you got a dick? My baby brother is only 4-years-old and he has a bigger dick than you."

Krystal, impressed with Sunshine's change of behavior, nodded her head in agreement. "I strongly advise you niggas to stop being disrespectful to Syndicate's daughter."

Jeff, caught off guard by what Krystal had just said, choked off the weed smoke he had just inhaled. "What did you say?"

Sunshine smiled at Krystal respectfully. "You heard what my girl said. Syndicate is my father and it's a new day, so fuck what you goin' through." Both Sunshine and Krystal walked away pridefully, while Porky and the others starred in disbelief.

Syndicate's uncle, Clept, squatted down next to him in the back of the car wash shooting dice, angry that he was losing heavily. "So, what's this shit that your mama talkin' about Sunshine being your daughter?"

Syndicate picked up a pile of money he had just won by betting on Young Tre, who was shooting the dice. "It's all true uncle Clept, as a matter of fact," Syndicate stood straight up scanning the car wash. "Sunshine, Sunshine! You and Krystal come over here for a minute." Syndicate yelled over all the loud music and chatter going on at the car wash.

Sunshine smiled triumphantly at the young gang members as she held her head up high and walked to the back of the car wash along with Krystal. Syndicate smiled proudly upon seeing the two young girls approaching. "Check this shit out everybody. In case you niggas haven't heard by now Sunshine is my daughter, so take it for what it's worth. Because all that weak shit is over with. It ain't going to be no more disrespecting Sunshine, and that goes for my young potna Krystal too."

Dmove looked up at Syndicate from his squatting down

position. "Nigga go on with all that noise. Everybody that's somebody knew about it last night. Let these suckas and fake ass niggas find out the hard way. I'm losing money and I'm tryin' to get mine's back," Dmove picked up the dice from off the ground. "What they hit foe'? I'm about to lash you niggas." Money hit the ground as bets were being made, as if nothing had ever been said.

Clept, standing next to Syndicate with a bottle of Hennessy in one hand and a wad full of money in the other one, felt insulted by Dmove's comments. "That nigga Dmove needs to get his facts straight I'm as real as they come and I just found out a couple of hours ago, that Sunshine is your daughter."

"Come on now uncle Clept quit trippin' off small shit blood. We giants out here nigga." Syndicate motioned for Sunshine to come forward. "Sunshine come over here and meet your famous pimpin' ass uncle Clept." Sunshine walked up and gave her Uncle Clept a hug.

"So, Syndicate is your daddy huh? Ain't that a bitch. After all this time he just now finding out." Clept smiled at Sunshine. "Well, it's better late than never. And I can see by your new clothes. that I don't need to tell you all that acting all fast and what not is over with? The family, we don't get down like that."

Sunshine, well aware of her uncle's reputation as a bona fide boss pimp, smiled shyly. "I seen the light Uncle Clept. You don't have to worry about me disrespecting the family's name anymore than I already have."

Clept counted off $500.00 from his wad of money and gave it to Sunshine. "Your daddy don' already made it clear that whatever happened in the past is in the past. I'll make sure that these watered down tennis shoe pimps get the message."

Sunshine gave her uncle another hug. "Thank you, Uncle Clept For everything.

CHAPTER 50

Ain't No Free Rides

December 30th, 1997 Friday afternoon 3 years later

Sunshine sat in the passenger seat of Krystal's dark blue Mercedes Benz, smoking on a blunt while they drove out east to drop off 9 ounces of crack to Krystal's crip potna Twin. "My daddy be trippin', talkin' about I'm not ready to be a part of the family business. Shit I want to do my part for the family just like everyone else."

Sunshine passed the blunt to Krystal. "I don't know what you're complaining about. Syndicate spoils you rotten all you have to do is say daddy I want this and daddy I want that. While the rest of us have to hustle our asses off or get cut off."

"Bitch, you got a lot of fuckin' nerve trying to talk shit. Riding around in your new Mercedes like you Ms. good pussy, got your own fuckin' luxury apartment. that my daddy put in his name, and he basically gave you a liquor store. While I'm sittin' here looking like your little flunky." Sunshine laughed.

Krystal passed the blunt back to Sunshine and laughed along with her best friend. "Bitch don't be a hater," Krystal nodded in the direction of a tall, cut up, light skinned youngsta, sporting a small afro. He was wearing a pair of blue corduroy pants, blue Nike sweatshirt, a pair of blue Nike shoes, and a blue bandana tied around his neck. "There goes my boy Twin."

Krystal drove slowly through the big yellow two-story Filbert Arms low income housing complex, cautious of the speed bumps, and all the little kids running around playing. East-Side Crips stood out boldly in their traditional gang colors, with blue bandanas tied around their heads, and hanging low from their right-side pockets. They appeared to be conducting their illegal business in an orderly fashion.

Slick, a fast talking, muscular, dark skinned crip, known for his smooth-talking abilities, smiled when he seen Krystal's blue Mercedes pull into the parking lot. "Cuz who are these lil' bad ass bitches riding up in here all clean like that?"

Twin waved a hand at Krystal acknowledging her presence. "They're here for me cuz. The one driving, her name is Krystal. The other one is that nigga Syndicate's daughter. Her name is Sunshine. Also present, Silky, a well-known factor in the crip gang. Known for his numerous gang shootings and suspected homicides, and a current rival of Syndicate. He stood up from the infamous hump that they were all gathered around just as Sunshine and Krystal exited the car. "Twin, what you doin' bringing these slob ass hoes out here? Just because you cool with these little hood rat ass bitches, don't mean they can't get touched."

Sunshine eyed Silky unflinching. "From what I heard, ain't nobody untouchable."

Silky's mind quickly flashed back to when Syndicate shot him in high school. "You lil' slob ass bitch, you better watch your fuckin' mouth, before you sign a check that your young ass can't cash. You not on the south side no more and your punk ass daddy, his slob ass name don't mean shit out here."

Dino, a short and stocky O.G., with a long perm and a powerful left hand that has left many friends and enemy's alike sound asleep, put his hand on Silky's shoulder to calm him down. "Rest on that shit Silky. Save it for that bitch ass nigga Syndicate and the rest of them slob ass niggas."

Dino aggressively pushed Twin forward who was standing on the other side of him. "Twin get these lil' slob bitches up out the east before one of the homies do somethin' to 'em. I don' already told you to stop crossing game with them south side hoes anyway." Twin quickly walked Sunshine and Krystal back to their car.

"Twin for now on, you can just meet me at Syndicate's liquor store. Because I'm not coming out east no anymore. I don't have time to be dealing with your retarded ass homeboys." Krystal angrily shoved the little black pouch with the 9 ounces of crack out the window into Twin's outstretched hand.

Twin reached into his front pocket and pulled out a wad of money tied in a rubber band and gave it to Krystal. "My bad Krystal I didn't know that nigga was going to be out here,' Twin smiled lustfully at Krystal. "But forget about that nigga Krystal. What's up with me and you? When we going to stop playing this little cat and mouse game?"

Krystal started up her Mercedes and smiled sweetly at Twin. "Just because I do business with the enemy doesn't mean that I sleep wit'em. See you later Twin."

Sunshine looked over at Krystal as she drove away. "How come you don't hook up with Twin? He's fine as hell."

Krystal smiled back at Sunshine. "That's just it, he's too fine. Besides, Twin isn't interested in me as a person. He's only interested in getting inside my pockets and in my panties. But since you like him so much why don't you go out with him. I'm sure that you wouldn't have any problem affording him. Just make sure that he keeps buying his dope from me."

Krystal passed Sunshine a blunt and slid in E-40's new C.D into her Sony face off sound system. "My game is way too tight to be played out of pocket by some pretty boy. Besides, I'm enjoying being daddy's lil' angel way too much right now to have a boyfriend to contend with."

"So are you going to tell Syndicate about Silky and Dino running their mouths." Krystal took the blunt back from Sunshine and exhaled the Endo smoke through her pierce nose.

Sunshine waved her hand dismissively. "My daddy is a boss and them niggas are roaches. That wasn't the first time niggas don' got at me foul, because of my father. Syndicate told me a long time ago that his enemies are now my enemies. I expect them to be disrespectful so no, I'm not going to tell him about it. That's what weak bitches do, make somethin' big out of somethin' small. As long as they didn't put their hands on me or you, then it's all good. It's just another part of the game."

CHAPTER 51

Spoiled Rotten

Scientist, a tall youngsta, buffed, brown skinned with a long perm, and deadly on a microphone lounged inside Syndicate and Dynamite's recording studio. Worthy, Ray, Mac Twain, Tro, and Chip were with them, smoking on Endo blunts and drinking Hennessy. Sunshine and Krystal came waltzing in late.

"Where in the fuck y'all been? I told y'all to be here by 2 o'clock and its damn near 3:30.

Krystal flipped Scientist off. "Who do you think you are nigga, Tupac or somebody? Don't be yelling at us like that. I had some business to handle."

Scientist's eyes blood shot red and half closed, leaned back on the black leather couch. "Time is money and money is time. Y'all wasting a lot of both by being late."

Sunshine smiled playfully at Scientist. "Scientist I think that my daddy made a mistake when he told me that we were cousins. Because all of my family is from the keep-it-real tribe, and right now you with that bullshit. I know for certain that we're not being charged shit for being up in here."

Worthy, with a blunt dangling from his mouth, looked up from where he was working on his sound equipment. "Not everyone is as privileged, as daddy's lil' angel. I have niggas on hold as it is trying to reschedule their studio time, because you walk up in here whenever you feel like it. So, when you're late or don't come as expected it fucks off everyone else's schedule, and money. Which like Scientist said, it's bad for business."

Sunshine stormed off towards the sound booth followed by Krystal and Scientist. "I don't know what you're complaining about Worthy, the only business that takes place in here is gamblin' and weed smokin'. Anyway, what good is it having parents that own a recording studio if you can't take full advantage of it?" Sunshine laughed along with the others lounging around the studio. "Come on Krystal. We better get to work before Worthy kicks us out for not being professional."

Worthy worked his sound equipment while the trio adjusted their head gear. "You two go ahead and laugh. When Syndicate opens up his nightclub and I stop droppin' beats to manage the club, we'll see who laughin' then." Worthy spoke to both Sunshine and Krystal through their head gear, before dropping banging ass beat after banging ass beat for the trio to rap to.

Sunshine, Krystal, and Scientist put on a private concert in the sound booth for the next 3 hours. Worthy nodded his head appreciatively. "Yeah, Yeah, that's it! Y'all on point that's what I'm talkin' about! Bring it to'em now, Sunshine and give'em the gas! Make'm feel your pain!"

Chip stood next to Worthy smoking on a blunt. "Shit they tight. I didn't know Sunshine had gas like that. I'm goin' to holla at Syndicate and see if I can produce a couple of their songs."

Worthy took his head gear off and spoke over the loud-speakers. "Good job everybody that's a wrap."

"So, what's the name of y'all group?" Tro asked eagerly at the same time Sunshine, Krystal, and Scientist walked out of the sound booth still full of energy.

Krystal smiled brightly and sat down on the couch next to Los. "The Untouchables."

Chip sat back on a big wicker chair and smiled. "I like it. The three of you were puttin' it down up in there. That was the first time I heard you rap Sunshine. I was impressed you remind me of Yo."

Sunshine, standing next to Mac Twain smoking on a blunt, rolled her eye rudely at Chip. Still not forgiving him for the way he used to disrespect her back in the day. "Thanks! Come on Krystal, we got to get goin'. I told Dynamite and Sugga that we would help them get the house ready for the New Year's party tomorrow night.

CHAPTER 52

Cream

New Year's Eve 1997

Dynamite and Sugga rubbed their bodies up against Syndicate seductively out on the dance floor, while dancing to Tupac's "All Eyes On Me". Syndicate stood in the middle of the two beautiful women with his hands held high in the air waving them from side to side.

Sunshine and Krystal stood off to the side of the dance floor, smoking on a blunt while watching the grown folks get their freak on out on the dance floor. "Look at my daddy out there getting his New Year on with his two women." Sunshine laughed, as Young Tre walked up.

"Come on Krystal lets show these niggas how real hustlas get down." Young Tre grabbed a smiling Krystal by the hand and led her to the dance floor.

C.P., a medium height, muscular, dark skinned youngsta, with a small afro and the reputation of being quick to squeeze the trigger, slid up next to Sunshine. He was dressed in a Dallas Cowboy football Jersey, a pair of black FUBU jeans sagging off his ass and a pair of blue Nike' air Jordan shoes. "What's up Sunshine? Why you not on the dance floor, shakin' yo sexy ass and bringin' in the New Year like everybody else?"

Sunshine appraised C.P. closely and slung her long curly hair back over her shoulder. "I see no one has ever taught you the proper way to ask a girl to dance?"

"Gangstas don't dance, we boogie." C.P. took Sunshine by the hand and led her out to the dance floor.

Sunshine and C.P. took over the dance floor like two long lost lovers. "Say lil' nigga you doin' way too much over there! Step your young ass back up off my daughter and let her breath!" Syndicate yelled from across the room.

C.P. took a step back from Sunshine and without missing a beat yelled back at Syndicate. "Come on now Unk, we just gettin' our boogie on like you, and everybody else. You know that I wouldn't do anything to disrespect the family!"

Sugga playfully punched Syndicate on the arm as the song came to an end. "Syndicate stop acting like an old man and leave Sunshine and C.P alone. They're only dancing." Syndicate, Dynamite, and Sugga headed up the stairs as E-40's "Hurricane" blasted out of the speakers.

Jazzy sat at the bar with Erin, with an angry look on her face as Dynamite walked up with Sugga. "Damn bitch what the fuck is wrong with you? Why you all frowned up?" Dynamite made an ugly face to go along with Jazzy's.

"It's your friend Star." Jazzy pointed to a very drunk Star making out with Dmove in the corner of the room."

Dynamite smiled. "Damn bitch, don't tell me you got a thing for Dmove?"

"Let's see how funny you think it is when you find out what she did," Jazzy turned to Erin. "Go ahead Erin and tell Dynamite what you told me."

"Damn bitch. I thought you were going to tell her. That's the only reason I told you in the first place." Erin said. Angry at Jazzy for putting her on the spot.

"Look I don't give a fuck which one of you bitches tell me. But one of you hoes better tell me something'." Dynamite said. Getting impatient with her two friends.

"Star, she told me that she slept with Syndicate on the night that Mondo was killed." Erin spoke hurriedly.

Dynamite's heart turned to stone upon hearing the news that Star slept with Syndicate. "That Bitch did what?" Dynamite yelled over the music causing heads to turn as she stormed off to where Star was making out with Dmove.

"Watch out Dmove, unless you want your ass beat too." Dynamite shouted to Dmove's back.

"Hey, hey what's this?" Dmove put his hands up in surrender as he backed away from Dynamite.

"Star, you punk rock scantless ass bitch! How come you never told me that you slept with Syndicate? Bitch you was one of my bridesmaids." Dynamite stood all up in Star's face, not giving her any room to move.

Star, influenced by the alcohol, was full of courage. "Bitch what you all up in my face for? Why your man didn't tell you?"

As if slapped in the face by Star's words, Dynamite headbutted Star in the face breaking her nose. Blood squirted all over Star's face as Dynamite unmercifully banged her head off the wall again and again.

"What the fuck!" Syndicate yelled before making his way through the crowd over to where Dynamite had Star down on the ground pounding her face in. "That's enough Dynamite she's out. Syndicate grabbed Dynamite roughly off an unconscious Star.

"Let me go Syndicate and fuck you too! You cheatin' ass nigga." Dynamite struggled to break free of Syndicate's hold.

"What the fuck are you talkin' about? Ain't nobody cheated on you," Syndicate looked over at Star who was just starting to wake up and put two-and-two together. "Aw fuck, that was a long ass time ago Dynamite! Way before we was even married. That bitch don't mean shit to me."

Alright everybody the fighting is over. Ya'll can go back to enjoying yourselves. Worthy turn the music back on!" Sugga yelled as she tended to Star.

"Why in the fuck you didn't tell me Syndicate? All this time that bitch been all up in my face with her little secret." Dynamite now more hurt than angry.

"It wasn't nothin' to tell you Dynamite. The bitch came by the house one night when you were visiting with your father and came on strong to me. I was young and dumb baby girl, the last thing I ever wanted to do was hurt you. And it only happened one time. That's why I didn't tell you." Syndicate looked into Dynamite's green eyes.

"I'm not some soft bitch Syndicate, that's going to break because some bad shit happens. You could have told me. I would have been mad, but at least I would have known." Dynamite pulled away from Syndicate's hold.

"Come on now Dynamite. Tt's the holidays. Don't let something that happened 10 years ago, when we were kids be the reason that we fucked it all off now. What we don' built together with Sugga is too good to throw away on a one nightstand, that happened before we was even married." Syndicate talking fast trying to get back into Dynamite's good graces.

"Save your speech Syndicate. You know damn well I ain't

going nowhere. I know that bitch is the one that came on to you. But if you ever do it again, I'm going to show you how this shit feels." Dynamite arched her eyebrows to Syndicate.

"I'm man enough to admit that I can't take it, Dynamite. I'll kill a nigga if he even gets too close to the pussy." Syndicate gave Dynamite a passionate kiss on the lips.

G Gunna and Poppa Fly walked up to Syndicate each holding a 5th of Hennessy and high as a kite. G Gunna put his arm around Syndicate's shoulder. "What's up Syndicate, you alright? Nigga other than Dynamite whoopin' on Star this party is on hit. I can't wait for the club to open up. We goin' to have that muthafucka crackin' every weekend."

Poppa Fly took a swig of his Hennessy. "Dynamite got mad hands, she knocked Star the fuck out."

"Yeah, we going to have to change Dmove's name to Captain Save a Hoe. That nigga damn near carried Star in his arms up out of here." G Gunna laughed.

Syndicate eased his way over to where Jazzy and Erin where chilling by the fireplace. And put his arm around Jazzy. "Big Time is going to be one of a kind. It's not going to be some little hole in the wall club like the Elk's. It's going to be more on the level of "The Game" only Federal niggas and top notch bitches allowed," Syndicate laughed to himself. "I'm going to have a big ass neon signs that reads No Suckas Allowed under Big Time's name."

Jazzy's heart ached at hearing Big Time's name. "So, when is this fancy club called "Big Time" going to open?" Jazzy managed a smile despite the pain she still felt.

"It's going to be a little while still sis. I'm giving it Big Time's name, so I have to make certain that everything is perfect. You know how that nigga used to trip if everything wasn't up to par." D.Dogg laughed. Remembering his Brother.

Jazzy laughed kindheartedly. "You don't have to tell me. I know how difficult Big could be."

Erin looked over at Syndicate nervously. "I hope you're not mad at me Syndicate for telling Dynamite about you and Star?"

Syndicate looked respectfully at the pretty white girl. "Naw Erin I ain't mad at you. I know you were just trying to be a friend to Dynamite."

Erin smiled back at Syndicate. "Thanks Syndicate, for understanding."

"Not a problem Erin. Now go and enjoy the rest of the evening." Syndicate smiled back at Erin.

Syndicate stood in the middle of the room in between Dynamite and Sugga. "Alright everyone it's almost midnight so fill your cups up. I want to make a toast."

All the guest gathered around with their cups filled. Syndicate raised his champagne glass to all those gathered around. "To the game god for blessing us to see another year come and go.

May he continued to bless us accordingly and allow us to see many more fruitful years to come."

"Here, here!" The crowd cheered as the clock ticked seconds from midnight. "10,9,8,7,6,5,4,3,2,1, HAPPY NEW YEAR!!." Shouts of well wishes went out throughout the house. Loved ones and friends gave out kisses like it were candy. Others rushed out of the house to their parked cars to retrieve their guns, so, that they could continue the celebration with the tradition of firing shots air.

Gail stood on the porch with Nutts, Winky, and Clept. "My god where did all those guns come from. I'm surprised the neighbors don't call the police. It sounds like there's a war going on out there."

Clept laughed out loud. "It ain't nothin', but a gangsta party Gail. But believe me it would definitely be a war if the police pulled up right now." The four elders watched as others went outside and joined in bringing the New Year in by shooting off their guns.

The party inside the house continued until late the next day.

CHAPTER 53

God Bless The Game

Present Day 1999

Syndicate groaned with pleasure as Sugga deep throated his big black dick. "Goddamn Sugga them honey lips feel so goddamn good on my dick."

Sugga continued sucking on Syndicate's dick while Dynamite buried her face in between Sugga's nicely shaped butt cheeks and licked her sweet black pussy. Sugga moaned as she held onto Syndicate's hard dick and looked back at Dynamite going to work manipulating her clit with her fingers and her tongue.

"Shh shit, Oh, good god Dynamite, we going to have to change positions. I can't concentrate." Sugga moaned.

"You're such a big ass baby Sugga." Dynamite giggled as she crawled on top of Syndicate who was laying down flat on his back and guided his dick inside of her.

"Yeah that's a good girl Dynamite. Put Daddy's black dick inside that lil' sweet white pussy and ride this muthafucka." Syndicate looked over at Sugga who was busy playing with herself. "Come here Sugga and bring that sweet pussy over here and sit on my face."

Sugga, facing Dynamite, sat on Syndicate's face and started grinding her pussy into Syndicate's eagerly awaiting lips and mouth, while Dynamite grinded her pussy down over his iron hard dick. Syndicate held Dynamite by her sexy white hips as he drove his dick deep inside of her, while Sugga smothered his face with her hot, sweet, tasting pussy.

Kissing passionately and lusting for each other, Sugga and Dynamite rolled over onto the bed in a 69 position. Burying there pretty faces in the other one's hot pussy.

Syndicate, admiring the pure beauty of the show being put on by his two women, maneuvered so that he was behind Sugga's sexy honey colored ass. And stuck his dick deep inside of Sugga's sweet pussy at the same time Dynamite licked on her clit.

"Oh, oh, Mmm goddamn, the two of you are making me cum." Sugga moaned as she buried her face back inside of Dynamite's pink pussy.

Sugga and Dynamite both cried out to the lovemaking they were getting. As Syndicate took his dick out of Sugga's tight pussy and put it in Dynamite's mouth before putting it back inside of Sugga. Dynamite kept her little legs wrapped tightly around Sugga's head as she licked and sucked on Sugga's pussy and Syndicate's dick one after the other.

"Aw goddamn this pussy is good," Syndicate yelled. "Sugga won't you and Dynamite change positions so I can fuck Dynamite doggy style."

Sugga laid down on her back with her legs wide open. As Dynamite went down on her. Looking down at Sugga's beautiful moaning face while Dynamite ate her out. Syndicate's dick was bulging uncontrollable as he entered Dynamite's wet pussy. Holding onto Dynamite's sexy hips and sweating profusely, Syndicate fucked her hard and fast. "That's it Daddy. Just like that. Oh, god yes I'm cumming!" Dynamite yelled.

Syndicate fucked Dynamite for all he was worth. "Oh, hell yeah baby that's it. Sugga get your ass up here I'm about to bust." Syndicate pulled his dick out of Dynamite's pussy and put it back and forth inside Dynamite and Sugga's mouth. "Aw, aw, aw, goddamn!" Syndicate yelled out loud as he shot his load all over Dynamite's and Sugga's pretty faces.

Syndicate walked out of the bathroom holding two wet face towels and smiled at the sight of Dynamite and Sugga going back at it in a 69 position. "I ought to film the two of you having sex on the webcam and put it over the internet. Www.professionalwoman gonewild.com. I bet I could make millions. I need to pick my game up and start pimpin'."

Sugga paused from her lovemaking with Dynamite and look over at Syndicate. "That's what you're not going to do. I wish I would let you pimp me and have my body exposed to all them pedophile rapist. Them perverted, nasty ass men out there."

Dynamite sat up in bed and lit a cigarette. "Syndicate you're so full of shit. Having me and Sugga on the internet, having sex for all or anyone to see? That's the last thing you want to happen."

Guilty as charged, Syndicate smiled, just as his cell phone started to ring. "You got me fucked up. As long as they're paying then it doesn't matter to me who watches."

Dynamite reached for the cell phone. "Yeah right." Dynamite answered back at Syndicate before picking up the phone.

Syndicate stood at the foot of the bed playing with Sugga's little black painted toes. "I hope that it's not someone callin' about Sunshine. That girl is way out of control. She's like a fuckin' beast out there on the streets." Dynamite picked up Syndicate's cell phone off the nightstand and tossed it to him.

On reflex, Syndicate caught the cell phone with one hand then proceeded to answer in a rush. "Yeah what up? Who this?"

The caller, a little taken back by Syndicate's rude behavior, responded in kind, "Nigga it's me, Nutts."

Syndicate relaxed, glad that it was Nutts and not someone

calling about Sunshine, laid back in bed in between Dynamite and Sugga. "Blood what's up? Why you callin' me on a Sunday morning? You already know that all I do on Sunday's is lay up between Dynamite and Sugga all day long."

Nutts, not liking to be scolded even in playing, spoke harshly. "Yeah well nigga put your pants on, because something came up that's more important than you laying up in bed all day."

Hearing the seriousness in Nutts voice, Syndicate stood up off the bed butt ass naked with his gold rope hanging around his neck. "What's crackin blood? Holla at your folks."

"I got good news and I got bad news. The good news is that my hitters caught up with that Richmond nigga, Leland and one of his boys who was unfortunate to be with him. The bad news is that my boys made him shark bait at the bottom of the Bay." Nutts spoke as just another day at the office.

"Damn Nutts, I didn't need for you to bury the nigga for me. That's what the K-Squad is for, to handle family business." Syndicate shook his head disapprovingly.

"Yeah I feel you Syndicate. No thanks necessary for taking care of them niggas that left you in a coma for two months." Nutts tone registered his feelings as unappreciated.

Syndicate having a lot of love and respect for Nutts reversed his stance. "That's my bad Nutts. I didn't mean to come at you sideways. That was one love on your part for feedin' the sharks for me. The shit was just personal for me you know?"

"It was personal for me too Syndicate. I'll get back at you later. I have to tie up some loose ends." Without feelings, Nutts hung up the phone.

Dynamite stood next to Syndicate in her pink panties. "What's going on?

Syndicate reached down on the floor and picked up his boxers. "That was Nutts. That nigga Leland and some other nigga that was with him is buried at the bottom of the Bay."

Dynamite, a little annoyed that Syndicate isn't more upbeat about the news, paced the floor excitedly. "It's about time someone touched that nigga. And what's up with you, actin' all depressed and shit?"

Syndicate shook his head disgustedly while he continued to get dressed. "I can't believe this shit. We been together for what 17 years and after all this time, you still don't know me do you Dynamite?" Syndicate walked out of the room without looking back.

CHAPTER 54

Young And Dumb

Dmove sat in the passenger seat of Sunshine's brand new customized red Hummer Truck, in the parking lot of Weber Town mall, smoking on a blunt. "Girl what the fuck is wrong with your young ass? Riding around with all this goddamn dope in the car. You know that shit ain't cool. You takin' way too many unnecessary chances. Riding around in this high profile Hummer, flossin' and shit. You already got the police and the jackas all over you. And that's even without you ridin' dirty."

Sunshine reached over and snatched the blunt out of Dmove's mouth and threw it out the window. Smokin' all that weed don' made your black ass paranoid. So, if you scared go to church, nigga." Sunshine reached under her seat and grabbed a blue backpack, reached inside, and then pulled out four Kilos of cocaine. "Here nigga now get your scary ass out, so I can drop off the rest of this shit to the family."

Sunshine, feeling untouchable, reached in her ashtray and picked up a fat blunt and fired it up.

Dmove reached over and snatched the blunt from Sunshine and took two hard puffs. "Say what you want to say about me Sunshine. All I'm sayin' is that you need to slow your ass down some. This ain't how we do business, all out in the open and shit for the whole world to see. You shouldn't even be touching the dope. You need to have C.P. or somebody else, that you trust to drop this shit off for you. Word to the wise, Sunshine don't let the little power you got go to your head, because just like yesterday, it can be gone tomorrow."

Dmove placed the four kilos' in two Footlocker bags and stepped out of the Hummer. He then passed the two Footlocker bags to a youngsta sitting behind the wheel of a green El Camino that was parked next to Sunshine. The youngsta in the El Camino drove off slowly with Dmove following close behind in his Lexus.

Later on, Krystal sat inside her immaculate three room apartment, sitting on the sofa, watching Poetic Justice on D.V.D when Sunshine walked through the front door. "Bitch where in the fuck have you been all day? And why haven't you been answering your cell phone? Worthy and Scientist been blowing me up all day askin' me why we weren't at the studio."

Sunshine tossed the blue backpack on the couch next to

Krystal, picked up the remote, and flopped herself down on the big bean bag on the floor, and without a word to Krystal switched the D.V.D. To watch B.E.T.

Krystal instinctively unzipped the backpack sitting next to her and pulled out a brown rainbow sandwich bag. "Sunshine what the fuck is this?" Krystal yelled while opening the sandwich bag and dumping out 9 ounces of cocaine. "What the fuck you doin' bringing this shit in the house? Why didn't you drop all this shit off like you were supposed to? Don't tell me you were with your lil' boyfriend, C.P., fuckin' all day without handling your business?"

Sunshine walked over to the couch and put the 9 ounces back inside the sandwich bag. "Young Tre ran me through an obstacle course, before he would let me drop his package off to his people. If it wasn't for my daddy, I wouldn't even be fuckin' with that nigga. He be trippin'. I didn't feel like dealin' with C.P. after that so I told him that I would drop his shit off tomorrow. And for your information, me and C.P. are just potnas like you and Twin." Sunshine giggled.

Krystal picked up the backpack and threw it at Sunshine. "What the fuck is wrong with you, Sunshine? You be doin' way too much. Why don't you just take them over to him right now? Syndicate will have a fit if he finds out that there's dope in here."

Sunshine put the sandwich bag with the 9 ounces back into the backpack. "Just relax, my daddy won't find out unless you tell him. So, stop worrying Krystal I promise you that they will be gone first thing in the morning."

Krystal picked up her purse from off of the cabinet. "Bitch fuck that, I can't let you keep doin' this. I gave Syndicate my word that I wouldn't keep any dope in this house. I'm tired of you making me out to be a liar. I don't like it one bit Sunshine. I don't know what's wrong with you, but you really need to get yourself together. Just get that shit out of here!" Krystal gave Sunshine a hug. "I have to go to work, I'll talk to you later."

Sunshine returned Krystal's hug with an ugly frown. "Work! What part of the game is that? Ain't you the fuckin' manager? Come on Krystal, its Saturday night we need to be out flossin' on these low budget hoes and not stuck in some liquor store." Krystal slammed the door behind her leaving Sunshine at a loss for words.

Syndicate and Sunshine sat inside the safe house at the kitchen table counting drug money at 3 o'clock in the morning. "So, what's going on with you Sunshine? I been gettin' a lot of bad reports on how you been conducting yourself in handling the family's business."

Sunshine frowned while she continued to feed money into the money counting machine. "They're all just either jealous or they're just mad, because you put me in charge of the dope game and not one of them."

Syndicate picked up a $5,000 dollar stack of money off the

table and held it in his hand. "I doubt that very seriously. Everyone in the family has a genuine love for one another. We been through a lot of hard times together and now we all eatin' from our good fortune."

"I bet if I was a boy, they wouldn't have any problems with the way I was conducting my business. It's only, because I'm a girl that they're trippin'. They don't like having a young woman for a boss." Sunshine babbled on.

It's not because you're a girl, Sunshine. No one ever complains about Dynamite and she pushes a hard line. It's because you're not thinkin' and your out of control. That's what got everyone is trippin'." Syndicate tried to be patient with his young daughter. Knowing firsthand what it's like to come from the bottom to the top.

Sunshine bundled up a $5,000 stack and pouted like the lil' spoil girl she was, in an effort to get her way. "So, you're going to take your friend's side over mine?

Syndicate's cell phone started to ring. "They're not friends Sunshine, they're family," Alarms went off in Syndicate's head as he recognized Dynamite's cell phone number coming across the screen. "What's up baby? You and Sugga alright?"

"It's not either of us Syndicate its Krystal. Someone followed her home and forced their way into the house. They beat her up pretty bad. I'm at the county with her Aunt, Heavy, right now." Dynamite spoke quickly from her cell phone.

Syndicate looked at Sunshine angrily as his heart went out to Krystal. "I'm on my way. I'll be right there."

Dynamite stood outside the hospital with a concerned look on her face. "No, Syndicate you better not. The police are here, and they found 9 ounces of coke wrapped up in a plastic bag, in the back of the toilet. They're asking a lot of questions about you. They know that the house is in your name."

Syndicate's mind went racing with thoughts of revenge on whoever was responsible for hurting Krystal. "What the fuck was she doing with dope in the house? She knows better than that. Fuck the police! What room is she in?" Syndicate demanded

Knowing better than to argue with Syndicate at a time like this, Dynamite gave him the room number. "She's on the 2nd floor, room 223."

Sunshine stood frozen afraid to move. "What's wrong? What happened?"

Syndicate grabbed stacks of money off the kitchen table and hurriedly stuffed it in a Nike gym bag before putting it back in its safe. "Somebody ran up on Krystal and forced her inside her apartment. They beat her up pretty bad."

"Oh, my god was she raped?" Sunshine yelled.

"I don't know, but we're about to find out. Come on let's go!" Syndicate rushed out the front door with Sunshine right on hi tail.

"What the fuck is this?" Syndicate shouted upon seeing Krystal handcuffed to the hospital bed with her pretty face all battered and bruised.

Krystal's aunt, Heavy, still tipsy from a night out on the town, sitting next to Dynamite in Krystal's hospital room, went belligerent at the sound of Syndicate's voice. "They arrested Krystal, Syndicate! Ain't that a bitch? Punk ass police! Punk ass nigga runs up in her house and breaks her jaw and these fagots got the nerve to arrest her. They need to have they sorry asses out there lookin' for the nigga that did this to my niece!"

Officer Smith, a lanky gray haired white cop stepped forward, "Don't you worry Ms, we're going to find whoever did this to your niece. I can also see that you don', had too much to drink. So, I advise you to calm down before I arrest you for being drunk in public," Officer Smith turned to face Syndicate. "The reason why the young lady was arrested is, because we found 9 ounces of cocaine wrapped in a rainbow sandwich bag, in the back of the toilet. She already stated that whoever did this to her was looking for drugs. In this case, left us no choice, but to arrest her for possession of sales.

CHAPTER 55

It's A Cold Game

With Sunshine coming clean on the way over to the hospital, Syndicate was well aware of who's drugs it was that was hidden in the back of the toilet. "So, that's why you got her handcuffed to the bed like some big time felon. Because you found some drugs in the bathroom?"

Officer Corona, a big fat Mexican cop trying unsuccessfully to be hip, stood next to Krystal. Krystal was laying in the bed with her jaw broken and face severely bruised, and looking terrified. "It's not like all we found was a couple of $20.00 dollar rocks. We found 9 whole ounces of pure cocaine, which doubles in street value to around $20,000 dollars. She's looking at some very serious time."

Dynamite, feeling helpless, tried in vain to defend Krystal. "You can't prove the drugs belonged to Krystal. For all we know the police could have planted the drugs there."

Officer Smith waved his hand in the air cutting Dynamite off short. "You can save that argument for the judge."

Syndicate walked passed officer Corona and squeezed Krystal's hand that was handcuffed to the bed rail. "She's not goin' in front of no goddamn judge."

Officer Corona, well aware of Syndicate's reputation as a notorious gangsta, nervously reached for his gun. "You want to explain that Syndicate?"

Syndicate gently brushed the side of Krystal's beat up face. Recognizing the fear in her eyes of not wanting to go to jail for Sunshine's mistake. Yet at the same time knowing that she wouldn't betray the code of silence. "The apartment and the house belongs to me. Krystal had no idea that there were drugs in that house." Syndicate looked at Sunshine then back at Officer Corona. "Nobody in their right mind would take a beating like that for nine ounces of coke."

Fear and terror took hold of Sunshine seeing that her father was about to take the blame for her disrespecting the game. "No daddy you can't do that!" Sunshine yelled out to the surprise of everyone in the room.

Syndicate turned on Sunshine like a rattle snake spitting out poison venom. "Sunshine shut the fuck up! Dynamite get Sunshine the fuck out of here right now, and go find me a bails bondsman to bail me out of jail after these muthafuckas arrest me."

Dynamite, knowing when and when not to ask questions, grabbed Sunshine by the arm and rushed her out of the room. Syndicate winked back at Krystal who tried without success to force a smile on her swollen face. "Un-handcuff my young potna I'm the big fish you punk muthafuckas been tryin' to catch. So, let's go." Syndicate turned around and put his hands behind his back. Officer Smith took his handcuffs and placed them on Syndicate's wrist. "You're right Syndicate. You are a much bigger catch. Unhandcuff the girl." Officer Corona did as he was told and unhandcuffed Krystal from the hospital bed.

After his arrest and dressed in his Orange county jail jumpsuit, Syndicate sat behind the glass window arguing with Dynamite, who was sitting on the other side of the glass with a phone to her ear. "Why in the fuck am I still here? How come you haven't bailed me out yet?"

As if talking with a personal client and not her husband, Dynamite maintained her composer and remained business like despite Syndicate's hostilities. "I already told you Syndicate that you have a no bail hold."

"This shit is crazy, they playing me way out of pocket. How in the fuck they goin' to put a no bail hold on me? I haven't even been to court yet. These muthafuckas is acting like I don' killed somebody!" Syndicate exploded.

Dynamite fought hard to control her feelings. "I don't know

what's goin' on Syndicate. You have a court date for today at 1 o'clock this afternoon. So, there's nothin' we can do before then to get you out."

Respecting the game as it is, Syndicate calmed down. "Damn they not wastin' no time getting me in front of a judge. "I barley been in here 24-hours. It normally takes 2 or 3 days before they take you to court." Syndicate looked up at the wall clock. "10 o'clock. I go to court in 3 hours and these punk ass deputies still haven't told me that I have a court date today."

Dynamite breathed heavily trying to relieve some of the stress she was feeling. "Don't worry about none of that Syndicate. The important thing is that you have a court date today. So now all we have to do is get the judge to give you a bail so that we can get you out of here."

Syndicate, hoping for the best and expecting the worse, gave Dynamite a reassuring smile. "I hope that you can make somethin' happen and get me a bail. I need to tighten up my circle and get all my business in order before, it's time for me to lay down for these white folks."

Dynamite, getting her first real taste of just how deep the game really is., started to feel the pressure of a life with Syndicate behind bars. "Being that it's only your first offense, hopefully the judge will give you probation or some county time."

Syndicate laughed kindheartedly. "I see that you don'

relapsed back into that spoiled lil' rich, naive, white girl that I first met." Syndicate's toned turned more serious. "Dynamite these muthafuckas been tryin' to get at me for years. They not about to let me get off with probation or some punk ass county time."

Dynamite gritted her teeth and flared her nose up thinking about all the trouble that Sunshine has caused Syndicate and the family. "Sunshine, that little bitch. I could break her neck for being so careless. I tore into her young ass somethin' decent. Could you believe that she had the nerve to break down and start crying talkin' about how sorry she was. I told her sorry sweetheart, but sorry doesn't fix shit."

Syndicate smiled to himself. Remembering how eager Dynamite was to prove herself worthy of being a bona fide gangsta bitch. "She's just like you were Dynamite at her age. Couldn't nobody tell you shit either."

Dynamite let out a small grunt grudgingly respecting Sunshine's gangsta. Yet at the same time not ready to forgive her for disrespecting the family or the game. "I admit I was wild as a juvenile, but I wasn't a renegade to the game like Sunshine. I always respected the rules that were put in place long before I ever arrived on the scene." Dynamite eyed Syndicate closely. "And so will Sunshine, if she wants to stay a part of the family's business."

During court, Syndicate stood in the courtroom next to Dynamite in his Orange jumpsuit shackled at the waist. "A flight risk?" Dynamite answered in shock at the reason as to why Syndicate was being denied a bail. "I beg your pardon your Honor. Not only is this not a murder case, my client has a spotless criminal record without so much as even a parking ticket. He's a businessman, a homeowner with a wife, and a daughter. He's a very active and outstanding member of his community. My client poses no threat to the community and has no intentions of jumping bail if given one."

Judge Peavy a very stern, heavy set, black man, sat back in his chair comfortably. "We have a very different perspective on what an outstanding member of the community is counselor. In this courtroom, outstanding citizens don't place 9 ounces of cocaine in a young woman's bathroom. Let alone without even telling her about it. And yes, it's true that your client doesn't have a criminal record so to speak. But Mr. Syndicate is no stranger to this court or the legal system. I'm well aware of Mr. Syndicate's family gang ties and their criminal activities. Bail denied counselor.

Dynamite stood perplexed not wanting to believe what she was hearing. "Your Honor may I please ask you to reconsider your judgment on the grounds that if Mr. Gaines is given a bail, he may be released to my custody. I am an officer of this court and will personally see to it that Mr. Gaines is present for any and all of his court appearances."

Judge Peavy looked sternly at Dynamite before leaning

forward in his chair. "Counselor it's very admirable of you to want to help your husband. But please don't make a fool of this court again or I will hold you in attempt. My decision has already been made. Is there anything farther counselor?"

Feeling defeated, Dynamite shook her head no. "No, your Honor." Content, Judge Peavy leaned back in his chair. "Good. So, Syndicate stays here."

"Objection your Honor!" Dynamite yelled cutting off the Judge. "The defense would prefer that you use my client's legal name and not his street name."

Without any emotion, Judge Peavy continued. "Mr. Gaines, it says here that you are charged with possession of more than an ounce of cocaine for sale. Which is a felony in the state of California and carries a maximum of 15 years in prison. How do you plea?"

Dynamite looked over at Syndicate. "My client pleads not guilty your Honor."

Judge Peavy nodded his head in agreement. "I'll set it over for a preliminary hearing for May 22nd."

"Hold on a minute your Honor!" Syndicate spoke in a loud and clear voice. "What kind of deal would you give me if I plead guilty right now and saved us both a lot of time?"

Dynamite looked at Syndicate like he was crazy. "Excuse me your Honor may I please speak with my client for a minute."

Judge Peavy, just as startled as Dynamite, nodded his head.

"By all means."

Dynamite no longer able to hide her emotions grabbed Syndicate by his chin and made him look at her. "Syndicate what the hell are you doin'?"

Syndicate pulled his head away from Dynamite. "These muthafuckas ain't tryin' to give me a bail and I'm not tryin' to stay stuck in this punk ass county jail for months and months dragging this shit out. When the final outcome is goin' to be the same, and that is I'm goin' to prison."

Dynamite's heart started to break from hearing the truth in Syndicate's words. "My mother can get you a bail she has connections and the longer you fight your case the better deal you get later."

Syndicate gave Dynamite a look she knew all too well. That his mind was made up. "The only deal that I'm going to get is the one that I'm going to get right now."

From experience, Judge Peavy could see that the conversation between client and lawyer was over, "So, have the two of you talked things over?"

Dynamite, not liking it, but respecting Syndicate's decision, "Yes, your Honor my client would like to resolve his case today. If the court is willing to offer something reasonable in return for a guilty verdict."

Judge Peavy looked at Syndicate with contempt. "If Mr.

Gaines were to plead guilty today, I would sentence him to a mid term of ten years."

Dynamite cut her eyes to the assistant D.A., who was sitting with a smirk on her face. "Not only is ten years unreasonable it's also unacceptable. As I said before your Honor, my client has a clean criminal record. Not only that I think it is totally unethical and should be illegal to sentence my client based on the people he knows or any unproven rumors that the court may have heard from biased sources. Therefore, seeing how it is that my client is ready to make amends and take responsibility for his wrong doing, the defense ask that the court sentence my client to a low term of five years."

Judge Peavy nodded at Dynamite respectfully admiring the fight in her. "Seven years' counselor. That's the best deal you're going to get in my courtroom today or any other day."

"Objection your Honor, the people feel that ten years was a very reasonable offer to begin with!" Shouted the assistant D.A.

"Overruled!" Judge Peavy shouted back. "So, what's it's going to be counselor?"

Dynamite held her head up high determined not to cry. "My client pleads guilty your Honor."

Judge Peavy nodded his head. "Does he waive his rights to have a trial by a jury of his peers?"

Dynamite, on the verge of a breakdown, gathered her strength and pulled herself together. "Yes, your Honor my client waives his rights to have a trial and would like to be sentence by your Honor today."

"In that case, Mr. Gaines I sentence you to seven years in the state penitentiary. Bailiff take him away. Next case!" Judge Peavy retrieved the paperwork for the next case and dismissed Syndicate without a second thought. The bailiff escorted Syndicate back to the holding cell with the rest of the prisoners. While Sunshine and Sugga sat in the front row of the courtroom with tears in their eyes.

CHAPTER 56

The Game Don't Stop

"He took seven years." Dynamite informed the rest of the family who were waiting outside the courtroom.

"This was only supposed to be his arraignment. All they were supposed to do was read him his charges and give him a bail." G Gunna shouted.

Dynamite wiped the tears from her eyes. "The Judge wouldn't give Syndicate a bail, and Syndicate said he didn't want to sit in the county jail for months and months fighting his case. So, he told the Judge that he wanted to be sentenced today."

Poppa Fly gave Sunshine a cold hard stare. "That's some fucked up shit that Syndicate about to do seven years for some weak shit he didn't even do. The only good thing is that the Feds didn't pick it up."

Dmove walked up to Sunshine and pointed his finger at her.

"This little bitch is going to get us all arrested."

Dynamite, understanding that now was the time for her to say fuck her feelings and take charge of the situation, walked over and put her hand around Sunshine who was sitting with her head down. "It won't serve anybody any purpose to be disrespectful towards Sunshine. Not only is she family, she's also Syndicate's daughter. I know personally that she feels worse about what happened to her father and Krystal than any of us. So, let's not pass judgment. Every one of us here don' made mistakes. Now let's get up out of here. There's way too many ears and eyes watching us."

Sunshine went to visit Syndicate, before he gets transferred to prison. "Daddy I don't want you to go to prison." Sunshine cried over the phone while she talked with Syndicate sitting on the other side of the glass window.

Syndicate let out a small laugh. "It's a little too late for that sweetheart, they shipping me out tomorrow. They don' had me sitting up in here for the last 4 months stressin'. If I had known that it was going to take this long to get up out of here, I would' ve fought my case."

Sunshine sat with tears running down her young pretty face. "Daddy I'm so sorry that I did this to you. I miss you so much."

Syndicate, long ago making peace with his fate, waved his finger disapprovingly at his daughter. "Don't ever let me hear you say that your sorry about anything ever again Sunshine. You're just young in the game baby, that's all and that's nothin' to be sorry about. It's also called growing pains, and we all go through them. I don't want you thinking that you got me locked up. I don' did a lot of dirt and a lot of wrong over the years and now it's time for me to pay up. So, I don't want you blaming yourself for my being here. I'm here, because I'm married to the game, for better or for worse."

Sunshine wiped the tears from her eyes. "I love you for taking responsibility for my disrespecting the game. But I will never forgive myself for putting you in this fucked up position." Tears ran freely down Sunshine's face. "Oh, daddy only if you would have let me ride my own beef. Then you wouldn't be going to prison."

Syndicate's heart ached from seeing Sunshine hurt so much for him. "And what lesson would you have learned then? That as long as you don't snitch and do your time that it's ok for you to do whatever you want to do? Then what? You get out and become even more disrespectful than you were when you got locked up? No, this way you can really feel that what you do doesn't only affect you, but also the whole family. I been hearing that the family is upset with you and rightly so. You need to understand that everyone is hurtin' right now. Once all the smoke clears and everyone adjust to my being gone, they will get over it. So be strong and keep your head up, making mistakes is part of the game. Now let me talk to Dynamite before my visit is up."

Sunshine stood up to leave with tears in her eyes. "I love you daddy."

Syndicate gave Sunshine a big smile and a wink as if he had not a worry in the world. "I love you too, Sunshine."

Dynamite, who had been standing behind Sunshine the whole time, took the seat in front of the glass window and picked up the phone. "Sugga sends her love, says that she doesn't want to see you behind the glass, because it hurts too much not to be able to touch you. And that whenever you get to where you're going she'll be the first one in line for a visit."

Syndicate smiled at his wife. "Tell Sugga I understand I don't like not being able to touch her either and that I'll be lookin' forward to seeing her when I get to where I'm goin'." Syndicate turned his attentions to Dynamite. "And what about you? Are you ready to ride this out with a nigga?"

Dynamite look at Syndicate like he had punched her in the stomach. "What the fuck kind of question is that? You already know that I'm a ride or die bitch. I'm down with you wherever you go."

Satisfied, Syndicate nodded his head. "So how is everything working out with Sunshine and the family business?"

Dynamite sighed. "It's working out ok. Everybody is still weary that she's gonna go back to bein' reckless. Other than that, it's nothing." Dynamite laughed out loud. "Young Tre told me that I might as well go ahead and make her a part of the K-Squad since she's more of a killa than she is a drug dealer."

Syndicate's spirits lifted hearing that everything is under control. "Yeah, well that's what I wanted to do in the beginning. But no, you were the one who didn't want her to be a part of the K-Squad."

Dynamite, suddenly feeling sad and all alone, put up a brave front for her husband. "And I still feel the same way today, so stop worrying about Sunshine. I have everything under control. You just worry about taking care of yourself and watching your back so that you will come home in one piece."

Syndicate, not wanting Dynamite to have any doubts about his heart, gave up the syndicate family gang sign and smiled. "And that's somethin' you don't have to worry about baby girl. Ain't nothin' changed, but the scenery. I still don't give a fuck. This is the syndicate family foe' life."

One of the deputies stuck his head inside the little visiting room. "Alright Syndicate, visit is over. Time to tell your folks good-bye."

Frustrated by the interruption, Syndicate yelled back at the deputy. "What you talkin' about officer, I still got ten more minutes!"

Triggered by Syndicate's hostilities, the deputy yelled back at Syndicate. "I said that your visit is up now get off the goddamn phone!"

Syndicate held up a finger signaling for the deputy to hold

on. "Fuck! Wait a minute!"

Dynamite sat on the other side of the glass glowing like an angel. "I have a surprise for you Syndicate. I was gonna wait until I came to see you at whatever prison they send you to. But I know that you would want to know now."

Syndicate stood up to leave as the deputy moved in closer. "Well then hurry up and tell me. You see this muthafucka is on my back, tryin' to rush me up out of here." The deputy stepped in closer to Syndicate. "That's it Syndicate time's up let's go."

Dynamite stood up with the phone to her ear smiling. "I'm pregnant." Syndicate stood speechless with the phone in his hand.

"Visit over." The deputy reached over and turned the phones off with his key.

"I love you Syndicate." Dynamite whispered with the phone still to her ear.

"I love you too, Dynamite." Whispered Syndicate in a state of shock as he hung up the phone and watched the love of his life walk away."

Pelican Bay level 4 prison 9 months later.

"We're not in D.V.I. no more blood. This here ain't no fuckin' goddamn Reception Center. We in a fuckin' war zone now blood. These crazy muthafuckas in here stay on lock down 24-7." E-Ru the piru from the Sacramento Meadowview blood gang whispered to Syndicate. While they walked through the rotunda along with the other convicts transferring from D.V.I.

"Gaines second tier cell 239." One of the guards yelled from inside his cage.

Syndicate picked up his bedroll from off the ground and look over at the youngsta standing with his face against the wall. "That's me E-Ru, stay strong blood. I'll catch up with you later."

Syndicate carried his belongings up the stairs to the second tier. Aware of the guard with the big riot pump shotgun walking back and forth across the isolated cage high up in the wing, looking down at everything and everybody. Convicts gave Syndicate cold hard stares from the small windows as he passed by their cells.

Without giving a second glance as to whom the convicts might be inside the small cells, Syndicate continued, on stopping in front of cell 239. "Pop cell 239." One of the guards yelled. Cell 239 instantly opened and closed with Syndicate stepping inside.

The convict inside the small cell sitting on his bottom bunk. Looked up at Syndicate as the door slammed behind him. "I see you finally made it."

Syndicate looked at the older convict and smiled in recognition. "O.G. Suja! What's up blood?"

The End

About the Author

Dean Roberts was born and raised in Stockton. California. He is the father of two sons and two grandchildren. Dean is an ex-gang member, ex-convict, and a 17-year recovering drug addict. He now resides in Sacramento, California where he works as a Certified Drug Counselor, helping others rehabilitate and change their lives, just as he did.

Dean is a Professional Writer and Poet. This is he first published book and plan to publish others. Stay tuned!

Disclosure

This is a fictional book and all the characters and story lines are and all fictional.

.

Made in the USA
Las Vegas, NV
28 February 2022

44770561R00295